STAINLESS

· RUSTY KNOB · BOOK THREE ·

STAINLESS

Wicked Reads
PO Box 29
Nelson, PA 16940

www.ericachilson.com/wicked-reads

Printed in the United States of America

First Printing,

ISBN-13: 978-0-9979899-0-8
ISBN-10: 0-9979899-0-4

NOTE TO READERS

Characters from all of Erica Chilson's series make an appearance in Stainless. Timeline: Unleashed epilogue – Hero (M&M of Restraint) & Warped epilogue (Blended, coming late 2016) While it's not necessary to read M&M of Restraint or Blended, these characters being shown/mentioned are for readers who have read all the series. Not knowing these characters or the events mentioned will not have an impact on the main focus of Stainless. Francis Parker and his partner-in-crime, Sage Fisher, will be series regulars in the Blended series, and this is one of the major reasons I felt the need to showcase specific characters from all three series, so readers will know they can follow Franny and Sage to Fairport to hear their HEAs.

Foster brothers, Kaden Marx and Brennan Kennedy, are at a precipice for change. While Kaden has made a career out of higher education as a way to drag his feet from reentering the real world, Bren has been in the thick of it.

Join Kaden as he learns a valuable lesson– how having four degrees isn't a measure of your true worth, nor is it a gauge for your maturity. Hyper-focused on the six-year age difference he has with Wynn, Kaden is blinded to the fact that Wynn is now a mature man ready for a stable future by his side.

Will Kaden and Wynn mature together, or will Kaden continue to stunt both himself and their relationship?

Over the past four years, Bren has held down a steady job, tried his hardest to please a wife who never wanted him, and raise their child in a cohesive manner. Unable to stay on this destructive path, Bren is making choices to ensure the happiness of his wife and child, not realizing he's been placing the one person he truly wants in the friend-zone– Jackson.

The happy smile is a façade, for beneath it is a dark secret that has the ability to tear all of Rusty Knob's major families to shreds. The terrifying past collides with the present, taking Brennan's future down a dark spiral, where the truth is finally revealed and deep betrayals are felt.

Kaden Marx and Brennan Kennedy move back to Rusty Knob, attracting change in their wake… but whether it's for the greater good remains to be seen.

FAMILY TREES

KENNEDY

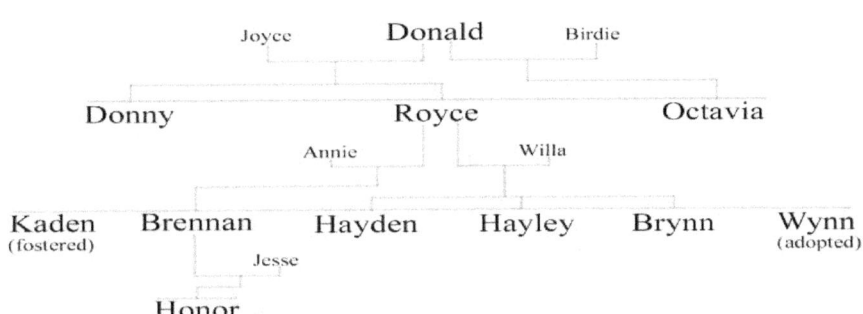

Joyce — Donald — Birdie

Donny   Royce   Octavia

Annie — Royce — Willa

Kaden (fostered)   Brennan   Hayden   Hayley   Brynn   Wynn (adopted)

Brennan — Jesse

Honor

GILLETTE

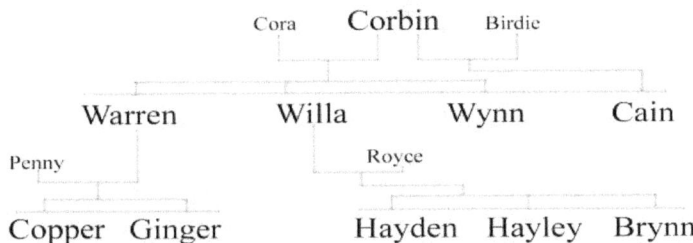

Cora — Corbin — Birdie

Warren   Willa   Wynn   Cain

Penny — Warren

Willa — Royce

Copper   Ginger

Hayden   Hayley   Brynn

MARX   ROSS

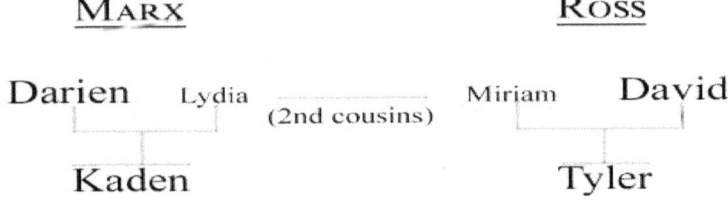

Darien — Lydia — — — Miriam — David

(2nd cousins)

Kaden   Tyler

FRANKLIN

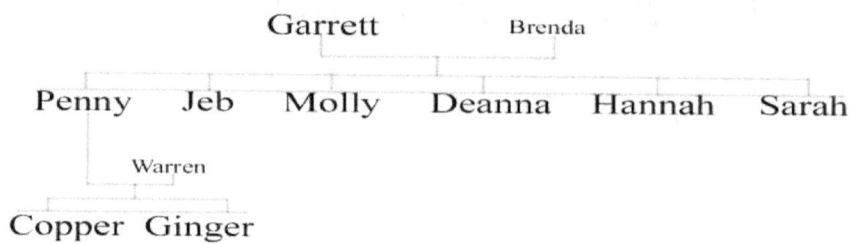

Garrett — Brenda

Penny   Jeb   Molly   Deanna   Hannah   Sarah

Warren

Copper   Ginger

PROBST

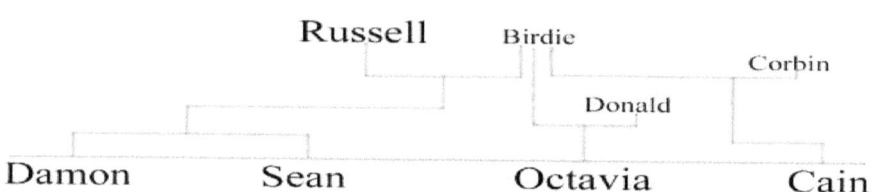

Russell — Birdie

Corbin

Donald

Damon   Sean   Octavia   Cain

BISHOP

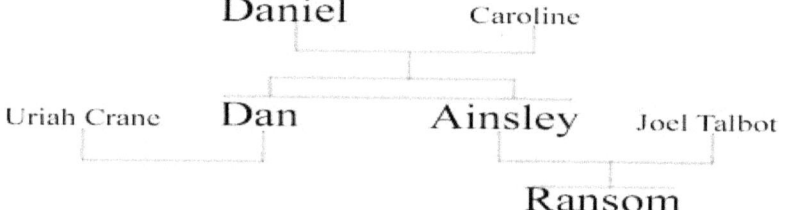

Daniel — Caroline

Uriah Crane   Dan   Ainsley   Joel Talbot

Ransom

Rusty Knob/Blended Series Crossover

FISCHER

Byron

Ginny Jamison   Opal   Audra

Francis Parker   Sage   Gemma

CHAPTER ONE
Brennan Kennedy

"You're doing great, Mrs. Hoffman," I encourage as I steady the woman, placing my hand firmly on her back to remind her not to slouch while performing squats. "One more rep– you can do it."

"If you say so." With an exerting grunt, the forty-something woman tries to finish a set for the first time. "My God, Brennan, how you push me."

Chuckling sardonically, I help the woman to her feet, then hand her a towel to wipe away the sweat beading along her neck and enhanced décolletage. I do what any red-blooded man would do, pretend I'm the cloth as it wicks away the moisture.

"Thank you, Brennan." Mrs. Hoffman blushes a beautiful shade of pink while I flatter her with my appreciative gaze. Breasts swelling more as her breathing deepens, her nipples bud against her sports bra.

"Hard work should always be admired." Voice light, I can't help the flirty tone from sneaking in. "You've improved since I've taken you under my tender loving care."

"Tender?" Mrs. Hoffman's lips slide into a smirk. "It's a good thing my husband is willing to give me a massage after our workouts." Swatting me with the damp towel playfully, she calls me a beast.

"Mr. Hoffman appreciates the results." I waggle my eyebrows exaggeratedly and preen a bit when she pats my torso.

"Charmer," is her parting comment as she sashays her firm ass to the locker room, where Mr. Hoffman is waiting to ravish his wife.

"Playing cupid again, are we?" Tony hops on the Stairmaster, a taunt and a challenge in his actions. My coworker is equally jealous and covetous of me. "That old man is gonna have a heart attack one of these days after you get his wife's motor running."

Gazing heavenward, I grab a clean cloth to wipe down the equipment in my area. "You know nothing of marriage, bud." With a swift kick, I eject him from my machine, ignoring how amazing his calves look. "Most people cheat because they are missing something inside of themselves, not within their marriage. Mrs. Hoffman is crazy over her husband. She just needed her confidence built back up so she felt what Mr. Hoffman was already trying to tell her."

"Then what's wrong with your marriage, *bud*?" To add insult to injury, Tony whips off his shirt, showing off years and years of hard work turned into muscular perfection. Professionally, Tony is a work of art, but he doesn't even get a twitch out of my dick, which is why he's perpetually pissed at me.

Working in a gym is a blessing and a curse. As the resident bisexual, it's my job to make sure everyone feels good about themselves. Surprisingly, even the straight guys ask if they're looking good enough to date.

Morgantown, West Virginia is like an oxymoron. As a college town, we're not as backward as Rusty Knob. Most of the clientele of *Sweat it Out* are students or those employed with a degree. They're a bit more open-minded than the folks in my hometown, but not by much. The fact that I'm a man's man who still loves pussy puts their minds at ease. They simply ignore the other half of my persuasion until they ask for advice on what to wear– *how the fuck should I know?*

I'm the only one who knows Tony wears women's underwear underneath those tiny shorts and craves sucking dick. His cowardice outweighs his physical strength.

I won't deny it; the fit women have my tongue dragging on the ground. Roundness: tits swaying in sports bras as they jog on the treadmill and bubble butts jiggling in yoga pants as they tackle the Stairmaster. Don't even get me started on the visceral reaction I get from camel toe– gross to everyone who doesn't want to get in those pants.

On the flip side, I have a thing for the geeky guys who look like I used to. Awkward, unsure, a bit insecure, and it makes me feel like the man when they come to me for guidance. But in the end, their hard work makes me proud yet sad when my geeky clients evolve, especially those who turn into muscle-heads. The bodybuilders don't do a thing for me– it's not what flips my switch. Even I wish I had backed off a while back. Now when I look in the mirror, I feel like my excess size is trying to compensate for my lack of height.

When I was soft, my wife didn't want me. Now that I'm hard, she doesn't want me either.

No shit, right?

Perils of falling in love and marrying a lesbian. I'm pretty sure if I grew a vagina, Jesse still wouldn't have me. Every time my dad looks me in the eye, he's biting back, "*Son, I told you so.*"

I haven't been laid since we found out our daughter was conceived, since I'll forever pretend that I didn't cheat on Jesse the night before we got married. It would take a heinous motherfucker to do such a deplorable thing.

Never happened.

Ever.

It was a goodbye.

For now.

I never talk about Jesse– our relationship is sacred. "My marriage is what it is." I shrug one shoulder, counting the minutes until the end of my shift. I love my job, just not the cock-measuring politics. "I don't wear the ring because I have to create an illusion, just like servers–"

"And strippers and whores." Tony raises an eyebrow, waiting for me to deny it.

No can do.

"For the Mrs. Hoffmans of the world, I'll gladly put up with being solicited day in and day out." Tilting my head to the side, I size up Tony. "I've never been unfaithful to my wife. I can look my fill and make my clients feel desired and wanted, but I never act on it."

"More's the pity." Tony's checking me out at the same time, tiny shorts failing to disguise the reaction he has to me –nothing on my end.

Raising an eyebrow like a villain, "Challenge?"

"Fuck, yes!" Tony shouts, startling nearby patrons. "You're such a fucking cock-tease, Bren." He snaps my ass with a towel. "If you hadn't bulked up, you would have found yourself on the wrong end of a bad situation."

"Laps?" I lope off toward the exit with Tony following me like a faithful puppy. "Is there a right end of a bad situation?"

"Yeah," Tony answers both of my questions. "Being the assailant."

"Jesus," I hiss, feet padding quickly down the stairs. "You're a sick fuck, bro. A real sick fuck."

With a wink, Tony brushes by me, making sure too much of his body comes in direct contact with mine. "I'm always up for who can do the most laps, because even if I lose, it's still a win for me."

"How so?"

Walking backward, wearing the most devious grin I've ever witnessed, Tony terrifies me sometimes. "You. Soaking wet. In nothing but a Speedo." Laughing evilly, he hammers the final nail in the creepy coffin. "I let you win just so I can watch those powerful thighs and arms move you through the water, and how your round girly ass sticks up like a shark fin."

"Bro, I'ma drown you." I warn with a lunge.

-*-

It took half a semester before I realized higher education wasn't for me. I'm more of a guy who likes to work with my hands– use my body as a machine. After this personal trainer gig is up, I'll be apprenticing at Kennedy Construction. Sitting in lecture halls, discussing things that I'll never apply in real life, it felt like I had fire ants crawling on my flesh.

I am a married father, a homeowner, with a fulltime job I adore– I don't need a degree to prove my worth, and I sure as shit don't need a degree to be happy.

I'm not Kade– *Mr. I'm Going to Stay in College Until I have a billion PhDs*. My brother is more worried about appearances than just accepting who he is and being happy. Kade was qualified for whatever job he wanted two years ago, yet he won't go home and stay home.

For the past four years, I've been working as a personal trainer and stay-at-home dad. Right after high school graduation, I'd bought a house for Jesse, me, and the baby, with a room for Kade to sleep. It took even less time for Kade to vacate our place, which he was only using three times a week while he worked on his graduate degree, than it did for me to turn college-dropout. By the third awkward night, Kade had found an apartment to call his own. It didn't take long before Wynn and Jack decided dorm life was too claustrophobic, after having all of Rusty Knob as their domain, before they invaded Kade's efficiency apartment and made it their own.

Poor Kade– it's Wynn and Jack's apartment now, but Kade pays for it, which means I'm actually paying for it.

If it wasn't for those idiots, I would have moved back to Rusty Knob, forcing Jesse and our daughter to follow me. I'm just biding my time until Wynn graduates next month, then I'm moving home, with or without them.

But not without my daughter.

"You're late," is my wife's barked greeting as I walk in the front door after a ten-hour shift at the gym. "I missed my art class earlier because Becca was sick and couldn't babysit. Answer your phone next time– it could have been an emergency."

Sighing deeply, I think to myself how this is exactly what a man wants to walk into when he comes home. But then I remember this was my choice, and I pushed Jesse into it. After how I was raised, I dreamed of a nuclear family.

My mom died, taking my baby sister with her, and then our lives turned to hell when the Probsts set their sights on us. Using extortion to gain control of our family's wrongful death settlement, the last hope of me ever having a mom, dad, and siblings went out the window. Now my family tree is exactly the stereotypical bullshit people use against West Virginian natives.

Since I didn't have it as a kid, I wanted it as an adult– a wife being the only person I'd ever touched sexually or loved, with a gaggle of kids who were happy to see me when I came home from work.

I wanted it, yet I failed to give that to myself or my daughter.

'Treat the wife as if she's always right, even when she's wrong' is not my usual style. *If Momma ain't happy, ain't nobody happy. A happy wife is a happy life.* I don't subscribe to any of that unbalanced thinking, because it breeds bad behavior I don't want my daughter to witness. Jesse is my best friend more so than my wife, and we don't do that enabling bullshit. But, tonight, I'm too tired to argue.

"You're right, Jesse." I step into our living room, shutting the front door behind me, then allow my gym bag to drop to the floor with a harsh sound of finality. "A class you attend at the YMCA is more important than the job that's paying our bills."

My petty, passive-aggressive bullshit causes fury to radiate from my wife's cold, blue eyes– I know I've overstepped our boundaries. Jesse contributes financially, and her art does matter. I just don't have the time to deal with her tonight.

"It's not like–"

"Don't!" I warn, raising a single fingertip, instinctively knowing my wife will bring up how none of us *need* to work.

Blood money.

Goddamn blood money I'd give back in a heartbeat if it meant I could bring my mom, unborn baby sister, and granddaddy back to life. They died, and the money we received brought nothing but terror into our lives. At first, everyone had their hand out, saying they were Kennedys so they deserved their cut.

My dad was a shell of a man– a walking zombie –and Uncle Donny was no better. To lose one person, you grieve. To lose the heart, the future, and the patriarch of your family, that is debilitating. I was a small child who grew up way too quickly, because I had a job to do– someone had to take care of my dad and uncle by showing them life was still worth living. Then we had the bright idea to do good with our unwelcome wealth, and we began revitalizing Rusty Knob and educating its natives.

Probsts.

Every time Jesse brings up how neither one of us *has* to work, I see red– the crimson wash of blood staining my hands. It was only a blink really– a two-second view of an object tearing my dad apart. Dad was larger than life to me until that very moment. A superhero brought down by the villain I thought was an ally. With the scent of terror and piss filling the air, that blink in time will last a lifetime. Blood ran down Dad's body to pool on the floor around his knees, with Sean's sated cock laying against Dad's thigh– that destructive piece of flesh painted with my father's blood and shit.

Sean, the guy who wanted me to call him Uncle Sean– the guy who would laugh and play with me– he had committed the most heinous crime one human could do to another, with the added torture of doing so in front of the man's brother, woman, son, and best friend.

Blink.

It only takes a blink to change the trajectory of your life.

A car exploding into a fiery ball on a freeway, with blood money to erase the loss, as if human life has a monetary value.

Blink.

The terror of a 'not a boy, yet not a man' having to make the decision to leave his father to protect the twins, then run into the night, using the Kennedy blood running in his veins to direct him across their land and through the woods to Gillette Holler.

Blink.

A sight that can never be unseen, removing all traces of innocence and altering how sex is viewed as a weapon, violence– an act of dominance instead of an act of love.

Blink.

Every time anyone brings up how much money I have, I remember the metallic flash of a gun butted against the nape of Dad's neck, and the sheer terror on Uncle Donny and Willa's stunned faces. White as a sheet is just a saying– one we visualize. But one can't truly know the horrific impact of seeing a loved one's complexion turned to a shade of death unless they witness it firsthand.

Blink.

The loud crack of gunfire next to my ear, where it took seconds in the ringing silence to realize Dad was still a live, and it was just Corbin meting out justice.

For nearly a decade, I've hidden the nightmares spawned by the red-wash as the front of Sean's head exploded outward, painting the sofa, spraying across the floor, and blowing all the way to the kitchen cabinets, with his brain matter splattering Dad's back and Uncle Donny and Willa's faces.

Blink– I had to blink dozens of times until my mind brought reality into focus, because at first I couldn't compute the macabre scene.

Why?

The lust and greed of green.

If the Probsts would've brought Octavia forward, telling Dad and Uncle Donny how Granddaddy had been naughty by getting another man's wife knocked up, none of that would have happened.

Kennedys are an honorable people, and Octavia would've been given a third of Granddaddy's money without hesitation. But the Probsts were greedy, violent people, and they didn't want their own half-sister to have her cut– they wanted it *all*.

Money is the root of all evil, and even the attempt by my wife to bring it up almost drops me to my knees.

On the verge of throwing up, I issue weakly, "Just go."

Without a backward glance, Jesse leaves our home, with her blonde ponytail the last thing I see. Slumping down onto the sofa, I stare at the door she just exited.

Passing ships in the night.

I work days at the gym while Jesse stays home with our daughter. Our next door neighbor's home-schooled foster kid pops in once a day when Jesse wants to run errands or help out during art classes at the YMCA. As soon as I come home from work, I'm a stay-at-home dad. Jesse bolts like lightning, not coming back until the wee hours of the morning just before I head out to work.

Jesse works until last-call at an artist bar. She sets up her easel, along with a few other artists, and they paint while being observed. The patrons drink and eat to make the house a profit. The finished pieces are sold, and the artists are tipped– combined, the tips and the sale of their paintings are the wages. Some of Jesse's pieces have sold for a pretty penny.

Jesse is damned good, and I'm proud of her, but I miss her more.

I was home late tonight because I don't have the luxury of a babysitter doing my duty for hours on end during the day. I took an hour for myself to challenge Tony to let off some steam, then he and I just sat in the sauna and stared at the insides of our eyelids to de-stress.

For eighteen years of my life, Jesse was my best friend. Just Jesse, Franny, and me. Jackson and Wynn hovered on the outside, never truly wanting in, with a few of our basketball buddies breaching the surface from time to time.

We lost Francis to California, where he's finishing his design degree and will never look back. Jesse was just as artistic, but her medium was oils instead of fabric.

I'm not sure what I added to our friendship besides being the one who posed in Frantastic Designs while Jesse memorialized the moment. The weakling is now the brawn, without an ounce of artistic ability, and the only common denominator between us is my purple stripe on the rainbow.

Small town. Small circles. No common threads needed besides proximity. With the distance of time separating us, highlighting how truly different we are, we've slowly drifted apart.

It didn't used to be like this. When we were first married, Jesse and I shared a bed but not sex, many laughs, and a life– a future.

We were closer than close, able to tell the other anything, no matter how damaging it may have been. I'm only faithful in our marriage because of my beliefs, which have nothing to do with Jesse. Never once did I ask her to remain celibate, and this was without judgment or explanation.

I'm Jesse's husband.

I used to be her life-long best friend and sometimes lover.

I am not her father.

But in the past few months, Jesse has turned into a nag who expects me to be a mind-reader. To read a mind Jesse doesn't even understand herself.

Just as I told Tony, a cheater cheats because of something within them. When Mrs. Hoffman began training with me, she refused to voice her issues. She felt undesirable, completely blinding herself to the actions of her adoring husband. While training, she would express how he wasn't attentive enough, but it was her inability to see outside of her insecurity to notice what Mr. Hoffman was actually providing. He could have doted on her hand and foot and she would have been dismissive and oblivious. It took me flirting with her to light a spark, when neither of us truly wanted the other. With the spark lit, Mr. Hoffman's fire engulfed the insecurities until it was too hot to dismiss.

I'm not blind, nor deaf, nor dumb. Jesse's the one pulling that bullshit now. I never judged, nor will I ever. Jesse's resentment, her assumptions of how I feel without asking me or hearing me, that is on *her*.

My wife is one of the reasons I celebrate my bisexuality, because I can't stand head-games with people who don't even realize they're playing them. Just like Mrs. Hoffman, why should their partner have to solve them like a broken Rubik's Cube? Most men are exactly what they seem. The ones who aren't, I don't plan on fucking anyway. As for the emotionally stunted women, no fucking way. Never again. I won't allow my daughter to grow up to be like that.

Most fathers worry about having a daughter who is promiscuous, while I'm worried she'll be a manipulative head-case. I don't care who my daughter has sex with as long as she doesn't jerk him around on a leash, mess with his head, and make him feel like a moron.

My dad was my mom's 'yes man', and I will never go down that road. Willa and Dad seem to draw strength off of each other, and that's what I want out of my partner.

The wife is always right, no matter what, and we're all to tee-hee and blush and feel guilty, even when she's dead *wrong*, because God forbid the wife got upset. Meanwhile, I'm not exactly sure how my wife, who is three months younger than me, who has grown up in the same town, went to the same schools, and has had the same life experience as I have, suddenly became wise beyond her years while I remained an idiot the instant we were married.

I will not raise my daughter to mother her misfortunate husband, unlike how Jesse was raised to treat me. Immediately after we married, I was no longer the friend, but the bumbling husband without a brain in his head, and my friend was suddenly a genius wife who is always right.

I may not have a mother, but I refuse to allow my wife to treat me like her son. It's been a struggle I've refused to relent on, because my self-respect is involved.

Our marriage was supposed to be built on friendship and our mutual adoration for our daughter. Regardless of the bizarre balance Jesse thinks we should have, our marriage won't crumble because of our sexual orientations, or from one of us finding someone we want to be with instead. It will crumble because one of us refuses to communicate with the other.

To admit my depression is to admit defeat. The end of my marriage won't be the failure; the dissolution of our friendship will be.

That's all on Jesse, because Lord knows I've tried.

A light thud has me on my feet in an instant. Without hesitation, I find myself down the short hallway, standing outside of my daughter's bedroom door. Resting my ear to the wooden panel, I listen to her chat animatedly with her doll babies.

All stress dissolves with the sweet cadence of Honor's voice.

CHAPTER TWO
Kaden Marx

"We need to eat." Try as I might, I can't remove Mr. Octopus Hands from my body. "We need to cook, or at least order some takeout before Jack gets home from work. It's only fair."

Blue eyes shining with lust, Wynn sits on my lap, grinding my dick into his fleshy behind. "Jack will be home soon," he reminds me, and not for the reasons one would think. The little shit is an exhibitionist, just begging for an audience outside of little ol' me.

Remember my Durango? Wynn even came out with spectators.

All activity thus far has been by the cover of darkness, thanks to the fact that we live in a two room apartment. One giant room housing the efficiency kitchen, the couch and TV, and two beds trying to be as far apart as possible– the only privacy is in the shitter, but there's no lock on the door.

I can't complain since I split half of my time here and the other half back at my house in Rusty Knob.

Wynn keeps edging closer and closer to the point of no return with Jackson, not realizing what he's up to until it's too late. I'm good with whatever, but Wynn's conscience might not be.

My ex-roommate, Dan... yeah. I'm the voyeur to Wynn's exhibitionist, so I *get* it.

I spent three years watching Dan have sex with just about every girl on Penn State's campus, not realizing he knew I was watching while jerking off. By senior year, Dan unexpectedly fell for a guy– a guy he paid to give me a lap dance. In a burst of jealousy and possession, Dan tore Uriah wide open. Dan became obsessed with Uriah, to the point the scholar almost flunked out.

I was Dan's best man when he married Uriah, and let's just say the bachelor party will forever be showcased in my spank bank.

I spotted Wynn as a freak from the time he first sprouted wood– innocently addictive. There's no way in hell I'm not going to give him everything he desires.

"C'mon." Fingers wrapping around Wynn's thick wrists, I try to pry him off of me. He just twists his fingertips into my shirt, getting a better hold. "It's not fair how we mistreat poor Jackson— he's not our bitch."

"You're the hog." Wynn leans forward, nipping at the tip of my nose with his front teeth. "This place is spotless thanks to yours truly."

Chuckling underneath my breath, living with a man who thinks he's auditioning to be the next Betty Crocker and another who is compulsive, bordering on obsessive about cleanliness, is both a blessing and a curse. It's like having two witty, snarky, intelligent yet smoking hot wives who take care of everything, but the downside is they are both on the rag at the same time and I fuck neither of 'em.

The buddies join forces and try to put me in my place on a daily basis.

Filthy fucking pig is exactly what I am. It's my lease, and they are here under my sufferance. So they can bitch until the landlord complains, and all it will sound like is music to my ears.

Only fifteen pounds lighter than me, and an inch shorter, yet somehow he's stronger than I am, there is no way I can move Wynn without his consent. "Up!" I say more firmly, when I usually indulge Wynn in whatever the hell he wants. I'm the driver at all times, but the adorable passenger is giving the directions.

"You're leaving in the morning." Wynn actually pouts, pale skin pinking beautifully, and it takes everything in me not to throw him on the floor and screw him into the next millennium. "For three whole days."

"Little shit," I snap, not enjoying this guilt trip game Wynn plays. He's a twenty-two-year-old pain in my ass, and waiting for him to grow up is slowly killing me. "We've been doing this bullshit for four years, true? So get off of me and deal."

"I. Want. You." Wynn's chiseled features come closer and closer with seductive intent. The little bastard knows exactly how to strum my fiddle, and it's terrifying to contemplate when he finally masters the instrument. "I want you, Kaden. Now."

Head jacking backward, I grunt sharply, "Christ!" as Wynn grinds his ass against my erection.

"Fuck me." Wynn's heat-seeking pink tongue locates its target in record speed. The reverberation as he speaks into my mouth makes its way directly to my cock. "Or let me fuck *you*."

The day Wynn figures out I'm waiting on him to take it, is the day I'll die and go to heaven. All he has to do is tear open my fly and sit on my dick, or jerk my legs apart and impale me, and I'll let him do whatever. But the little shit is too selfless and polite to figure it out, so I'm good for now.

I made a promise to myself when Wynn was still a kid, how I'd never take from him– *ever*. I'd give, he'd give, and we'd both receive.

I'm not *taking* Wynn's virginity– he has to give it to me.

Shivering with a mix of anticipation and intense arousal, "Youscareme," comes out in a jumbled mess as teeth attack my throat, leaving a necklace of marks behind.

Laughter vibrates my damp flesh. "I'm no longer Teenage Wynn, remember?"

"Adult Wynn is way scarier," I admit without hesitation, while curling my fingernails into the sofa cushion to stop myself from totally annihilating his ass. "Smarter. Stronger. Older."

"But you'll always be smarter, stronger, and older than I am, Kade– no fear."

"Bullshit." I jackknife off the sofa cushion as Wynn's mouth travels south, further and further south. The sound of my zipper lowering is deafening in our cavernous apartment.

At least Wynn's no longer pinning me to the cushions… but his skilled mouth renders me immobile.

"How was school today?" Blue eyes roll up to stare at me through thick lashes. "Good day, I take it?" Fingers wrapping tightly, I'm engulfed in a firm hand, right at the base of my cock, nails digging into my nuts. "Bad day, maybe?" my voice breaks.

Wynn blinks, clearly annoyed by my evasion tactics, but he doesn't look away. Saliva-slickened lips widen, ruddy skin pulling taut until white, as my flesh passes between and into the seductively evil recesses of Wynn's mouth.

Brain blanking, just like every other man on the planet, I forget what my malfunction is as soon as lips wrap around my cock. Wynn learned this nifty trick in *how to short circuit a guy's brain via blowjob 101.*

As with everything, Wynn excels in oral ministrations.

"Christ!" I gasp out on a laugh, back arching, fingers curling into the cushion to stop from gripping blond waves. "Do whatever the fuck you want, Wynn, but I ain't gonna last."

When we have privacy and unlimited time, Wynn works me from back to front, missing no inch of flesh from my tailbone to my bellybutton. But we're on a time crunch against the clock, because Jackson will be home from the hospital at any second.

Shit quality but still mind-blowing intensity, I pop the instant Wynn adds teeth. "Motherfucker! I'ma punch you for that one day!" I scream loud enough to alert the Thai restaurant beneath us. "Knock all your goddamn teeth out."

Jerking like I'm having an epileptic fit, Wynn taunts me with maniacal laughter while nicking the head of my dick until blood is drawn. Body beaded with sweat and lit by aftershocks, all I can do is gaze in wonder as Wynn tucks me back into my jeans, and then pats my package like it's a good boy.

"Something to remember me by as you rub one out while you're in Rusty Knob." Wynn rises to his full height, staring down at me sprawled on the sofa like my world just burst into flames at my feet.

Weak, I reach for Wynn, wanting to give him pleasure too… and get some vengeance.

"I'm good." Wynn jacks up his pant leg, then cups the wet spot growing over his bulge. No doubt, while giving me head, the horny bastard rubbed the heel of his palm on his jeans until he popped. "You gotta get up and cook us supper while I shower."

Mouth slack, "The fuck?" falls out.

"Don't you remember? Jack's not our bitch." Wynn's taunting laughter flows as he swaggers across our apartment.

Completely lax, I stare at the ceiling while listening to the shower flowing. It takes me a few more heartbeats before I get it. "Wynn Erastus Gillette! I'm not *your* bitch!" is bellowing out of my throat just as the front door opens.

"Hmm… somebody ought to explain that to Wynn." Always cute as a button, especially while wearing scrubs with storks carrying babies printed all over the light green fabric, Jackson smirks at me, knowing exactly what just went down. "Jesus, I'll have an order of whatever you just had."

"Be careful," I warn, then deadpan, "My meal bites back."

CHAPTER THREE
Brennan Kennedy

"Daddy?" Honor's big brown eyes gaze up at me from her jungle-themed toddler bed. Tunnel-visioned, all I see is Honor, and any regrets I have from the past mean absolutely nothing.

Nothing.

Honor is my everything.

How Dad managed to survive without Hayden and Hayley for a few years of their childhood is beyond me. The lying. The worry. The very real fear. The weekend visits under the guise of an uncle and cousin wanting to bond with the last of their kin. I couldn't imagine having to adopt my own children back, fearing the court would say no, which was the main reason I married Jesse.

Honor is mine, and the thought of saying she was my niece like Dad had to with Hayley... just remembering how gut-wrenching that time was gives me a case of the sweats. Now that I'm a father, there is no way I could have survived it.

"How's Emma and Bridget this afternoon?" Curling to the floor, I sit at the side of Honor's bed, fascinated by every breath she takes.

With warm brown hair and eyes, Honor is all Kennedy, more so than my brother and sister are with the Gillette in them overpowering the genetics. Chubby fingers curl around her Barbies–gifted by Grandma Willa and Aunt Hayley.

Bridget Barbie is sporting a Mohawk and a dress with tiny cherries on it. Emma is clad in khaki shorts and a t-shirt with a puppy on the front. Any guess on who picked out which doll?

"You be Andy, Daddy." A gift from Uncle Kade, Andy Ken is thrust into my hand. For every Barbie bought by Grandma, a Ken materializes via Uncle Kade, and Mommy sneaks in Skipper to rub everyone the wrong way.

Jesse always let me be Skipper when we played together as kids. Jesse was Ken, Franny was Barbie, and I was Skipper. Neither of them let me play with my own toys. While it may rub Willa and Kade wrong, it warms my heart because the gesture is meant for me.

Uncle Hayden is the purveyor of all things literature, while Uncle Warren and Copper are obsessed with showing up with Matchbox cars and Tonka trucks. Ginger's still a baby, but she slobbers on Honor's toys and then hands them back to her. Aunt Penny and Uncle Wynn don't stick to a theme, but the newest was a cash register and a basket of plastic food– some snarky asshole tagged it with a Circle K emblem in Sharpie.

Franny designed Honor's bedding and shipped it from California– there's a few unicorns hiding in the foliage of the jungle animal theme, and the lions' manes are actually feather boas. There's no half way with Francis *Frantastic* Parker.

Jackson– Jack doesn't buy my daughter's affections. He gives his free time whenever he can, so I can get a few hours to myself to get in a jog, or just sit in the park without someone needing something from me by making demands. Dad does the same, trying his damnedest to give Jesse and me time alone together without interruption.

"What do you want Andy to do, baby girl?" I settle onto my side on the carpet, reaching up with Andy like it's a puppet show.

Honor slides from her bed to sit next to me, folding her stumpy legs underneath her skirt. She reaches for the scenery set Jesse painted for her on poster board, then snatches up some doll furniture.

"Puppies like the park." A handful of hard plastic puppies– all choking hazards for a three-year-old –materialize out of nowhere to be unceremoniously dumped in front of the poster board park scene.

"Let me guess, Uncle Kade?" Kade doesn't get the concept of age-appropriate, stating Honor isn't a fucking moron because tiny plastic toys don't taste as good as cookies.

Honor's chubby for a reason, and Uncle Kade's visits have been restricted because of cookies and bad toys.

Uncle Kade says Honor looks just as pudgy as her daddy used to, always said in a taunting fashion, then the animal crackers are passed out like crack– including to Daddy.

"Uncle Kade lubs me." Honor smirks at me sweetly– the little minx. "He said I can have as many real puppies as I want when we come home."

"What?" I try to keep my composure, eyes bugging out of their sockets. Andy takes a header to the floor when my hand goes numb.

"Isn't this our home, Daddy?" Chubby fingers arrange Andy in a doll-sized deck chair, then puppies are piled in his lap. Emma's plastic hand is patting the top of a golden retriever's head.

"If only I could nail your mommy down, we could answer that question."

Elusive bitch.

Honor tilts her head in exactly the same way her mother does just before I'm nagged, and I shudder in horror.

Universal truth: all the flaws you can't stomach in your spouse will be reproduced in your child. Wonder what Jesse hates about me that is reflected in Honor? Probably everything.

My belly growls loudly, signaling the tank is empty, and Honor giggles in response. "Let's fix some grub, eh?"

"Hot dogs!" Honor claps while hopping to her feet.

"Fine, but it has to be kosher dogs. I can't do another night of that cheap hot dog flavor."

"Cheese! Hot dog! Cheese!" I ignore the loud chanting, which will go on until she gets her hot dog cut up into tiny wheels, dotted precisely with ketchup, with a side of shredded cheese out of the bag.

Hehe.

The cheese is actually shredded carrot.

"Whatever my princess wishes." I tap her on the butt. "Go on out to the kitchen. I'll be right there."

"'Kay, Daddy!" Drunk running in a zigzag because the girl clearly has my shitty coordination, Honor bounces off the hallway walls while giggling up a storm.

Love her to death, but Honor will never be an honor student.

"Uncle Kade says Honor is too smart to eat toys, but she thinks carrots are cheese because both are orange." In one fell swoop, every plastic puppy is deposited into a tote I hide in the top of Honor's closet, filled to the brim with cheap, choking-hazard toys Kade brings because that's what asshole big brothers do. He's also notorious for toys with sound, which lose their batteries the instant he leaves, and Play-Doh.

Yes, the bastard always brings Play-Doh, and permanent markers.

Kade is all about revenge.

My punishment for licking a *mine* stamp on his baked goods, then eating them in front of his emaciated ass.

"Hot dog! Cheese! Hot dog! Cheese!" All the women in my life are demanding. I find Honor trying to fix her own supper in the two minutes it took to clear her bedroom of Uncle Kade contraband.

Caught red-handed with a kitchen chair shoved up to the refrigerator, Honor freezes when she catches sight of me.

"We've had this conversation before, baby girl," I softly reprimand, never once raising my voice to my daughter. Why is it so hard not to think she's cute? It takes all of my willpower not to laugh at the stunned O expression on her cupid bow mouth. "When you're a little bit older, you can help Daddy and Mommy cook. But not yet."

The house I bought straight out of high school is nothing to write home about, but it's served its purpose well for the past four years. The bedroom, which was originally Kade's home away from home, is now mine– I didn't want to sleep in our marital bedroom, because the ghosts of good times from Jesse's and my past would have haunted me.

My wife used to be *in* love with me, cock be damned.

Next to the backdoor from the kitchen leading into the minuscule backyard is a puppy playpen– Perty's from when she was a tiny pup always underfoot and we were terrified to step on her. Call me a bad daddy if you will, but it gets the job done. Chuckling underneath my breath as Honor chatters about absolutely nothing, I situate the canvas octagon into the center of the kitchen where a table and chairs should be.

"Up– up and away we go." Hands scooping my baby girl up by the armpits, I swing her over the top of the playpen, and plunk her behind on its canvas floor. Immediately she begins zipping and unzipping all of the windows, which will occupy her for all of two minutes. Honor can easily let herself out through the doors or over the top, but she sees it for what it is– a boundary line.

Hillbilly is strong in my daughter's blood.

"Hot dogs and cheese– my princess gets what my princess wants." I go about the arduous task of sorting the contents of the refrigerator. Since Jesse and I are hardly home at the same time, never eating together, there are cartons and containers of food made by Jesse, Becca, and me. I only touch what I've put in there. One time– it took one time of accidentally pitching some mashed black beans and getting my ass handed to me to learn to leave it alone.

I spy the rice I made last night, always needing a healthy dose of carbs to offset my weight-training, and I grab for a fresh pack of '*adult*' hotdogs. Nuker going, I sizzle the dogs in a pan.

"We good with some apple sauce tonight, baby girl?" Daddy and daughter plates go on a tray for when our food is ready.

Honor finishes rolling up one of the window coverings in her puppy pen, trying as hard as she might to get the Velcro tab to stick to the canvas instead of its mate. "Peaches?" Hard at work, she figures out Velcro only sticks to Velcro, smiling up at me beatifically like she just cured cancer.

I'm going to have to have Wynn design Honor's future playhouse like the inside of the puppy pen. "Peaches it is, then."

Startled at the sound of the front door slamming, my back goes ramrod straight after a shudder rolls down it.

"Mommy!" Honor's to her feet and reaching her chubby hands out of the top of the playpen in an instant. "Mommy's home."

With the flick of my wrist, the gas is shut off to the burner, allowing the residual heat to finish cooking the hot dogs. I keep my back to Jesse as she greets our daughter, but her voice is tight with rage.

What'd I do now?

Jesse's shift at The Voyeuristic Artist doesn't start for another hour, and I have no idea where she ran off to in a rage earlier. I try to relax my muscles, knowing Jesse gets even angrier when she thinks I'm trying to intimidate her with my size, when it's not fury having me flex, but depression having me clench tightly in fear.

"Would you like to join us for supper?" I ask my wife, voice soft yet hesitant. "I can add another dog to the pan, and I have rice in the microwave."

"I wish you wouldn't feed her hot dogs," Jesse snaps. With the fridge door open, she squats to take inventory of the disaster area. "Why do I have to do everything around here? This is disgusting."

"Because I'm damned if I do, and damned if I don't, so I don't," is on the tip of my tongue, but I know better than to rile Jesse up more.

Plastic containers become projectiles, landing across the kitchen into the sink, and the takeout cartons plunk into the nearby garbage can– including the cheesecake I was saving for a snack tonight.

Ignoring my wife, I go about fixing Honor's and my plates.

"You should take care of your own shit, Bren," Jesse chastises while going batshit cray-cray on our refrigerator. "Look at this!" A hand is thrust into my face with a Pyrex measuring cup filled with '*something*' sloshing over the side. "What fucking idiot would do something like that?" implying *I'm* the idiot. "It's not covered and it's stinking up the fridge."

I bite back a laugh and the word *cunt*, mind running in two different directions, split between fury and amusement. "I look at the fridge as a work fridge. Tag and date it. Once a week it gets emptied. It's up to the owner to take care of their own shit. Thanks for pitching the cheesecake I bought *this* morning, which is why I stress we take care of our own food."

After quickly looking at the teriyaki sauce, I place the measuring cup in the sink and twist on the tap. Eyes flicking up to mine, I meet my wife head-on. "I take care of what I put in the fridge, but there is someone who doesn't. That someone had teriyaki marinated tofu last week, and we both know I can't stand it. So you're calling yourself an idiot– angry about yourself. Get it under control, Jesse."

"Don't condescend to me." Jesse glares, rising to her feet to intimidate me. Meanwhile our daughter has stopped being happy– stopped playing with her puppy pen.

No one knows what I've been through and what I've seen but those who were with me. I've never spoken of it, never gone to a therapist, and always maintained I'm perfectly happy. Honor will *never* go through it. Ever. Maybe not sharing this part of myself with Jesse has destroyed us, because she feels I never truly let her in, but my nightmares are for my mind only.

Leaning in, I whisper in Jesse's ear. "The next time you swear in front of Honor, the next time you try your damnedest to pick a fight with me, will be the last. You hearing me?"

"You do not get to speak to me that way," Jesse warns, pink face flushed crimson red with rage.

"I've said nothing irrational, Jesse." I don't voice who is being the nutjob. "You and I are going to have a serious talk and get things settled. Wynn graduates the first week of May. Jack's going to commute to graduate school– med school, whatever you call it– from Rusty Knob."

"Yes, because our lives revolve around theirs," Jesse says snidely, resentment thick in her voice. "You just assumed we'll move back to Rusty Knob and be a happy family, but you never asked me what I want."

"I assume nothing," I remind my wife. "If you'd stop running, you'd find out how I've wanted to ask you what you want, and make sure you get it. But you've been playing hide and seek with me since before last Christmas. It's gotta stop."

"I can't say what I really want to say in front of our daughter." Guilt flashes over Jesse's features as her eyes dart toward Honor.

"No fear, Jess." I try for levity in my voice, because Honor can read my emotions better than her mother can. I use a conversational tone, when I'm anything but. "Dad and Willa are going to take Honor, not this weekend but next. So clear your schedule."

"Trust me when I say you're not going to like what I have to say," Jesse warns.

Smiling privately, I issue my own warning. "Trust me when I say you have no clue what I'm going to say, Jesse, and without Honor around, I *will* speak my mind."

"There's nothing you need to say to me," Jesse snarls, pulling away from me to stalk across the kitchen to begin washing out the dishes she tossed in the sink– her measuring cup of shame first.

I count to ten as I finish plating our food. After walking the tray into the living room, I hesitate before lifting Honor out of the playpen. "I hope your maturity level rises before our chat. You acted older when we were kids than you do as a twenty-two-year-old wife and mother. There's never been anything you couldn't say to me and have me judge you. All of our problems rest on your juvenile behavior."

"Stop spouting Kade's psychobabble." Jesse glares at me over her shoulder, and I hate how that feral look goes straight to my cock. If only... if only my wife was attracted to me, loved me, saw me for the man I am... If only, we'd be happy together.

"Nope, not Kade. That was a direct quote from the advice your father-in-law gave me last week when I was upset after you called me an insecure faggot who couldn't make up his mind on which team I wanted to be on– which was rich coming from a lesbian married to a man."

"If you weren't such an indecisive bastard, we wouldn't be in this situation. Pick one– gay or straight, and stop waffling."

"Ha!" I snort in disgust, channeling Kaden. "Bisexuality is not indecision, and I'm not betraying the straight folks or the gays by not picking their side. I am what I am, and it ain't indecisive. I find it gross how *you* are throwing that bigoted bullshit into my face."

I pick up Honor, refusing to look at Jesse. Our daughter curls up to my chest, resting her cheek on my shoulder so she can look at her mommy as I walk into the living room.

Jesse's words have my feet halting. "You should have picked Jack."

Heart breaking, I pull Honor from my arms, placing her on her princess throne at the toddler table. If I'd picked Jackson instead of

Jesse, and had allowed her to get the abortion she wanted, the abortion it took Franny, Jack, Kaden, and me to talk her out of *at the clinic*, there would be no Honor, and that has my stomach threatening to spew out my mouth.

"You're such a vicious cunt," I quietly seethe to Jesse, not fearing Honor knowing what it means, since she's never heard the word before. "Go to work– I don't want to look at your face until we have our *little* chat."

Lowering to sit onto the tiny seat at the table, daughter and daddy have a dinner date of hotdogs and shredded *cheese*, with peaches for dessert. We ignore the banging of pots and pans as we chat about whatever nonsense spews from a toddler's mind.

Jesse's a good mother when I'm not around, and used to be a good friend before Honor was born. I don't know what is bothering her. It took both Kade and Dad to reassure me that it wasn't me, but something internal Jesse was battling inside of her own mind. If only… if only she'd let me in, I could help her by being the best friend she's trying to forget she has.

CHAPTER FOUR
Brennan Kennedy

All's peaceful as Honor lounges on her unicorn pillow in the center of her puppy pen, which is now situated in the living room. She's softly singing a lullaby to one of her babies while staring at the ceiling fan spinning above.

Every time a new thought pops into my head, I jot it down on my notepad. After cleaning the kitchen until it shined like Wynn Gillette had a hand in it, I've taken inventory of what I do and don't like in the house. It's my version of getting what I want in my forever home, and allowing some nice amenities for my future tenants.

First thing first, dishwasher. Second, a French door style refrigerator. Third, no microwave over the stove range, because Honor won't be able to reach it until she's almost grown, and any self-respecting ten-year-old should be able to make popcorn and pizza rolls. The exhaust fan was never powerful enough to suck the cooking fumes away either.

"Ready to play some shoot-'em-up?" Already bathed for the night, I tug my sleepy baby girl out of her playpen and place her next to me on the sofa, propping her back against the cushions. Her greedy fists are reaching as her impatient feet kick the sofa cushions.

Bad dad move #2 for the day.

I hand Honor a broken controller with no batteries, and then point out which character is hers, when in reality it's Jackson's avatar. I grab two headsets, using a splicer so they are both connected to my controller, activating bad dad move #3 for the day by allowing Honor to listen in as we play our nightly bouts.

"We're ready," I say to Jackson, who's always ready and waiting for us. "Let in the rest of the guys."

Bad dad move #4: Halo.

"How's my sugar doing tonight?" Jack's voice never fails to elicit a shiver out of me, no matter how much I try to ignore it. When I lost my best friends to graduation and marriage, my coulda-been-boyfriend took their spot.

"Jack!" Honor shouts so loud the feedback of the mic reverberates sharply in my ears. "Jack, I played with puppies at the park today."

"Really?"

"No, you didn't." I look at my daughter crosswise, knowing it's a lie yet the truth at the same time. Either Honor's a genius or a moron.

"Dude, pull that mic away from Honor's face, ya hear?" Jack orders me, voice holding laughter instead of anger. "In a few, I'll let the guys in. How was your day, bud?"

"SSDD," flows quickly without thought. "On all fronts– work and home. Can't wait to go back to Rusty Knob. Tony's still trying to get some, my clients believe I'm in the world's oldest profession, and my wife is acting younger than our daughter."

I always call Jesse my wife when speaking to Jack online with Honor listening in. The girl knows her mommy's name is Jesse, picking up Jessica or Jess too, but doesn't register *my wife* yet.

"Deliver any babies today, Mr. Midwife?" I murmur with a taunting air, finding it bizarrely adorable how Jack went from liberal arts to midwifery. Yet not surprising with how caring and giving the man is. Jack already has a lesser degree in nursing, but wants a long list of certifications that require continuing education. I don't know what letters will be after his name, but Jackson Duncan will be in school for a few more years yet while doing practical at Kentwood General. He's been commuting back and forth already, with the hospital closer to Rusty Knob than to Morgantown.

Willa had a baby three years ago, quickly getting knocked up as soon as Dad conned her into his bedroom. But something was wrong with it, and Willa had to do a natural delivery of a stillborn baby boy who was malformed and not viable. The loss wrecked us all, but it hit Jackson in a different way. It was at my baby brother's funeral where he whispered to me he wanted to be a midwife. There was nothing anyone could have done, but it still struck a chord in Jackson.

Yet another one we've lost that I'm forced to mourn on Dad's timeline. Another grave to visit. More reason to bleed agony. Dad still hasn't gotten me on board with mourning for twenty-four hours straight, when I mourn in my own way each and every day. To me, it feels like taking a searing hot knife and slicing into a healing wound, and then shoving a dirty finger into it to get it infected. Just as the inflamed emotions soothe, Dad forces us to do it over and over again every year on the anniversaries. He employs guilt to keep me coming back to the graveyard haunted by those we've lost.

Willa's seven months along again, terrified out of her mind even though her doctor said she's just fine with no risk factors. Last time, the egg or the sperm wasn't viable, allowing the baby to grow but not to full-term. The doctors cautioned for an abortion, but Willa wanted the baby with her for as long as nature allowed, even knowing he wouldn't survive. I won't lie, I'm terrified I'll have another person to mourn instead of celebrate.

Penny had Ginger a few months ago, and none of us were comfortable until after she was born. It made for a nail-biting nine months, which overlapped into Willa's pregnancy now. Fear eclipsed all joy.

I can't wait to take a deep breath again, and then force the women in my family on birth control so I don't have to go through this bullshit again. Jesse really went off the rails when this started, not letting me near her. That was when I moved into the spare bedroom.

"You there, bub?" Jackson gains my attention. "I said I delivered the biggest baby to date. A little girl who weighed almost ten pounds. Poor momma, but I managed to keep the skin soft enough not to tear so we didn't have to do an episiotomy."

"What's that?" Honor babbles like she's keeping up with the conversation. I have no idea what Jack's talking about, and I don't want to know, either.

I bark a laugh, pure irony pouring out. "I just– I just can't–" it takes me a few seconds to regain my composure. "I can't get over the fact that the gay guy who used to call straight people breeders, the one who was angry with me because I was bi, is now the same guy whose profession is getting up close and personal with tiny humans pushing their way out of vaginas like a twisted version of the movie Aliens."

"You suck!" Jack lobs my way while chuckling sardonically.

"I did, and you wish I would again," I volley back, causing a strangled sound to vibrate into my headset via Jack's. "What are my brothers up to tonight, studying?"

Jackson snorts, causing Honor to giggle at the sound– thank God she doesn't get why he made the noise. "They've been in the bathroom for the past two hours– it's always like a choose-your-own-adventure in there, never knowing what you're going to get. I had to piss in the kitchen sink, and then disinfect it before Wynn caught a whiff."

Face twisting up with revulsion, "What are they doing in there?"

"Bubble baths!" Honor suggests, thumbing her controller like it does anything.

"Yeah, while raising their periscopes." My daughter joins my laughter, making it funny because she has no idea what's so funny.

"We only have a shower stall… and toys. Lots and lots of toys. Latex toys with suction cups, and a rattlesnake trap of a dishwasher not used for dishes." I can hear the blush riding Jack's voice over the headset, and I can't imagine the expression on his face. "Letting the guys in now."

"Yay!" Honor shouts, while I murmur, "'Kay."

One after another, gamertags pop onto the screen.

Musclebound and *Nurse_Jackie* were already logged in.

"You're going down, Bren. Down. Down. Down. To sexy town!" *TheGaySage* shouts into his mic. Franny's roommate turned housemate and on-and-off-again lover has a vicious tongue sharper than a knife's blade. But we don't realize Sage is insulting us because his quips go right over our underdeveloped minds. Only his tone gives us a hint. Tonight he's as playful as ever.

Wreck&Ruin logs in next, saying nothing because he'd rather listen to us. We met Kieren Mason through Sage Fischer– they're related in a roundabout way. Sage's stepmother is Kieren's aunt, but they also share another person whose name we're not allowed to voice. Weston– Kieren's baby brother is Sage's the one-who-got-away, but almost-landed-him-in-prison-and-fifty-yards-away-from-a-classroom. Bad position for the future teacher-man.

"Thanks for letting me play, guys. My girlfriend is out to dinner with her father, so I'll have to logout when she calls me after she gets home."

PreacherBy-blow.

Tobias Kline is an acquaintance of Sage and Kieren, and yet another roundabout relation to Kieren somehow or other. Kieren's foster uncle's baby uncle– yeah, wrap your head around that. The guy isn't much older than we are, and he's the best Halo player I've ever met. Without a vicious bone in his body, Toby is efficient while being compassionate. He actually apologizes while we wait to respawn.

"Teams– capture the flag. I want to be a leader, so we'll have to switch out to team-only mic action." Toby brought in our oldest player, a guy who is knocking on forty's door, but is the most zealous gamer I've ever seen. *FarmvilleForLife*'s real name is Roarke Walden, and he brought the last of our players.

"Sage is our leader," is said in unison– one voice soft, one naughty.

TheEmpath and *TheTrickster*.

Zane Zeitler and Torian Spencer, a pair of cousins who are a few years younger than I am. They can't be beaten, no matter what, because they are in perfect synchronization, like they share a hive mind. They're not allowed to play with Roarke, because he's able to connect to the hive and annihilate us.

The most baffling thing of all, Zane and Torian are notorious celebrities and Roarke is their ex-cop bodyguard. I Googled their asses and found miles of controversy. Zane is whiter than the whitest person I've ever seen, even his hair, while Torian has rich coffee-colored skin and husky eyes. They have the same button nose and jawline– other than that, they're total opposites.

Never thought I'd meet two guys with more money than I have.

"I want Nurse Jackie," Zane whispers softly.

"No," is an immediate denial rolling off my tongue. "Jack's mine– always on my team."

"Dude, stop waving your flag!" Tori lights into me. "We're talking Halo, and Nurse Jackie takes great direction, with Sage making sure we do it."

"Or else." Sage chuckles evilly in a voice deeper than how his tiny, effeminate body should be able to produce. "If the '*honest, I'm straight*' guy is gonna say shit like that to me, then let's play it my way. Bren, Jackson, me, and Tori, because he's hiding in Bren's closet."

"Hey!" the kid in question bellows, causing his cousin to snort. "I like girls."

"We *know*," Roarke stresses, failing to hide his amusement. "But your eye also follows Caleb's baby brother around like the petrified country bumpkin is prey– *and* his older sister."

"They look just alike!" Torian interjects. "It's creepy, so I look at 'em."

"Sweet cheeks, you flirt with me nonstop on Facebook," Sage delivers the kill-shot.

"I flirt with everybody– doesn't mean anything. I'm devastatingly charming."

"You're a spoiled brat." Zane snickers when he's usually very reserved. "I think you channel Cortez just to piss off my mom."

Evil laughter flows into all of our headsets.

"Toby, how the fuck do you put up with this shit? Come back home," Kieren pleads, voice cracking with intensity. "Auggie and Tina need you."

"I don't hear you asking me to come home," Sage pouts.

Kieren ignores him. "Boys, your conversation is going over my head. Can we not make everything a political statement?" Kieren begs. "Please? I have to deal with this shit constantly, and Sage's 'I'm gay' rhetoric drives me up a wall. I know too many intimate details between Sage and West–"

"Na. Na. Na." Sage sounds like he's going to have a seizure. "Na. Na. Na." Honor joins in with her singsong voice, causing Sage to change his tune until they are singing together quietly in the background.

"Sounds good," Zane and Roarke mutter at the same time, with Zane continuing. "This will prove once and for all that Tori and I are just *that* good. We don't need the other as a crutch. Red team: Roarke, Kieren, Tobias, and me, verses the blue team: Sage, Bren, Jack, and Tori."

"Red versus pink," Sage interjects, and Jackson is instantly accommodating our leader by changing the color.

"Jesus Christ," Kieren snarls, showing his latent homophobia, while Tori whines, "At least make us purple."

"Pink," Sage and Jack say in unison, causing Tori and me to say, "Purple," over top of them.

We remain pink.

"If Dad was playing, every team would be gray." Zane cracks a joke, causing Roarke to choke on whatever he was drinking.

Proving how there is no bounds to the internet, our reach is from California, to West Virginia, New York State, and all the way north and east to Massachusetts. Together, we have a full game, with no need to allow outsiders in. Our skills vary, but our game's a bloodbath, with Honor as our mascot.

"Jackson! We're on the same team!" I shout, aghast. "Quit tea-bagging me."

Tori's cackle is loud with evil intent. "You let Ren sneak right up behind you and assassinate your ass, bro– ya oughta keep a better lookout for our team, which is why your boy is sitting on your dying face."

"Fromunda cheese." Jack has me laughing so hard I snort.

"Keep your head in the game," Sage warns to get us back on track. "We're losing."

"Too bad we can't hear what the other team is saying." Jack drops a shotgun at my respawned feet as a consolation prize. "You're welcome."

"Pfft... I want your sword."

"NFW, buddy."

"They're gloating," Tori informs us. "I can hear Zane all the way from his bedroom, and he is one quiet mofo, so you know he's excited. Sneaky f'er is probably near one of us, just lying in wait."

"What the– Zane has our flag!" Sage is furious. "Git yo ass in his bedroom and take the controller out of his hands."

"Cheater." I snicker.

"The albino is a lot stronger than he appears." Tori's voice shifts from playful to dead serious. "We train on the mat, and it's always a draw."

"Game over," Jackson mutters, not sounding too put out. "Zane scored with an assist from Tobias."

"Train?" My interest is piqued.

"Musclebound, no." Sage shuts the conversation down. "Time to regroup and plan a strategy. As losers, we get to pick the map. Battle plan session– now."

After two hours, Honor's snoring while holding onto her controller, and Toby's tapping out because some chick named Spyder is calling him. A few minutes later, Kieren's muttering something about Spanky needing the TV to binge-watch The Vikings. Then the rest of our New Yorkers logout at once, going on high alert like the sky is falling over Dominion, New York.

"So... is the sugar baby napping with her headset off?" Sage sounds sheepish– not a good sign.

"Yup." I tug my baby girl into my lap, cradling her against my chest. "What's up?"

"Francis and I are headed east– Kieren's hosting a family reunion."

"Real accommodating family, ya got there," Jack murmurs, not bothering to contain his laughter at Sage's expense. "The guy doesn't sound like he's too fond of you."

Sage chuckles without humor. "I'm going to sneak into town and say hello, but not go to the party because Chief Mason has it out for me."

"Obviously," I tease. "Popping an underage cherry will do that to a guy."

"Mine was popped first," Sage reminds us. "I just returned the favor."

"And forever made a manly man's baby boy a bottom for life?"

"I'm *that* good," Sage says without a hint of arrogance. "No one should complain– the kid was just drafted into the NFL without stepping foot into an institution of higher learning."

"Damn," Jack and I mutter together.

"No more talk of Weston– it kills me." Sage takes a deep inhalation of breath, and it's so pained I hurt for him. "This is the last summer before I'm a working man– substitute since no one any-fucking-where is looking for an English teacher. Yeah, so I'm doing a fly over Fairport, then I'm headed to stay with the snooty Sages of Boston. I'm hijacking my baby sister, and thought maybe I'd take a scenic drive south to visit you dumbshits in person, with a layover to check out the sights in Dominion, New York. You've got enough kids running around to entertain my sister, Gemma, and give her a taste of life outside of the manor's walls. Rusty Knob is about as far removed from Boston as Jupiter is."

"For real?" I lean forward, heart beating out of control because I'm so excited. "You're bringing Franny to us! Oh, my God." I hug my sleeping daughter's form closer, missing Francis so much my breath catches. "Thank you."

"It's a secret– Francis doesn't know. So keep this between us."

Jackson whispers through the headset. "Is it gross if I admit I just got so excited I almost pissed my pants while popping chub?"

"I'ma start calling you puppy."

"Snooty prick is picking up words from *our* Franny, I see." Jealousy burns in my blood like flowing lava.

Jack's next words have me losing my shit. "I'll blow you in thanks if you get our boy back on Rusty Knob soil."

Gut twisting, I'm not so sure I like the sounds of that. I want to be Jack's hero.

"Oh, sugar– that will be my pleasure," Sage purrs. "So pleasurable."

"Hey!" I snap, literally *snapping*.

"I may be small, but I'm not proportionate. There is more than enough of me to go around, Brennan. No sense in getting jealous over Jackson having the pleasure of my flesh. You can suck my hairless sack while he bobs my knob."

"Holy fucking Christ." Jackson makes a wounded animal sound.

"Did you just come?" I accuse, fingers turning to claws. I glance down to see I've scratched my controller. "You know that's not why I was getting pissed, Sage."

"Good of you to admit that, buddy." Sage's laughter fades to silence as he logs out of Xbox Live.

"Wanna come over after I tuck Honor into bed?"

"You sure?" Jack whispers.

"Yeah, we could watch something on TV." The loneliness is killing me, and Jackson is the antidote. "Get you away from my brothers for a few hours."

"They're now loading the dishwasher like perverted savages. Gimme twenty– I gotta shower off real quick," Jackson mutters sheepishly, logging out before I can respond.

"Oh, my God!" I shout into a dead mic. "You did come!"

CHAPTER FIVE
Brennan Kennedy

Why am I nervous? Jack's been coming over three or four times a week since we moved to Morgantown. After I tucked Honor in, I took a quick shower and changed my clothes.

"What do I put on?" I murmur to myself.

The remote slips through my sweaty palms to land on my thigh as I try to navigate the DVR. After a quick rub on my track pants, I'm able to hold onto the remote, shaking be damned.

"Jesus, every show makes it look like I've got a hidden agenda." I leave it on ESPN, not seeing what's on the screen, and then lean back against the sofa cushions like I'm just chillaxing after a long day.

The knob turning has gooseflesh beading along my arms. "Hey," Jackson breathes as he shuts the door behind himself. "Did Honor go down without much of a fuss?"

"Yeah, she's getting settled into the sleeping schedule now." I scoot over a bit on the sofa. "After I changed bedrooms, she was confused."

Jack sits next to me, palms running along his thighs, betraying how he feels the awkwardness settling in around us. After a deep breath, he toes off his sneakers and then folds his legs, always sitting cross-legged on the sofa. "What are we watching?"

"I–"

"Seriously?" Jackson chuckles at my expense. "Do I need to go get us a couple brewskies? Maybe belch as I shove my hand down the front of my pants for some nut scratchin'?"

Cheeks blooming bright red, "It was just on," I mutter as my excuse while gesturing to the TV. Then I hide my face behind my palms as soon as what's playing registers in with my brain. "I didn't know what to put on, so I flicked it to ESPN, and then never looked to see what was playing."

"Women's beach volleyball?" Jack hits me upside the back of the head. "Look at those asses– so firm yet jiggly. Those tops are small enough to be considered pasties, making thirsty babies' bellies rumble everywhere... Does this turn you on? Seriously, I'm curious."

"I'm not looking," I drawl out in a voice tight with mortification. "I'm sure dude's beach volleyball or diving would get you to pop chub, so behave."

Grinning like a villain, Jack leans down to whisper right in my face. "Being bi must be like being ambidextrous, right?"

"Um... okay?" I quickly grab for the remote before my body takes notice of the luscious tits and ass on display. "Here," I thrust the dang thing into his awaiting hand. "You pick."

Jack types in the channel number without going to the guide and looking up what's on right now. A commercial for trash bags is playing. Wiggling deeper into the cushions, he gets comfortable. "Did it turn you on? I'm not judging; I really am curious."

"Yeah, if I watch it long enough," I answer without hesitation. "Doesn't mean I get aroused for everyone, though. I'm not a man-whore anymore."

"You've been repenting for your past transgressions like a goddamn monk." Jack takes a deep breath, gathering courage for some reason. Sex has been a no-no conversation between us since we did each other the night before I married Jesse.

I learned every square inch of Jackson's body, inside and out, repeatedly from dusk 'til dawn– whatever I did to him, he did to me. Jack was my first and only with a guy, in every sense of the word. I took his virginity, but Franny beat me by a few weeks as the first guy Jack ever gave head– just thinking of that makes me want to cry like a hypocrite.

I have no idea who Jack's been doing since, and I made Kade and Wynn promise to never tell me. Kade understood, but he still called me an immature coward.

"Ask me anything, Jack." Leaning backward, I close my eyes and drape my forearm over my face.

Jack mutes the TV, so I know I'm in for it. "How many girls have you been with? What's it like? Who was your first? How old were you?"

Laughing without humor, I squeeze my eyes shut tight. "Nine, even if it seems like it's higher– it's not. No splitting hairs. It's not nine cock in vag– it's nine anything with a girl. I consider any sexual contact as sex. Jesse was my first, and we were fifteen– obviously she trusted me and it felt good to her, or she wouldn't have come back for hundredths. Three of the girls was me vetting them to see if they were interested– they weren't, and I didn't fuck 'em unless they were."

"Interested in what?" Jack turns sideways on the sofa to look at me, and I kind of miss being his size, fitting into smaller spaces and being comfortable all the time. I'm still short, just not as flexible from the bulk.

"Getting a bit tipsy and fooling around with Jesse. The remaining five of those girls were threesomes. Sure, I wanted them, but I wanted to make Jesse happy more. So I found girls who were bicurious or horny enough to mess around with both me and Jesse. The times you caught me with a girl is because I had to get her hot enough to whisper the idea into her ear."

"I can't imagine how freeing it would be to just put yourself out there." Sadness infuses Jack's voice. "I try very hard to wrap my mind around wanting to touch a girl as much as I want to touch a guy. Then I feel kind of terrified for you, because of the total sensory overload you must be under."

"I'm no hornier than the average guy." I snort when I think of my brothers– fiends. "I think there is a balance, like you're probably attracted to a few types of guys, but I'm only attracted to a small number of guys and girls. Make sense? It's not like even one out of ten our age– maybe one out of thirty from the people older than us. I might go a week before someone gets any reaction out of me– besides those who already do, that is."

"Damn. Here all this time I thought you were attracted to everybody, and it's even less than I am." Jack tugs on my arm, not allowing me to hide behind my forearm. "Don't be embarrassed."

"I'm not." After taking a deep breath, I release the pent-up truth of it all. "I'm ashamed. Some of those girls I didn't want at all. Some I wanted to mess around with. All I did for Jesse. It was a twisted form of loyalty I had with my wife. I regret it."

"I-I-I–"

With Jackson tongue-tied, I decide to explain. "Don't get me wrong– I *want* girls. But I feel ashamed about why I did it. It wasn't because I wanted to date, or even fuck 'em. I did it to keep Jesse, when she wasn't mine to keep. I used them. Jesse used them– and she used me, even if she didn't mean to."

Jackson whispers so softly I struggle to hear him. "You haven't had sex since me, have you?"

"No," I breathe back.

"After the constant sex for three years, you punish yourself by not having any for four? If that's not a Royce Kennedy move, I don't know what is."

"I never want to have another threesome again– it's not for me. I'm sure it's fun for most, but I've already been there and done that, and found it to be toxic for me. Jesse and I made no promises about remaining faithful. I've been good to prove that I can be to myself, because I won't use anyone ever again, and I won't let anyone use me."

"How many guys have you wanted?" Jack treads carefully.

"A few," I admit after a few heartbeats. "There's lust at seeing someone from afar, and then there's *want* from knowing someone personally. Many from lust, but very few from want. I'm not giving names, so don't ask."

"Yeah, I get that." Jack laughs without humor. "Francis?"

"No– he's your type, not mine."

"You have bad taste, bro– *bad* taste." We share a laugh over Jackson making fun of himself. "You placed Franny in the category as your brothers, though, so I get why you're blind to his virtues."

"In my world, the only ones who are versatile are off-limits, and the rest are tops. It's not bad taste– it's a preference."

"Oh, so I'm your last resort?" Jack acts offended but his eyes are sparkling with mirth and his lips are twisted into a shit-eating grin.

"Nope, you're the only contestant at the pie eating contest, and we're all different flavors of pie."

Throwing his head back, Jackson tries to laugh without sound flowing out so he doesn't wake Honor– that small bit of consideration makes me love him all the more. "There's always Tony."

"God, no." I shudder in mock-horror. "Not my type. *Ever*. He'd die and go to heaven if he ever met my brothers."

"Tony's not their type, though. They only like big guys when it comes to each other, not when they're ogling other guys."

"Narcissists." I snort, thinking back to the hilarious conversations I've had with Penny and Warren about this subject. "They get off on looking at each other like mirrored bookends. Then they point out who they think is hot while in public, like they're shopping. It's fucking bizarre."

"You don't live with them– sometimes I think Wynn's tracking me like prey, but he doesn't realize it. Kade is respectful by acknowledging it, but he keeps a safe distance. It's like the creepy elephant in the room."

Startled, "They want to fuck you?" spills out from between my lips.

"They're perverts– it's not about me. I get it, can't explain it, and ignore it. As I said, Kade hedges around it because Wynn's blind."

I murmur, "As usual," not as creeped out as I thought I would be. "Do you want to fuck them?"

"I get that they're your brothers, Bren... but really? Any guy would be so lucky." *Shit!* "When we move back to Rusty Knob, the pool is going to get even smaller," he reminds me.

"You know it doesn't matter." I try to assuage Jack's fears, basically telling him there's no one else for me. Bi or not, I've never truly wanted anyone but Jesse and Jack, and neither are a consolation prize. But instead of smiling and playing along, I only seem to make Jack frown.

"What's wrong?" I shift toward him. "What'd I say?"

"Nothing," he answers so quickly, I know it's a lie. "Let's watch TV." Closing me out, he settles back against the cushions, feet on the floor, not at all how he sits when he's comfortable.

I stare blankly at the screen for a few minutes before the show registers. "Hoarders? For serious? You turned it here by memory alone."

"For serious." At least the humor is back in his voice. "I love this show– Wynn got me hooked."

There's a middle-aged woman sleeping in a mound of trash inside her home, with Lord knows what beneath her, and everything is covered in cat shit and black mold. "I could see why Wynn would like it, but why are *we* watching it?"

"Have you ever watched the show Intervention?" Jack keeps a straight face.

"Also a favorite of Wynn's via Kade, no doubt." I roll my eyes, having no idea where Jack is going with this.

"Bud, you and I have to talk about the state of your daughter's bedroom. Channel your dad again, and box that shit up and donate it."

"I'm not buying it!" I whisper-shout in outrage. "It's my family. Our favorite toy is the puppy playpen– I'm a simple man."

I spiral deep, drawn to the laughter bright in Jack's eyes. Catching myself leaning forward, I jerk upright, only to grunt in pain. "Christ," I hiss between clenched teeth as I try to reach the cramp.

"What's wrong?" Jack's hands flutter in the air. "I can fix it."

"I'm not pregnant," I gasp, turning surly because of the pain. With every inhalation, my muscles spasm. "Motherfucker!"

"You do realize I had to learn everything before specializing, right?" Jack's narrowed stare is none too pleased with me at the moment. "You're not hydrating or resting your muscles, you buffoon."

"I don't like bothering the massage therapists at the club, because their hands and wrists ache." Leaning forward, I try to stretch out my back by resting my cheek on my thigh.

"What is this insanity in which you speak?" Jack wedges himself between my ass and the back of the sofa, then his fingers are wrenching my t-shirt over my head. A sharp inhalation has me gazing over my shoulder.

"I know," I mutter in shame. "I overdid it. I hated being so scrawny, and I enjoyed the high of working-out. Now I wish I hadn't bulked up so much. I've only been doing cardio and some light lifting to stay firm."

"Why do you look self-conscious right now?" Jack stares at me with a gobsmacked expression. "Explain?" Healing hands locate the knot immediately.

"Argh," I groan, body going lax as Jack's fingertips press with brutal accuracy. It hurts like a sonofabitch, but it's relieving the spasms. "Deeper– sorry."

"Sorry about what?" comes out breathless.

"The massage therapists bitch about their bodybuilder clients because of how taxing it is to work the kinks out of our muscles. So I'm apologizing in advance, because you'll be transferring my pain into your own hands come tomorrow."

"I know what I'm doing," Jack mutters flatly. "I know you know what muscle is what in order to train, but I know why it does what it does. So where is some lotion or oil?"

"There's hand lotion on the bathroom sink…" My blush is so brilliant my speech pauses. "Or grab the baby oil next to my bed."

"Now that you have a kid, it doesn't look so perverted buying it, does it?" Laughing, Jack crawls over my back. "Get comfortable."

"I am," I project down the hallway as he walks away. "I can't sit upright." Spreading my legs a bit, I hug the back of my thighs to stretch out more. I need to do more yoga and less lifting.

"You didn't make your bed today." Jackson clues me into which product he grabbed. "I'd do the same thing if it wasn't for my bed being in the corner of the living room, with an OCD roommate."

"Kade still a filthy hog?" A grunt is pulled from me because Jackson presses on my back as he shifts to sit behind me. "He used to beat me up if I didn't do his chores around the house."

"Fuck yes– the only thing that man cleans is his sex toy collection." Jackson pauses, weighing his words. "I love living with the freaks, though. I'm not one who would ever want to live alone. I'd get lonely. Gonna miss 'em when I move back in with my parents."

The soft powder scent hits my nostrils, immediately forcing my blood to flow to my groin. Everyone thinks I'm being a good daddy by buying Honor unscented, expensive baby oil, but that's not why. When a boy starts using what he uses at puberty, it gets ingrained in his mind.

Cheap baby oil equals orgasms.

"Uh… that feels so good." Slack-jawed, words just babble out. "Marry me." Jack's fingers still on my back, so I make it into a joke. "You'd be perfect if only you could cook."

The fingers go back to work. "I cook– why do you think your brothers keep me around?"

"You've never cooked for me," flows almost inaudibly.

"I've never had the opportunity."

"Ah– are you happy to be going home?" Jack's lubed hands land on my back, and I can't contain the groan that escapes. "Christ, don't stop."

"I won't– yes and no on going back to Rusty Knob. Feels like I'm going backward, sleeping in my old bedroom after spending four years on my own. But I can't get my own apartment and live alone, and I won't trust a random roommate." Jack attacks a knot with vicious intensity. "You've been in pain for a long fucking time, you cocksucker. Don't pull that shit again, damn you."

"Promise," I mutter in a moment of weakness, too blissed out on Jack's touch and from the euphoric pleasure-pain radiating throughout my back. I could give a shit less about the fact that I'm drooling on my thigh. "Talk to me, Jack. Don't care what. Trust me– living with someone doesn't mean you won't be lonely."

Biting fingertips work their way down along my spine, causing my eyeballs to roll into the back of my head. A sound too close to orgasmic spills from between my lips, and my cock is throbbing for attention inside my pants.

"Married life isn't what I thought it would be." I find myself the one with a loose tongue. "After growing up as I did, with no momma, and having a year with Willa in the house, I had expectations on what I thought it would be like. I wanted to eat at the table as a family– to start our days together, and share our experiences over dinner. Laugh a lot. Dry tears. I never expected anything sexual. I would have cooked if Jesse didn't want to, without a single bitch– cleaned everything too. I just wanted someone to come home to, to raise my daughter with… my best friend who loved me as much as I loved him or her back."

"Bren?" A warm body envelops me from behind, arms sliding underneath my torso. "Shh… it's okay." His soothing words make me realize I'm crying.

Shit.

The comfort is like nothing I've ever experienced before, and I find myself pouring it all out. "I have to talk to Jesse, because we have a bunch of shit left to work out before we can move back home."

First Jack stiffens, then he pulls away, and the rest of my words dry up before I can release them– important words I needed Jackson to hear, but was too nervous to say until now– now he doesn't want to hear them.

Healing fingers go back to work, tirelessly kneading on the knots in my back. Patient yet sad, Jackson doesn't say anything else. I suddenly realize he's closing me out because Jesse is now a no-no topic of conversation, like sex used to be.

What I wanted to talk about affected *us*– Jackson and me.

Our future.

I wanted to tell Jackson that I'm not mourning the loss of my marriage, but my lifelong friendship with Jesse. More so, I wanted to tell Jackson how I never chose between Jesse and him. I chose Honor. As a baby, a child, then a young woman, I need to be the most influential person in my daughter's life, yet that doesn't negate how I feel about Jack. At the time, Honor's life depended on me supporting her mother in all things. Now it doesn't. The biggest obstacle is working out our differences so Honor can have a happy life, however we live it. I hoped to have Jack's input on my solution, but he keeps shutting me down.

"Can I explain," I beg, breath hot against my knee. "Please, don't be mad at me."

"I don't want to hear anything about Jesse, Brennan." Jackson's chastisement is punctuated by a vicious jab of his thumb into my right shoulder. "Do you want to hear about the endless string of blowjobs I had in college? Hmm? Do you wanna know how I learned to deep-throat even the biggest of dicks?"

"Fuck no!" my voice is filled with silent horror.

"Then shut up about your wife."

"It's important," I try again.

"I don't give a fuck– I don't wanna hear about it. Got it?"

"Fine," I mutter in defeat, not wishing to argue with the man jabbing me in the back with all ten fingers and both palms.

"I'm done." Jackson pulls away from me, and I'm left bereft at the sudden loss. "If you continue to not hydrate and work your muscles to the point they spasm, I'm never going to do this for you again. But if you drink your fluids, stretch, and only maintain muscle mass, I'll do this for you a couple times a week."

"Really?" My voice squeaks with awe and a little bit of hope.

"Really– promise me," Jackson demands.

"But you're mad at me?" I flip around easily to look at him over my shoulder, when half an hour ago it would have murdered me to do so.

"Being mad doesn't change anything– I've been mad at you since you first kissed me back in junior year of high school. Promise me."

"I'll take care of myself," I vow, voice solemn.

"Good." Jackson moves from behind my back, but I snag his wrist in my palm to keep him from leaving me.

"Let me return the favor."

"Why?" Jack's eyes narrow, suspicious of my motives.

"At least let me rub your arms, wrists, and hands, because they will ache because of me, and my hands are perfectly content at the moment."

"Why?" he tries again to pull the truth out of me, when he didn't want to hear it a few minutes ago.

"Because I want to touch you. No one touches me but my daughter and random hugs from my family. All I do is lie in bed craving you– thinking about us." My voice gets softer and softer as I speak, while I slowly tug Jackson closer. "I wanna make you feel good too. Please."

Jack slumps to the sofa cushions, acting put out and annoyed, but his lips are curving up at the corners in a satisfied smirk. He flops his arm onto my lap. "Get it over with, so you'll quit bitching about it." The words are pissy, but he no longer sounds angry with me.

Smiling slyly, I slide to sit behind him like he was behind me earlier. I'm going to give more than a hand massage. With my thighs bracketing Jack's hips, I marvel over how small he feels, when I used to be that size too. Groaning, I get off on our differences now.

"What are you doing?" Jack protests, yanking his t-shirt out of my grasp.

"I can't rub your back if your shirt's still on."

"You said my arms," Jackson reminds me, voice warbling for some unknown reason.

Settling my hands on his biceps, I show Jack how his sleeves are in the way. "Ditch the shirt, Duncan."

"Thanks for humiliating me, *Kennedy*." The shirt lands on the floor, and the same sound Jackson made when my shirt was yanked off flows out from between my parted lips. I know why I made it, but why did Jack?

"What?" Jack whispers. "Stop looking at me and get to massaging– you must find me repulsive."

A puff of air billows out my nose– 100% shock. "Jack? You have no clue what I'm thinking about, so shut up and let me enjoy the moment."

Tentatively resting my fingertips on his back, I just stare in wonder. My breathing is increasing the longer I look. Jack's skin is pale perfection– so dang soft I want to rub my cheek against it.

"So soft," I purr, scared to move my hands, knowing it will betray how they quiver.

"I know I'm a fat ass, Bren. No need to press the knife in deeper." Jack hangs his head in shame. "With all the courses I've been taking, all I've done is sit and get chubby. Without basketball, I've grown a pot gut and moobs. I don't know how it's possible to be simultaneously scrawny and fat, but I manage it."

"Shut up!" I snap before I can stop myself, then I moderate my voice to something less furious. "I hate how I look, not finding it the least bit attractive."

"Don't fish for compliments when I'm the one freaking out because I don't look like I did four years ago when you last touched me."

"I don't look the same, either," I remind him.

"Yeah, you look a billion goddamn times hotter. I've spent the last few years watching you evolve, wanting to climb you like a tree. Meanwhile, I've atrophied."

"Promise me something?"

"What?" Jack says hesitantly.

"If you want to get fit to feel better about yourself, only do cardio– swimming, cycling, or running –and some light lifting to firm up your muscles. We can do yoga together, because I suck at it. But don't build an ounce of bulk– promise me."

"Why?" Jack might not know where I'm leading or why, but his breathlessness means he senses the direction.

"Earlier, you asked me if I had a type– this is it." Jack's gasp pulses in my dick. "Now shut up and let me feel how soft you are."

Taking a giant leap and feeling no guilt over it, I lean forward to press my chest to Jackson's back, wrapping my arms around his torso. The overwhelming sensation of our bare skin touching coalesces into a feeling of absolute rightness.

Lust roars through my veins, demanding I accept the gift that is being given. With every exhalation, I inhale Jack's potent scent. Our nipples harden at the same time– mine against his back, and his pressing into my forearm.

Never once have I denied wanting Jack, and he's never hidden his desire for me. We've just never given in but once forever ago.

Groping with no finesse, my hands are everywhere. Needing more, I curl my fingers along Jack's jawline, and turn his face to the side until his lips reach mine. Craning my neck forward, I complete the connection.

Jack's whimper flows into my mouth, plump tongue following it. Wiggling impatiently, trying to crawl between my lips, he grinds his ass into my cock. In this moment, it doesn't matter how much head Jackson's given and received in the past few years, because I know my dick's the only one he's ridden.

With a hungry growl, I reverse our position until Jack's underneath me, pressed to the sofa cushions. Mouths fused together, Jackson takes hearty pulls on my tongue, no doubt giving head with the same enthusiasm.

Breaking free, I trail my damp lips along his neck, traveling down until I can suck on his fleshy nipples. With a big mouthful, I nearly come all over myself.

With a rough yank to my hair, Jackson has my eyes connecting with his. "Told ya– I have tits, yet my ribs still show. How is that fucking possible?"

"Are you under the impression that turns me off?" My voice is thick with incredulity. "Because I'ma 'bout to blow a load in my pants like I did during our first kiss."

"Christ!" My hair is released and my lips are attacked. Questing hands shove beneath the back of my pants to cup my ass, nails biting into the flesh. "Your cock feels so good grinding against mine. Get the pants outta the way– I wanna feel how hard I'm making you."

Well, that's a new development– dirty, demanding mouth.

Fumbling between us while my lips try to seek out Jack's nipple, I huff out a laugh. "Don't shut up now– keep talking."

"You're hairier than before– Jesus, I wanna comb it with my teeth. It holds your scent better– stronger."

"Fucking pants," I whine, trying to wedge my hand down the front to pull them down.

"Daddy, are you having a tickle fight with Uncle Jack?" The playful tone in my daughter's voice has us both freezing.

"Ugh..." My guilty gaze flicks to connect with my mini-me, who happens to be standing no more than ten inches from my face as I'm poised over Jackson.

"Sugar? What are you doing outta bed so late?" Jackson gains his composure quicker than I do, which says how shitty I must be in the sack. "You need a drink? Gotta go potty?"

Honor just shrugs her tiny shoulders in response. "Can I join the tickle fight?"

Jackson crawls out from beneath my frozen body, tugging up his pants as he goes.

"Daddy gave you a raspberry on your boob." Honor points at the huge suck mark I left behind, giggling like we're playing.

"Hmm... I guess Daddy did." Jackson tugs my shirt on in a hurry, which thankfully covers the damp front of his sweatpants. "How about we take a trip to the kitchen for a glass of water, then a detour to the potty, and end our journey where I tuck you back in bed?"

Honor grabs for Jackson's outstretched hand, smile so bright it's blinding. As soon as they walk out of the living room, I relax my muscles all at once, landing on my belly on the sofa. With a violent gust, all the air whooshes out of my lungs on impact.

"Universe, what evil deed did I enact in a past life that has you punishing me eternally?"

No one answers me.

Even after being interrupted by my daughter, my cock is still armed and at the ready. Of course, Honor thought nothing of what she just witnessed, because she's been exposed to her grandparents touching each other, to Penny and Warren being fused at the lips, and Wynn and Kade crawling all over each other like horny monkeys.

Honor will grow up in a different world than I did– where it's okay to have two mommies or daddies, instead of a mommy and a daddy. Where she'll have an aunt and uncle, but also have a pair of uncles too.

I feel not a single ounce of shame or regret over what my daughter walked in on since nothing was showing, and not one iota of guilt over touching Jack instead of Jesse.

"Hey?" Jackson's hand lands in the center of my back, fingers massaging already stiffening muscles. "Honor fell asleep instantly."

"I gotta work this shit out with Jesse." I try again to explain, but Jackson flinches away like I just lit his hand on fire with my touch. "Please listen."

"I gotta go." Jack straightens to his full height, and then strides to the front door. "I can't touch you while you're married to Jesse."

"I know– me too."

"So I guess that means we have nothing left to say." Jack turns away from me, but he can't hide how devastated he looks.

"You have to let me get the words out, Jackson." At least that made his hand still on the doorknob. "Jesse and I have some shit we have to work out before we move back to Rusty Knob."

"Save it– I can't listen to this shit." Before I can get a word out, the door is already closing behind Jackson's retreating back.

After slamming my head into the armrest a good dozen times, I decide my fate hasn't changed. "I thought men were easier than women," I mutter to the universe, and yet again it doesn't answer.

"Ha!" But my wife does. "I came in the backdoor because I saw Jack's car parked out front."

"Hell!" I scramble to sit up, but Jesse shoves me back down where I started.

"Did you have sex?" Not a trace of judgment is in her voice.

"No," I mutter guiltily.

"You should." Jesse leans down over me, running her hand along my back, touching me for the first time in six months.

"We were going to– I think. But Honor interrupted." Groaning in both pain and mortification, I hang my head.

Jesse laughs just how she used to, but it feels like a nasty trick. I only get glimpses of my best friend from time to time, but then she's replaced with a harpy.

"Maybe tie Jackson down next time, so he can't get away and will actually listen to you." I relax into the touch, trick or not. Jesse makes a sound in the back of her throat– zero sexual interest, all appreciation of my hard work and dedication to transform my body. My wife does like how I look. She just doesn't want me.

Tugging on my wrist, I allow Jesse to pull me to my feet. She snorts at the mess I've made in the front of my pants– a huge wet spot that only seems to keep growing. Bobbing up and down, my dick is pointing straight out, seeking any attention he can get.

"Go to bed. Here," she passes me Jackson's t-shirt. "Sniff this–" she fetches my baby oil from between the sofa cushions "–while using this."

Gobsmacked, I stare after my wife's retreating form, with her laughter trailing behind her. Shameless, I do as Jesse bid, and I blew the top of my head clean off.

CHAPTER SIX
Kaden Marx

Finger trailing along the lines of Wynn's face, I try to touch lightly so I don't wake him. Ordinarily, we're up at the crack of dawn, but he doesn't have any classes until this afternoon and I'm driving back to Rusty Knob to stay for a few days. We were up late studying last night– actually studying, and I know the kid needs his rest.

It's a different experience to have unlimited access to Wynn when he's silent and still, and never in the light of day. Poetry in motion, my boyfriend is always animated. If I try to touch him, he's greedy and tries to touch me back. A kiss always leads to orgasm.

We've spent our time trying to get off quickly in the main room, racing the clock for when Jackson gets home, or holing up in the bathroom for a few hours of play. But the sensual side of things has been lacking, because we have to do it under the cover of darkness, trying to be quiet enough because we're not selfish assholes who wake our roommate.

In a few more weeks, I'm going to feel like I've died and gone to heaven. Wynn's moving in with me in my home in Rusty Knob– *our* home, where we'll start our life together.

I'm not complaining. Peeking underneath the sheet, I make sure my movements are fluid enough not to wake him. It's just a novelty to watch Wynn at rest, with his flaccid cock nestled against his sack like a baby bird in a nest. He's always hotter than hell, libido set to sex, sex, and more sex. The only soft dick I see is a sated one, but it usually rises for round two, three– ten –before I'm ready.

Four years of college basketball and a family discount membership at Bren's gym have Wynn filling out more than I could have dreamed. Somehow the stocky gene bypassed Wynn, maybe because of his height, so all of his muscles are lean and stronger than steel. Biting my tongue, I curl my fingertips into my palms to stop myself from outlining the valleys of flesh.

I have no idea what I did to deserve Wynn. But he wants me, so I'm not giving him back.

A page flipping draws my attention, and I spy Jack sitting cross-legged in the middle of his bed with a heavy textbook propped up on his thighs. I'm pretty sure if Bren saw Jackson in the wild, he'd lose his shit. The guy always puts on emotional armor before he heads to Bren's house, so my brother isn't seeing the man I see. With mussed up brown hair and hazel eyes hidden behind black frame glasses, Jack is too adorable to describe.

This is nice– I love peaceful moments like these.

"Kade," Wynn murmurs in his sleep, voice thick with lust. No doubt the brat is dreaming of me moving inside of him. Catching my undivided attention, I watch as Wynn's cock slowly fills with blood. Curving to the left, precum beads out to land on the epically sexy tattoo riding Wynn's hip.

Gade.

Wynn surprised me, memorializing our first time in the Durango, where I had teased him by calling him Gade.

"You're Gade, is what you are. Gay for Kade. Now stop staring at it, you little shit. You're not that innocent to think sex is a staring contest with a dick."

Smiling privately, my eyes gaze down the length of my body, but I have to tug up my thermal to see it first. Riding just above the base of my dick is a tattoo.

Little Shit.

I'm Wynn's for life, because any new lover would think I was saying I had a shriveled up dick. Wynn got off on the mortifying factor of the gesture.

"Mmm… more– harder." Wynn moans, shamelessly wiggling his ass against the mattress. "Ah! The stretch is…"

To see this in the light of day– to experience it for real instead of in a dream state.

Growing impatient, I have to shove my thumbs into the holes in my sleeves, ensuring the fabric covers my palms to stop myself from waking Wynn with my touch. Like an emo from fifteen years ago, I have to wear long-sleeved shirts underneath everything, and I even wear them to bed. I've jabbed holes into every cuff to keep the sleeves from riding up and showing off my scars.

Only Wynn has seen me naked, and I don't want to freak Jackson out. I don't care if he sees me, but we're not friends like he is with Wynn, so I don't want to burden him with my story. Plus, my side and my hip have fresh cut marks– not from the past few months, but even with my therapist working with me, I've still cut myself since I've been with Wynn.

It's looking in the mirror that does it– I see Dad. The rest of the time, in my head I look like I used to– like *me*. So I can't handle seeing my dad while trying to understand that it's me in the mirror gazing back. In my thoughts, I'm still a gangly kid with a pockmarked face, with every bone showing.

My therapists says I have Body Dysmorphic Disorder. Staring at my scars is painful because I don't want to see the truth, so I cut myself to force reality.

I'm working on it.

"I love you!" Wynn practically shouts, a bit of cum dribbling out the tip of his dick. Normally, when this happens in the middle of the night, he'll wake up and attack me. At this rate, I'll have the pleasure of witnessing Wynn having a wet dream.

Fuck– that's hot.

A sharp intake of breath gains my attention, eyes connecting with Jack's, and I realize I won't be the only one to bear witness. Pale face washed with a crimson kiss of embarrassment, beneath that is agony.

"What's wrong?" I mouth, not wanting to wake Wynn and miss out on this epic adventure. It's not like Jack hasn't heard Wynn come a billion times before.

Mouth gaping open, I go into shock watching Jack pad across the floor to stand next to the bed. It's not that the guy is skittish, just reserved. I know he gets some once in a while, but we don't talk about shit like that– ever.

Wynn knows every sordid detail, I bet.

"I want that." Jack points down at Wynn, looking devastated. "I want it so fucking bad it's killing me."

"Wynn? Or you want to have a wet dream?" I try for amused, and it works because Jack rests his hip on the edge of the bed. "Hate to break it to ya, buddy, but I've heard you come in your sleep before. I won't embarrass you by saying what you groaned while doing it."

Even Jack's ears blush.

The generational divide is wide right now, with us bookending our twenties. They're still horny bastards fueled by runaway hormones, and I'm settling down into amused contentment.

"I want a blowjob– just a blowjob." Jackson's confession startles me. "That's all. I need to be touched."

"When you came home from Bren's last night, you were pretty wrecked." More like sobbing, but I don't want to kick a man when he's down. I figured it would take ten seconds of manipulation to get my brother to spill.

Bren doesn't confide in me anymore. Instead, he walks into Royce's office and shuts the door. Since Royce has no clue what to do about any of it, he comes to me. So, yeah, I know all of Bren's secrets, even if he doesn't think I do.

Parents– never trust 'em. What they say to you about your siblings, they say to your siblings about *you*.

"Bren's never going to leave Jesse," Jack whispers with tears lacing his voice.

I beg to differ, but I can't say it. Goddamnit!

"I think we're having a bit of a failure to communicate situation here," I murmur instead.

I don't have kids yet, but I plan on upholding the family tradition of fostering pains in the asses like me. I can't hold Bren's and Jack's hands and walk them through this. I'll stand by with an extinguisher while they light themselves on fire. Maybe laugh while grabbing a few marshmallows. Sure, I could take the matches away, but how would they learn fire hurts?

So, instead of fixing Bren's problems, I lie in wait with the burn salve while they torch and burn their lives to the ground. My future profession pretty much gives me license to say, "*I told you so, dumbass. What did you learn from your lesson so you won't do it again?*"

"Bren and I almost had sex last night." Jackson's face turns a putrid shade of green.

Well, shit!

"Almost?" I drop the sheet, realizing I was displaying Wynn's goods to his buddy. They are gorgeous goods, but Wynn should get a say in the matter. "Why not close the deal?"

"Bren kept wanting to talk about how he and Jesse have a bunch of shit to work out before we all move back to Rusty Knob, and it was making me feel sick."

"Bub, trust me when I say whatever you're thinking, Bren meant the complete and total opposite." Idiots. I know exactly what Bren's plan is since I was the one who came up with it in the first place. I had Royce feed it to Bren like it was his own idea. "You're not a child anymore. Act like an adult and talk it out."

"Bren has toyed with me since I was sixteen– I'm done. *If* he ever gets a divorce, he'll know where to find me."

"*If*? Surely Bren's told you how Jesse has been seeing someone on the sly, too cowardly to introduce her to the family."

"What?" Jack gasps, and I get a sick kick out of how upset he is with himself for feeling happy over Jesse being a cunt. Wynn and

Jack are selfless souls, not understanding the subtle nuances of the human condition. Right-fighters, not realizing what is right for them may be wrong for someone else.

As for Jesse, more power to the woman– I hope she gets lots of pussy. Jesse deserves a happy life just as much as Bren does. Whatever woe-is-me tale Bren spins, Jess can spin one as well.

Wynn was close to breaking shit when Royce relayed this bit of intel. Now Jackson looks guilty for deriving sick pleasure from Bren getting what he deserves.

My immature puppies are so cute. They should own why they feel what they feel. It's so much more freeing to not give a shit.

I change the subject to more interesting topics, feigning ADHD when their teenage angst bullshit rears its ugly head. "What's up with the blowjob request?" My eyes flick down to take note of how Jack is still sporting wood, even after trying to discuss emotional shit. If he starts up again, I'ma wake Wynn.

Mentor? Sure. BFFs sharing our hearts desires? No way in hell. I hear enough sob stories during mock group therapy drills. I'm the boss at spinning woe-is-me, always causing my classmates to cry. Dr. Lansdale sometimes questions if I'm actually a sociopath– jesting, of course. Then he says I ought to write dark literary fiction and warp impressionable readers' minds.

"I just want a blowjob." Jack shrugs his small shoulder, pretending he's not embarrassed.

"You asking?" I deadpan.

Jack doesn't break. "You offering?"

I just stare, refusing to blink.

Jack breaks.

"I used to get a lot of head from my nursing school buddies," Jack admits. I raise an eyebrow, intrigued. "I know how cliché it sounds, but nursing is predominantly gay."

"No shit?" Now this conversation is getting juicy. "Really?"

"At least it was in my class– lots of women and some straight dudes too. But study sessions ended when they left, and then we pretty much had a suck-fest. I miss it."

"Lots of fun, eh?" I don't even bother hiding how the sheet is tenting. I'm completely shameless. "You miss it?"

"Yeah." Jackson blushes so red, his ears glow crimson.

"Shoulda sealed the deal last night with Bren, then." My dig hits home. "Then miscommunicated after. True?"

"No," Jack snarls at me, showing teeth. The sheet bobs, fabric rubbing against the abrasion Wynn left as a parting gift last night. "I'm not going to fuck around with Bren while he's married. Either Bren wants only me, or I'm out."

"You're out? You want a spit-shine? But the guilt is going to suffocate your ass because you'll wish it was Bren on his knees. You get that, right?"

"Get off of Team Bren, and just be real." Jack stares me down, showing more backbone than I thought he had.

"I'm Team Everybody, bub. Wynn's selfless. You're caring. Bren's trying everything he can to fix his shit. I'm over here with a bucket of water, just watching your lives burn. But I can't tell you what to do because I respect you enough to let you make your own mistakes."

"Advice would be good." Jack doesn't even blink.

"I keep trying to hand everybody the bucket of water, but they just won't take it." I roll my eyes skyward dramatically and stare at the ceiling. "Step-by-step guide, brought to you by Kaden Marx." I shift on the mattress, trying not to disturb Wynn. I tug my shirt back into place when my scars peek out at the wrists. "Step one, which you'll be a fucking moron and do last, no doubt– listen to Bren. Step two, don't fuck around because that'll hurt more than you realize."

"Kade." Jackson sighs deeply, sounded exhausted. "It was fun fucking around in college, because we all knew what it was. I've avoided temptation ever since for a couple of reasons. I didn't want to hook up with a coworker and have it ruin our jobs when it went to shit. But the biggest reason was I didn't want to find someone I might fall for."

"See, you're on Team Bren, too." I wink to be a rat-bastard. "So go get your dick sucked from a random, but be careful. I don't mean on the protection front, but having shit taken from you you're not willing to give. There's a lot of nasty people running around."

"Do you have any idea how bizarre your advice sounds?" Jackson has the balls to laugh at me.

"Hey! It's good advice," I bellow, waking Wynn.

Rolling around, sucking air deep into his lungs while stretching, Wynn doesn't have a modest bone in his body. His foot hooks on the sheet, dragging it off us. Making a wounded sound, I press my junk to Wynn's thigh to hide it.

"What's up?" Wynn stretches from the tips of his toes to his arms straining overhead, naked as the day he was born. His cock is hard, drying precum dotting his belly. Smiling, he murmurs, "What?" again.

"I forget," Jack stammers, eyes on my man's dick. I own the fact that Wynn is this comfortable, and that I'm getting turned on by Jack getting turned on by Wynn.

"Jack wants a blowjob, but he's too much of a pussy to get one from Bren," I blurt out just to see what happens.

I'm a sadistic bastard. Toss the cards in the air and see where they land. Poke a wound until it festers. Toss your horny roommate at your equally horny boyfriend. All in a day's work for a therapist-in-training.

Practical, hands-on experience.

"I'll do it," Wynn mutters without hesitation, voice still groggy from sleep. "Stand up." He stretches again, offering his dick on a platter. He wipes at his mouth with his palm, getting ready.

"You... what?" Jackson looks at me with his jaw hanging to the floor, waiting to see if I'm going to turn into a raving, jealous bitch. All I can do is laugh at the monster I've created. God, Wynn is magnificent. "First, Kade gives horrible advice. Now, you're trying to give me head."

"It's a blowjob— I didn't offer to have your baby." Nothing is a struggle with Wynn. He flows like water to sit upright in bed, still not bothering to cover us with the sheet. When I try to cover my own ass, his toe mysteriously decides to hook into the sheet again. Then his thigh moves, giving Jack a flash of my junk. I make like a drag queen and tuck between my clenched legs.

"Why was my advice bad?" Scrunched eyebrows betray my confusion.

"You just told me to fuck around on your brother!" Jack's all aghast. "Then Wynn offers to suck me off. Your *boyfriend*."

"If you're so insulted, why are you popping chub?" Wynn's eyes flash to Jack's groin.

"I thought— I thought you guys were in love with each other?" Jack is so confused, it's precious.

"We are," Wynn and I say in unison, but I continue. "His dick, brain, and heart seem to be having a disconnect." I tap all three, with Wynn pressing into my hand when I get to his hard-on. "Slut," I mutter with affection, earning a chuckle. "I have the glorious honor of telling him what his dick wants because it's hooked to my brain."

"Pfft..." Jack is not a believer.

"It's true. Wynn– he's a selfless fixer. You're having a problem and he offered the solution. That doesn't have a dang thing to do with me."

"The thought of Bren fucking another guy makes me want to destroy things." Jack's nails curl into his palms, knuckles turning white.

"I'm not going to explain color to the blind, but Wynn and I are on the same page, Jackson."

"What would Bren think if I touched one of his brothers?"

"Maybe Bren would finally take a shit or get off the pot, is what I'm thinking." Nuts aching, I untuck after covering the area with my palms. "Jealousy always levels the playing field. *But...* I have a better suggestion."

Eyes staring at his buddy's bulge, Wynn licks his lips. "You don't want me to suck you?" Wynn actually looks offended, dick shrinking a bit. But Jack's visceral reaction has us all harder than steel.

"I didn't say that," Jack gulps out, voice quivering. Through his sweatpants, he has a death grip on his dick. "Didn't say that at all."

"Hear me out– we'll celebrate Wynn's impending graduation by going out to a club, yeah?"

"Really?" Wynn sits up like a puppy begging for a treat, eager and wagging his tail. "You said I wasn't ready, refusing to go on my past two birthdays."

"You're ready now." I don't voice how I was terrified Wynn and I are toxic for each other when it comes to our adventures, but I don't have to worry this time because all of Wynn's focus will be on protecting our little buddy. "The three of us will go, and Wynn and I will pick out some stud to suck Jack off in the bathroom."

"That's it?" Wynn's wheels are spinning. "Can we at least watch?"

"Jack's ass belongs to Bren, and whoever gives it away is going to have to deal with me." I pin them with my unflinching stare. "I mean it. Messing around is one thing, but letting a stranger *inside* you is another."

"I just want a blowjob." Jack's voice is shaking like a leaf. "Really."

"Good, because I'll kick your fucking ass if you give it up to anyone but Bren." My eyes flick to Wynn. I trust him, and I'd forgive him. But he's been so eager for penetrative sex, he might slip up.

The kid has been optically stalking his best buddy for months, not even realizing his divining rod is pointed at Jackson. That's why I said Wynn's dick is connected to my brain, because I'm not sure he'll ever be able to communicate with it outside of knowing what he wants from me. It's a terrifying responsibility I'm shouldering, but Wynn's navigating while I drive.

"Okay, to prove I'm the best advice-giver on the planet." I wedge myself off the bed, still cupping my junk. "I have to get going soon. I'm already late as it is. So while I shower…"

After yanking on my pajama bottoms, I play marionette with my puppets. Wynn laughs, having no idea what the hell I'm up to as I arrange him until he's sitting on the side of the bed, with his feet on the floor, with Jackson next to him.

"I had four years of roommate fun to take the edge off. So while I shower, you kids do what most junior high idiots do— watch the other rub one out." They're stunned and I'm relieved. I'm too tired to service Wynn this morning. "I expect to hear you both coming, so make it loud and sexy."

I don't look back over my shoulder as I walk toward the bathroom, terrified yet aroused at the fact that whatever I see would probably have me joining them on the bed. Terrified because I'd lose control and end up fucking them both, and that's unforgivable on two counts.

"I'll be jerking off in the shower, so you better listen for me, too."

"Oh, God!" Jack shouts, realizing I wasn't joking. "Are you okay with this?"

Wynn *finally* turns bashful. "Kade's letting me relive his past experiences. He likes to hear my fantasies, and this is one of 'em."

God, I didn't think I could love Wynn any more than I already did, but I manage it.

Most people are so narcissistic, they don't realize their partner has had experiences they will never go through. They're greedy, selfish, taking what isn't theirs while not giving the same in return.

If you're mature enough, selfless enough, you'll share what carved you into who you are. Give it freely, not have it taken away from you by demand or squashed before it's been experienced.

If Wynn and I are to truly understand one another, we'll have to get a taste of what made us who we are.

Jerking off while watching Dan was the highlight of many years of my life, and I want to gift the experience to Wynn. I did it without him, so I give him the same respect, not wanting him to feel like he has a disapproving father standing over his shoulder. Wynn needs to learn there is no shame in owning his own body, and enjoying the pleasure it gives him.

Content yet happy for them, I stay in the shower until I hear their garbled song of climax, and then I add my own.

CHAPTER SEVEN
Brennan Kennedy

"What are you working on?" Jesse comes into the living room, and I quickly snap my notebook shut like I'm up to no good.

"It's a surprise." I smile to lessen the denial. "It's one of the things I wanted to talk to you about, but it's not ready yet." Nervous, I doodle on the cover, not realizing what I'm writing until after I blink a few times.

Duncan.

"Got Jack on the brain?" Jesse laughs, the laugh that feels like a trap because it's the sound of my best friend. Since the kitchen yesterday afternoon, she's been more herself. "I'm not good with surprises, Bren. But I am patient."

Sitting on the sofa, I look up to Jesse with a huge grin on my face. Jesse is *not* patient at all. "Are you headed out to work?" Wednesdays are our mutual days off. Until recently, we'd hang out and spend some quality time together.

"No," is all Jesse says, no explanation necessary. Her smile is replaced by a look of immense guilt.

"Whatever you're doing, whoever you're seeing, wherever you're going, I truly hope it makes you happy." No one could ever doubt the sincerity in my voice.

Jesse turns her face to the side, but not before I see tears sliding down her cheeks. After quickly brushing them away, she turns back to me. "Yes– happy… but sad too."

"Yeah, I get that." We speak in code, but we understand each other perfectly.

Jesse is spending the day with her girlfriend. Whoever she is, I know she's not a casual fuck. Jesse showed no guilt with her past flings– this is different. The real deal. Permanent. Best friend, lover, and partner rolled into one perfect person for Jesse.

Forever.

I could be an ass and throw a fit, but what good would this do when she'll be my daughter's stepmother? I loved my mother, but there's no denying how much I adore Willa. What kind of parent uses their resentment to remove loving people from their child's life? It's not a competition– it's just one more person to love my daughter almost as much as I do. Jesse's girlfriend probably loves Jesse more than I can imagine, so I'm not going to vilify the woman.

"Bren, I put Honor down for her nap, so you should have about an hour to work without interruption." Jesse speaks to the floor, refusing to look at me. The sob hits my ears a second later, gutting me.

Gutted.

Moving quickly before she can stop herself, Jesse is launching herself into my arms, holding us both together. Familiar lips meet mine for a moment, then move as she speaks. "I love you."

My *I love you* falls on deaf ears, because Jesse is gone in a flash, leaving behind her goodbye.

"Christ." I scrub my palms over my face, brushing away tears I hadn't realized were falling. Then I slump forward to rest my elbows on the coffee table on either side of my notebook. "Guess I better get back to work on this more than ever."

Drawing a rough sketch for the cupboard placement, I jump out of my skin when a heavy palm lands on my shoulder.

"You okay, bub?" Kade musses up my hair, trying to pretend he's not a sappy fool. Giving up, he leans down to engulf me in a back-slapping bear hug. "I came in the kitchen door... I heard that last bit with Jess."

Pulling away, I take a deep breath, releasing it on a laugh. "I thought you'd be home by now, being Dad's part-time bitch."

"Dick." Kade drops down next to me on the sofa, causing me to lose my pencil. After some searching, I find it sticking out beneath his mammoth ass. "No funny business down there, bub. It's virgin prime real estate."

Never failing to force a laugh out of me, I'm actually glad to see Kade. "What do you think of right here for the cupboards?"

"Nope." He yanks the pencil out of my hand. "This eraser sucks ass, baby bro." Taking his time, I'm surprised to see he actually has a natural talent besides asshattery. "I'm assuming we're outfitting this kitchen with your boy in mind. Let me work on it for a minute– Jackson's almost as OCD as Wynn when it comes to what goes in which cabinet."

Concentrating on drawing, I can feel Kade wants to say something that's going to freak me out. "Just rip the Band-Aid off."

"This miscommunication bullshit between you and Jack is for the birds." Kade's shoulders tighten beneath his t-shirt, and it terrifies me. "He sobbed half the night, using his pillow to absorb the sound. Then this morning he said he wanted a blowjob."

"A blowjob?" A cold sweat flashes across my skin. "From you?"

"No. Yes. I don't know who. But Jackson said he wanted one, so I had to come up with a solution on the fly because Wynn was more than willing to be accommodating. Then I offered up my boyfriend to the sacrificial gods of mutual masturbation to take the edge off."

"What?" I lean closer. "Come again?"

"Yeah, they came!" Kade rolls his eyes at me, purposefully being a douche. "When I get back from my tour at the center, I have to take my slut and your brat to a club. We're going to pick Jack out a willing mouth and get him sucked."

Red hot fury flows in my veins, and I'm about to bust my skin like the Hulk. With at least six inches of height on me and years of reading my body language, Kade's got me pinned to the sofa with a hand smothering my mouth before I can react.

"My niece is sleeping," Kade reminds me in a cold and calculated voice. "Don't bitch at me about anything Jack does, because I've been keeping dick out of his ass for the past four years for you. But now I've got a big fucking problem. Wynn's gaining confidence in knowing what he wants… and your boy has one *sweet* ass."

Wrenching my head to the side, I dislodge Kade's sweaty palm from my mouth. "Wynn and Jack?" is all I can get out.

"I've got it handled," Kade assures me, sliding to sit back on the cushion next to me. "This new development is putting a wrench in my future plans, and I won't let anything take Wynn and me off course. Got it?"

"What do we do?" Head in my hands, I thought losing my wife to her girlfriend was bad enough. Now Jack is going rogue with my brothers. "How do we stop it?"

"I know you think guys are simpler creatures." Kade laughs quietly, but it's the evilest laugh I've ever heard. "Bullshit, buddy. Jack has been festering for years, and he's going to make you pay. I tossed Wynn at him because they love each other and won't harm the other. The alternative was worse– some drunk asshole may make you jealous, but he could take something from Jack he's not willing to give. You feel me?"

"I guess it could be worse." Slightly relieved, I fall back to rest on the cushion. "After I talk to Jesse and get all of that squared away, I'll force Jack to listen. What's a couple of random blowjobs between now and then? It's not like he's dating someone."

"*Exactly*," Kade stresses, but I was being sarcastic. "I'll do my best to protect Jack from himself, but you've got to get him to listen."

"I don't know how you do it." I mutter in mystification.

"What?"

"Watch Wynn with someone else."

Kade shifts on the sofa to face me. He pauses, really thinking over how to answer me. "I watch everyone, how they say something other than what they're thinking, because their body language is telling a different story than what's coming out of their mouths. Human nature dictates that we are all liars, especially to ourselves. I'm not going to lie to myself. I'm not going to lie to Wynn, and I'm not going to allow him to lie to me."

"You think I've been lying to Jack?"

"No," Kade answers solemnly. "To yourself. Wynn and Jack watched each other jack off this morning. Does that mean they somehow love us any less than they did a few minutes before? Or does it mean they love us more for allowing them to spread their wings and fly where the air current takes them?"

Jaw dropping, "I–I–"

"Because I can tell you, Wynn was all over me after that. I had to fight him off to get out of the apartment." Kade looks so smug, I'm fucking jealous. "I'm not advocating an open relationship, either. We have rules we abide by, and to break them is to break our trust. But I'm not going to get jealous and stifle Wynn like I own him and have a say in what he does with *his* body."

"I don't think I could handle that, Kaden– I really don't." I feel like a shit heel for admitting it, like I'm not as enlightened as he is.

"That's good, because Jack isn't built for it, either." Kade silently laughs at me, eyes looking more green than brown. "This shit between Wynn and Jack? It's no different than Franny and Jack in high school. It's safe and exploratory. Wynn? That kid is a freak. But he's *my* freak, and I find it precious how he gets so turned on he can't think straight."

"I seriously didn't want to know that." I shudder in revulsion. "For the love of all that is holy, no details."

"You and me, it's like we're the same age now." I blush from Kade's praise after begging for it for over a decade. "I think it was because you got married, had a kid, and got a job instead of sitting in classrooms and hanging onto your youth. So we want the same shit outta life right now, but our puppies don't."

"Puppies?" I'd be mildly insulted for Wynn and Jackson if I didn't find it hilarious.

"Eager and stupid," Kade says without missing a beat. "Untrained. The trick is to let them navigate while you drive, so they can't wreck our future before it even begins. Just pull the dang E-brake. I wouldn't let those assholes go anywhere together without supervision. Naïve is an understatement."

Getting a clue, I add my two cents. "Prey."

"Yes!" Kade pats me on the back like I'm a good boy. "Wynn and I are going to be happy every fucking day of our lives together, even if the world is burning down around us. All give, no take."

I look at Kade crosswise, biting back a sharp bark of laughter. The '*virgin*' is giving me advice. "If everyone is giving, how the fuck does anyone get what they need?" Which is why he's still a virgin.

"By understanding your partner and being a selfless person. We're in luck, because Wynn and Jack are natural caregivers. I'm a selfish asshole in all things but Wynn. I've made it my life's mission to learn what Wynn wants and why he wants it. I give it to him because that's what I want. This only works if neither takes."

"Yeah, but if you're not allowed to take…" I gesture, pointing out the vital flaw in Kade's plan.

"*Receive*," Kaden stresses, making me feel like a dipshit. "Everyone is always saying it's fifty/fifty, but it's all or nothing. I give my all, Wynn gives his all, and we both accept what was given freely."

"No demands," I mutter, conjuring up how I felt every time Jesse made me feel small over something that meant absolutely nothing in the grand scheme of things. It seems so petty to think back on it now, but the wound is still fresh.

"Thank you for the advice. I get it now– when I talk to Jack, I have to do so from his point of view. The conversation isn't about Jesse and me divorcing, but what I have to offer Jack in any capacity he'll have me."

"I'd start by being his buddy and stop editing what you say to him." Kade rises to his feet, and then looks down at me. "Sometimes I say the most bizarre bullshit to Wynn, just to test to see if he'll judge me–"

"And he never does," I interrupt.

"Never." Kade looks smug, and instead of being jealous, I feel happy for him.

"But what if he did?" I try to wrap my mind around having absolutely no fear of rejection.

"I never judge him, and that transfers over to how he treats me. The little shit judges everyone else, though." Kade laughs sardonically. "Might take a while between you and Jack, with so much water under the bridge. Remember, when someone judges, that says more about them than the one they are passing judgment on."

"In theory," I mutter, willing to give it a try. "You're going to rock your job, Kade. Really."

"Can I tell you a secret?" Bubbling over with excitement, Kade doesn't give me time to answer. "Miriam Ross has a couple of jobs she wants to hand out to me and Wynn when we get back, and I'ma tell her no."

"What?" I half shout. "Seriously?"

"Yeah." Kade grins. "Sometimes life changes its path, and I don't want to be a guidance counselor anymore. I think I'd rather go into private practice. As for Wynn, it would probably be a cold day in hell before he sets foot back into any building operated by Kentwood Area School District."

"Fuck, I want to watch her face." Chuckling as I imagine it, I shake my head back and forth.

"I like Miriam as a person, but not what her position stands for." Kade shrugs.

"Yeah, but maybe you could change what it stands for, Kaden." My words have his face going blank for a few seconds, then he blinks out of it. "Maybe your path hasn't changed after all."

"It has," he mutters in a daze, trying to hide just how much he *really* wants it. "I-I– I gotta get going if I plan on getting anything done at the center today."

"I'll see ya in a few days." I stand to give him a back-slapping hug. "Call me if anything is new in Rusty Knob."

"Will do." Kade walks to the front door, and something strikes me as odd.

"This is the first time you've ever visited without your arms loaded with gifts and cookies."

Kade makes a funny grunting laugh as he shuts the door behind himself.

"Deny it all he wants, Kade's gonna take that job." My smile washes away when I realize why Kade paid me a visit in the first place. "I can't judge– I still have a wife."

Mind spinning, the best defense is offense. I'm going to bother the piss out of Jackson, to the point he'll feel so guilty he won't go through with it. "Dammit! I ain't gonna play mind games with him. Gonna be real."

I'm reaching for my cellphone before it even registers in with my brain. Jack picks up on the third ring. "If you could have anything your heart desired…"

"Anything?" Jack's incredulity emotes from across town.

"Okay, maybe not anything." I laugh at myself. "If you could have a dream kitchen, what color would it be?"

"What?" Jack breathes, causing me to shiver. "Why?"

"Just play along, buddy," I coax, grabbing for my notepad. Handjobs and blowjobs not forgotten, but there was nothing to forgive in the first place. "Kitchen, what color? I'm helping Dad design the plans on a rental house, and I need ideas… but it has to be exactly what *you* would want."

Okay, so Kade said we're to never lie, but he also said human nature makes sure we do. My baser self and I get along famously for the next half hour while Jackson describes the fantasy house I'm going to make his reality.

"Daddy?" Honor's voice enters the living room before she does. I quickly glance at the clock and realize she's been napping for close to two hours, which has never happened before.

"You feeling okay, baby?" I ask in a soothing voice, worry pounding in my veins. Then I see her. "Uncle Kade!" I bellow, positive he can hear me as he's driving like a bat out of hell toward Rusty Knob.

Honor shuffles into the room, sheepish as all get out, while dragging a giant stuffed unicorn by its horn. Her cheeks are covered in melted chocolate, and she's wearing a hot pink feather boa and plastic high heels.

"My word– how the– what?" I tilt my head to the side, noticing a bag of cookies clutched in her other hand. "How did that get in here?" The unicorn is at least four feet long and three feet high, and Honor can barely drag it.

"Uncle Kade surprised me." Her face lights up like it's Christmas morning. "He came in through my window."

"He did, did he?" Bastard said he snuck in the back door.

"There's a present for you too, Daddy!"

I'm on my feet and charging down the hallway before Honor's words even register. Sure as shit, there's a box in the center of the room, wrapping paper torn to bits off it. I fall to my knees, examining the paper.

Wedding bells?

The fuck?

"I tried to open your present for you." Honor has no shame. "But I couldn't get it open."

"It's an adult present, baby." I shudder in horror, terrified to find out what's inside, and glad Kade had the brains to duct tape every seam on the box. With effort, I hoist the box in my arms. "Let's stable your unicorn in the puppy pen. I think he'd like that as a home. We'll even get him a plastic bowl to drink from."

"Yay!" Honor has to walk backward while tugging the unicorn down the hallway for leverage. I could help, but I won't. She loses a high heel at the halfway point, and I snatch it up to add to the treasure trove of no-no gifts. Mommy will shit a brick if she catches our daughter dressed like that. I retrieve the second shoe at the mouth of the hallway.

"Unicorn needs a harness, baby. I bet Uncle Kade meant for that boa to be for the unicorn." Parenting on the fly– I am the master.

With Honor and her presents tucked away safely in the puppy pen, minus the cookies, I plop the box on the countertop and grab a knife. My hand shakes as I slice through the duct tape.

"Oh, Kade," I sigh, gathering courage to lift the flap on top of the box.

"What, Daddy?" Honor peeks at me over the top of the playpen, her chin resting on her hands as they grip the surround support. Her unicorn is standing several inches taller than her, also staring at me to see what Kade gave me.

"Here goes nothing." I reach in with my eyes squeezed tight, flinching like I'm going to be bitten.

"A book!" I take a deep breath and open my eyes at Honor's exclamation. Then a half sob, half laugh is torn from me.

How to Survive Divorcing Your Lesbian Wife.

"They have a book for everything nowadays." I chuckle while leafing through the pages, noticing Kade has highlighted passages throughout in different colors.

I grow balls and look in the box– a stack of books. One right after another. No wonder the box weighed as much as lead.

Two Mommies & Two Daddies: how to help your child cope. Including a children's edition for age 8 & below.

Relationship Rescue by Dr. Phil McGraw. My snort echoes around the kitchen, causing Honor to giggle, then make horsy noises because unicorns don't exist.

Homeowners Guide: Kitchen, Bed, & Bath Floorplan designs.

Bisexual's Guide to Dating, Relationships, and Sex.

"For serious?" I almost drop it like it's hot. **The Ins and Outs of Anal Sex**.

A printed page is glaring up at me from underneath the last book. *Who needs Liberal Arts? Study life by living it and educating yourself on shit you don't understand. Get your degree in Trial & Error. READ THE BOOKS, dipshit! Read 'em! Now lift this piece of paper for your reward.*

"That's not scary at all, now is it?"

"No, Daddy." Toddlers clearly don't get the concept of rhetorical questions.

"Yes, it is, baby girl," I murmur. "Yes, it is when you're dealing with Uncle Kade." Laughter echoes around the kitchen as I stare down into the box. Everything has a sticky note attached.

Adventure One: It's time for big boy slick, Hoss. Toss the baby oil– you're not 12 and it eats latex for breakfast.

I love Kaden– sometimes. Right now is one of those times. The biggest bottle of Gun Oil imaginable is waiting for me to play with it. Beside that is a purple lifelike dong... and a package of Chips Ahoy!

Adventure Two: The Ins and Outs of Anal Sex + Dong + Suctioned to shower stall + Gun Oil = world's best orgasm.

Adventure Three: RELAX– here's a cookie as your reward for playing Kade's Choose-Your-Own-Sexual-Adventure game.

CHAPTER EIGHT
Kaden Marx

I could have made this hour drive twice a day for half the week to take classes, so I blame my laziness for splitting my time in Morgantown and Rusty Knob. In actuality, I love living this double life, which is about to end. It's like I have two families that give me their undivided attention.

Absence makes the heart grow fonder, they say...

It works, especially once you've made them dependent on you. I leave Rusty Knob behind for four days at a time, where Wynn acts like it's been years. He basically kisses my ass and is so damn thrilled to see me. Then the rest of the gang clamors to fit in visits with me around my class schedule. Everyone is accommodating, happy to see me, and puts me first.

When I get back to Rusty Knob for my three-day tour at the Community Center, everyone needs me. *Kade, can I have a minute? How do I do this? Will you help me organize the evening courses?*

Miriam comes around at least twice each visit, feigning interest in my life, and always hands out a job offer before she goes. Warren can't wait to go out and do buddy stuff, like fishing and hiking, because he's a family man now. All the kids run around my legs, tugging at my arms, and beg me for undivided attention. Then there is Royce, who takes me into his office and asks me for advice. He treats me like a grown man now, and that makes me feel both proud and wanted.

My therapist says I have issues with finding my place in this world, and this feeds into it. The celebrity status, dependent bullshit. But it's ticking its time down to the end, and I'll have to deal when it does in a few weeks.

I know everyone laughs behind my back, calling me the professional college student, thinking I keep going just to draw out this special treatment and waste money, like I don't know what direction I want to take in my life. But that's not why I continued to study even after getting my master's in education, double majoring in both counselor education and school counseling... and that was a year and a half ago.

No, I had to keep moving forward, proving myself worthy, and I've lied through my teeth when asked what I'm still doing in college. No, I'm not currently attempting to forge ahead with getting a PsyD degree– I doubt I'll complete it, but I couldn't stop myself from trying.

I'm the only Marx left of my bloodline– the throwaway faggot nobody wanted to lay claim. I'm not the boy I used to be, but that doesn't mean I'm not as broken. I grew up without a mother, and I was able to survive the loss because I had my dad. I was able to survive my grandfather's sneers and slurs because I had my dad. My dad would put his own father in his place to protect me, because he thought me a worthy son. But dad left me too, didn't he?

I didn't survive the loss of my dad.

I was a skinny, zitty, awkward gay orphan in a hillbilly town where being masculine was the norm, and nobody wanted me. No matter how big and brawny I get, it's still obvious from the way I speak, the way I move, and my mannerisms that I'm gay. There's no hiding it. Added on top of that, I was the kid who tried to kill himself, the psycho kid who was a pervert for already loving a boy he shouldn't.

I was terrified of going to Penn State– *terrified.*

Between my bent pride and self-preservation, I had to leave Rusty Knob in order to survive. No amount of love from Royce and Bren, or reassurance from Miriam, could make me feel at home in a town that saw me as less.

Worthless.

My granddaddy didn't graduate from high school, barely getting a sixth grade education. My dad did graduate from high school, but my momma didn't. While there is nothing wrong with honest hard work, I left Rusty Knob to find my people, only to drop into a place where I was shunned for my roots.

Kaden Marx belonged nowhere.

My roommate, Dan Bishop, he made me put down roots. He made me feel comfortable in my own skin. He protected me from those who made fun of me, those who called me a cousin-fucker, inbred, faggot, and worse.

It took me six months to train myself not to speak like my fellow hillbillies, simply to protect myself from the bullies. College, even a gigantic university like Penn State, is no different than elementary school. You have to find your people, or the rest will devour your soul.

I never did find my people, because they were back in Rusty Knob, a fact I didn't come to terms with until recently, thinking them less because I felt like less when facing my peers.

I left Rusty Knob to get a degree, to prove myself worthy. I stay in college to prove to my peers I'm not some backwoods, illiterate imbecile. The educated part of me is at war with my roots, and I recently realized to be a proud West Virginian, to be proud of the hard work my kin did to provide me with the life I'm leading today, means I can't be ashamed of the fact that they weren't educated. They were smarter than me because they were able to survive on next to nothing by doing the work no one else wanted to do.

Dr. Marx has a ring to it– a ring that will finally make me feel like a man.

Becoming a teacher wasn't enough. I experienced a county-wide lynching over my sexuality. Sure, I'll admit that I tested them with Wynn, and he played along knowing damn well that was what I was doing. Kentwood County, Rusty Knob, even Miriam, they all failed my test, because being gay with a degree still wasn't good enough.

Nothing has a guy running back to school for a hit of validation like having dog shit flung from an open window as a truck slows to a crawl. In the face, with it going into my open, gobsmacked mouth, while walking my innocent dog. The humiliation was ten-fold with the slurs coming out of the mouths of people who were born to this land the same as I was. Just because I was born gay made me less in their eyes, and no amount of muscle, strength, height and weight, or education was going to change the fact that I love men.

Wynn.

I sheltered Wynn from the worst of it. The smashed mailboxes, the piles of shit –human shit– on my front step, and the slurs painted on my front door and keyed into the doors of my Durango.

Ignorance is the absence of education, but bigotry is based in fear. They were terrified they may end up like me, terrified their sons would be bashed as they were bashing me, so ignorant to the fact that they themselves perpetuated the cycle.

It's easier to go for another and another degree than it is to go back home and educate the children of the ignorant assholes who terrorized me.

The bitterness inside me is toxic, and so very real it's like a living organism dwelling deep in my belly.

My family and friends, I let them think whatever negative shit they want about me. My real reason for splitting my time between Rusty Knob and Morgantown was because if I hadn't, I feared everyone but Jack would have fled back to Rusty Knob within a month of moving to Morgantown.

Five of us went to college, and only two of us stuck it out, with Bren and Jesse quitting immediately and Jack veering off to another profession.

Wynn fit in great at school, with his basketball team, and in class, but the social life of a college student was not for him. We're tied to our land, needing space, and being compartmentalized into a dormitory, where Wynn could sense every single person in his space… he needed a place to call his own, with people he trusted, and he found that with Jack in my rented apartment.

Bren needed to get away from Royce to grow into a man. Lord knows, Royce is the best person on the planet, but he's nosy and overbearing, and wants to do everything for us. Bren needed to learn how to do it on his own.

It was a kill two birds, one stone deal for me: I needed to finish out my graduate degrees so I could move along to licensing and certification, and I wanted to become Royce's understudy as the ultimate mentor to our family members.

Not to sound arrogant or anything, but I've been doing a mighty fine job.

I want a blowjob.

Maybe not a good enough job, because my subjects do exercise their freewill.

Idiots.

As I pull up to my house, I breathe a sigh of relief that Warren is at work and Penny is at the center with the kids in tow. If they're home, they're on the front porch, and that means it will be a good hour or two before I get inside my house.

There is a downside to my double life. If I want some peace and quiet, I have to accommodate those who need me first.

Hopping out of my car, I quickly go about stowing all of my recent purchases. Wynn is a cheapskate of the highest order, so I go shopping while he's in class. I also have the delivery men secure all of my Amazon purchases on the back porch for when I come home. I'll take care of all of this later, because I have to switch out my clothing first, then get to the center.

Even after four years, the loneliness descends as I enter the house without being greeted by Perty. Sometimes I catch myself calling out to him, expecting to hear his nails tap on the hardwood floor, or hear the snorting sound he makes because of his smushed in snout. I miss how he'd wag his entire body in greeting, one leg, then the other, coming off the ground in a welcome home dance.

Willa stole the very dog she despised, and now she won't give him back. Perty is the Community Center's mascot now, following his new master everywhere, including sharing Willa and Royce's bed.

I'd get another dog, but I don't want to feel as if I'm replacing Perty. Plus, I was totally annihilated online when I was asking opinions on the subject. Note to self: never ask opinions on the internet.

I never want to live alone, finding the three nights I sleep here too upsetting. I'll sit with Warren on the porch until I can barely keep my eyes open, and then stagger my way to bed. It's so peaceful to sneak back to the apartment to find Wynn softly snoring in our bed and Jack muttering in his sleep.

After losing first my mom, then my dad, and finally my grandfather last year, I'm the only member of my family left on this planet, and when I'm alone it hits home.

Fuck changing out of my clothes– I can't do this right now.

After charging back to my car, I ignore the fact that I'm a selfish gas-hog for driving five streets over. I have presents to distribute after all.

"Good Lord," I groan as I pull up to the curb outside of the center, finding Miriam Ross waiting for me. The woman can't take a hint. Just seeing her face makes me think of my parents, then she tells me how proud they would be of me, it makes the grief that much more.

Miriam was my dad's best friend all through school, but she's also my distant kin. She never fails to regale me with how my parents met, and it makes the hollow ache in my chest throb.

I'm a Rusty Knob native with land to my name but no Marxs to put on it. My granddaddy left me everything when he passed, and we were finally on good terms, so I felt good about it. Right now, the only use the land has is for Warren's expanded hunting ground– greedy bastard is using Gillette, Kennedy, and Marx land, then brags about his trophy-worthy kills.

Miriam and my momma were second cousins, but I never knew her or her family because Granddaddy was an old-school bastard. Momma left what little family she had left behind. When she died,

I was cut off completely from that side of the family. I met Miriam when social services first came a'calling.

Lydia Marx was a typical momma, even though I don't remember her much at all. Dad reminded me several times a day up until he died when I was sixteen. I lost Momma when I was only four years old. We didn't have a lot of money, but we were happy. Dad used the family truck to get to work, so Momma rode her bike to town for errands while Granddaddy watched me.

Momma was struck down by a hit-and-run driver, leaving her to die on the side of the road like a deer carcass. It was dusk, and anyone from around here knows how powerfully blinding the sun is when it's sinking beneath the hilltops, like a laser through your windshield. So there are two theories: accident, where the person thought they hit a deer, which happens weekly for those in the hills, or a drunk who was too out of it to know the difference.

Doesn't matter how it happened, or who did it, knowing wouldn't bring back my momma. But the grief for me is more guilt, because I think of Lydia Marx as a stranger my dad told me stories about.

Seeing Miriam makes it real, draws my mom into reality. Witnessing the longing for my father written across Miriam's face every time she looks at me... well, that just about brings me to my knees.

"Woman, are you stalking me?" I demand of Miriam as I exit my vehicle.

"I saw you drive by." The take-no-prisoners woman leans against the stone façade of the Community Center with her arms folded over her chest, wearing a flawless pant suit.

"You saw me drive by?" I hit the clicker on my fob to engage the security system. "In Hillock Corners? What did you do, run to your car to catch me?"

Miriam shrugs. "It's kind of hard to miss a black Land Rover driving through town, Kaden." She pulls away from the building to join me in the center of the sidewalk, a smirk flirting with her lips. "Yours is the only one in the county."

"Yeah, because I'm an asshole, that's why," I mutter defensively.

"I drive a brand new Cadillac, Kade." Miriam looks me over from head to toe. "What's up with you?"

Unable to stop myself, I quickly rumble, "I only bought the car because Bren wanted one. I'm a selfish asshole who forced him to buy a Jeep, and then bought the car he wanted. I flaunted it in his face and wouldn't let him even drive it."

"Ah!" Miriam's head goes backward as she hums the singular word. "You're the only one who thinks you're a selfish asshole, Kaden. You work so hard to prove it to yourself. I bet Bren saw right through your bullshit."

"What do you want?" Scowling, I charge away from her. "Leave me alone, lady. I'm not going back to that hellhole you run."

"Kaden, wait!" Miriam grabs my arm, forcing my feet to stop. "I come around to see you because I genuinely enjoy your company. You know this, but you won't admit it. I keep offering you the job, not because you think I'm trying to buy you off over what had happened, but because it's good for all of us. You want it, I want you there, the kids need you, and I replaced all of the homophobic misogynists on the school board with the mothers and fathers of our LGBTQ kids. We can change futures, Kaden."

"I bet that went over real well with the parents," I grumble begrudgingly, but deep down I'm in awe Miriam pulled it off.

"Half of the parents are to the kids who are out, and the other half are parents to the kids who aren't, that's how I got away with it." Miriam's touch lowers from my arm to squeeze my hand. "Kaden, the main reason I come around is because I knew your father, and I think he'd want this for you. He'd be so proud of you, son."

Unable to handle it, I jerk out of Miriam's grip, and leave her behind on the sidewalk. She's unrelenting, so even if I'm being a rude piece of shit, she'll be back around in the next few days anyway.

As soon as I set foot into the main door, Penny is on me. "Thank God you're here." She runs right up to me and engulfs me in a welcoming hug. As she pulls away, she says, "You're waaaay late, by the way. But I'm just glad you're here."

Wynn's words ring out in my head. *Pregnancy isn't a disability.* He was so upset with Penny that night when he argued with her over her lost potential. But it wasn't graduating that made Penny into a woman– it was Copper.

Pregnancy didn't derail Penny's future– it changed it.

The grown woman pulling me through the center to my office is unrecognizable from the hillbilly girl from five years ago.

Copper penny hair swings around her jawline, intelligent brown eyes beg me to help, and perfect diction spills from her mouth…

Change has come to Rusty Knob.

Penny is only one example of what we're trying to accomplish.

I have two master's degrees, with a BA in elementary education, and I'm slowly but surely headed toward a PsyD degree, and I can attest to the fact that higher education stunts your growth as an adult.

Wynn, for as mature as he was growing up, he hasn't evolved in the past four years. He goes to school, he plays, and he studies, no different than his senior year of high school. I don't begrudge Wynn that after his past, but he and I are still not in the same stage in life. I'm hoping this summer, after we move back to Rusty Knob and into my house, getting him away from all of that will allow him to grow more.

Jack had a wake-up call, and has since joined the working class, understanding the pressures and stressors of adult life. Bren grew up around the time Jessica got pregnant, and for a while, I felt he was more mature than I was. Hell, he's always been more mature than I am. Behind that happy smile was always a kid with agony in his heart.

Penny– a hillbilly girl from Franklin Holler with a high school education and two children–not only is she my equal, she's Royce's equal.

"Royce and Willa are three hours away getting an ultrasound to make sure the baby is okay. After two lost babies, Royce is understandably not with it. So I need your help." Penny shoves my ass in the chair behind my desk, and then sits in the chair facing me.

Heart pounding out of my chest, I can't survive another loss like the last one. "First, is the baby okay?"

"Precautionary stuff all mommas-to-be get." Penny shifts, pulling out an iPad from somewhere. "Baby Royce had a congenital anomaly, and there was nothing anyone could do. I get why they're terrified, but this baby is perfect. So don't you stress too, because I need your head on straight."

"Okay, good. So what's the emergency?" I reach over to flip the lid on my laptop, getting it booted up.

"Patty–"

"The young momma from our domestic violence group?" I interrupt, already getting upset. I lean forward, nails biting into the edge of my desk. "What did that fucker do?"

"Whoa– slow your roll. Patty's safe, Kade." Penny brings something up on her tablet, reading off it. "Okay, so this is what I did while you were away. Shit hit the fan last night. I placed Patty and the kids in the women's shelter at the church. My ladies are keeping them nice and safe and away from undue influence."

Undue influence– that's my girl.

"I didn't know which lawyer to contact, because this isn't just some simple domestic violence case. We need a restraining order, but her husband's the town cop. No judge is going to issue it. Bryant is already screaming bullshit at the top of his lungs. He's saying Patty is an unfit mother, but in the next breath he's saying he doesn't even know if the kids are his because she had sex with some dude before she ever met him."

"Classic bullshit. Bryant was isolating and manipulating Patty– I picked that up in the last group session. She was blaming herself, saying he couldn't help it because of the pressures of his job. If only she would've had supper on the table on time, or kept the kids quiet, or not spent so much time with her mother. The usual."

"Kade, Bryant is threatening to take their kids away from her if she doesn't go back to him. He was running his mouth around town, saying she doesn't have a job, so how can she take care of the kids. But she doesn't have a job because he didn't want her to have one."

"Damned if you do, damned if you don't– the strategy of every abuser," I muse.

"Bryant will prove Patty is a whore somehow, swaying public opinion because she fooled around before they got together. He'll call her a slut and lazy and a good for nothing woman. But she can't prove his abuse, because verbal doesn't leave physical scars, and he's a respected cop who covered his tracks. So what do we do?"

"We do what we're doing. Patty's job was a stay-at-home mom and wife. No court will force a mother to live with her abuser because she can't afford to be on her own. This is another threat all abusers make. We'll call a lawyer, and then find someone with a beef against Bryant. Somewhere out there is someone who isn't the town cop's biggest fan– but they have to be someone without a criminal record. Preferably an ex-girlfriend."

"How do we do that?"

"Consult the Fates," I say without cracking a smile.

"Kaden." Penny growls, causing a smile to stretch wide across my face. "I hate it when you call them that."

"The church ladies are our greatest source of gossip." I point to my office door. "Go forth and gossip."

"With pleasure." We share a grin. "It's my only talent."

"Whoa… whoa… whoa…" I stop Penny in her tracks. "Schedule?"

The mature mother of two rolls her fucking eyes at me like a toddler. "I emailed it to you earlier, but here's a verbal rendition. No classes scheduled tonight because Willa's pregnant, Royce is smothering her, you just got back in *late*, and we have a private birthday party being hosted in the common room from six until nine tonight."

"Thank you," I say with all sincerity.

Penny returns the sentiment. "We need you here in Rusty Knob every day, Kade. No more playacting the teenager." Penny walks out of my office, then shouts over her shoulder. "Come home, stay home, and bring Wynn with ya, ya hear?"

Shouting back, "I hear," comes out more as a laugh.

Leaning back in my chair with a smile on my face, I open up my email, looking to see if Penny's fibbing me or not. An email from one of my professors catches my eye, and I can't help but open it and fall down the rabbit hole.

My therapist says not to engage, but I can't help it.

Dr_Carlin@wvu.edu
To:director@revitalizerustyknobwv.com
My dimmest minion,

Would you stop running home to Papa? You have papers to grade and a lecture to lead, or did you purposefully forget your duties as my TA? You can't honestly believe working at that institution of ignorance is more important than what I require of you?

Is it something in the water that has you going back? I know your hot piece of ass is currently across town from me with that pudgy baby catcher, so I don't see your constant need to go back to Oxidized Handle.

Is jailbait blondie having another litter of Kennedys, is that why? As we discussed in our class, no doubt the last stillbirth was due to inbreeding– should have aborted. Don't you hillfolk believe the developing cells have feelings or some such horseshit? You made that deformed monstrosity feel pain, didn't you?

Shame on you, Kaden. Tsk-tsk.

The family tree must look like someone tossed the names on a page and shook it up. How many times do the same people need to replicate? Is your foster father and his cheating sister-in-law trying to repopulate the earth? Is the breeder your sister-in-law, your foster mother, or your foster aunt? I mean, it's so confusing for someone who wasn't raised in a 'Holler'. Are the children your foster siblings, your nieces and nephews, or your foster cousins? Is Wynn your foster brother... you are a bad boy, aren't you?

Do you want to be Dr. Carlin's good boy, Kaden? You do, don't you?

It's a good thing two cocks can't reproduce, because your genetic code sure as shit should never mix with that illiterate coding infused in the Gillette's genes.

Your IQ drops ten points every time you go back to the cesspool of ignorance you call home. Getting close to being borderline deficiency at this rate, considering you forgot to do your JOB!

How does it feel to know everyone hates you when you pull into town? Do they stare at the giant cocksucker driving his fancy ride he didn't pay for, while waving his unimpressive degrees in their faces? Is the shit slung still warm when it slides down your cheek?

You are a great disappointment to me, Kaden. Return to me at once!

If you miss one more alumni cocktail party, I'm going to go across town and drag your trophy cock to represent you in your stead. You know how much the ladies and gays love your "partner". We have money to earn, and your 'going nowhere in life fast' boy-toy can shake his moneymaker to pay his way.

NOW!

–Dr. C.

Breathing deeply, my nostrils flare and air whistles past my lips. Fingertips curling against my keyboard, I try to get myself under control. My therapist keeps pressing that Dr. Carlin is abusing me, manipulating me, trying to sabotage me for his own amusements. But it's a conflict of interest as she used to be under his control a decade or so ago. Without Dr. Carlin, Dr. Amherst wouldn't be a therapist.

Dr. Carlin wants the best out of me, so he's challenging me by testing my mettle. That's all. No abuse, because the truth hurts.

I need an injection of funny, or else I won't be able to function at work after how harsh Carlin was with me. I quickly bring up Facebook, looking for the most decadent recipe video I can find, because it's humorous to send it to Penny because she burns water.

Mmm... my salivary glands go haywire when I spot a recipe loaded with chocolate sandwich cookies and peanut butter cups.

Knowing the video won't be enough, I scroll for the top comments, looking for the step-by-step recipe.

Joan Hill: This poison is what's wrong with 'Merica. Fat fucks.

Ron Porter: Too much sugar. Diabetes, anyone? I'm going into shock just looking at the video.

Kaylee Danvers: Oh, holy mother of God, this looks divine!

Finally someone who appreciates a dessert for how it's meant– a treat. I quickly click to open the replies, hoping someone was nice enough to post the recipe for her. Forget sending this to Penny as a joke– Willa. This is going straight to Willa. I need me some chocolate to soothe my ruffled nerves. After two negative comments, I can already feel my blood pressure rising, the vein in my forehead beginning to throb, and the back of my eyes have pressure pushing forward.

Ron Porter: Look at your profile pic, @Kaylee Danvers. You are a fat little piggy, aren't you? Do you feed your kids these chemicals from a trough? Bet you don't care because each are from another baby daddy, you stupid whore.

Becca Tallman: Haha! @Ron Porter, you win the internet comment of the day. Kaylee looks like a slut. Look at those floppy tits hanging out. Forget a moment on the lips, forever on the hips. For Kaylee, it's a moment in her gushy, stretched out vag, eighteen years on the tit, another ten to life in our over-bloated prison system because she fed her kids processed sugars via the government's dime.

Kyle Web: What is wrong with you people?!? She's a beautiful, intelligent woman with healthy children. Not only that, she's married with two jobs listed. Don't you give a shit that everything you're saying is dead wrong?

Ron Porter: Dead wrong? Here's dead for you, @Kyle Web- go kill yourself, you stupid douchebag, and take @Kaylee Danvers with you. Both of you are a leech on the system. Get a job, and get the fuck off Facebook.

Kaylee Danvers: Irony, you're online… attacking me. Don't you have better things to do than make terroristic threats on a fucking dessert recipe?

Becca Tallman: This is why people shouldn't breed. Don't you see what your existence is doing to the environment? Go kill yourself, so someone who will make a difference can suck up the oxygen you're wasting.

"Jesus fucking Christ, what is happening to the world?" I cry out, hating how this bullshit infects every post. No matter what. With my eyes closed, I quickly click to my timeline, unable to witness the destruction of humanity.

Heart beating out of control, I steady my breathing to the point I can no longer feel the blood rushing through my veins.

I need some inspiration, something light, but I know my feed is filled with political posts meant to divide. Liberal versus conservative. Man versus woman. Straight versus LGBTQ. People of color versus white. Millennials versus each other and the world. Stay-at-home-moms versus working-moms. Poor versus rich. Higher educated versus undereducated. North versus south, east versus west. Country versus country. Continent versus Continent. Religion against religion against atheists.

People can get offended over an inspirational saying. Last week, a war erupted over a video of a kitten playing with a toy mouse. The internet is reaching its boiling point, and it's taking me with it.

Ping!

Shaking like an addict, I'm unable to not answer the call of a Facebook notification. I *must* look. It doesn't matter what, it requires my immediate attention.

Corina Gaffer made a comment on your post in Mid-Atlantic Pugs group.

I'm clicking before I can stop myself, needing to know what else could possibly be said in my hornet's nest of a post. Heart beating uncontrollably, like I'm on the verge of a heart attack, I wiggle in my seat, unable to stop from defending myself.

After missing Perty so much every time I go home, I posted an inquiry about locating another Pug puppy. It was all above board, politely asked, simply stating I wanted to be a pet parent again, and I was attacked immediately.

Kaden Marx– Mid-Atlantic Pugs group: Does anyone know of any reputable Pug breeders in the West Virginia area? I'm looking to adopt again after my SIL stole my beloved pooch because Perty was so loveable.

712 comments. 14 likes. 3 loves. 7 wows. 93 laughs. 1248 angry faces.

Like a pitch-fork carrying mob, the majority of those comments are heinous, as if I asked advice on how to euthanize pets, instead of wanting to adopt one. The rest of the commenters were trying to either be helpful or defend me, but they were easily bullied as I was. The newest comment was no different than the previous hundred.

Corina Gaffer: @Kaden Marx, you don't deserve a dog if you're looking for a breeder. It is your duty as a human to adopt an adult dog who is in need of a good home. You are the reason puppy mills exist. All those ill puppies being inbred– your fault for being willing to pay money for a dog. You should donate the cost, and then some, to a rescue shelter. Why are you so much better than the rest of us? Thinking you deserve a pedigree puppy, probably so you can show it off to your friends and then dump it at a shelter when it becomes too much work. Word of advice: don't reproduce. One of you is bad enough on this planet.

"It's not my fault," I whine. "I'm no better, so I won't get a puppy. But I don't deserve people being mean to me."

Fingers poised over the keys, curser blinking more of a promise than a threat, I try to stop myself from replying. It never does any good. Anything I say will be warped and misconstrued to fit a commenter's agenda. There is no defending myself on the internet, even when it involves my own emotions. Everyone knows me better than I know myself. With freedom of speech, they feel they have the right to be an abusive asshole, and I have no right to form my own opinion, feel what I feel, or think what I think.

They will abuse and troll until their words are coming out of my mouth, then they will feel like they won. No matter what, I lose.

I only wanted a puppy.

Fingers flying over the keyboard, I give into my unnatural urge to put total strangers in their place because they were mean to me. How dare they? I'll give them a taste of their own venomous medicine, especially since I just learned, from the recipe video, the nasty trick of looking up the asshole's profile.

Corina, your bitterness is giving you wrinkles. Keep spackling on the makeup– it only accentuates the cracks. I love how you have seven purebred Pugs, and you sold a litter of puppies at five grand a pup last month. Should I school you on the definition of hypocrisy? Here's a link explaining how you're a backyard breeder, making you a tiny step up from being a maggot-infested puppy mill. I'll head you off at the pass. Yes, I am a white man, but I'm a highly educated, gay orphan from an economically depressed region where I volunteer my time, so that cancels out whatever bullshit you're going to try to use against me–

Dan's ringtone pierces the silence, stilling my fingers on the keyboard. My ex-roommate saves me yet again. "Hey," my fingertip hovers over Enter.

Twitchy.

"Don't do it," Dan orders, causing me to look around to see if he's somehow watching me spiral out of control.

"Don't do what?" I ask in a false calm, finger getting twitchier with every comment added on my thread. Now some douche-noodle is blaming me for the world's overpopulation of dogs, like Dr. Carlin did when he found out Willa was pregnant again. My professor said with the world being overpopulated, only the smartest should reproduce, and Royce was the most selfish piece of shit for putting a strain on our ecosystem.

"Whatever you're doing, don't do it," flows a comforting tone from the other end of the phone. "You know I have a spidey-sense when it comes to you doing something fucking stupid."

"Aren't you mediating today?" My fingertip caresses the Enter key, nearly pressing it in. "I thought you told me that last night."

"Talk to me first, Kade, then I'll tell you," Dan negotiates.

Fucking lawyers.

I love Dan with every fiber of my being, but I wouldn't call him my best friend– I can't. Dan was my savior, when I never wanted to admit I needed one in the first place. Dad, then Royce, then Dan, and I've been going it alone since, with Royce and Dan tag-teaming me when I get out of hand… like now, when it comes to being a keyboard warrior.

I needed them to make me strong, so Wynn wouldn't see me for who I truly am.

No one would want the real Kaden Marx.

My finger twitches violently, but I don't pull back from the keyboard.

I didn't earn my way into Penn State. Miriam hooked me up, selected my classes, and even picked her friend's son to be my roommate, but Royce paid for it. I thought Dan was just a roommate, but it took three and a half years to figure out he was my babysitter. Not that he didn't love me back. He took care of me, not out of obligation, but because that is who he is, and he liked me.

Dan really liked me– the *real*, raw and ugly me.

Dan made sure I took my meds, pretended he was Bren when it came to alone time with sharp objects, and advised me when I was panicking. Then, he offered a sexual outlet so I wouldn't break the promises I made to myself.

"Kaden, c'mon?" Dan tries to get me to come out of my trance. "I know you're up to something stupid. I can feel it."

My world imploded when Royce was assaulted and left for dead. I took care of Bren the best I could, but everyone in Rusty Knob shoved my ass back to Penn State so I wouldn't flunk out. But the real reason was they were having to take care of me, when Royce, Willa, Bren, and the twins needed their support instead. I was a hindrance that was going off my rocker with fear– fear of abandonment.

My momma left me. My daddy left me. My granddaddy didn't want me. Miriam was obligated to take me, so I chose Royce because he chose me instead. But when Royce was harmed, and I didn't know if he'd recover, I lost it. Like really fucking lost it.

Knowing the real me, Dan offered, and I cleaved onto him like a lifeline. I'm relieved my boyfriend isn't jealous over our unconventional relationship. Dan and I love each other in a way I can't explain– a form of dependency that I'm terrified to relinquish.

Dan is a living, breathing form of suicidal tendencies, with the ability to give sound advice, and sometimes force me to take it.

I've been waiting a decade to return the favor, to help take care of Dan like he's done for me.

"How's Uriah?" I ask absentmindedly, because it's the nice thing to ask, not because I care with my eyes glued to the laptop screen as trolls engage in battle on my post.

Twitchy finger.

"Delete whatever you posted. Not just your comments, but the entire motherfucking thread." Dan knows me too well, already having done an intervention junior year of college when I was at the height of my assholeness on the internet. But I was worse back then, because I was on a campus, and I didn't need Facebook or threads. The debates were face-to-face.

"It's not worth it," Dan warns, somehow sensing I'm a hairsbreadth away from pressing the button. "You can't handle the fallout. They don't know you, so it doesn't matter what they think."

"I don't know what you're talking about," I mutter, acting flippant, eyes drinking in the vile comments.

"I still have your log-in and passwords, Kade," Dan warns, and I sit up and take notice. A sense of relief flows through me, because Dan will take care of it if I don't have the strength.

I shut the lid to my laptop with an audible snap.

"Good," Dan murmurs soothingly, and I relax further. "My client is currently bitching at her husband, to the point I left the conference room with a warning that I would quit if all wasn't quiet when I returned."

"Will that work?" I mutter, voice incredulous.

"They're like children– everyone going through a divorce that isn't amicable acts like immature children. They respond well when I place firm boundaries. Their marriage wouldn't be in the gutter if they knew how to communicate in the first place."

"You sure you don't want that BDSM book I picked up for you," I tease, then get a good chuckle out of Dan's growl, sounding the alpha male he pretends he's not. "Yes, Mr. Omega, your beta will behave."

"Good. Uriah's being Uriah." Dan's tone has me sitting up straighter, hope flowing through my body. Maybe I can help pay off a bit of the emotional debt I owe Dan by helping him. "It's like he's been replaced with a body-snatcher."

"And that's a bad thing…" I lead Dan, not wishing to insult him by saying Uriah is batshit crazy on a good day. In Uriah's case, crazy is motherfucking hot, the most intelligent person I've ever met, and compelling.

"Yes, when Uriah's acting like a Stepford Wife. Hell, yes," Dan snarls.

"Eww." My face scrunches up in distaste. "How can I help?"

For once, Dan opens up to me, letting it pour out, believing in me enough to help him with his marriage, and I feel lighter because of it. After our call ends, I open my laptop and delete the thread.

They don't know me– fuck 'em.

But before I log out, I do ask for the complete recipe, promising myself I'll delete any negative replies on my comment. But within seconds, assholes are hijacking my comment, and a portion of the calm Dan gave me dissolves. I'm a heartbeat away from losing my shit, when an angel gives me the recipe.

Uriah Crane: Check your email, bub. These fuckfaces don't deserve the recipe. If you delete your comment in the next thirty seconds, I'll make you a batch of goodies for when we meet up next week.

Maybe I don't want to help Dan after all– Stepford Wife makes tasty treats.

Did I fail to mention Uriah witnessed my meltdown after I came back to school after Royce's attack? I was so out of it, I didn't know Uriah existed until weeks later. He was there for me too, so I behave.

I delete the comment, then check my email, forwarding it to Willa. Then I get my ass to work.

It takes three hours to find a reliable lawyer willing to go against a cop, and another twenty minutes of dealing with the guy's personal assistant to nail down a time to meet. Around the time my belly is growling, I hear a ruckus coming from the reception area.

Wandering through the center, I marvel over all we've done. I'm at one end of the block of interconnected buildings, and Penny is at the other. My office is just off the common room, used for group meetings and social events. Then there's the kitchen, the study center, the workshop, and finally Penny's domain– the reception area.

Every time my eyes light on the history of Rusty Knob posted on the walls, I get choked up. "Ugh!" a grunt is forced out of me when bony arms encircle my waist.

I look down into Gillette blue eyes and see a happy future for all of us. "Rockabilly, I've missed you." I peck a quick kiss to the top of Hayley's pink mohawk, and then hold her out at arm's length.

"Lemme get a good look atcha, Rocky." I tug one arm, then the other to rotate her a bit. Inheriting Wynn's height, she's going to be the tallest person in the Kennedy family tree, and prettier than her momma. Hayley and Hayden will be twelve this summer, and it makes me think of Penny.

When Penny was twelve, Warren sunk his teeth into her. Wynn was this age when I first noticed him– God, just thinking about that makes me feel sick.

The first boy to go near Hayley will come up against a wall of grown men who take Hayley's future seriously. The only consolation is that Hayley doesn't give two shits about boys. Her guitar is her best friend.

"Stop it!" Hayley struggles to get out of my grip, only to hug me again. "I look exactly as I did four days ago, ya big dummy."

"I'm looking atcha because I missed you, *ya big dummy*," I tease back, jutting out my chin. "Hey, big dummy number two, get over here."

Somewhere in a swarm of Penny's little sisters is Hayden. He's going to be a short little fella for life, but adorable nonetheless. Somehow the wrong twin got the height, and I'm happy there is no resentment surfacing.

"Hey." Hayden manages to escape, giving me a crooked smile and a husky voice. Every time I see him, I have to blink. Wynn's face is resting atop Bren's body. I can't imagine what it would be like to see yourself reflected in someone's face, which makes me feel guilty because my dad never got to see me grow up to look just like he did.

"Can you help me out here, man?" Hayden hitches his thumb over his shoulder. "I just spent seven hours with them at school, and I need a break. This summer, ya gotta give me some work as an excuse."

"Done." I agree, shaking the little man's hand. "You sure there isn't one in the bunch you got your eye on?" His immediate blush is explanation enough.

Hayden leans in close, not caring in the least that his twin sister can hear him, because Rockabilly is the keeper of all of his secrets. "Hannah," he whispers, choosing the only sister with hair the color of pennies. "But I can't hang out with her 'cuz her sisters are always around, and I don't wanna hurt their feelings and get 'em to fighting with each other."

Judging by the way Warren behaved as a boy, and how Wynn behaves as a man, Hannah better watch out. Warren was messing around with girls when he was Hayden's age. The boy was a pussy magnet.

I catch sight of Jeb, the only boy in the Franklin family, glaring at Hayden– good, an angry cock-block.

"Okay!" Penny shouts, looking exhausted. "Jeb, go help Daddy at the shop, and while you're there, tell Warren to get his ass up here."

"Will do, sis." Voice deep, face freckled, Jeb is twenty and perpetually pissed, a condition caused by being the big brother to four boy-crazy little sisters. Brennan will want to get his hands on the boy to train him– the kid is built like a brick house.

With one last warning glare, Jeb leaves.

Hayden murmurs, voice quivering like a leaf. "Jeb says I act like Warren."

Head hitching back, I release a baying laugh at how history is trying to repeat itself.

"Hey!" Hayden tugs at my sleeve. "I don't, though. I'm nothing like Warren. We don't even look alike. I'm book-smart and get straight As. I play sports and plan on going to college. How is that *anything* like Warren?"

Should I answer that?

Rockabilly whispers into her twin's ear, causing the poor boy to break out in a sweat and his eyes to bug out in shock. His tiny mouth forms a perfect O, and then he laughs.

"It's not so much that you act like Warren," Rockabilly explains out loud. "You attract girls like Warren." She leans into me. "I would like some peace from them too. Can I have a job this summer, Kade?"

"I'll hook ya both up." I mess up their hair, earning a swat or two.

"If your last name is Franklin, go get in my car," Penny orders. "If your last name is Kennedy, since Kade has finally graced us with his presence, you're with him for the rest of the day."

"Sweet!" The twins high-five each other.

"Your parents will be home in an hour, so don't get too excited." Penny bursts their bubble.

"Whoa… whoa… whoa…" Warren dodges four teenage girls as they skip out the front door. "Where's the fire?"

"Where's my kids?" Penny isn't fucking around. "I've got to take the girls home, get the kids fed, and then you and I will switch off so I can be here to make sure the birthday partiers don't destroy the place. Chop! Chop!"

"Schedule me ten minutes in there somewhere, babe." Warren shoves his tongue down his wife's throat before she can protest. When he pulls away, she's blushing, and not at all angry anymore.

"I wanna grow up to be Uncle Warren," Hayden murmurs in awe, and Rocky displays how she earned her title. She punches her brother in the ass for being an ass.

"My kids?" Penny tries again.

"Leave Kaden and the twins here for a bit. I'll get the kids settled in at home and supper started. When you get back from taking the girls home, I'll run up here and relieve Kade. Okay? Does that work?"

Obviously touched, Penny still loses her patience. "Yeah, but where the fuck are my children?"

Just to be a pain in the ass, Warren finally acknowledges my existence instead of answering his wife. "Hey, bud. Welcome home." After a few hard hits to the back in a bro-hug, Penny is about to lose her shit. "Come along and say hello to your godchildren."

This is standard operating procedure for Warren. I follow him out the front door, only to burst out into laughter. Copper is sitting in his big boy car, bopping his head to music only he can hear, hair swinging with the movement.

Copper is a super cool dude for a little man of four and a half. He's stocky, with thick straight hair to his jawline, cut just like his mother's and the same color too. He's wearing aviator sunglasses and a t-shirt with a skull on the front. He looks right at me, honks the horn, and then waves at me with two fingers like his daddy does.

Copper's chill.

"Here's your kid, sis." Jeb materializes out of nowhere to hand Ginger off. "Your asshat of a husband is getting on my last nerve, and you force me to work with him day in and day out." As I said, Jeb is perpetually pissed off, stoic, and never cracks a smile. "I'm going back to work since Warren won't be there."

After another warning glare at Hayden, we all watch Jeb stride down the sidewalk toward Franklin Auto. Penny turns, handing me Ginger, and says, "That boy needs to get laid something fierce."

"He needs to take the stick out of his ass," Warren adds his two cents. "Then maybe he could get laid."

"Which team?" I ask while nuzzling a patch of baby powder-scented bright red hair on an otherwise bald head. "Hayley might be the same size, but you must have grown a few ounces in the past few days, baby waby. Your hiney is definitely heavier."

I pass the three-month-old girl to her daddy, because Kaden Marx doesn't change diapers.

"Team? No clue." Warren takes his daughter from me, and then snaps his fingers at Copper. The boy executes a perfect three-point turn until he's facing the direction of home on the sidewalk. "I keep hanging up nudie calendars in the shop office, but the boy won't look at 'em. I'm not discriminatory either– one's twelve months of hot firemen."

"By hanging up calendars…" Penny trails off with a snicker. "Warren means he hung up twenty of them with naked girls sent by auto parts advertisers– they aren't even the current year. The twenty-first was firemen in full turnout gear, sent from Rusty Knob's Volunteer Fire Department as a thank you for the donation. What Warren meant by hot, is that it included burning buildings– tragedies that struck Rusty Knob. Not exactly spank bank material."

Penny gives us a wave, and then disappears around the end of the block to where her car-full of sisters is waiting.

"We share an office, so I wanted to be comfortable in it," Warren whines. "The firemen calendar is a nice reminder of what could happen if you don't change the batteries in the smoke detectors every three months. Let's roll, little dude."

The twins and I watch Warren walk slowly while holding his newborn daughter, as his son drives down the sidewalk.

"I give the best gifts," I mutter with pride, hooking an arm around each of the twin's necks, then I steer them back into the reception area.

"We're getting a pair of cars on our sixteenth birthday, right?" Hayley bats her eyelashes at me, looking just like my little shit when he wants something.

"Not a chance, Rockabilly... Not a chance." I hug her to my side. "You have more money than I do– buy your own dang car."

"Kade?" Hayden pulls out the world famous Gillette charm. "Can I intern at Franklin Auto this summer."

"I thought you wanted to get away from Molly, Deanna, Hannah, and Sarah," Rocky reminds him.

"Yeah, I do," Hayden mutters sheepishly. "But I could file paperwork in the office or something."

"You guys are pure entertainment for me." I hug them both. "Comedy gold."

"I don't get it," Rocky whines, causing Hayden to snicker.

"Homework," I order, steering them to the study center. "If either of you needs a calendar, look at your dang cellphone."

"Perv!" Rocky punches Hayden in the ass again for being an ass.

CHAPTER NINE
Brennan Kennedy

Bren: *You owe me one.*
Wynn: *Why?!?*
Bren: *Our mutual 'brother' paid me a visit this morning.*
Wynn: *Oh.*
Bren: *All Winnie the Pooh has to say is oh.*
Wynn: *Oh, shit?!?*
Bren: *I need you to get Jack here ASAP. Both of you. Under the guise I need help with a project I'm working on. Then I want you to take your niece for a few hours so I can talk to Jack alone.*
Wynn: *Maybe I'm busy...*
Bren: *Like what? Jacking Jack off.*
Wynn: *Oh, shit! I didn't jack him off. It wasn't as bad as you're making it sound. Sorry.*
Bren: *Show your remorse by getting your ass over here.*
Wynn: *k*
Bren: *You know I hate that shit with the text-speak.*
Wynn: *That's why I do it. K?*
Bren: *Our asshat brother is wearing off on you.*
Wynn: *Be there in 20, 'cuz I gotta jack Jack off with my mouth first.*
Bren: *Dick.*
Wynn: *Exactly. In. My. Mouth. Sorry. Not sorry. L8R.*

"Your uncle wouldn't really do that, would he?" Honor's head pops up, confused as to whether or not she should answer because I've been talking to myself for a few hours. Sprawled out on the floor, she's using markers on an old ratty sheet to make Mommy a wall-hanging.

Kid got her artistic talent from Daddy– poor Mommy.

"Is that a kitty?" I lean forward to examine the four-legged creature with a mane of hair. "A big kitty? Lions roar."

"Hayden." At three and a half, Honor's already perfected that pissed off female tone of perpetually being offended by men– just like Mommy.

"Good job, baby girl. Mommy's gonna love it." Blushing, I swallow a laugh over insulting Honor's drawing while she insults poor Hayden. I flip another page in my notebook, eyes glued to the blueprints laid out on the coffee table.

Honor's a good girl who is content to be in the same room with her daddy. A few minutes later, she abandons the sheet because it's more fun to string every toy she can find across every walking surface in the house. But I've got to get some serious work done, so I can't follow her around. At least she stays within earshot.

"Door! Somebody's at the door!" Running in her drunkard zigzag formation, Honor bounces off the wall. "Oops." With a giggle, she jerks forward, speed never consistent. "Door. Door." Then she falls to her behind on the carpet like her feet are made of rubber. "Door."

I'm laughing so hard by the time Wynn and Jack enter, I have tears pouring from my eyes.

"Door. Door. Door. Door." Wynn is barking like a dog, laughing just as hard as I am. "All that excitement, and she didn't make it." He plucks Honor off the floor, swinging her around. "Weee… the piggy goes weeeeee…"

"More, Uncle Wynn!" Honor giggles as she flies through the air. "More."

"Ya know–" Jackson gestures around ground zero. "This wouldn't happen if she didn't have so many toys."

"You'd think, right?" I snort. "But that means she'll just find other shit to get into."

"Like what?" Jack challenges, wearing a shit-eating smirk. Before his ass lands on the cushion next to me, he's wincing. Plucking a spatula from beneath his behind, "Oh," he drops it to the floor.

"There's a potato masher, a set of graduated measuring spoons, and a whisk around here somewhere." I reach down by my foot and return with a prize. "And this."

"A salad spinner? Really, Bren?" Jackson looks around, taking note of the Bundt pan near the DVD fort holding an array of unicorns in various sizes. They're using the butter dish as a trough.

"At least she can't reach the knife block I have stowed above the stove. I had to rescue a value pack of frozen chicken thighs a few minutes ago."

Wynn's wrestling the little monster in question. "Little young to fry chicken, ain't she?"

"She's in the explorer program." My double entendre has Jack choking on his own spit. "We no longer have chairs in the kitchen because she uses them to get into the freezer."

"Chicken? Jesus Christ, at least go for the ice cream." Wynn tugs Honor until she's propped up on her butt. "Always go for the ice cream."

"Honor was conceived from a slow swimmer sperm with a fucked up tail, I just know it."

"Oh, my God!" Wynn cracks up.

"Last week she managed to get in the trash in the amount of time it took to take a piss– coffee grounds, egg shells, leftover spaghetti. Every-fucking-where. It was two minutes. Tops."

"You're a bad dad," Jack drawls out.

"Don't I know it." I bump my shoulder into his while chuckling. "But I'd rather steam-clean the carpets than go through the misery of explaining why I have a hose to piss out of because I can't trust her to behave while I drain the snake."

"Have you been holding it?" Jack accuses, right on the money.

"I'm good."

A punch lands in the center of my chest, and Jack's hand has got to sting. "I told you to stay hydrated."

"My piss is clear and no cramping to be found, Nurse Jackie." Grabbing for his hand, I crack all of his knuckles. They rip like a zipper, but it must take the sting away. "Thanks for asking."

"That's why you invited us over, isn't it?" Jack and I both take a few moments to appreciate Wynn's obsessive compulsive tendencies. Making quick work of it, Wynn has separated kitchenware, toys, electronics, and toiletries into separate piles, and he and his minion are hard at work hunting down all the shit that's scattered about.

"Partially the reason. Partially that I really do need help with my project. But mostly because I wanted to hang out with you."

"Sappy, much?" Voice flippant, skin flushed, the pleased curl of Jack's lips betrays the pleasure my words bring. "What's the project? Same one we were talking about over the phone?"

"Yeah." I show him the blueprints. "I designed the house with my shitty artistic skills, but the concept was all mine. Our foreman brought in an architect to map out the blueprints, and the shell is already built, along with all the rooms but the kitchens and baths, and the added details need to be fleshed out to personal tastes."

"Wow!" Jack turns to the side to stare at me, face filled with wonder, and I actually feel like I accomplished something for once. I'm just the uneducated meathead daddy, while everyone else has degrees and future career plans. "You did this?"

Gesturing with my hand, "The house itself, but not laying it out on paper or hammering the nails– no."

Wynn shuffles over on his knees, dragging Honor because she's attached to his foot. "It's amazing." He smiles at me, reading me like an open book. "If you'd go home more often," he taunts Jack, "You would've noticed it being erected."

"It's in Rusty Knob?" Jack's button nose turns red, eclipsing his freckles. "Where at? It's a duplex. Did your dad need more rental housing? It's pretty high-end for that. Three bathrooms? Four bedrooms? What is that giant space? A full basement?"

Now it's my turn to blush, but Jack doesn't want to have this conversation yet.

Wynn chuckles underneath his breath, then takes it upon himself to pick up the rest of the mess. "C'mon, baby. Let's put this stuff away for Daddy, then we can work on your artwork."

With a big inhalation of air, I drag the coffee table closer so I can show Jack the details. "Most people have kids, right? So three to four bedrooms are ideal. As for the bathrooms, who wants their guests roaming around in your personal shit, or in the room your children use?"

"Jack?" Wynn projects from the kitchen. "Think of what's in our bathroom right now. Anyone but you, Kade would have been too mortified to allow to see it."

"What's in there?" I ask, and Jack blushes even redder. "I take it I don't wanna know– anyway, believe it or not, I saved up a lot of money working, with Jesse working, and not having to pay tuition and loans. You know I hate tapping into my *money*." I turn sheepish. "I'm going to rent this house–" I gesture around us. "Then use the money for upkeep and taxes on the place, save up the profits for upgrades. It's not going to be used to line my pockets."

"That's a good idea." Jack leans forward, really studying the blueprints. "Is this going to be a rental, too?"

"So I saved up money... and bought a plot of land off Dad. I wanted to show him how fiscally responsible I could be, ya know? Independent of blood money. Anyway..." I rub my sweaty hands off on my thighs. "There was a copse of trees next to Dad's house on a few acres, and he sold it to me. I left a thick tree line for privacy, and it's the last house on the street with only Dad as a neighbor because the hill incline is on two sides and fields on another."

Jack's jaw drops. "This is *your* house?"

"Yeah– it is," I croak out. "Kade gave me unlimited access to my trust, but I'm being responsible. Whatever I spend, I'm looking at it like a mortgage I gotta pay back. But I'm not going cheap because I want quality so it will last."

"A duplex?" Jack's eyes are narrowed, mind spinning its wheels.

"Yeah, I need a lot of your input on some stuff, 'kay?" I don't mention who shall remain nameless, because I need just as much input from her and her girlfriend. At least Jesse has been on board with this idea from its inception, but too cowardly to bring her girlfriend to meet me so she can make some decisions too. "A duplex." I point to the single room that connects both sides of the house.

"I don't get it." Jack leans forward, squinting his eyes. "That bedroom is half in one side and half in the other, with a door into a hallway on each side."

"Honor's room, with access to the entire duplex, and infallible trust in the residents of the other side of the building not to breach Honor's bedroom door to the other hallway."

"Took him long enough!" Wynn chuckles at Jack's mind-blown expression. "Kade keeps saying it was his idea, that he led Bren down this path. But I don't buy it. This is 100% Bren's brainchild, so he deserves a billion pats on the back."

Expressions wash over Jackson's face at lightning speed: fury, sadness, happiness, rage, and settling into a pinched, pissed off look. I ignore him, watching Wynn and Honor instead, as they lay on their bellies to work on the wall-hanging.

"Because we're not allowed to have a specific conversation, let's help me figure out what needs to go in the master bathroom and kitchen."

"I'd suggest a walk-in shower if you made the space big enough." Wynn offers his input from the floor. "When we get home, Kade's giving me free reign to play carpenter." He laughs at some inside joke none of us get but him. "I'm knocking out the spare bedroom, so the entire upstairs is the master suite, and I'm going to have a walk-in shower for adventure time."

"Adventure time?"

Shaking his head, "Don't ask," Jack blushes crimson.

"Oh!" The contents of this morning's gift box pop into my mind. "Yeah, we need a walk-in shower."

Jackson scoots a few inches away from me on the sofa, then grabs a throw pillow to cover his lap. "Kade's house is kinda small, so what if you guys want to have kids in the future?"

Wynn stares at my child for a few silent moments, then rumbles, "I don't want to reproduce. We have enough Gillettes running around, and I can see myself reflected in them."

"That's a shame, because you're so pretty and perfect, Golden Boy," I tease, grinning. "What about Kade, though? He's the last of his kind."

"It would be a shame never to have a mini-Marx." Jackson looks more comfortable, less rosy-cheeked and aroused. "It's kinda connected to my job, ya know? I have resources to help same-sex couples have biological children."

"You want kids?" Surprise colors my voice as Jack and I both look at Honor, who is behaving now that she has a playmate.

"Yeah, I'm an only kid and I'd love to make my parents into grandparents." Jack looks away, skittish all of the sudden. "When I'm older."

"Kade has issues," Wynn finally responds, voice quiet. "He's already filling out the paperwork for foster care, wanting to give back what he was given. So he's ditching the home office downstairs, and moving everything into his office at the center. The family room is going bye-bye too. We'll have two bedrooms downstairs for emergency placement foster kids."

"Where the hell are you going to watch TV?" comes from me, because I have skewed priorities.

On the other hand, Jack is a bit more selfless than I am. "Are you okay with this?"

"Why do you think I'm getting the upstairs to myself?" Wynn raises an eyebrow at us. "I'm terrified, to be honest. I don't know if I'm ready, but Kade is. It's emergency, so they will need someone who can talk to them– Kade. Then they will be placed into a foster home, with relatives, or back with their parents. It's a no-attachment scenario, and I'm going to struggle."

"You're not okay with this, are you?" I scrub a hand over my face, hearing Kaden say how he had a vision of how their life will play out, and now I'm scared he's not seeing it clearly. Kade has always been fragile, and I worry if this doesn't pan out with Wynn, he'll be in his own emergency situation.

"I think it's amazing." Wynn's eyes shine so bright, he's throwing shadows in the room. "Kade is incapable of seeing who he is, inside and out. To him, he's gross and selfish. But he's not." Wynn rests his hand in the center of Honor's back. "I'm on board, but I'm terrified I will get attached to each and every kid and not be able to let it go– let go whatever happened to them and not be depressed when they move on to a permanent home."

"So you do want kids." Jack calls Wynn out.

"No, I want *Kade's* kids. Adopted? Yes. But I think it would help his dysmorphia if he had his own biological child. Take that loneliness away, because there hasn't been anything any of us could figure out how to do it."

"That bond–" Honor looks up at me, sensing I'm talking about her. "Is suffocating at worst, and more important than breathing at best. Kade– no matter how much Dad and I let him into our hearts, he'd pull away from us. Turn into a jackass mid-hug. He won't be able to give himself to a foster kid, only because he will have to be the one giving them everything while expecting nothing in return. His own kid– there is nothing to expect in return, because they are *it*."

"I actually get that." Wynn grins at me. "Willa's and Penny's kids– their existence is the gift. Fostering and adopting kids may also take the guilt away of having his own someday. Kade gets pissy when people have kids, because there are so many across the world who need a family."

"He's a head-case," I mutter. "He's going to either be the best therapist, or the very worst."

"They're all head-cases." Wynn snorts. "Trust me. They're snooty bastards who love their cocktail parties and expensive meals out. I've met Kade's classmates, professors, and therapists. Most are pretentious, and all are batshit crazy."

"Dysmorphia?" Jackson's voice warbles with confusion. "I've lived with the guy for four years, half a week at a time. What?"

"Is it normal for people to wear long-sleeved shirts–" I turn to Jack. "To bed? I haven't seen Kade without a shirt on since I '*accidentally*' walked in on him when he was twenty. That was what? Eight years ago."

"What's under the shirt, Wynn?" Thoughts are playing out on Jack's face, and I see it's finally sinking in.

"Besides a gorgeous body?" Wynn sits up, then trails his fingers through Honor's baby-fine hair. My daughter is a greedy girl, and her face is blissed out. "Thick scars from his wrists to elbows– thank God he missed the arteries with the hunting knife."

"Oh." Tears are lacing that singular word. Jack quickly looks away but continues. "Mentor KM said he had been where you were– that's why you get each other so well."

Wynn snorts. "Kade *gets* me. I don't have a clue most days on how to get him. My problem was environmental, whereas his is deep in his psyche. What's under the shirt? A thousand cut marks down both sides of his torso, from ribs to hips. The scars are thin and wispy, time lightening them until they resemble feathers. But the newer ones are still pink and angry. That's what's under the shirt."

"Is something wrong with his junk? You were dead-set on exposing him, but he wouldn't let you."

My head cranks so quickly to the side, it makes a crunching sound and stiffens my neck muscles. I glare at the side of Jack's face, watching the blush flow up his cheeks and forehead.

Wynn just shakes his head minutely in my direction. "Kade's shy– I was teasing him. I know you think we're like swingers or something, but we've only touched each other. I figured with you, he'd be less uptight about it and know I was teasing. There's nothing casual about Kade– and his junk is perfect."

"Kade and shy?" Jack raises his eyebrow. "I don't see it."

Wynn quickly looks down at Honor, then back up at us. "No D inside A action after five and a half years together?" The expression on Wynn's face is murderous. "Kade's a shy control freak with dysmorphia. But he also likes watching–"

"And listening." Jackson clutches the pillow to his groin, and I know every single sign of arousal in the man. His pink button nose is glowing with lusty thoughts.

Wynn snorts, then it flows into laughter– a laugh so sexual I shiver in a combination of revulsion and curiosity. I never want to hear it again.

I don't care if they know shit about each other I don't know. I don't care if they fool around. I don't care if Jack gets that blowjob he's after.

It's written in human nature to lie to oneself.

Jackson is getting Karmic satisfaction after I screwed my way through junior and senior year without taking his feelings into account. Only it hurts more because I'm a grown man and this is real life, not teenage angst bullshit when I didn't know any better.

I change the subject before I murder someone.

"Baby? Why don't you go grab the gift Uncle Kade squeezed through your window this morning. I'm sure Uncle Wynn and Uncle Jack will get a kick out of it."

Zigzag running, Honor's rocketing toward the kitchen.

"No more toys!" Jackson seethes. "Did you forget what this place looked like when we entered?"

"It's Kade." Wynn shrugs. "We fight about it constantly. You *know* my thoughts on excess. If you think Honor is the only kid he does this for, you've got another think coming."

Wynn has marker ink on the side of his face, and Jack and I share a smile but don't tell him.

"Kade's like a demented Santa handing out gifts every freaking day. Copper now has a motorized car he rides around the sidewalks like he's cruising for chicks."

"You're kidding, right?" Jack's eyes flick between Wynn, me, then back at Wynn.

"Wish I was–" Wynn bursts out laughing at the display my daughter makes.

Walking backward, trying to get leverage, she keeps falling to her tushy. Panting from exertion, she's dragging the puppy playpen with the giant stuffed unicorn inside the ring from the kitchen to the living room to show everyone what Uncle Kade brought.

Honor loves it.

The struggle is real. We watch Honor for a good five minutes as she gives up on the puppy pen, and tries to wedge the unicorn out of the zippered door. Giving up on that, she drags the unicorn over the top by its horn, falling to her ass in the process. After some major huffing and puffing, Honor pulls the unicorn to the center of the living room, crawls on its back, and holds the feather boa like reins.

"Giddy up!" She kicks her heels into the sides of the unicorn, making it rear up.

"I'm speechless." At first I think Wynn's talking about Honor's joy, but then I follow the direction of his gaze. "That's Perty's puppy pen. You put my niece in a dog containment octagon?"

"Did you not see this house when you walked in?" Offended, I gesture around the living room. "That hand-me-down pen is a lifesaver. I place it in the hallway with the bathroom door open, so I can take a shower or a shit without worrying she's harming herself or the house."

"Ya gotta do what ya gotta do, bud." Jack pats me on the back to take the sting out of Wynn's judgmental words.

"Uncle Wynn?" Honor hangs off the side of the unicorn, fists gripping the boa. "Wanna tickle fight?"

Jack's snort is so loud, he has to hide his face against my shoulder.

"I'm gonna get you!" Wynn curls his fingertips and tickles Honor's sides until she's shrieking like a banshee.

"Daddy gave Uncle Jack a raspberry on his boob." My daughter, the tattletale.

"Say what?" Wynn's face whips around to stare at us, and Jack lifts his shirt real quick, showing off a hella big suck mark.

"Lord, have mercy!" I hiss, about to lose my shit. "Let me see."

Shameless, completely fucking shameless, it's only fair I get to have a tickle fight too. I tackle Jackson to the couch, touching any body part that comes in contact with my hands. He's laughing, bucking around, trying to knee me in the nuts hard enough to graze me but not harm me.

"Honor, go get a glass of water." Wynn's words barely register. "We gotta cool your daddy off."

"No!" I yelp, finally getting Jack's shirt up so I can look at my masterpiece. Sensing my daughter has left the room in search of her cup, I pepper a kiss to the swollen area, getting off on Jack's groan. Then I pull away like it never happened. "Kissed it and made it better."

Tomato-red, Jack clutches the throw pillow like a talisman.

"Here, Daddy!" Honor thrusts her sippy cup into my hands. Praise Jesus for spill-proof cups, or I'd be drenched right now.

"Thanks, baby." I pretend to take a sip, then hand it back to her.

"You guys go over the blueprints," Wynn offers. "I'll read to Honor, and then put her down for a nap. No can do on taking the little scamp on a date. I've got a late afternoon class today I can't miss."

"Oh, thanks." I whisper, sounding dejected.

"I drove myself." Jack reads me like an open book. "I'm on call in case one of my mommas is about to pop. But usually it's uneventful. So I have nothing planned for the rest of the day."

"Cool." I reach for the blueprints like my heart isn't beating out of my chest.

"You guys are so transparent– it ain't even funny," is Wynn's parting shot as he leads Honor down the hallway.

"Blueprints," Jack warns. "I didn't come here to talk, Brennan. I mean it. I didn't come here to fool around, either." His expression is stark, lips pulled into a thin line. "As long as you're married to

Jesse, my body is off limits, as is any conversations about your wife. Got it?"

"Yeah," I breathe, coming up with contingency plans B – Z, since A is off the table.

"The kitchen sink should be under the window, so you can see Honor playing in the yard." Jack runs his fingertip along the blueprints. "I like this common area you've made off the back doors of each side of the duplex so Honor can play from one house to the next. But there is no way you're going to want to sit out there and have Jesse." Jack stumbles over my wife's name. "What if you're enjoying the sunset, and Jesse comes out– ruining it?"

"Three yards." I find a compromise, which is why I wanted Jackson's help in the first place. "The small one for Honor to play, with a view from the kitchen windows of both sides. We could use the side doors leading to the garages to make a fenced in area where the other household can't have access, and neither can Honor unless she's led out there."

"It doesn't have to be fenced in. Fence Honor's yard, then run a divider all the way to the edge of the yard at the boundary line, separating the yard in half. There's no neighbors and you don't want to block the amazing view of the hills. Privacy, ya know?"

"Yeah, privacy is important," I agree.

Resentment so thick he's almost choking on it, Jackson reveals his earlier anger. "Especially when your sworn enemy is your neighbor who shares your walls and Honor."

"I'm sorry. It has to be this way–" my words are cut off by a hand covering my mouth, and a face being buried against my neck.

"Shut up– don't talk," Jackson rumbles against the side of my throat, sweet breath tickling me. "Just listen."

Wynn ghosts by, lightly stepping as to not disturb us, then he slips out the front door. But I'm not going to shut up, and it's Jack who's going to listen.

CHAPTER TEN
Brennan Kennedy

Pulling away from Jack to stand up, I decide to get him lubricated for the conversation to come. "Do you want a drink now that the teetotaler isn't in the house?"

God love Wynn, but he really is a very judgmental person. Selfless, loving, compassionate and giving, yet a right fighter in the extreme, and only his point of view is the right one.

I can understand how alcohol is a trigger for him, but to tell us we can't have a drink ever again in our lives… Corbin is a recovering alcoholic, and Willa and Warren are regulars at NA meetings, but that doesn't mean the rest of us are budding abusers for having a taste.

Wynn's kneejerk reaction has caused us all to act shady. Like I'm sure Royce and Kade will share a beer while shooting the shit around the bonfire tonight, but neither can tell Wynn about it. Nothing tastes better than a cold beer after working in the yard, and Wynn turns into a bloodhound after coming home from class to find out Kade or Jack joined me.

Jesse got me hooked on wine with certain meals, and she's not going to stop doing that just because Wynn says so. We all want Honor to have a realistic view of the world, so she doesn't go nuts and not know how to handle it when she comes into contact with drugs and alcohol. This is exactly what Wynn needs to be around now. He doesn't have to partake, but he needs to see it's okay to have wine with dinner or a spiked Arnold Palmer after mowing the lawn.

Glaring at us and making us feel guilty, like we were on an episode of Intervention, Wynn dumped the punch down the drain at the Christmas party Jesse and I hosted this past year. Kade pounded a beer in front of Wynn, and then dragged him off for a dropdown, knockout fight. It ruined the party.

"I'm on call, remember?" Jack moves me along to contingency plan C. "But I guess nursing one won't hurt."

"*Nurse* Jackie." I chuckle at my bad pun while crossing to the kitchen. I drag the unicorn back into its pen, and then shove it over to where our kitchen table should be.

"That never gets old." Jack laughs with me. "It's not like I don't hear it at the hospital."

"Pick your poison." I lean into the refrigerator and fiddle with the childproof thingamajig keeping Honor out of the booze drawer. "We're out of wine, not that you like it anyway. We've got Amber Bock or Strongbow cider. As always, the Guinness belongs to Kade."

"Cider," flows in from the living room. I grab a couple, snag the magnet opener off the fridge, pop the tops, and then make my way back to Jackson. Instead of leading off on how I have to chat with Jesse, I go straight in for the kill.

"How old were you when you figured out you were gay?" Standing over Jack, gazing right into his eyes, I hand him a bottle. "On a cellular level, I knew Franny was gay since preschool. I thought nothing of it." Lifting my cider, I don't look away as I take a drink. After swallowing thickly, Jack follows suit to wet his throat.

I can tell I've baffled yet put Jack at ease, so I sit down next to him and shift so we can look at each other without wrenching our necks. He makes it easier by toeing off his sneakers, and then sitting cross-legged on the sofa, sitting sideways to face me. I follow suit, yet again wishing my legs weren't so bulky so the short bastards were more flexible.

"I guess, I can't say I felt different, because I was just feeling what I was feeling and assumed everyone else did too."

"It's not normal versus different," I remind him. "Nothing was wrong with how you were feeling."

"Yeah, I know." Jack takes another sip, and then slides the bottle in his hillbilly cup holder– between his thighs to nestle up against his crotch. I've never wanted to be a bottle as badly as I do right now.

Focus.

"Thirteen? Fourteen? Everyone was noticing girls, and I just wanted to hang out with them, not kiss 'em. Didn't see what the big deal was until it was time for gym class. It was eighth grade before they made us take showers after class. First shower was highly enlightening."

Jackson takes a big gulp of his cider, nose painted pink with a blush.

I have to ease Jesse into this conversation, because it's important, even if Jack doesn't think so. "My dad and momma, they were together all through school, so I thought that's how it was supposed to be."

Jack moves to open his mouth, so I thrust my bottle between his lips to shut his ass up. His glare makes my cock sit up and take notice, so I tilt the bottle and force him to take a sip.

Backtracking, I watch, fascinated by how his tongue darts out to capture a drop of cider on his lip. "Franny was my best friend since preschool. I was Honor's age, not knowing there was anything bizarre about him wanting to dress in pretty clothes."

"Baby drag queen in training," Jack murmurs fondly.

"Have you seen him all decked out?" I lean forward, turning animated. "Francis is absolutely stunning." I make an explosion sound. "Mind blown."

"He posts his designs on Facebook, but I've never seen him decked out." Jackson smiles, envisioning it.

"I'll grab my phone and show you later... anyway, as I was saying. He was my best friend. Nothing he did was weird to me. I wasn't always super friendly, and sometimes when I am, it's just a bullshit lie. So it was me and Franny taking on the world in kindergarten. But the thing was, I was the shortest in the class and chubby, and Franny was being bullied for wearing blouses by some older kids."

Jackson looks away, knowing exactly where I'm headed, but he doesn't stop me this time. Whether he hates Jesse because of jealousy or not, she does have her virtues.

"I wasn't strong enough, so they started bullying me too–"

"Jessica," Jack mutters begrudgingly.

"Right. She was the tallest in our class at the time, taller than the third graders beating us up. She had long blonde hair she wore in a ponytail, and it would whip around her head while she wailed on kids for being mean to us. She was our superhero. So our duo turned into a trio until we hit junior year."

"I know– you didn't even know anyone else existed." Jack takes a hearty pull off his bottle, so I reach over to rub his foot to keep him connected to me and not off in his head somewhere toxic.

"My mom was bossy. A nag, and I don't feel guilty for saying that. She had my dad's balls in her purse, and I thought that was normal. So our pecking order was Jesse, Franny, then me being their bitch. Our dynamic worked. I blame modeling after my parents for a bit of my troubles, but not all of it. The rest is on me."

"What troubles?"

"My mom died. Puberty hit. My dad was dealing with Willa marrying Uncle Donny. I was trying to get Wynn to like me, and he wouldn't give me the time of day, so I put all of my attention on Franny and Jesse. I saw Franny as my brother, but Jesse reminded me of my mom, and that led me to… right here, right now.

"I was like a baby bird imprinting or something, I don't know. I do know what I felt was real– I do know that. I fell hard for Jesse. We started messing around when we were thirteen, screwing by fifteen, and I knew I was going to marry her and have kids. It was just what it was going to be."

Jack makes a gutted sound in the back of his throat, but the truth is either going to soothe it or make it worse.

"Jesse was into me– I've been with enough girls to know when one is horny and getting off on me. So I didn't suspect a thing. Kade came home for good, getting ready to take over his job at the little school, and he was setting up the LGBTQ group on Facebook. Jesse and I were fooling around in her bedroom and Francis barged in all excited to say he just joined. Jess dropped the lesbian bombshell while my hand was thrust down her pants."

"Are you fucking serious?" Jackson displays all of the pent-up rage I've never allowed myself to feel.

"Yeah, I am. While wearing a goddamn promise ring and everything, she tells me she's a lesbian and doesn't know if she wants to be with me anymore– wants to mess around with girls. To say my world died at my feet would be an understatement."

I reach over to the coffee table to grab my cider, and then drain it in a single gulp. "Gimme a minute." I stalk back into the kitchen, arms braced against the countertop with my head bowed, ignoring the tears streaming down my cheeks. After a few cleansing breaths, I grab another cider from the fridge, and stalk back to the living room.

"That same night, Duane had a party in his backyard, and I got shit-faced. Obliterated." After closing and opening my eyes, I look to the ceiling for some help from above. "I thought I'd follow my dad's path, true? Marry Jesse, only ever lie with her, and make babies in a house I built. So I fucked Dori Sylvan that night to nail the coffin shut."

Jack doesn't say anything, but his face reveals how I feel on the inside.

Tormented.

"Dori was a dirty talker, telling me how she used to fool around with her friends, and it gave me an idea. I was so pussy whipped by Jesse, I would have done anything. I mean, *anything*. I was only sixteen at the time, what did I know?

"It took me a few nights of screwing to butter Dori up. I dragged Dori to Jesse's house in the middle of the night, and we snuck into her bedroom. It was my first threesome, and Jesse was way into it. She treated me better than ever after that for a while. But then Dori started only wanting me, I only wanted Jesse, and Jesse only wanted Dori. So what was one more fuck, and another, and another, on my path of making sure I could stay in Jesse's bed by bringing willing girls around."

Sighing, Jackson rests his elbow on his knee, and then cups his forehead in his palm. "Christ, Brennan."

"Yeah, I know," I breathe out in a gust. "I'm not the same person I was back then. An idiot teenager who thought he was doing the wrong thing for the right reasons. I wouldn't change it, because I know I wouldn't know any better any way you look at it. I was running off pure desperation. I was *in* love with Jesse, and she was my world. Best friend, girlfriend, lover, protector."

"I don't get it. Are you actually straight?"

Ironic laughter flows from my throat, so pain-filled it makes my eyes water. "We had our cliques, and it wasn't until after I was bugging the piss out of Wynn every weekend that he finally let me in. Pretty sure Dad told Wynn to befriend me– I was hard to ignore when we were in the same house. So you and I didn't know each other at all aside from seeing one another in class. I didn't join the basketball team until junior year so I could be around Wynn, with Francis following me as our scorekeeper."

"I remember you being everywhere, but totally lost in your own world. Once we learned you had money, the kids were like leeches, so you ignored us."

"Not ignored– I wanted friends who liked me for me." Scrubbing my hands across my face, I clear my throat. "It all happened the summer between the end of tenth and the beginning of eleventh. Kade moved home and started up the group. I enlisted Franny to seek out who to add– the fag test. Jessica came out to me, and I discovered I belonged in the group as well."

"How?" Jack grins, but it's warped with confusion.

"Up until then, the only gay guys I'd been around were my foster brother and the kid I saw as my brother– not including Wynn. Again, brother. I can look at them objectively and see how guys would find them hot, but to think of them sexually turns my guts. So Miriam Ross brought her son to the house to help Kade set the group up, and he brought his boyfriend–"

"Our ultimate traitor, Josh Truman," Jack fills in for me, still pissed over five years later.

Josh Truman and Tyler Ross were dating, and Tyler refused to come out of the closet while still in high school, so using his phony alias, Josh outed every member of our LGBTQ group on Facebook, including his own sister, Libby. Josh took off to Rhode Island for college, leaving Tyler and the rest of us to pick up the pieces.

"Yeah, the one and only. Kade and Tyler were in Dad's office– I tried to join them but Kade kicked me out. So I was just hanging out in my room, and Josh cornered me in there. We talked about basketball and flirted for a bit, and I was popping chub the whole time. So I kinda figured out I didn't realize I liked boys too because the only gay guys I'd been in contact with were like brothers to me."

"What am I, chopped liver?" Jack deadpans.

"If you remember right, I hit on you something fierce once Wynn brought you around." Reaching over, I bop Jack on the nose. "We didn't hang out until then. I really didn't know you at all. I developed a bit of a crush on you, stalking you around school once we hit junior year. I flirted with Virginia Duncan relentlessly in the group, and Jesse figured it out."

Jack growls, and I huff a laugh.

"I didn't sic Jesse on you with the blowjob, Jack. Honest– I didn't." I close my eyes, trying to press down past agony. "We got in a huge fucking fight. We were together, and she never forgave me for cheating on her, even if it led to us fucking around with girls together."

"If I had known what was going on, I would've suffocated Jessica with my cock."

"Ha! It was both of our faults. We were toxic together. Jesse started blowing all of my friends to hurt me, and I hooked up with three girls who didn't want to do her too. So she blew you, saying she wanted to make sure you were gay so I wouldn't get hurt. Then she came back and said you were totally into and loved it."

"I did not!" Jack snarls. "I was hard at first, but then I lost my wood and couldn't get off."

"Yeah, I know." After taking a deep breath, I let the truth out in a rush. "She was trying to hurt me. Jesse and I had another huge fucking fight because she thought I was getting off on Morgan Prescott more than I was on her during our final threesome. I don't know how, but I got Jesse crying, revealing my best friend again, and she came clean about you."

Voice incredulous, "How do you not hate her?" Jack raises a hand to stop me from answering. "How are you still in love with her?"

"That's the thing– one of the things I wanted to tell you and you wouldn't let me. And this isn't a new fucking occurrence between us, Jackson. You put up walls on off-limits topics, and this has always been one of 'em. But it's important you hear this shit– it's important I get it out. Because I am loyal to Jessica, and I couldn't share this shit with anyone *but* you."

Jackson's features warp, turning green like he's going to be sick, and then the guilt washes it away.

"I haven't been in love with Jesse since the beginning of junior year in high school. She knows it and I know it. There was too much between us that couldn't be fixed, and none of it had anything to do with our sexuality. Friends don't do friends like that. Ever. But I kept holding onto the glimpses of my best friend shining through.

"You asked why I don't hate her– because I get her, Jackson. I get how Jessica felt. She was a teenager who had just come out of the closet, with her best friend pining away for her, and she didn't want to lose me. Shit just went off the rails from there, snowballing. In the past few months, as she's pulled farther and farther away from me, the real Jessica is shining through again. That's why I can't hate her, because I'm not an asshole. I get it."

"I don't think I'll ever be able to like her," Jackson admits, and I know he's speaking the truth.

"We all make mistakes, Jack. Play head-games. I waited until after Jesse and I were done with our sick games, both of us getting our shit together, before I kissed you behind the barn. Jesus, here I was the man-whore of Kentwood, promising to turn over a new leaf, and I was grinding against you until I popped."

"You definitely proved you weren't straight that night, and made me a believer in how great being gay was going to be." Jackson blushes so bright, I can feel the heat radiating off of him. "Dude, you hooked me and I haven't been able to get away from you ever since."

"Same for me," I answer without hesitation. "I didn't want to ruin it with sex. We were teenagers and motherfucking stupid. I knew that if I fucked you, it would have been a crash and burn. I didn't want to lose Wynn by hurting his best friend, so I decided I'd rather be your friend, instead of some mistake you regretted from back in high school."

"That wouldn't have happened, Bren, and you know it."

"I didn't, though. I didn't know you, Jack. *At all*. I was hot for you. Every other person I had fucked left me. My world was upside down, because I thought I would be a one-woman-man for life, and when that didn't happen, I lost myself. What I found was that I was bi. I was done being a fuck-up. I learned my lesson just before I found you, and having sex wasn't a chance I was willing to take when it could have cost me losing you."

"I'll buy that, but come senior year, where we'd been hanging out non-fucking-stop for over a year, you still didn't make a move. You drove me insane, to the point I wanted to tear your nuts off."

Stomach twisting in knots, I fear I'm going to be sick, remembering exactly how it felt at the time. Suffocating agony with every breath I tried to take, and I had just dealt with it because I didn't want to be a hypocrite. "Mistakes, Jack. Even you've unintentionally made 'em. Not that I blamed you– you had every right."

"What? What are you talking about?"

"Kade assured me teenagers have no impulse control, so what I did was a kneejerk reaction that was probably unavoidable." I close my eyes, because I can't admit this to Jack's face. "I was going to ask you to prom, like a fucking idiot. I thought it would be this epic romantic gesture. We were already getting hazed, bullied, and bashed by the townsfolk, so it didn't matter anyway. I came to your house to ask you out, and found you giving Francis head."

"God, no." Jack's voice warps in horror, but I still can't open my eyes.

"Asshole that I was, after finding the guy I wanted screwing around with my best friend– Franny and I have never been the same since, by the way –I ran straight to the only other person who ever gave two shits about me."

Jack makes an animalistic baying sound in the back of his throat, like he's wounded by the truth. "That's how Honor was conceived."

"Yeah, that." I finally open my eyes, because I've never been surer of anything in my life. Staring Jack down, I let it all pour out.

"You and me, if we had hooked up in school, we wouldn't be together now. It's a fact of life. You would've gone to college and found someone worthy, because I wouldn't have grown up as much without going through this shit."

"I don't believe that–"

"It's true. We would've screwed around and not gotten to know each other. With Wynn being shoved up Kade's ass, it's given us time to spend together. With Francis in California, I don't have him as a crutch anymore. Jesse being Jesse… for the past four years, you and I have become better friends to each other than we were with those fools– admit it," I challenge. "Even with your no-no topics, we have a mature friendship, instead of just being tossed together by age group and lack of options."

"You're probably right, I guess," Jack admits lamely. "Lord knows, Wynn and Kade spend more time messing around than talking, and I have a feeling you and I would probably do the same." The '*I hope*' goes without saying.

"My dad says there's no such thing as coincidences– this was supposed to happen, Jackson. I was supposed to have Honor. I was supposed to grow up fast. I moved here to get away from Dad so I could learn to be my own man. I might act and feel older than my age, but I like who I am now, when I hated who I used to be. That guy wasn't good enough for Nurse Jackie."

Jackson's chest is rising and falling rapidly, closing in on hyperventilating. "Do you regret saying goodbye to me the night before you got married?"

"Goodbye?" I reach over to cup Jack's face, not fearing rejection. "It was to keep us going, so you'd know what you had to look forward to in the future when we were both ready– never a goodbye. I was showing you how much I loved and trusted you."

"Bren," Jack breathes, leaning forward to press his mouth to mine.

CHAPTER ELEVEN
Brennan Kennedy

What starts out as a banked fire turns into an inferno. Weeks of crushing turned to months of flirting, turned to years of denial. Gasping into my mouth, both laughing and making a sobbing sound, Jack curls his fingers around the nape of my neck to use as leverage to pull himself into my lap.

As much as I'd love to lose control, I won't allow it. Wanting to savor the moment, nothing matters more than the heavy press of Jackson's weight on me, the sound of his breath hitching in his throat, his musky scent flowing into my nostrils, and the feel of his lips and hands on me.

No more mistakes– this is the beginning when I've yet to end it with Jesse, so I can't allow it to go any further than learning how we both tick now as adults. I wouldn't destroy it back then by sleeping with him, and I won't now.

Laughing into Jack's mouth, "I can't believe I'm shaking." My fingers vibrate along the curve of his back to accentuate my point. "I've missed this feeling– being touched, not feeling alone. I've missed it with you."

"Christ!" Jackson tears his lips from mine, fingers twisting in my hair to pull himself up further. With rough movements, my face is shoved against the side of his throat, and I take what is offered. Mouth opening, I lick a long, wet line from his jaw to his shoulder, nudging the collar of his t-shirt out of the way with the tip of my nose.

Jack rears up on me, rocking his ass into my crotch while pressing the front of his body into my belly. Grinding, rolling his hips, he roughly gasps out, "Your stomach should be illegal– my God, I can feel your abs through our clothes and it's like running my dick along a washboard."

Rearing over me while taking advantage of my stomach, it puts Jack above me. So I wrench his shirt out of the way and take my pleasure from nuzzling at the suck mark I placed on his chest last night.

"I hate how I've always had little girl tits." Jack snarls, but forgets his malfunction when I suck his nipple into my mouth.

"My muscles are always so tight I can barely bend, but you seem to be getting off on frotting with my abs– so have at it." Taking me at my word, Jack shoves me backward on the sofa, and then grinds his dick so hard into my stomach, it's going to leave a bruise.

A naughty chuckle flows from between my lips to vibrate against Jack's chest. Just to be a shit, I suck as much of his tit into my mouth as I can, making him both groan with pleasure and growl at me for embarrassing him.

Retaliating, Jack has my back arching off the sofa cushions when his hand wedges between us to squeeze my hard-on. Fingers working my fly, "I want to ride this– I'm going to fuck myself on your dick."

"Yeah–" every reservation I have flows right out the window, because if Jack wants it, so do I. "Hurry!"

"Ahem…" A soft cough ricochets around the living room, taking a moment to filter into my lust-fueled haze. It takes Jesse's, "Bren," to clue Jack in that we're no longer alone. "I was just going to stay in the kitchen, figuring you'd both blow before you got to the main event, because I want that for you. *Really*, I do. But that last bit had me stepping in."

Jack releases a string of very audible misogynistic slurs as he pulls away. Laying half on, half off the couch, I stare at my wife from upside down as she stands in the entryway from the kitchen to the living room.

Jesse's not mad, not that I expected her to be. She's holding onto her elbow while her other hand twists at her hair– classic uncomfortable, nervous gesture of hers. She keeps eyeballing Jackson, like she's waiting for him to murder her– which he is probably contemplating.

"You're home early," is my lame reply, when all of my attention is on Jackson zipping my pants back up. I can feel his fury licking at my flesh, but I know he's merely pouting on the outside. "Honor was settled in for a nap, but knowing her, she's probably playing in that toy store we call a bedroom."

"I'm not judging– if Honor caught you, she caught you. But next time, either wait until she's on a playdate, or take it into your bedroom." Jesse has her, '*I'm the wife, so I know more than my dumbshit of a husband,*' voice in full action, but for once I agree.

"I didn't expect this to happen," I admit, wanting to kick myself. "So I won't argue with you."

Jesse's sarcastic grin is priceless, causing me to chuckle– we've been conflicting like oil and water since kindergarten. Our words harming more than physical punches.

Hand wrapping around my wrist, I'm hit with vertigo as Jackson pulls me to sit upright. "I have rosacea," Jack is muttering, causing me to take a good look at him. In a mix of lust and mortification, his cheeks are so flushed I fear capillaries are going to burst. "I'm just hot, is all." Turning his back to us, arm movement suggests he's adjusting himself.

Not being modest, I do the same thing while Jesse watches me like a hawk– I don't even get a blush out of her.

"I thought you were going out, being your day off and all." Turning to the side, I give Jackson some cover while he collects himself. I reach forward like nothing major has occurred, and begin rolling up the blueprints. The notebook is next, waiting for me to submit the changes via text message to our foreman.

Jesse leans against the entryway with her arms crossed over her boobs, too leery of Jack to enter her own living room. From the time she got pregnant with Honor, until we got married, Jack was brutal toward Jesse. It took Jack screaming in the middle of the clinic to guilt her into keeping the baby.

What kind of vicious cunt would murder a piece of Brennan?!?

That was one of the worst days of my life. Kaden was the voice of reason, saying it was Jesse's choice, but there was no reversing an abortion. Jesse could be a mother, or not be a mother, simply by either raising Honor with me, or allowing me to raise her by myself.

Honor was never just Jesse's and my daughter– she belongs to all of us.

My wife is hesitant with good reason. "After last night–"

"Last night?" Jack's head whips around like he's under demonic possession. He eyes me with suspicion and a healthy dose of disgust, like I've been confiding our secrets and conspiring against him.

"I came home while you were leaving last night," Jesse explains. "So I thought it was time."

"Aren't you nosy, always stalking from the kitchen?" I snort at the personality change Jackson always goes through around Jesse. He's behaved the past couple of years because we had to create boundaries. It's funny, but it's not.

I ignore the bullshit. "Time for what?" I stand up and walk to the center of the room, keeping myself between them. Jesse is an athlete– strong and fit, yet another reason why we get along for the most part. Jack… Jack would get his ass kicked if it came to blows, and I would end up defending him against my wife, who has every right to feel insulted and strike back.

"What's up, Jess?" Her terrified expression has me walking toward her to take her by the elbows. "Are you okay? You're shaking."

Jesse flashes me a wane smile, eyes refusing to look over my shoulder at Jackson. "This is kind of a big deal, so I wanted to do it with Jack here." She hesitates, and the floor vibrates beneath my bare feet as Jackson walks over to us. "I know it's sudden– only a few months… but I feel it."

Jesse curls a fist between her breasts, signaling she feels it deep in her heart.

"She's here?" My voice pitches high with excitement, so happy for Jesse. I know I'm baffling Jack, but Jesse will be my best friend first and foremost. If she's happy, the guilt and shame will dissolve.

My daughter's life will be exponentially better if her mother and I get along, with both of us loving the life we're leading, and that's only possible if we can compromise with our significant others. Meaning Jack has to knock his shit off and get with the program.

We're parents, not teenagers anymore.

"Can I meet her?" Eager, my voice is light and barely a whisper. Jesse tilts her head toward the kitchen, and I follow her lead.

A tiny girl is crouching down next to Honor's playpen, weaving the feather boa into a collar around the stuffed unicorn's neck. She senses my attention, and quickly rises to her feet.

Jesse's girl is nothing like I expected. At five foot tall, if she's lucky, she's pudgy with a mass of brown curls. Resting on her freckled nose, square glasses cover her eyes. Round cheeks are flushed bright pink. She's wearing a flower dress and leggings. Everything about her is at complete odds with Jesse's tall and lean athletic Barbie appearance.

Jesse found her own version of my Jack.

"Hi." I approach her, hand at the ready for a shake, keeping my steps light and trying not to intimidate her with my size. "It's nice to finally meet you."

"Hey, Bren." She greets me like we already know each other, but this is the first time I've ever laid eyes on her. "It's good to see you in person."

"OH! My God!" Jack shouts while brushing past me. For a terrifying second I freeze, worried he's going to attack her. "Libby!" Jack is hugging the girl, rocking back and forth and laughing. "I have an ally! You have the worst taste in women."

Turning to look over my shoulder, I catch Jesse slumping into a chair just inside the living room. Her barely audible, "Thank Christ," has me smiling with confusion. She shrugs, shoulders reaching her ears, just as baffled as I am.

With Jack and whoever the hell Libby is engaged in a hug-fest, I weave my way back into the living room to plunk my ass at the dinette set that's butted up against the wall to the kitchen.

"Any clue what's going on?"

"Yes and no," Jesse murmurs, eyes glued to her fingertip as it runs along the grooves in the top of our table. "You know Libby– you've just never spoken to her in person. I thought it would be the same with Jack, because I didn't think to ask Libby if she knew him."

"How?" I grab Jesse's hand so she'll concentrate on me instead of her outlining. Jack's chattering, just like he always does when he's happy, while enlisting Libby to help make coffee.

"I should check on Honor." As evasion tactics go, Jesse has a good one. She and Kade both have titanium-lined emotional shields they hide behind.

"I'll get her." Jack has evolved from jackass to hostess.

What?

The playpen is dropped in the center of the living room. The cider bottles are tossed in the recycling bin. Then Jack wanders down the hallway with my blueprints and notebook.

"Had I known–" Jesse stares at Jack's retreating back. "I would have introduced Libby sooner."

"I didn't know *Jackass* was Jack." Libby struggles to slide onto the bench seat that runs along the wall, so I pull the table toward me a bit. "Thanks."

"Lemme guess– Jesse always called him Jackass?"

Jesse stares at the ceiling while wearing a blush and a faint smirk, fingers drumming on the tabletop. She's awful at the innocent routine.

"You don't know who I am, do you?" Libby's laughter is light, and it makes both Jesse and me join in. "It's nice to meet you, Bren Kennedy. I'm Wood Kent."

Mind spinning, it's been years since I heard the ridiculous names we picked out for our LGBTQ group. Even back then, I owned who I was by using my actual name.

"Gimme a sec– I'm thinking. Wood Kent. Furrow Creek High. Two years younger than the Rusty Knob kids. She was questioning her sexuality." My eyes pop wide when it finally hits home. "Kent Wood's little sister. Libby Truman! We were just talking about your brother. How is Josh doing?"

"I'm sure you weren't saying anything good about him." Libby snorts unladylike, and I can see what Jesse sees in her. She's unlike any of the needy, attention-starved girls I brought into our bed. She's geeky, laidback, and comfortable in her own skin.

"No, Josh was the good guy in the story– honest." Libby and Jesse both raise an eyebrow in my direction. "I take it he's still a prick. Anyway, how did you guys meet back up?"

"Online dating," Jesse and Libby say at the same time.

"No way!" I lean back in my chair, not buying it at all.

"Way," Jack mutters, carrying a chattering little girl who's telling him a story about the time Copper stole her Ken doll. He deposits her into the playpen, and goes in search for the unicorn she's demanding.

"I work in the hospital cafeteria," Libby explains how she knows Jack. "Lame, I know. But there aren't too many jobs in the area. My mom's an administrator at the hospital and she hooked me up. Josh was the family overachiever, leaving me to be the underachiever."

"Pfft..." Jesse's bangs billow from the force of her breath expelling. "You like your job, and you know it. So who cares if you're not an engineer? There's a job for everyone. If we didn't do those jobs, the college-educated idiots would be lost without us."

"Hey, I heard that!" Jack sets a tray on the table, laden with coffee and a confiscated package of Kade's cookies.

"You don't count." Libby grins at Jack, glasses sliding off her tiny nose. "Nursing is not a bullshit degree."

"Wynn's is a bullshit degree." Jack slides in next to Libby on the bench, glaring down at his tummy touching the table. I move it some more toward me. "His is utterly worthless. Kade's been trying to convince Wynn to get certified in Industrial Arts. He's missing a few credits he can take online, and then getting certified to teach. Otherwise, Wynn can wipe his ass with his bullshit degree."

"They fight a lot about that, don't they?" Jesse picks that up immediately, and I hear Kade from this morning explaining how Miriam has a job waiting for Wynn if he'd take it.

Kade's lying to himself– he is so going to do what Miriam wants.

"Yeah, they basically fight and f–" Jack's eyes land on my daughter, who is cuddling with the unicorn and hanging onto every word we say. "Fudge. They eat a lot of fudge."

"Jack!" Jesse squeals, batting him in the center of his chest with her palm, forgetting to hate him for two seconds. "That is so bad."

"What?" Jack blushes, not getting it, so we all just stare at him until he does. Palms covering his face, "That was *so* bad. Bad. I didn't mean it that way– I fudged up."

I change the subject for Jack's sake, before Honor hears her first gay slur. "How did you guys meet up, and what's this about online dating?"

"We'd chat a bit while Jack ordered his lunch. It took a few months of that before we realized who the other one was– I finally looked at his lanyard and saw Duncan. So now Jack makes sure our breaks coincide and we eat together."

"Online dating." Jack points at himself. "That was all me. Royce is right about there being no such thing as coincidences. Libby and I sat down one day and made her a profile because the dating pool was nonexistent for her. It never dawned on me who Cutie was."

"Kentwood Cutie?" I turn to my wife, who looks guiltier than hell for online dating while still married to me. "Nostalgic," I murmur fondly.

"Irony." Jesse actually smiles at Jack. "In your quest to steal my husband, you inadvertently hooked me up with your new friend. So instead of dying alone like the harpy you think I am, you found me the love of my life. So I guess I owe you a thank you."

CHAPTER TWELVE
Kaden Marx

"Is your mom still craving hot and spicy?" I ask the kids as I lead them into the house. I get a bit worried that Willa and Royce aren't back yet because it's now after five. Especially when Royce lost his dad, Annie, and their baby when they were going to a baby-doctor appointment. Then after losing Baby Royce. So I occupy myself and the kids by doing something nice for Willa.

"Yeah, Momma's obsessed with hot chips lately." Rocky slides onto a stool at the kitchen island, like she's waiting to be served.

Hayden tries to flow onto the stool, but he's too short. None of us laugh when he stumbles and has to crawl to get on. "Daddy had to run out to the store last night and get Momma chips and ice cream, so he brought back like fifteen bags so we wouldn't run out."

Chuckling, I wander over to the pantry and discover it bursting with junk food. "Royce didn't let Bren and me eat like this– man's turning soft in his old age." I grab a bunch of cans and whatnot, and then set them on the counter

"We're not allowed to touch it." Hayden doesn't have an ounce of resentment in his voice. "I like Momma's homemade snacks better anyway. What are we making?"

"Black bean enchiladas?" I grab one of Willa's precious special order pans from the pot rack, taking extra care to only grab rubber tools– or whatever they're called. "She made them last time I ate with y'all. Seems simple enough since I can't cook for shit."

"I'll cut up some veg," Rockabilly volunteers. "Hayden knows how to make the sauce real good."

Using my powers of manipulation, over the next half hour, I manage to get the kids to make the enchiladas while I pretend I know what I'm doing. Putting them in the oven constitutes as the one who actually made them, right? I want all the praise from Royce for being sweet and helpful to Willa.

I'm not a total shit– I cleaned up the kitchen and scrubbed dishes by hand so there wasn't a mess. I need credit for that too.

The kids are setting the dining room table, and I'm pouring salsa in a dish to be all fancy like, when the front door opens. I freeze for a heartbeat, scared it will be bad news, but then I remembered my nuts dropped almost two decades ago and I need to man-up.

"Something smells good!" Royce's jovial voice has my shoulders relaxing. I take a deep breath, put the salsa jar down, and then wander to the entrance. I'm not surprised to find the kids swarming their parents. At almost twelve, they still haven't gotten to where they don't want hugs anymore. They're all over Royce and Willa like leeches, sucking up affection and love.

Most people would wait while the happy little family came together in relief and homecoming, but it's been four days, and I want some attention too. So I charge right into the cuddle party and demand some.

What I get is what I wanted when I first arrived back in Rusty Knob earlier today– a big wet lick across my face, a cold nose pressing into my palm, and a wiggly behind welcoming his daddy home.

"Perty!" I pick up the overexcited pug for some cuddles. "Daddy's home– have ya missed me?" I accept kisses and give nuzzles. "You're Daddy's boy, aren't ya? Willa's a meanie for always taking you in the car with her, and having you sleep with her, and taking you to work, and carrying you around like you can't walk, and never letting your daddy have you back. She's abusing you."

Laughing, Royce pats me on the back a half dozen times, then he leans in for a hug, not giving a shit that Perty is wiggling between us and barking happy barks. "Welcome home, son. Stop going back and forth, will ya? Then you can see Perty all you want, but he ain't your dog no more."

"You're so mean to me." I pout, causing Royce to laugh harder. "I take it you got good news today?"

"Sure did." Royce beams. "Willa's far enough along now that even if something bad happened, the baby could live outside the womb. Not that everything ain't going as it should. But at least that was a comfort."

Willa gazes at me, tears glistening with a mix of fear and relief. She sniffs the air, tasting it on the back of her tongue. "Mexican? Mmm... I'm starved." Then she looks at Hayden. "Thanks for making supper."

"Hey!" I shout, outraged. "I made it!"

"Sure ya did." Willa pats me on the cheek, big belly brushing against my side. "I'll be taking Perty back." Then my dog is lifted out of my arms, and the traitor burrows into her side, ass sitting on her baby bump. "Thanks, Kade– for watching the kids and supervising supper. I'm starved and emotionally and physically exhausted."

Mollified, I don't complain as she walks away. "I'll go pour the tortilla chips into a bowl." I stalk off, pouting.

Dinner consisted of Royce giving every detail of their doctor's visit, which was the best birth control on the planet. I'm positive Rockabilly will never procreate. We were told to clean up the mess, as if I'm a kid in this house and not a twenty-eight-year-old professional man. Pride bent, I did as I was told just because Perty gave me his undivided attention as long as I was in the kitchen and accidentally dropped snacks were involved.

Now the traitor is laying on Willa's upraised legs, with his behind butted up against the baby bump, snoring up a storm. His new master is concentrating on an adult coloring book with a billion gel pens scattered everywhere. The twins are watching a television that's way too loud. Royce is staring blankly into space. While I'm just trying to decide if I want to sit here and do nothing, pester Warren and the kids since Penny is at the center, or go home and be alone.

Being alone is the last thing I want, but I feel like an interloper. A decade ago, Bren and I were the kids and Royce was all about us. Now Willa is the lady of the house, and she and the twins are Royce's world.

Bren has his own family now, and he's getting ready to branch it into two. He wouldn't be sitting here like he wanted to turn back the clock and be the center of Royce's attention.

I need to grow up and learn I can't go backward. I can't pretend I'm a teenager because I'm still studying for another degree. I need to go to my own house, carve out my own life, and hope and pray Wynn isn't doing as I am– holding onto the past instead of making a future.

With my hands braced on the arms of the chair, I slowly rise to my feet. "I–"

"Bonfire?" Royce is turning to look at me before I'm fully upright, somehow sensing the negative thoughts spinning around in my head. He doesn't wait for me to answer. He's out of his chair and out of the room before I even register what's going on.

I look at Willa crosswise as I leave, because she's laughing at how startled I look. The kids and the dog don't even react, lost in their own worlds.

Confused, I quicken my step through the house, and then pop out the kitchen door to the backyard. I spot Royce ghosting into the barn, and by the time I near it, he's coming back out with two bottles of beer in each hand.

I don't know where I stand with anyone anymore. I'm the last Marx. Royce isn't my dad, but he can't be my friend because he took me in and tried to raise me. Bren is my foster brother, so he can't really be my friend either. The rest of the gang sees me as a mentor more than a friend. Then there's Wynn, who is still too dang naïve and young for my liking, but he can't be my friend because he's my boyfriend. Everyone needs someone they can bitch about their significant other to, but not me.

Even though Warren and I were buddies in school, we have absolutely nothing in common anymore besides the occasional stop at the fishing hole or a hike through the woods. I can't bitch about Wynn's immaturity to his own dang brother, adoptive father, adoptive brother, or his best friend.

I'm a man on a deserted island.

"Here–" Royce hands me two bottles of beer, one for each hand. "With Warren and Willa not allowed to imbibe, and Wynn getting testy when he sees anything with alcohol in it, I've got to hide it in the barn fridge."

Royce lights the fire in record speed. Seriously, he should take up with the fire department. I'm sure you have to know how to start a fire to put one out.

I sit on the ground with my back to the log, resting my arm on my upraised knee. I dangle the beer bottle from my fingertips, mind still stuck on all the bullshit.

Satisfied with our tiny fire, Royce settles in beside me, and then gazes with reverence at the flames. "I have to tuck my stash in a cooler and get it out of Wynn's barn when he comes home to visit. I'ma have to find a new location once you guys move back."

"Jack and I trust Bren with our stash. So maybe that's what you'll have to do. Give your son your booze." I chuckle at how ridiculous this conversation is. "I get not wanting temptation around Willa. But when Wynn moves into my house, I'm not going to edit myself for him and turn sneaky. I'm not an alcoholic, so he can either deal with a few bottles in our fridge, or he'll be sleeping in his old room in your house."

"Nice," Royce drawls out, chuckling. "I'm not going to give you advice on that front, only to say you're going about it the right way. Don't be a doormat."

"Does it bother you how you have no friends?" is out of my mouth before I can stop it. I'm mentally kicking myself in the nuts, so I try damage control. "I mean, friends who aren't genetically, financially, or emotionally dependent on you."

"I knew what you meant, dumbass." Royce shoulder bumps me. "I'm not as single-minded as before, ya know? My sons all moved away at the same dang time. As fun as it was having the twins, they didn't offer stimulating conversation back then. Willa– sometimes ya gotta get away so you appreciate when you're around 'em."

"Ha! I was thinking just that when I was driving into town today. How being away for a few days keeps it fresh. But I think I could settle with being apart during the workday and call it good."

"You still need to get out without Wynn once and a while. Willa has her friends too, ya know? She and Penny are no longer like oil and water, but buddies they are not. Penny sticks with the younger mommas at church, and Willa spends time with a few of the women who come into the center. You need a life outside of your spouse, Kade."

"I have no friends," I breathe, pretending my voice doesn't warble.

"Bullshit." Royce takes a sip of beer. "Once you're out of school, age means jackshit. Warren and I get along really well. I spend a lot of time with Penny's dad, Garret. Hell, even Corbin and I have found an alliance of sorts. You and I–" Royce pats my thigh. "I've always said I wasn't your father, because I never wanted to replace him. Sitting around this bonfire, talking about adult shit, you and I are friends, Kaden. Whether you realize it or not."

Maybe I want you as my father, I think but don't say out loud.

"I'm so sick and tired of not having grandparents, aunts and uncles, a momma and daddy, siblings, actual nieces and nephews. I feel like an imposter or interloper imposing on your life."

"Knock it off, Kaden," Royce says none too kindly. "That is the bullshit narrative playing out in your head speaking. You have us, and you know it. You need to grow up, son. You can't go back and forth between Morgantown and Rusty Knob so you feel special because everyone falls all over you. You're not a kid coming home for the weekend from college anymore."

Looking away, I don't comment on it, because I didn't think I was so transparent.

"When it was Daddy, Annie, and me, with Donny next door, we used to sit on the porch and make fun of the assholes when they came back to visit after moving away. How they expected everyone to drop whatever they were doing because Joe Blow was home from college or was visiting from some major city, like they were a goddamn celebrity and their shit didn't stink as much as ours."

"I'm revoking your playtime with Corbin, Royce," I taunt, grinning.

"My point." Royce squeezes my thigh to keep me focused. "While you feel special, or validated, coming on in here expecting special privileges, the rest of us are going about our days and find it annoying as fuck. You're not a visiting dignitary– you're just another Rusty Knob native like the rest of us. So shit or get off the pot. You're not a kid, Kade. Grow up and man up."

"Good talk." I reach behind me, resting my palms on the log for leverage to rise to my feet.

Royce yanks me back down. "I ain't finished. We can see right through you, bud. That car you drive, bought with Bren's money, we were more concerned with you trying to get us to think you were a piece of shit, than actually thinking you were a piece of shit. That crap you pulled with Wynn so you'd get fired, it was a self-fulfilling prophecy. You didn't think you deserved the job, so you sabotaged yourself, so when you were fired you were proven right. Now as Miriam is trying to give you the job of your dreams, you pull your resentment around you like a warm wool coat on a cold winter's day. Grow. Up."

"I don't want to be the guidance counselor, thank you very much." I shift, but don't get up, knowing Royce would just drag my ass back down anyway. "I didn't enjoy being an elementary teacher, either."

"Bull-fucking-shit, bud. You're like a kid magnet. Only now you're bribing them with toys to boot." Royce sucks in a large gulp of air like he's gaining momentum. "You do this to yourself. We all love you. We all want you around. We see you as family, blood be damned. We know you loved your job and want this new job. But it's you who refuses to deal with it, accept what you want, and realize you deserve it merely on the fact that you're a human being."

"Being birthed doesn't entitle anyone to anything. People are dying all over this world. Children are abused, starved, and without families, yet everyone is reproducing instead of taking care of the kids we already have. New houses are being built while others are being torn down. Every person should sacrifice for the greater good. Humankind are assholes."

"You can only do your part, Kade. You can't police the world. It's not your right to dictate the choices of others because you're not in their shoes– their money is not your money. You can't adopt every child, or tell others they can't have children of their own."

"It's the most selfish thing a person can do. Egotistical and narcissistic. *I'm so fucking fabulous, I want to duplicate myself.* I can understand accidental pregnancies, but planned ones?"

"Kade, what am I going to do with you?" I've never heard Royce sound so disappointed in me, and it draws tears to my eyes. "The propaganda machine has gotten to you more than I thought."

"What are you talking about?" I demand.

"Your issues made you easily brainwashed." Royce sighs, sounding exhausted by me. "You loved your father beyond comprehension. Are you saying he didn't deserve to express his love with your mother by creating you? That it isn't in a man's instincts to ensure his bloodline lives on?"

"It's still selfish," I mutter, ignoring the way my heart squeezes painfully and the reason behind it.

"Your parents made you because they wanted you. I fostered you because I wanted you. The love we felt for you was the same. You can't give so much of yourself that you're left an empty husk. You can't take the agony and guilt of billions of people onto your shoulders. You can only do what you can do, and take responsibility for that alone. Get fifty fucking degrees if you want, but until you realize it doesn't change how any of us sees you, it won't matter."

I narrow my eyes and stare at the side of his head. "You've been gossiping about me with your therapist again, haven't you?"

Royce looks away, humming slightly. After a few moments, he turns to stare me dead in the eyes. "I don't expect you to know what you want out of life, Kaden, because it's an organic thing. But I expect you to accept what you do want as of now. You're not a selfish person if you take what you want."

"What if–"

"People with lives don't give two shits what others are doing in theirs. I worry about you, Kade. But as you can see, I've got my hands full with two kids and another on the way. I've got more than two hundred lives dependent on me with my employees and their families, and then there are the folks who go to the center. I've got a grown son going through a divorce and a granddaughter. I can't have the one person I need to be by my side testing all of us instead of helping me support it all."

"You've got Bren for that, Royce," I mutter, feeling heartbroken. "You don't need me."

"Bren's in transition, and I want his whole focus on his family and getting it to function. Even when he's ready to take on more responsibility with the business, that doesn't mean I won't need you just as much. You are at the center, and Bren is with the business. Apples and oranges."

"You'll never love me like you love your birth sons." Which is why I'll never have my own children, because I wouldn't want my future foster children to feel like I do about Royce's birth children. I love them, but sometimes I envy their connection to Royce more.

They're the original, and I'm just the generic replacement part.

"Goddamn it, Kaden!" Royce hits me– he motherfucking punches me in the shoulder. Wincing, I grab my arm and glare at him. "You're such a needy asshole. A validation-seeking, patience-testing, attention-whore."

"Speaking my virtues, are you now?" I mutter sarcastically.

"The fact that you're not offended by what I just said, says a lot about you, doesn't it? I didn't pick my kids out. They came outta their mommas as they are. It was a crapshoot, a lottery. I love them because they're my children. When it came to you, I knew exactly who you were. I *picked* you. Don't you get that? I wasn't obligated to love you– I love you because you're *you*."

Stunned speechless, I watch as Royce charges to his feet, more than furious with me. "As soon as you finish up *this* degree, you have to get your ass back to reality. You want to work at the center, which is only open in the evenings. You want to be with Wynn because he's your future. You also have always wanted to be a counselor. Secretly, you've always wanted children of your own."

"I know I'm a selfish asshole, Royce," my voice warbles with guilt for feeling as I do. "But even I'm not *that* selfish."

"Fostering children changes *their* world, but having your own children changes *yours*. While it looks selfless to foster, it's a selfish act as it makes one feel better about oneself– I would know. Either way, being a parent is about giving more than you have to give, but you still manage to give more. So stop testing people, playing head games with yourself, and thinking you're a piece of shit, and do what you want to do but are too cowardly to admit."

Eyes locked onto my foster father, I watch as I drive the man to drink. He pounds back two beers like he's in a chugging contest, takes my two away since I never opened them, and then stomps away to the barn. When he pops back out, he's glaring at me.

"Whether you get your shit together or not, I'll still love you–always will, no matter what. But I don't like your warped sense of reality and narrow-mindedness. You've spent eight years locked in the vacuum known as college, where everyone has a hive mind and a singular opinion, and you've been indoctrinated to bleed guilt over the acts of others. Kade, it's time you joined the real, big bad world, with real, big bad problems. Because the people preaching to you, they do nothing to change anything. They lock themselves on campus and don't leave. They judge others, when they are most guilty of inaction and instigating division among the most impressionable."

"People with lives don't give two shits what others are doing in theirs," I quote Royce as he walks away from me.

"I'm glad to see you were listening, son." Royce turns to me. "I'm just an uneducated hillbilly– what do I know, right? I'm in the thick of *actual* life, not playacting it from inside a campus designed to keep the outside world out and me safe in my educated ignorance. I've lost more than anyone should, but I've given back more. I've volunteered. I've fostered and adopted children. If some asshole does something shitty halfway around the world, I will not apologize for it. Got it?"

"I–"

"I'm preparing for my fourth living child out of six," Royce explains. "I will not feel guilty, nor will I adopt one hundred more to offset guilt people like you think I should feel. I take care of what's mine, and I also take care of others. It's not selfish of me to want children. Just as it's not selfish of me to want a purebred pet when there are too many in shelters, or to buy a new TV when someone, somewhere doesn't have one. Those responsibilities rest solely on the assholes of this world who put us all in these situations. If I thought the way you think about yourself, I might as well lie down and die, because I wouldn't deserve to breathe the oxygen in the air because somewhere, someone else was already dying so why should I get to exist."

"I wasn't– I wasn't saying that about you, Royce," I stammer, gut twisting on itself. "God, you're the most amazing person I know."

"And you–" Royce points at me. "Are the most amazing person I know. You need to fucking remember that and stop being a goddamn, brainwashed martyr."

CHAPTER THIRTEEN
Kaden Marx

Shoulders slumping, head held down, I shuffle up the sidewalk to my front door, ignoring that I'm sniffling. Royce didn't want to be around me after he yelled at me, not that I blame him. So I didn't dare go back in the house and say goodbye. I'm not in the mood for Warren's upbeat, sarcastic attitude, but I don't want to be alone. All of the people I want to be around are an hour away, living their lives without me.

Lifting my foot to the first riser, I release a girly meep because I almost stepped on someone's thigh. My head jerks up, slinging tears with the movement. "What are you doing here?"

"Willa called as soon as Royce took you out to the bonfire." Wynn tries to soften the meaning of his words with a sympathetic smile. "She said he was going to hand you your ass."

"So it was a premeditated ass-handing." I slump to the step to sit next to Wynn, and he automatically hugs me to his side. I rest my head on his shoulder, sighing deeply. "Do you know what the conversation was about?"

"Yeah," Wynn's whisper is lost as a car drives by. "Royce loves you, you know? Maybe more than any of us."

"Pfft…" I roll my eyes at the ludicrousness.

"It's true, dummy." Wynn head-butts me, but not enough to hurt. "Ya wanna know why? Because he sees himself in you. Even you'll admit you don't see yourself clearly, so don't argue with me. You've become more moody, melancholy, and worried about what others think the more you continue with your studies. Those people you're with, they're toxic to you. Infecting you like a disease. Those groups filled with people in pain, begging you to take it all in. The professors spewing their own personal rhetoric instead of actual facts to educate us… They talk a big game, never practicing what they preach. But you—"

"What about me?" I mutter in an accusing tone.

"But you *will* do something about it. So it's like they're egging you on to take all of the problems of the world on your shoulders. The same thing would have happened to Royce. I'm not saying you're easily manipulated, just that you are when it comes to being selfless."

"I am *not* selfless." I laugh sardonically. "If only you were inside my head. If I was selfless, I would have left you alone."

"That!" Wynn shouts, causing the neighbor dog to bark. "That right there is exactly it. What the fuck is wrong with us being together? What?!? I'm a grown man, graduating college in less than a month, and I have plans for the future. What is wrong with us being together when we love each other?"

"You're still a kid," I mutter, regretting it as soon as I say it.

Wynn's laughter is beyond ironic. "I'm the same age you were when you started teaching, you motherfucking hypocrite. You're keeping me a kid in your head, the same way you're calling yourself a selfish asshole. It doesn't matter how much we age, it's impossible for us to be the exact age at the same time. The six year difference is nothing now that we're in the same boat. You think nothing of Willa, who is months *younger* than you, being with Royce, who is our *father* figure."

Sniffling, I stare down at my hands and say the first idiotic thing that comes to mind. "I want another dog because your sister stole mine. I'm lonely, and I didn't want Perty to be lonely, so I wanted to give him a dog family. So I looked into having him stud for a lady pug. I was in a message board, and I was attacked by hundreds of people, calling me out on how I should go to a shelter, and how no dogs should ever be bred– even once. They said I was responsible for every euthanized dog because I never neutered Perty. They called me a murderer and made me feel an inch big. All I wanted to do was give my dog a family– a dog family our family could share."

"Fuck 'em." Wynn shakes me. "That! That right there. You told Bren this… and yeah, he gossiped it to Royce, and down the grapevine it went. But I'm glad he did. That is what I meant about you being easily manipulated by assholes who do nothing but bitch and judge. If every dog was neutered, they would go extinct."

"They had an answer for that, too," I grumble, the fury still burning bright.

"They always do," Wynn snarls. "Always."

"Everywhere I turn, people are judging me. People are being abused. People are hurting… You do it to me too. When I buy something, you say it's in excess because we don't *need* it, even if I can afford it and really want it. It makes me feel bad about myself for wanting more than I need. Dr. Carlin said I was gluttonous for buying Copper that car– carbon footprint –but the kid loves it. I wasn't wrong, was I?" I ramble and ramble and ramble, and finally Wynn cuts me off.

"Dr. Carlin can shove his carbon footprint up his ass, because the bastard was bragging about owning two vacation homes and seven classic cars while shoving a champagne flute in my hand with his eyes glued to my crotch."

"Dr. Carlin is an asshole," I agree. "His ex-wife was arrested for using a phony charity to scam people of their hard-earned money."

"Then why do you care what he thinks of Copper's car? If anything, you should do the complete opposite of everything that asshole says."

"He has tenure," I grumble at the atrocity. I wouldn't have been fired if I had tenure.

"Miriam is promising you tenure this time around, so screw Dr. Carlin." Wynn orders, "Describe me."

My eyebrows scrunch in confusion. "What?"

"Describe me. Not how I look, but deep down. How do you see me as a person?"

Clearing my nose, I pretend I'm not sniffling. "You're caring. Selfless. Kind. Giving. Loving. You're the smartest person I know. You excel at everything you do with little to no effort. If I had to sum you up with one word, I'd say you are *good*."

"Willa located a woman two counties over who wanted to breed her pug because her adult children wanted a dog, and she loved her dog so much, she wanted to share the joy. Just one litter ever. Not a puppy mill. Not for profit. For love. This woman also had four shelter dogs, and countless others throughout her family. Is she a bad woman?"

"No," I mutter emphatically.

"But those assholes made you feel bad about yourself. Strangers who don't know you. Strangers who probably run dog fights for all we know. They don't know you, but you allowed them to change how you view yourself."

"But they were talking about *me*, not her. I won't stud Perty because it's wrong."

"You called me good. Am I a bad person because I already took Perty to the bitch? I stood there with Mrs. Baxter and watched as our dogs had a fun time in the yard. Sex is instinctive, and I'm glad Perty and Kalie got to enjoy it at least once in their lifetime, instead of being castrated as puppies."

"Dude, that's cold when you look at it that way," I murmur in awe, amazed how Wynn can always play the devil's advocate and get me to see all sides.

"Jack and I moved into your apartment because we wanted to throat-punch one out of every five students on campus. The ones who used intimidation, guilt, and bullying hatred to spread their opinions. It frustrates me to no end how I'm paying for an education, and instead of facts, the political leanings of my professors are tainting every lecture. It should be black and white data, while discussing the subtle nuances of any given subject, allowing for an actual multi-sided debate."

"Over the eight years I've attended, at two different major universities, I've seen several students bullied by the professor for having a different viewpoint, so I get it. But I value my education."

"I was in the yard while Royce railed on you– I lied earlier," Wynn admits. "So what I'm about to say, I want you to use in every single bullshit agenda your professors, counselors, students, and internet trolls have made you bleed about. Promise me."

"I– okay? I promise."

"This is all rhetorical," Wynn warns. "Am I a bad person because I took our dog to knock up another? Am I a murderer of dogs now because I didn't adopt? Even if I had adopted a dog, those others would have still been put to sleep. I could adopt every dog I could afford, but it will never be enough. Never enough. Even if I never own a pet at all, bad shit is still going to happen to pets everywhere. Because no matter how responsible you or I, or Royce, or the idiots next door are, there are going to be countless irresponsible people ruining it for all of us. We can do our part to clean up their messes, but not at the expense of not living this *singular*, very short existence we were given."

"Wynn, you've been reading my psych books, haven't you?" I laugh without humor, hating how he's using my tricks against me.

"I'll use whatever trick is at my disposal to get you to see clearly. But mostly, I've loathed all of your hypocritical colleagues, so this has been slowly building pressure." Wynn grabs my hand, pulling me to my feet, then he leads me around the outside of the house. Strong hands curve around my shoulders, and then push me straight down until I'm sitting on the back steps.

"Was Warren watching us, or something?" I murmur in confusion over our location change.

"No." Wynn sits next to me, and then takes my hand. He yanks my sleeves up until he can see my shame. "I thought we'd finish this conversation in front of Suicidal Tendencies."

"I-I-I–" I stammer, uncomfortable.

"These–" Wynn runs his fingertips along my forearms, and then jerks up my shirt to expose my sides. "I want the life we've mapped out, Kaden. God, I want it more than anything. I need you to stop seeing me as a little kid because you hang onto guilt. I want to live together, get married someday. I want to have jobs that change lives, and not feel ashamed because we're gay or because we want to play around. I want you to look in a child's eyes and see yourself reflected. But what I don't want to do is find you in our bathroom bleeding out because you can't fix every ache in the world."

"Wynn, no!" I cry out.

"I *get* it, damn you! I get it. Most people do nothing, and those are the ones who are calling you out. We have taken on the responsibility of this entire town and its inhabitants, and by God, that is fucking good enough."

"Wynn, don't go!" I charge to my feet, reaching for his hand and missing. "Royce is already pissed at me. I can't take it from you, too."

"We're not pissed at you." Wynn's feet stop moving, but he's half the yard away from me. "We're on your side." Pointing a vicious finger at me, "You're the one who's not!"

"What do you want me to do?" I shout, hands flailing in the air.

"Get. The. Dog. Kade." Wynn stares at me like he can't believe how dense I'm being. "Take. The. Job."

"Why?" I huff out, barely audible.

"Because you want it!" Wynn bugs his eyes out and shakes his head. "One of us could die tomorrow purely on accident, or be diagnosed with cancer. If watching my nephew be born missing half his skull doesn't teach you how fragile life is, nothing will."

Sucking in air, I drop to the ground to land on my ass. "That's not fair to pull that card out and play it, Wynn. Not fair at all."

"But it's my card to play, isn't it?" Wynn challenges me. "It happened to me– it happened to *us*. It's the same card some stranger would use to push their agenda, not having a care for where they got it from. Fuck the keyboard warriors. So I don't give two shits what's happening to someone else. Call me selfish, but I just want to be happy. But I can't if my boyfriend is hiding in the bathroom with his hunting knife because some internet troll called him out on a *puppy*, or his pretentious as fuck professor called him an ignorant hillbilly because Willa wouldn't get an abortion."

I didn't realize Wynn knew where the last two lines I sliced into my sides came from. Mentally, emotionally, and physically exhausted, I slump forward with my head in my hands. "What do you want me to do?"

Wynn raises his arms to the sky and bellows so loud every dog in the neighborhood starts howling. "I. Want. You. To. Fuck. Me."

"Right now?" I yelp.

Wynn's arms fall to his sides, and he whispers fiercely, "*No, not right now.* Your dog lost his virginity, yet you hang onto ours." Wynn laughs without humor. "I want you to fuck me because you want to, because I want you to, and because you finally accept that you're gay. I want you to prove you mean what you say." Wynn walks away, shouting over his shoulder, "That's why!"

"Don't leave me," I beg. "I'm sorry I ever thought you were too young for me. I'm the immature loser. Don't leave."

Wynn just shakes his head at me sadly. "I'm not going anywhere but for a walk around the block, because you need some privacy to talk to him." He points at my zombie gnome, then disappears around the side of the house.

I knee-walk twenty feet or so, and then sit on my ass in front of Suicidal Tendencies. Just as I open my mouth to confess, a shout fills the air.

"Get the puppy! Take the job. And Do Wynn– me," comes from multiple sources– four Gillettes to be exact, with a baby crying in the background because our fight disturbed the neighborhood. They better get used to it, because Wynn and I are passionate about everything.

CHAPTER FOURTEEN
Brennan Kennedy

"Nothing is sweeter than a sleepy, cuddly granddaughter." Dad rubs his cheek against the top of Honor's head. "Papaw missed his baby girl." Dad's lounging in his recliner, with Willa taking a nap upstairs, and the twins off on two separate sleepovers. He wanted uninterrupted Papaw time with Honor.

Jesse is hovering behind me, her discomfort so thick it should be visible in the air. I reach down to fix Honor's pigtail, and then step to the side to include my wife in the conversation. In a way, I understand Kade after twenty years of dealing with Jesse. We want them here– we love them no matter what. But they keep themselves apart from us.

"You're looking well, Jessica." Dad's always polite, but he gave up about a year ago on coaxing Jesse to accept that she's like a daughter to him. Dad's known Jesse as long as I have, watched her grow up, and loves and cares about her too.

"Thanks, Royce." Jesse blushes so bright, she looks like she's been set on fire, but not because of the compliment. She's uncomfortable in the extreme.

Giving up on that thread of conversation. "How's Kade?" Dad's face clouds over with pain. The bonfire and Wynn's second wave were all a premeditated intervention for Kade. He was getting more and more depressed, acting out by trying to prove he was an asshole, and we all wanted him back. Wynn was terrified a simple cut to release the pain would turn into a life-ending slice.

"Better– I think." Nodding my head, I sort out the events from the past three weeks. "Kade seems more even. There were a couple of heavy fights between Wynn and Kade, where Wynn had the internet cut to the apartment, and turned off the 4G on Kade's cellphone."

"*Damn*," Jesse whispers as she sits down on the sofa. I follow suit by taking the recliner facing Dad.

"Wynn found out Kade was taking courses to gather credits for yet another fucking degree. The fight was so bad Jack had to step in and call me to break it up. Kade was being forced by Dr. Carlin to attend three parties the faculty were throwing. Wynn said if Kade went to a single one of 'em, he would leave him for good. It was Dr. Carlin or Wynn."

Dad sighs deeply, resting his cheek against the top of my daughter's head. "Kade– he doesn't see it. Education is wonderful if it's used to learn, not when it's used to drag your feet and avoid life. Wynn said the majority of Kade's professors are amazing, but there are two or three who aren't."

"I've been talking to Kade," Jesse reveals, shocking us. "About some stuff, and he opened up a bit. So I called Wynn." Jesse looks down at her hands, refusing to meet our eyes. "It's easier sometimes to talk to an outsider. Ya know?"

No, I really don't. But I shake my head in agreement, and Dad joins me, just so she'll keep talking to us.

Outsider?

Jesse would be in the thick of it with us if only she'd walk in the door we've left wide open for her. While she's at it, she needs to drag Kade in with her too. Libby's already a part of the group after a few weeks. Twenty years, and Jesse still won't join us.

"It's the psych department. Dr. Carlin is notorious for finding a single thread in someone and plucking it to get a reaction. Only the fabric of Kade's mind isn't strong enough to handle it without unraveling." Jesse looks up and connects with Dad. "Kade needs to get away from there, Royce. He needs to come home. He's got enough degrees to do any job he wants to do– cut off his money if you have to, but get him away from there."

"I don't think it will come to that," I butt in before Dad can respond, because he's looking on the verge of being sick. "Wynn threatened not to take his last two finals if Kade didn't remove himself from school, and without those, he wouldn't earn his degree."

"Did he?" Dad's eyebrow hitches high, knowing Kade is a sneaky motherfucker.

"We went as a group, and we pulled Kade's funding since it was coming out of my trust." I chuckle a bit, remembering how Kade fought, threatening to prostitute himself, which made Wynn die with laughter. "Truth be told, as soon as it was finalized, he looked relieved. Before that? Ha!" I bark out. "Then we deactivated all of his social media accounts."

"I don't know if I would trust Kade," Jesse murmurs, causing me to smile.

"Wynn put parental tracking software on his cellphone, not that the fuck won't go buy another one."

"Oh, that's classic Kade, right there." Dad sounds proud of all the bullshit Kade has put us through over the years.

"Kade loves and loathes me, Jess. I was the annoying little brother who would butter his bread and cut his steak. I even took the forks away and gave him plastic plates and cups. I would sleep on the floor next to his bed. I wouldn't even let him take a shit without me, fearing he'd cut himself. I promised Kade I would take all of his freedoms away if he didn't cut the shit. Meaning, I would glue myself to his ass."

"Kade secretly loved you doing that." Dad chuckles, no doubt remembering the epic transition we went through when Kade first moved in with us. "So I'm guessing Kade's walking around with his head in the clouds right now, because everyone proved he is the center of their universe? True?"

"I just hope Kade grows out of this cycle, because I'm getting too old for this shit." I stand up, ready to move onto the next stressful portion of my day. Kade has sucked up the past three weeks. Now the other head-case can have my undivided attention.

"You?" Dad chuckles sarcastically. "*I'm* getting too old for this shit. It took everything in me not to punch him in the face as he talked about how selfish it was to have kids of your own, when my pregnant wife and two of my children were in the house. I don't think I can stop myself if we have to go through this cycle again."

"Kade's Wynn's problem now. No take-backsies." I flash a grin, and then tug Jesse from her seat. "Let's go look at our house."

"We'll be here." Dad snuggles deeper in his chair, eyes drifting shut. "Taking a nap– gotta fill up my sleep reserves for when the baby comes."

"Good luck, Royce." Jesse giggles underneath her breath because we've had three and a half years of no sleep whatsoever. She slips her hand in mine, needing moral support after giving her time to my dad, or maybe she knows what's coming.

After dealing with Jack shutting me down on the conversational front, then Kade's bullshit behavior, I'm not giving Jesse a warning. I had told her our talk would be when Dad took Honor for the weekend– *last* weekend. I'm not waiting any longer for this shit to fester.

"How come you didn't want Honor to see the house?" Jesse steps over the freshly dug area where the sidewalk forms will be laid tomorrow morning. The sidewalk originally ended at the edge of Dad's front yard, and it had to be extended to our lot.

"I didn't want her getting too impatient." I pull my old school tablet out of my back pocket. The paper is curled into a C shape. Everyone else would just use their cellphone. I pluck the pen from behind my ear, pretending to get ready. "We have a few last-minute adjustments, and you need to figure out what you want for furnishings. Jesse, we have too much to do to put our attention on a toddler running around a construction zone."

"Oh." Jesse's muscles relax, and her hand slackens in mine. I can almost hear her thinking, "*Thank God*." Too bad we really will be having that four-years in the making conversation she's been dreading.

The front walk extends to a large front porch with two entrances. We hop over the cement forms that were set this morning, just waiting to be filled when the cement truck arrives bright and early tomorrow morning.

I open Jesse's side of the duplex, not needing any of her input on my side of the house. "Just look around, and if you notice anything out of whack, let me know. I have a printout with the room sizes you can use when you order furniture."

We spend the next hour going room to room, and my appreciation over my wife deepens. On the outside, Jesse is tall, athletic, with long blond hair and bright blue eyes. She looks like an outgoing bubbly, empty-headed girl who only wants a free-ride from her looks. I'm sure a lot of people assume she got knocked up as a means to trap me into marriage and take me for all that I am worth. But that's not Jesse.

Jesse's a down-to-earth person. She's firm, opinionated, and private. But once she trusts you, she lets you in. She's organic everything. As an artist, she wants refurbished furniture and not a lot of clutter to distract the muse. I know Jack sees Jesse as a demon sent straight from the fiery pits of Hell, but she doesn't have a materialistic bone in her body.

"There's an attic space– you can either use that as your studio, or the basement. One has natural light, and the other will give you solitude."

"I'm speechless, Bren." Jesse wraps her arms around one of mine and squeezes. "I can't believe you designed this. I know I sound like an asshole, but I remember how we all were. Seeing us grown up is mind-blowing. So proud of you."

"I'm proud of you, too." I squeeze her back, then lead her down the basement steps.

"This place is going to feel massive, living here alone with Honor going back and forth." Jesse and Libby aren't *there* yet. They're going to date and see where it goes, not wanting to upset Honor if they moved in together only to have it fall apart. "We didn't need so many bedrooms."

"Ya never know what the future will bring, Jesse." I search along the wall with my fingertips, trying to find the light switch. I'm going to add a dual-switch to my list of needs. "Dumbass brother needing a place to crash when he fights with my other dumbass brother... baby siblings wanting sleepovers... parents needing a place to stay... having more kids."

"Out of that list, it's a guarantee that Wynn will be on your sofa at least twenty times. As for the parents and kids, zilch."

"You never know about space for more kids," I mutter with a shrug, and Jesse glares at me sideways. "Jessica," I say sharply. "I'm not talking about you and me, okay? Honor will be my only biological child, and I won't be asking to use your womb in the future. But I'm not a narcissistic asshole who won't think of my partner's needs. So before you start going off on not having any more children in your life, you need a partner who agrees first."

"Sorry," Jesse mutters lamely. "When I think about that kind of stuff, my mind goes back to how I felt when I found out I was pregnant with Honor, and I can't handle it."

"I get it– I do." I step into the basement, which is a blank canvas for Jesse to work with. "Mine is already outfitted with some gym equipment and gaming stations."

"Gaming stations?" Jesse stares at me, having never understood the restorative powers of shooting your friends' avatars.

"Jack and I can't share the same system and TV. That's not fair." I walk to the side, near the corner, and point out a door that connects our basements. "There's one here, one in the attic, and then in Honor's room. I wanted to make sure our bases were covered, especially in case of fire."

"I can't wrap my mind around how you try to think of everything." Jesse turns pensive for a few moments, like she's gathering strength, always walking around on eggshells with everyone. "Libby plays," she mutters sheepishly, and then walks away. "Don't steal my girlfriend, Bren."

"Wouldn't dream of it." I chuckle underneath my breath, knowing Libby plays for my team. "But Jack might." I joke about how he'll steal her time via friendship.

"No doubt." Jesse looks around, but I know her thoughts are keeping her elsewhere. "Jack and Libby have been shoved up each other's asses. I'm not masochistic enough to double date, so don't let Lib see your gaming stations."

Jesse rotates in a circle, eyes lighting on something that has her freezing in place. "Two camping chairs?" her voice warbles. "Two camping chairs facing each other. Bren?"

My wife doesn't turn to face me, but I can hear it in her voice that she understands.

"Without our daughter, locked in a massive duplex at the edge of town, in a basement that is virtually sound-proof." Jesse flips around to glare at me. "Anticipating a screaming match, Brennan?"

Instead of answering, I take a seat. Folding my hands in my lap, trying to look harmless, I wait for Jesse to lose her shit. I wait her out like you would a tantrum-throwing child, hoping she'll exhaust herself enough to be real and to be receptive to a solution.

But Jesse surprises me by sitting down and staring back at me, when usually she would have bitched my head off. "Let's get this over with. I want a divorce, an iron-clad custody agreement, and I don't want a cent of your money in settlement, alimony, or child support since Honor will be with us fifty/fifty."

"I know." I look down at my hands, knowing Jesse would say all of that. "That's why I built the house. A real man takes care of his family." I flick my eyes up to meet hers. "No matter what we've been through, we'll always be family, and I'll always take care of you in all ways. You were my best friend first, and I want her back."

"I know how everyone sees me, Brennan." Head jerking to the side quickly to look away, Jesse breaks our connection. "I know what they say. All those girls in high school, when they couldn't get to you, they tried to through me. You know it. I know it. Everyone knows it. They say I only wanted your money. Those other girls tried to get knocked up by you, and I succeeded."

Sighing, my mind searches through endless amounts of knowledge from the books Kade fed me, and from the conversations I had with both Kade and Dad. "Jessica?" I call, trying to get her to look at me.

Movements slow, it takes a few moments before Jesse gets the balls to look me in the eye.

"That says more about me than all those girls, including you. Like I'm only worth my money. Not a good friend, or fun to hang out with, or good in bed. That the only thing anyone wants from me is my bankroll." It's my turn to break our gazes. "That someone can't just love me."

"Bren," Jesse's voice warbles, and it breaks my heart that I just had to manipulate her to get her to see a different angle.

"I know you love me, Jess– I've never doubted it."

"I do," Jesse says with conviction. "I still do and always will– just not like I should."

"Fuck 'em. Fuck those people who form opinions about shit they don't understand. It's no different than Kade being suicidal over some assmunch who's never met him, giving an opinion on how Kade should live his own life."

The day we found Kaden typing furiously, arguing with faceless people about how gays weren't stereotypes, and it devolved into a political discussion, was the day we took his social media away. It was on a video for a quick and easy recipe, for Christ's sake. Arguing on the internet changes nothing. Minds will not change. The only thing it was changing was Kade– how he saw himself and how he was behaving. He was so angry he couldn't speak. The fury was so thick he was turning violent, and we feared he would take it out on himself. He couldn't let it go.

My brother and my wife aren't just two sides of the same coin. They're hanging out on the same side, frustrating the piss out of all those who love them.

"That's not what I'm doing," Jesse turns defensive, fingers tightening into fists as they rest in her lap. So much anger, and I have no idea where it's coming from.

"You shut me out and won't let anyone else in. You allow people who don't know you to change how you feel about yourself. You act like a cunt when you're hurt or when you try to test me, or when you're trying to make me prove my love or to prove to yourself you are a cunt. Sound familiar?"

"I-I–"

"Don't be Kade." Holding my wife's eyes, I pin her in my stare so she can't look away. "It's immature, and awful to be around. Learn six years sooner than Kaden. We need to be real, you and I, for Honor's sake. I'm not going to be baited into proving whatever's playing out in your head. I'm sick of the games."

Leaning forward, Jesse is seething, because the truth hurts. "I don't play games!"

"The fact that you don't realize you do is the problem. I didn't get it when we were kids, and I let it go because we were. You didn't know better then, and neither did I. But now that we're parents, I can't allow it to infect our daughter. Just be real, especially to yourself."

"Everyone thinks I'm a bad person!" Jesse screams into my face, which is why we're in the basement. Honor has heard enough of this for a lifetime. "*You* think I'm a bad person!" Jesse's voice strains from the violence flowing from her throat.

"*You* think you're a bad person." Three weeks of playing Kade's therapist is coming in handy right now. Same conversations, just different gender and situations. "The rest of us are too busy trying to live our lives, or are too self-absorbed in our own bullshit to give whether or not you're good or bad a thought. It's narcissistic to think everyone everywhere gives a fuck about what you're thinking."

Deflated, Jesse slumps into her chair, head hanging low.

"I love you, care for you, and want you to be happy. But I can't fight you all of the time. My dad doesn't look at you with malice, like you assume. Half the time, even when he's talking to me, his head is with the baby. Even Libby might be thinking of what she has on her to-do list or has to do at work. The world doesn't revolve around you."

"Trust me. Jack's thinking bad shit every time he looks at me," Jesse snarls, proving my theory right.

"You're toxic to yourself, Jessica. Inside your head you think you're worthless. Yet you make everything about you. So which is it? Are you *all*, or *nothing*?"

Jesse's face whips to the side, like I physically struck her. "Whatever… pretend your boyfriend doesn't hate me."

What does Kade call this bullshit?

Evasion? No, projection.

"Jack might look at you like you're a cunt, but he's judging you on your actions. You treat *me* like a cunt. You talk down to me, belittle me, and scream at me. Jack's on team Bren when it comes to you. You're always on team Jesse. I'm on team everybody."

"What's that supposed to mean?"

"If you can't read between the lines of what I just said, then explaining it to you won't matter either way."

"You hate me."

"Nope, but you want me to hate you. You do your damnedest to make me hate you." Leaning forward, I rest my elbows on my knees, and just plead with Jesse. "I wish you'd just be real with me."

"I don't get you," Jesse snarls, lashing out like a wounded animal. "You should hate me. Nothing I do seems to get to you. It's frustrating."

"I'm frustrating. Ha!" I huff an ironic laugh, but it's completely without humor. "Explain to me why I should hate you."

"Because I'm not straight," blurts out before she can censor herself. Face washed pale with mortification, I can tell Jesse wishes she hadn't said it.

Baffled, I mumble, "Why?"

"Because– because I ruined everything for you. If I had been straight, none of what happened would have happened."

"Jess?" I reach forward to take her hand. "When we got together, neither of us knew who we truly were. We were thirteen when we started fooling around– babies. I can't blame you for it, and you can't blame yourself."

"The girls?" Jesse whines, voice breaking with agony.

"That's on all of us– you, me, *and* the girls." Disgust twists my lips into a nasty smile. "That time in our lives murdered something in us. I wanted you to want me, and you felt guilty because you didn't. You wanted the girls to want you for you, and I wanted them to want me for me. You were a means for them to get closer to my money. We used them, but they were using us more."

"I'd never been more stressed in my life– honest." My best friend returns, even the pitch of her voice changes. She still looks pissed off, but not at herself. "I still have nightmares about it. We had to keep rolling condoms on you, because those bitches kept tearing them off."

"Got to the point where I refused to come, then I refused to even take my dick outta my pants." I've got to be real with her too. "You aren't them, Jessica. I would have given you anything you ever wanted without expecting anything in return, simply because you didn't want anything from me but me."

"But then I did to you what we were terrified would happen with them." The guilt in Jesse's voice is so thick she's suffocating on it.

In a heartbeat, I realize our marriage has always been a threesome, with the third wheel of guilt riding us. "I could make excuses– I was drunk. I was upset. I wanted to do something epically stupid to feel something. *Anything.* Sure, you didn't stop me when I didn't use a condom, when it was something so ingrained in us. But that doesn't mean you're to blame. Hell, in the back of my mind, I was probably trying to trap *you*. I don't regret it, and I never will."

"I don't regret it, either." Jesse smiles at me, and my heart simultaneously fractures and repairs itself. Then tears spring to my wife's eyes, and an agony so real shines through. "Jack and I hate me for the same reason– for the same reason you should hate me too."

"If you haven't figured it out yet, there is nothing you could do to make me stop loving you." I try to reassure Jesse, but all I end up doing is making her wince.

"Then you're an idiot," Jesse says bluntly. Taking a deep breath, she stares at the floor. "Jack hates me, because when he looks at me, he sees a world without Honor in it, and I make him sick. Your father sees it too, as does Wynn, and Willa, and Kade. Even the twins probably know what I almost did."

The self-hatred in Jesse's voice draws me upright. I take a good look at my wife, and I don't recognize what I see. "Jessica, you were only a teenager and terrified. If you had gotten an abortion, it was your choice. I understood it then, and I do now. I wanted our child, but I was just as furious with Jack over how he treated you. I was there with you, but I wasn't going through what you were going through. Try as I might, it was impossible for me to understand how you felt."

"I hate myself." Jesse's eyes laser into mine, nothing but torturous agony shining through. "You wanted me to be real with you, Bren. This is my reality. I see what Jack sees when I look in the mirror. When I look at my daughter, I see a perfect little girl who almost didn't exist because I'm a vengeful, narcissistic, selfish cunt of a human being."

"Jess–"

"You're right. It's impossible for you to understand how it feels to look your own daughter in the eye and realize she was almost your murder victim."

A death wail fills the air, and it guts me. Acting on instinct, I pull my wife into my lap and wrap my arms around her. Wailing, Jesse is inconsolable. All I can do is whisper how none of it is her fault, how any decision she made was the right one, how I know she thinks Honor is precious, and she's a better mother because of what had almost happened.

Laughing sardonically, "It's admirable how you truly believe it was my choice to make because it was my body, but maybe… just maybe, I wasn't capable of making that choice. How I was terrified of making that choice. How every adult I spoke to said it was the right choice for me, but I knew I'd regret it, and I didn't have the balls to go against what everyone else was telling me to do."

The agony in Jesse's voice is so deep, I'm rendered speechless. I manage to say her name, but little else. All I can do is listen as she finally gets out what has been destroying her.

"In theory, everyone is always saying how it's the woman's choice. But maybe I was a child who didn't know what I wanted right then, let alone five minutes later, or eighteen years down the road. I wasn't capable of making a decision, because I was set adrift with no one helping me decide, all because they feared looking politically incorrect."

"I didn't– I didn't want to push you with what I wanted."

"You wouldn't even tell me what you wanted!" Jesse screams, voice breaking.

"If you had gotten an abortion, it was the right choice. You didn't get one, so that was the right choice too. There wasn't a right or wrong, Jesse. Only a right or wrong for you."

"But it was *your* baby in my belly, and if I had had an abortion, you would have despised me. I know it. You know it. Only Jack had the balls to say it. You should have told me what you really thought, not some bullshit, so I could have made a fucking decision based on what we all needed."

"Jessica, I'm so sorry," I cry out, tears dampening my face, simply from the emotions pouring from my wife. Agony. Fear. Desolation. Resentment. "I was doing what I thought you needed, against what I wanted. I kept my mouth shut because I thought that's what all men should do. I really believe it's your right."

"My body is mine, no shit. But that doesn't mean I didn't need more than a '*do what you need to do, I'll support you either way*' when it came from you. You were my best friend, but you wouldn't give me the advice a best friend would give. That has nothing to do with women's rights and everything to do with feeling lost and alone without the support system I'd had my entire life."

"This is what has been between us this entire time?" I try to pull Jesse away, so I can look in her eyes, but she clings to me.

"Do you know why I've never hated Jack?" Jesse doesn't wait for me to answer. "Because when I had no fucking clue what I wanted, let alone what you wanted, Jack told me. Screaming at me in the clinic woke me up, made me realize what I needed to do. I would have gotten an abortion out of fear, not because it was right for me. Without Jack, there would be no Honor, and the thought of a life without our daughter in this world makes me physically sick."

"Jessica? You need to let the past go and learn from it. It's done. Over. Looking back will help you make better decisions in the future, but you're allowing it to dictate how you feel about yourself right now. That's not fair. I get it– I've always been on your side no matter what."

"You love me too much," Jesse whispers, voice rough. "You shouldn't." Flipping around quickly, before I can stop her, desperate lips are pressed to mine. Needing from me what I can't give her, Jesse tries to take it instead.

Lost, the passenger in a toxic journey, I allow my emotions to override my common sense. Lust roars in my veins, moving my body like a master pulls a puppet's strings. Panting roughly, sweat slicks my body, as a tongue invades my mouth and hands grip and pull me apart in every direction.

I want.

I need.

I love.

But I won't be used.

"Stop!" I try to pull Jesse away, but she's too lost in her destruction. Silenced, I give as good as I get. Mouths and hands touching places they shouldn't, the comfort and the familiarity yank me back into reality. "No!"

"Bren?" Jess moans, ignoring me.

"Jessica, stop!" I use my strength when I ordinarily suppress it. Hands wrapping around Jesse's upper arms, I pull her away from my mouth.

Eyes glazed with pain, Jesse slurs, "You don't want me?"

This is always the start to another fight we've had since junior year in high school. It always turns into war, leaving me feeling stripped raw and having to explain myself. If I don't want to touch Jesse to preserve my self-respect, then I'm a liar. I'm not bi. I'm just a fag in the closet who won't admit the truth.

Refusing to repeat the past, I grab Jesse's wrist, wrench her forward, and wrap her hand around the bulge in my pants. "This is *not* a reaction to being touched. This is me wanting you because you're you, because you have tits and a pussy, and you're the most desirable woman I've ever met."

Jesse flinches as if struck, no longer able to lash out and use her go-to defense strategy.

Leaving her hand on my throbbing cock, I release her wrist. "This is why I said no." I grab the waist of her yoga pants with my fingertips, then I thrust my other hand down the front of her pants. Fingers delving in deeply into her softness, I know what I'll find after nearly ten years of playing around.

Pulling my hand free, I show Jesse how my fingers don't glisten in the light. "You don't want *me*," I remind her. "Not because you don't love me, but because I do have a cock. Sure, I can force you to get wet for me, because I know how to work your body, but I deserve more... and so do *you*."

"Bren?" Jesse cries out when I nearly dump her onto the floor as I rise to my feet.

"I'm not angry with you, Jessica." I turn to face her, hoping my tone, my words, and the expression on my face are in agreement. "I get it. I do. No more games."

"I'm not playing a game!" Jesse turns defensive.

God love her– "Yes, you are. You're trying to fuck me to forget. Maybe even get knocked up with another kid because you're terrified of change, or to erase the past by not going to an abortion clinic this time around. Just so you won't feel guilty looking at the next kid."

"That's... harsh," Jesse breathes, voice warbling in agony.

"You have to drive right, straight through that shit and deal with it, Jess. There is so much I've been through that I don't talk about. It might have made me who I am, but it isn't who I am now."

"Other than your mom dying, what the fuck do you know about pain?" Jesse accuses, so off base I find myself laughing– the cruel sound causing my wife to shudder with fear.

"You're not my end all, be all, so you don't get to know." Turning away from Jesse, my feet lead me to the steps. "If what you seek is Honor's forgiveness, all you have to do is grow up and move on. Holding onto the past will destroy our daughter as surely as if you had aborted her."

CHAPTER FIFTEEN
Kaden Marx

"This doesn't look like a club?" Wynn accuses as he looks at the rundown bar known as Adam & Steve. I like the in-your-face, asshole vibe for calling out our Christian haters. "I hear country music."

As if a good shepherd would ever lead his precious lambs to the slaughter...

"Are we sure about this?" Leaning against my car, I stare down the little shits. Well, I look Wynn in the eyes since he's only a hair shorter than me, but Jack is a good head shorter. They grin at me, lips pulling taut across their dumbass faces. This is a *bad* idea. "Really?"

Wynn smiles at me like he has a juicy secret on the tip of his tongue he wants to share. "Since when did you become such a coward?" he challenges, making me want to fist his hair and shove my tongue down his throat.

We're in a public parking lot, Kaden. Behave.

"Since when did you want to go to clubs filled with music, booze, and horny bodies?" I volley back.

"I'm branching out." That smug smile is back, while Wynn's little shit of a friend smiles serenely. They're up to no good. "It didn't matter if I acted like I was ninety, forty, or like a four-year-old, because you're never going to see me as old enough. Never gonna be the same age as you at the same time, Kade. I give up."

"So somehow it's a good idea to take your buddy to a bar to get his dick sucked... when he'll probably be our brother-in-law someday?"

Jack laughs.

Wynn shrugs.

"I'ma call Bren," I threaten, not planning on it.

"Call him," Wynn calls my bluff. The brat actually gets his own phone out... and then dials. "We good?" My eyes bulge wide. "Yeah, I know you don't own Jack, but for some reason Kade thinks you do."

"Gimme that." I grab the phone out of Wynn's hand and press it to my ear. "Bren? Bren, you there?" I pull the phone away, noticing the screen is still black. I swipe at the screen and the security code pops up. "Oh, you little shit," is a warning growl as I lunge.

Wynn yelps, and then jogs across the parking lot to the entrance, his taunting laughter trailing after him.

"Don't bother trying to catch him," Jack warns, putting a hand on my forearm. "He's too fast for most of us. It's fine, Kade. Really."

"Does Bren know?" My loyalties are divided.

For the past few weeks, I've put my priorities in order as I packed up the apartment and said goodbye to my academic career. Wynn is my best friend– he has to be in order to be my partner. I have to be able to come to him for everything, and I realized my behavior was pushing him away. Jack isn't my friend by default– he's my friend. Period. Jack's awesome, and I want what's best for him. But Bren– Bren is my brother, and he comes before Jack's needs. Hands down. Forever. No matter what.

"I know you won't lie to me, Jackson." I do the hand on the shoulder trick I was taught to use to connect me to whomever I'm trying to manipulate– erm, I mean help. "What are we doing here?"

I look up to find Wynn chatting with a guy he probably assumes is a bouncer, wide smile on his face. The burly guy is just a dude hanging outside, probably waiting for someone. But Wynn's presence is attracting a few from inside the open door to pour out.

The idiot doesn't realize he's flirting. Wynn's naïve innocence makes my pants too tight.

"Kade." Jack levels me with a look, pulling free of my touch. Somehow reading me, he does the reverse, getting the upper hand so to speak. He rests his palm in the center of my chest, like he's trying to calm *me*. With a straight face in a serious tone, Jack's next words make me bark a laugh. "I'm getting that blowjob."

"Bren?"

"Bren knows– you know he knows because you told him an hour after I brought it up, remember?" Jack calls me out on my shit. My little roomie has been a thorn in my side, worse than any take-no-prisoners therapist. He's a nurse– nurses don't dick around. "This is for me, okay? This has nothing to do with Bren. He gets it. I get it. Wynn gets it. I know you get it when it comes to Wynn. So why not when it comes to me and Bren?"

"Team Bren," I mutter underneath my breath, face blooming bright red because the guy never ceases to hand me my ass. "Is this like a last hurrah? Because when it comes to you, Bren ain't willing to share."

"Same here." It's Jack's turn to blush, his button nose turning so red his freckles disappear. "Bren and I aren't together yet, so this is a goodbye to an era. In a few days, we're moving into the duplex as roommates with separate rooms. We're friending it."

"With benefits?" I raise an eyebrow, waiting.

"Nope." Jack's an idiot for lying to himself like that. Bren doesn't believe that shit for a second. "I give us a week– tops – before we can't take it. But we gotta try. I'm not going to build a life by going into it blindly. We have to be friends, Kade. *Real* friends get each other, in and outside of the bedroom."

"Why does that feel like it was directed toward me?" I accuse, eyes instantly seeking Wynn, who has a small following at the entrance– no one wants to go inside the bar as long as Wynn is outside of it.

Shit.

That's fucking hot.

Wynn's like a hillbilly version of a Nordic god, bright blue eyes and sandy blond hair, with long, lean muscles. It doesn't help matters that when he smiles, he truly means it. He's charming without being smarmy. He's sexy, downright sinful with his playfulness. Witty yet down-to-earth. Genuine. Good.

Mine. Thank fuck.

"Wynn and I are friends," I whine. "Really. We're doing buddy shit together now that I'm jobless and banned from higher education and the internet. We're down to only two orgasms a day, because someone got it into Wynn's head that I use sex to avoid real intimacy." I stare Jackson down. "I've enjoyed every second of it, though. The more time we spend on meaningless shit, the more of it I want."

"Which is why you're finally happy," Jack points out, smirking at me. "C'mon– let's go get me that blowjob. Looks like Wynn will be my wingman, drawing them in like flies."

"Yeah, he is goddamn gorgeous," I mutter, not in the least feeling jealous or possessive. I know Wynn's my biggest fan. I might not understand it, but I'm not going to argue with it, either.

It must be love.

"Jack?" I call him back to me as he walks across the parking lot. "You won't need a wingman. You'll ugh–" Rubbing at the back of my neck, I'm unsure how to say this without looking like a creep. "Um... just be you, and you'll have men dropping to their knees."

"You suck at flattery," Jack teases me. "But I'll take it wherever I can get it."

"I wasn't bullshitting you, Jackass." My large stride takes me to Jack's side in a few seconds. "Bren has–" *Cough.* I clear my throat so hard, I fear my nuts are lodged in my esophagus. "Bren has good taste. Between Bitch Barbie and Nurse Jackie, my brother is one lucky sonofabitch."

Blushing, Jack murmurs, "Bren has exceptional taste in men." He elbows me playfully to take the sting out of his next words, because I get Jessica, and Jack knows it. "But he has atrocious taste in women."

"HA!" We're laughing together as we approach the entrance, and Wynn turns to smile at us. Now I don't envy Bren, because his two lesser halves would have been jealous if Bren had been laughing and awkwardly flirting with one of their friends. Wynn– he's just happy to see us having a good time.

Stopping in my tracks, smile frozen on my face, I just stare at Wynn, marveling over what I did to deserve him. As Wynn stares back at me, every emotion he feels in the moment written across his face, I realize it has nothing to do with me deserving him.

Wynn chose me, and for some reason, he loves everything he sees in me. He makes me want to be a better man. He makes me realize only his opinion of me matters. I can't practice what I preach, how validation and respect and happiness come from within, because I have dysmorphia and what comes from within is skewed. Wynn is my compass, forcing me to see how my outside and inside look exactly the same as he sees them. With Wynn navigating, I know I'm driving us in the right direction.

Smiling, still innocently flirting up a storm, Wynn's arm hooks around my neck as I approach him. Tugging me close, he flutters a kiss beneath my ear, and then whispers, "Me too, Kaden. Me too."

Warmed beyond words, I distract myself by protecting our little buddy. Wynn and I both hook our arms over Jack's shoulders, and walk into the bar huddled up together with Wynn's fans following us back in.

"I'm gonna need a drink," Jack whispers in my direction, causing my eyes to flick to Wynn, who overheard. "I want this, but I need to loosen up a bit."

I picked a smaller hole-in-the-wall bar, not wanting to drop my guppies into an ocean with sharks circling. I steered us away from the university haunts, choosing the hometown vibe at Adam & Steve. I've been here a few times when Dan and Uriah come my way. Of course, Uriah hates it, loving the insane beat and ever-flowing free drinks at a club. But Dan and I chose Adam & Steve so we could sit back, have a few drinks, and reconnect, all the while watching Uriah tongue-tie the natives.

"Let's get a drink." Wynn shocks us dead. Our feet freeze mid-step, Jack and I stare at Wynn with our jaws hanging open. "If you're willing to change, so am I. I'm not a little kid, and I'm not going to turn into Corbin if I have a drink now and again. I get it– I've been a judgmental ass."

"I– okay?" my voice rises on an upward inflection. "I'll nurse a whiskey sour, because I have to drive and be responsible." More like I'm terrified of what would happen if Jack and Wynn really let loose, which is why we're in a bar where all the patrons are mature gay men. By mature, I mean adults twenty-one and over who would protect my boys, not childish, destructive fuckboys who would see them as prey.

"No beer for me," Wynn murmurs, blushing. I get why he doesn't want a beer, which is why I won't force him to smell one on my breath. Same reason I drink Guinness– no tinny, sickly sweet scent rolling off my tongue to remind Wynn of being tortured by an abusive drunk.

With a welcoming smile, a regular slides down a few seats at the bar to give us three stools in a row at the end. "Hey, fellas, this your first time here?"

"For these young'uns? Yeah." I chuckle as I sit next to the old-timer. Even a gay bar has a resident drunk who likes to drink and watch. "I've been here a couple dozen times. Like the atmosphere."

"Young'uns?" The guy is impossible to age, being that he has the classic signs of living a hard life. "You all look the same age to me."

"I like him." Wynn elbows me in the side for always making him feel like a baby because of our age gap, when it's me who feels like a pervert. "What do you usually drink when you're being sneaky?"

"Your nose for alcohol is like a bloodhound tracking a scent." I chuckle, watching all eyes flick in our direction. There's a few hot rural boys floating around, but the rest are over Royce's age. I can recognize how the three of us bellied up to the bar would look like dessert. "Beer? Dark. Imported. Never the cheap shit Corbin drowned himself in for decades."

"Usually we just drink hard cider, because you don't seem to have a nose for that." Jack tattles on us, amusement riding his voice. "I hate wine because Jess loves it, but Bren has developed a taste. When I go out after work, I usually have a few shots of whatever everyone else is having, then nurse a beer or two."

Wynn begins swaying on his stool to Trouble by Imagine Dragons, humming the lyrics softly, and Jack joins him. Like moths to flame, a few younger guys drift from their tables to the bar. Chuckling underneath my breath, I signal to the bartender to order our drinks, but he's going to serve us what he thinks we need, not what we want.

"Bourbon?" I arch a brow as three shot glasses are lined up in front of us, and the dangerously sexy forty-something bartender begins to pour. "Cliché? Or are we saluting our kin to the south? Why not go local with some moonshine while you're at it?"

"A boy's first drink should put some hair on his chest," the bartender says gruffly, but winks in my direction.

"Oh, I have hair on my chest," Wynn's voice is light and friendly, then the idiot pulls up his t-shirt to show off defined abs and a gorgeous, golden blond happy trail leading from between his pecs to the button on his jeans. "See." All eyes follow his huge palm as it rubs across his belly. "I've always been hairy for my age."

This is why I say Wynn is too young, and I don't mean his birth year.

"Hook baited. Lured. Bait bitten. Hook sunk. Wynn caught." Making a reeling motion with his hands, Jackson starts giggling like a little girl as Wynn looks at him sideways.

Wynn's, "What?" has the half of the bar that is paying attention roaring, with the other half joining in because they're that drunk. "Hairy is good, right? I'm no twink. I'm six-foot-four for fuck's sake."

"Hairy is better than good." The bartender pushes the shot glasses in our direction. "First one's on the house. Drink up, boys."

"I'm hairless." Jack is most definitely insulted. "Every time Wynn announces his height, he's taller than the last time," Jack points out, then reaches for the shot glass in front of him. "I'm waiting for the day he's seven-foot." Without hesitation, he sucks it back like a pro, proving he was a naughty boy in high school and thereafter.

Then there's Wynn, who is watching Jack like he's about to sprout horns or keel over dead. Jack laughs, turning to us with a grin on his face, and Wynn relaxes.

"I'm not pretty enough to be a twink, but my ass sure thinks I'm one," Jackson says without shame, causing the bartender to hitch his head backward and release a deep, intoxicating laugh.

Men get closer, scenting prey, waiting for the booze to kick in and lower inhibitions and expectations.

Jack getting a blowjob will be the easiest endeavor of his life.

"This is my only stiff drink tonight," I warn the bartender. "You can see why." I knock it back, enjoying the pleasant burn as it descends from my throat to my stomach. As soon as it hits its destination, the warmth radiates out. "Thanks," I say, pushing the glass back to the bartender with the tips of my fingers.

"I'll take another," Jack announces– man on a mission. "Make it a double."

"Is this like pot, where you don't feel it the first time?" Wynn renders me speechless. "Or is that a myth too?"

Jack makes a funny face, eyes bugging out then narrowing. "No on both accounts." He quickly drains the two shots the bartender laid out. Bang. Bang. "Myth. What the hell, Wynn?"

"You no longer scare me," I murmur, mystified.

"'Bout time," Wynn purrs, then his shot disappears. Everyone in the bar, including the dude just walking in the door, is mesmerized by the expression on Wynn's face as he takes his first sip of alcohol.

While everyone laughs, I finish what I started to say. "You utterly terrify me now. We're not experimenting with drugs tonight."

Face both blanching and managing to turn splotchy, "No," Wynn's still sputtering, shuddering too. "Not tonight."

"It's always all or nothing with Wynn, Kade." Jackson leans forward so I can see him better. "When you gonna learn?"

"Apparently Wynn will surprise me every single day for the rest of our lives," I mutter in awe. "Pot? Remember you're a Gillette and moderation is key."

"This boy's a keeper." The bartender smiles brightly. "Never get bored that way, but you never know what you're going to get, either."

"Petrifying," I whisper as Wynn requests a double. "No. Two is your limit, newbie. I'm not cleaning up your puke in my ride."

"Don't you mean Bren's ride?" Jackson taunts, chuckling sinisterly. "Give Wynn another, but no double."

The new arrival leans on the end of the bar next to Jack, but he's looking at all of us since there aren't any more stools. "I'll buy this round," he rasps, voice so husky it's barely audible.

Literally bellying up to the bar, "Thank you," Wynn chirps, suddenly too eager to drink now that he has one shot buzzing in his veins. "That's very kindly of you."

"I'll never get over the accent." Small with shaggy dirty blond hair hiding most of his face, I can't get a good read on the new guy. He's dressed in jeans and a t-shirt, but they're good quality. Nothing is cheap on him, but nothing leaves an impression either. The guy is meant to blend in until he wants to be seen.

New guy knocks back the shot with ease, hair still hiding his face from view, even with it tipped backward.

"Where are you from?" Jack turns to face the man, knee brushing against the guy's thigh, and it skeeves me out to see Jack touch someone other than Bren.

Wynn reaches for my hand, twining our fingers together to rest on my thigh. He's getting better at reading me. So much so it's scary, but a comfort too.

I sense his eyes are focused on Wynn, but I can't say for sure. "Here and there," the guy says noncommittally. "My family is from West Virginia, but I grew up in Virginia with my sister. After my brothers were out of the picture, it was just the two of us."

"I'm an orphan, too," I release to get a read on the guy, but he shows no reaction. Usually people who don't know you will wince in faux sympathy, simply because they're glad they hadn't been through that. Those who are orphans will truly feel connected to me.

The newcomer just looks at me through the fall of his hair, like he already knows me.

"You seem to be doing okay for yourself," is murmured almost inaudibly.

"I wish I was an orphan." Wynn's laughter shows he was joking, but the new guy's shoulders stiffen and his fingers clench on the bar. "Just joking. I don't have anything to do with my momma, but my daddy and I are trying to mend fences. There's just a lot of acreage to close in."

"Yeah," he grunts. Even though he looks like he's talking to all of us, I can tell his sole focus is on Wynn. I clench my boyfriend's hand, confused and worried about him. "I know all about either mending the fence or burning the wood for heat."

"Visiting family in the area?" Jack asks conversationally, and I concentrate on Wynn's thumb rubbing the back of my hand to soothe me.

"Something like that," the guy mutters noncommittally. "The pool table just opened up. Wanna play?"

"Sure." Jack slides off the stool, then looks over his shoulder at Wynn and me, giving us a wink. "I haven't played in a few weeks. But I never play with someone when I don't know their name."

"Cain," the guy reveals, a light-colored eye peering at me through the fall of his hair. Blue, I think, but most definitely a challenge. "Cain Probst."

"Cain, nice to meet you." Jack walks away, new friend in tow, and I strain to hear them. "I'm Jack, by the way, and they're Wynn and Kade."

"Hey," Wynn and I grunt, fascinated in the way one watches a car accident. I'm oddly jealous on several fronts, while Wynn is just rolling with it.

"Yeah," Cain breathes, acting like he already knew our names, or just didn't give two shits in the first place.

"What do you do?" pops out of my mouth before I can stop it.

"I take care of the family business." Cain's words were hard to hear when he was next to us. Now it's near impossible to make out what he says.

"What's that?" Jack's higher voice is easier to pick out through the din of the bar, but it's only because I'm attuned to it.

"C'mon." I tug Wynn from the stool, needing to be closer to hear. "Let's play pool."

Wynn chuckles, squeezing my hand as we weave through the bar to the back where four pool tables are spread out. All are taken, but the guys closest to where Cain and Jack are shooting pool only have four balls on their table. Wynn and I select our cues and chalk them as we wait– eavesdropping.

Arms curl around my waist and a chin rests on my shoulder. "Relax. What could go wrong?"

I turn my head, cheek brushing against Wynn's forehead. "You're so naïve."

"Jack has been going to bars since last year, a few times a week." Wynn kisses the corner of my mouth, and my eyelids grow heavy from the pleasure of it. "He'll get what he wants, then we can forget about it and go about our lives."

"You realize he's been hitting bars with a gaggle of nurses." I turn more so I can steal a kiss of my own. "Nurses are badasses, and Jack has never wandered off alone."

Wynn and I watch them play for a moment. Jack doesn't show the least bit of anxiety. He's laughing, chatting, and his body language is open. But I don't trust this Cain character. He doesn't look shady. He doesn't act shady. But he also doesn't look or act like anything at all. My inner alarms are blazing, and I don't know why.

"How's your instinct feeling right now?" I ask, curious.

Arms clench me tighter. "I'm worried, obviously." Wynn laughs without humor. "Feeling a bit awkward. Jack's ours, ya know? He's his own man, but this guy isn't one of us. I get him wanting something from someone other than Bren. But I would've rather just sucked Jack's dick myself."

"Same here," I mutter, completely understanding. This isn't about sex for Jack. Exercising his independence and liberation, and saying goodbye to both. "We're conditioned to ignore our baser instincts. I'm trying to figure out if what I'm feeling is because I'm jealous and feeling like this dude is stealing our Jackass, or if my instincts are trying to tell me something else– something more important. I'm feeling paranoid."

"C'mon." Wynn's arms pull from around my waist, and his front is no longer curled around my back, leaving me feeling chilled and anxious. "Our table's free."

After breaking, Wynn turns to me with a Cheshire grin. "We need a pool table in our house."

"Guys?" Jack calls to us, and our eyes flick up to him to find him pointing behind him at the bathroom. Cain is selecting a song at the jukebox. "I'll be in there."

"Gotta take a piss?" Wynn smirks, confused as to why Jack is telling us that he's got to go potty like Honor would. "Oh," Wynn huffs when he gets it. "Be careful."

"Will do." Jack turns and stalks off to the bathroom.

Cain turns to face us, calling out, "Enjoy the song." Yet again, the hair covering all but one blue eye, it all feels like a challenge he is begging me to accept while his focus is centered on Wynn.

"What?" Wynn stares at me. "It's country. What's the BFD?"

"The song hasn't started yet," I remind him. I line up my next shot, ignoring the unsettling sensation in my gut. "The song is to occupy us while he does our Jackass. About that pool table…" I change the subject to forget what's happening. "Our house is too small."

Hands shaking as badly as my voice, I scratch.

"Yeah." Wynn's trying not to look freaked out. "So no pool table, I guess."

"We could get a bigger house," I remind him, curling around his back like a cliché dude hitting on a chick.

"Nope." Wynn looks back at me, laughter and terror roiling in his eyes. "We're unemployed, we spent our trusts on education, and we're not begging off Royce and Bren."

"Ah!" I bite the back of Wynn's neck, causing him to gasp and grind his ass into me. "You're no fun. You know Bren would buy us a house."

"No. We'll go to the Main Drag and shoot pool." Wynn refuses to put up with my shit. "What the fuck is that?" He points at the jukebox.

Huffing a laugh, I stare at Wynn. "You've never heard of Marilyn Manson?"

"Not in a hillbilly bar– it's been a mix of country, southern rock, and rock so far." Wynn can't take his eyes from the jukebox, as if he's hearing shit. "Not all of us were emo bitches."

"Ha!" I tug Wynn into my arms, rocking him back and forth while murmuring the lyrics. "I don't care if your world is ending today, because I wasn't invited to it anyway. You said I tasted famous, so I drew you a heart. But now I'm not an artist, I'm a fucking work of art. I've got an F and a C, and I got a K too… and the only thing that's missing is a bitch like you."

"That's disturbing," Wynn mutters, pale face flaming with a blush as I sing to him. I'm going to have to do this more often, because the kid is hard as a rock, and his fans in the bar are staring at his crotch.

Whispering, barely breathing into Wynn's ear, I make the words flutter against his skin. "I've got an F and a C, and I got a K too… and the only thing that's missing is *U*."

"Why this song?" Wynn's brain is still working while mine is off on vacation. "Why did that guy want us to hear *this* song?"

"What's my name… what's my name? Hold the S because I am an AINT." As I sing, my mind spins, then something clicks and dread pools in my stomach. "What was that guy's last name again?"

"Cain," Wynn reminds me. "He said his name was Cain Probst."

Heart beating in my throat, I'm running before my feet check in with my brain.

CHAPTER SIXTEEN
Brennan Kennedy

Dad's in his glory. Practically everyone in town is surrounding the bonfire– the backyard is filled with the joyful chatter of playing kids. Penny's quartet of sisters is keeping watch as the twins, Honor, and Copper play the beanbag toss. The mommas are highly competitive with ladder ball: Willa, Penny, Jesse, and Penny's mom, Brenda.

Mind half in Rusty Knob, and half in Adam & Steve, I sit around the fire with the dads: Dad, Corbin, Garrett, and Warren. Sulking, Jeb looks like we're torturing him instead of feeding him pizza and including him in the conversation. I can't get a read on him, and he's only a little over a year younger than me. I feel bad, because clearly he feels set apart from us, and I don't know why.

Leaving Dad and Corbin to their debate over which type of barbeque is better, I sit next to the lone man at the party. "What do you do when you're not at the shop?" I ask conversationally. "Do you play video games? Fish? Go on dates?"

Jeb stares at me, and I can see distrust in his eyes. He reminds me so much of a mix of Wynn and Jack, it ain't even funny. Tall yet thin, Jeb has blond hair tinted with strawberry, and a smattering of freckles across his cheeks and nose. His eyes are lighter than Penny's, hints of gold instead of brown.

"Do you work out?" I don't reach over to grip his bicep, because that's a dick move. I'll either look like I'm hitting on him or insulting his physique. I only ask because I need a jumping off point for conversation. Jeb is a black hole when it comes to small talk. "Introvert?" I pull off the top of my head, after hearing Kade talk about that before.

"I like to read." Jeb stares down at his long, thin fingers. They're scrubbed raw and banged up with cuts and scratches. Noticing the direction of my gaze, "Motor oil has to be scrubbed off, and every liquid we use is caustic. Hydraulic fluid. WD-40... you get the idea."

"Gloves?" Jack would lose his shit if he saw Jeb's hands.

"I can't..." Jeb turns his head, unable to look anyone in the eye unless he's angry. I know he wasn't beaten as a kid. Garrett is a pushover of a man, and Jeb is his momma's only baby boy. Then there are the five sisters who think Jeb sets the moon. "I can't wear gloves because most of the stuff I do is with my fingertips, and the gloves are either too bulky or make it so I can't feel what I'm doing."

"I'll have Jack find something to soothe your skin, okay?" Just looking at his hands is painful for me, and they aren't my hands.

"Thanks." Jeb pulls at a hangnail, and I wince when it bleeds. "I like to read, and hauling tires is exercise enough. It's a fulltime job looking after them." He points at his sisters as they give out pointers on how to throw the beanbags. "So they don't end up like her." He points at Penny, who's laughing with Jesse. "Because of men like him," he snarls, glaring at Warren.

Warren looks at us, his middle finger slowly rising. Then he scratches at the few days' growth of blond whiskers, as if he wasn't telling his brother-in-law to fuck off.

"Pretty sure Warren and Penny are happier than a pair of pigs in shit," I mutter, and the rest of the dads overhear. Laughing, they elbow Warren and start razzing him.

"Wallowing in shit." Jeb snorts, still glaring at Warren with thinly veiled hatred.

"I don't know… if you want a different job to get away from your family, I can hook ya up. Or get you some new digs so you're not in the same house with all those girls. If you need a buddy to go jogging with, or fishing, or to just sit and stare out into space, I'll have your back, man."

If Jeb didn't hate Warren so much, I don't doubt for a second that Warren wouldn't be having this same conversation with Jeb. Warren is very outgoing and fun, and he'd try to make Jeb feel comfortable and welcome.

Jeb looks down at his hands, whispering so quietly the others can't hear. "Are you hitting on me?" His face flushes, and I don't know if he's embarrassed because he's straight, or because he's gay. I can't get a read on him.

"Nope," I say with all sincerity. "It's in my nature not to sit idly by and watch someone be fucking miserable. If I can help you out, I will. Kennedy curse, as they say."

"I might take you up on one of those offers," Jeb mutters. "Dad's shop will continue on whether I'm there or not, because of Warren."

"Sorry to tell you this, bro." I elbow him playfully. "But your rein of being the only cock in the hen house has come to an end.

With five sisters, you're going to have to put up with interloper brothers-in-law."

Jeb releases a growly sound, and it does things to me it shouldn't.

"I'm moving back here in a few weeks, and I'm going to be apprenticing under our foreman. So if you want another job, let me know. It will still be manual labor, but not with your daddy as your boss."

"I'll think about it." Eyes glued to hands, Jeb is beyond timid and unsure of himself.

"That's all I can ask." I pat him on the back, and I'm shocked when he doesn't pull away from me, like he does when anyone else gets into range. "You figure out what works for you, and try to find a bit of freedom while you're at it."

"Thank you," Jeb murmurs, blushing.

"Anytime." I look up, feeling eyes on me, only to find all of the dads looking at me with a mix of wonder and pride. Now it's my turn to blush.

I jump a little when my cellphone vibrates in my front pocket, the sensation teasing my half-hard cock. With a bit of a struggle, I manage to get the device out without breaking my dick in half.

"What the fuck?" I mutter as the image slowly comes into focus. Heart beating a rapid tattoo in my chest, it doesn't even register as Jeb pulls me to my feet to drag me behind the barn.

"No one else should see that." Jeb's voice quivers, like he's been in a similar situation. "To have that happen... but to take a video."

"I need Corbin," I whisper, eyes never leaving the screen as one of my worst fears plays out on video. "Hurry."

Now that I'm alone, I restart the video with sound. "Brennan— oh, Brennan?" Dirty blond hair is pushed behind delicate ears, showing off a younger, smaller version of the man who stars in my nightmares, mixed with the features of the people I love most in life. It's a terrifying combination. "Cheaters. Cheaters. The world is filled with cheaters."

The camera pans down, showing Jack lying in the fetal position in the middle of a dirty bathroom stall, with his pants yanked down to his knees and his dick and ass hanging out. "My momma was a cheater but no whore, and her husband punished her and her bastard daughter, then his *real* sons punished the bastard son." The camera leaves Jack's shuddering body to pan in on Cain's pale, tortured eyes. "Your daddy was a cheater, so Sean punished him. But your daddy only cheated as a way to get Sean to leave Donny alone. I get it, 'cuz my momma only cheated as an escape to get away from her husband. So here's my apology and a thank you, Bren."

Camera trained on a single blue eye, the sound of a zipper being drawn down has terror flooding my veins. "My momma didn't deserve what happened to her, what her own sons and husband did to her. I should thank Corbin for taking out the trash, because Momma's no-good husband and Sean were wastes of space. It's too bad Damon isn't in the ground instead of safe in prison. I've paid for sins I didn't commit, but this one... this is for you, Brennan. No one should cheat on the one they love."

Jack's pitiful whimper murders a vital part of my soul. Steam blurs the video as a stream of hot piss flows from Cain's dick to spray all over Jack's prone body. "Don't worry. Our brothers are safe and sound– tell my dad I want to see him."

The camera zooms in as Cain jiggles the last few drops of piss off the tip of his dick, to land on Jack's shoulder. Panning down, Jack's mortified face is the last thing I see as the video ends.

Shaking, I nearly drop my phone, but Corbin is there to grab it for me. The two of us have an odd relationship no one else understands, so I am more than willing to accept when he presses my head to his chest.

"We need– we need to tell the truth," I gasp, close to hyperventilating. My fingers turn to claws, gripping Corbin's shirt.

"Let me find him first," Corbin warns. "Cain wants to see me, so he'll see me."

"Jack?" I cry, knowing what I saw will never leave me– forever haunting my thoughts.

"You know Cain has an odd sense of justice. He can't understand anything but black and white after how he was raised."

"Raised, or abused? No sane person pisses on a guy's boyfriend as a thank you for taking out his abusers." Body wracked with shudders, "He was in the same room with Wynn, Corbin!"

"We'll call Kade." Corbin tries to reassure me. "It'll be okay. Jack's tough, and you can tell him all of it. Okay? Tell him all of it. It's all you can offer as an apology."

"What about you telling the truth?" I demand. "Please!"

"I've been working on it, Brennan." Corbin pulls away, face turning cold. "I think your family has destroyed mine enough. Don't make me destroy it even more because of your grandfather sticking his dick where it didn't belong."

"What about yours?!" I shout, pointing at the body part that created Cain.

"Chain of events, Brennan, and you fucking know that." Corbin stalks off, fury radiating off of him in waves.

CHAPTER SEVENTEEN
Kaden Marx

"Jack!" Slamming into the swinging bathroom door, I skid to a halt when I see Jackson's flip-flops sticking out the bottom of the stall. "Wynn, don't come in here!" My protest is too late, because Wynn charges past me to land on his knees.

"Don't look." Jack whimpers, trying to pull up his pants. The hot stench of ripe piss filters through my nose. At first I think Jackson wet himself, but I notice the piss is all over him.

"Is this a gay bashing?" Wynn stares at me over his shoulder in horror, where I'm frozen in the center of the bathroom. The unfathomable expression on his face proves how innocent he truly is– this is why I didn't take them to the university haunts. He pulls our buddy into his lap, then tries to look for injuries. "What did that fucker do to you?"

After grabbing handful after handful of paper towels, which I thrust into Wynn's outstretched palm, I tear off my t-shirt. For once, wearing my scar-covering thermal saves the day.

"I'm okay–" Jack weakly bats Wynn's hands away. As they grapple, the nurse not wanting to be taken care of, I surreptitiously make sure nothing more than revenge in the form a good old fashion gay-bashing took place.

Ruddy but flaccid, Jack's junk has a dribble of semen dried on it, so things did progress to a certain point. But there's no redness on his butt cheeks, so it didn't go that far.

"Why would he do this?" Wynn tears Jack's pissy t-shirt off the tiny guy's body like he's nothing more than a toddler. The fabric hits the waste bin with a splat. Struggling, Wynn shoves Jack closer to the sink so he can scrub him down. "I don't understand. I thought he was into you."

"Cain was enjoying it, but then he freaked the fuck out on me." Jackson wrenches away from Wynn, refusing to be fussed over. "I ain't dying. I've just been pissed on. I'm humiliated enough, let me keep some dignity by not treating me like a goddamn kid."

"We won't tell Bren." Wynn doesn't listen to Jack's protests, proving he wasn't lying about his height, because Jack has no way of stopping him. "We'll just work through this and deal. Okay?" Wynn's voice breaks, no doubt fearing we'll have another suicide-watch on our hands.

Jackson catches my eyes in the mirror as he scrubs himself in the sink, and I'm proud how courageous and together he's being. "Cain was into it. Neither of us wanted a boyfriend experience. Just a mouth-fuck. So he squatted and started sucking me off, and he was into it too. Then all of the sudden he started saying some odd crap." Jack waits a heartbeat. "About Bren and Wynn."

"What?" Wynn shouts, furious. "I don't know that asshole. He wouldn't even let me see his face– his hair was in the way."

Jack's grimace has me asking, "What did he look like?" Hazel eyes hitch in Wynn's direction, and it confuses the hell out of me.

"I'm sure you've figured out Cain was Sean Probst's baby brother– he can't be any older than Warren, younger even. I couldn't tell."

"What?" Wynn repeats, only this time it's a squawk. "No wonder he did this– Sean was a monster."

"Are you okay?" My feet unfreeze, and I find myself helping Jackson into my t-shirt. The height difference has it falling to his knees, so I say the fuck with it and wrench the pissy pants off of him.

"Thanks," Jackson mutters dryly, more pissed off at me than Cain. "Smelling like piss is bad enough, but now I'm in flip-flops and a t-shirt– that's it."

"Wynn?" I reach into my back pocket to grab my wallet. I count out a couple twenties and pass them to Wynn. "Go close out our tab and leave the rest for a tip. Tell the bartender we're leaving out the back."

The bills disappear from my hand and the bathroom door is closing behind Wynn before Jack and I disconnect our gazes. "What aren't you telling me?"

"You better call Bren." Jackson's composure fractures, tears fill his eyes to fall down his cheeks. "Cain recorded the incident with his cellphone."

"How do you know he sent it to Bren?" Stunned, all I can do is stare.

"Because Cain spoke to Bren the entire time he did this to me." Jackson gestures to his destroyed clothing. "Cain said it was a 'thank you' and an 'I'm sorry'. His parting words were how he wanted to see his father."

"What the fuck?" Waiting for the burst of adrenaline to crash, I recognize the instant Jack sways on his feet. I'm lifting him up into my arms before he can protest. Smelling like piss or not, I clasp him tight to my chest.

I failed my little buddy tonight.

"I'm sorry," I breathe as I charge out of the bathroom, and then make my way down the hallway to the back exit. "I'm so fucking sorry, Jackson."

"Kade?" Jack sniffles, and it kills me. "Cain– he looked… Cain looks exactly like Wynn in the face, but he's short like Warren. Do you understand?"

"The picture is getting clearer by the second." I stride up to my car, to find Wynn waiting with the door open and a blanket in his hands. We settle Jack on his feet between us, and completely strip him down to nothing but flesh. Wynn swaddles Jackson, and then pulls him into the backseat.

There isn't a jealous bone in my body as I watch Wynn hold our friend, making promises he has no way of keeping.

"I'm calling Bren now," I warn, and Wynn looks at me oddly through the rearview mirror. "He already knows, Wynn… Bren already knows."

Since Adam & Steve wasn't far from our apartment, I decide to wait to call Bren until we got home. I don't like keeping anything from Wynn, but I need to figure out what the hell is going on first.

Wynn wouldn't relinquish his hold on Jack, even after the man protested. Now they're locked in the bathroom, giving me some much needed privacy with my brother.

"What the fuck?" I demand as soon as Bren picks up. "Where are you?" Pacing, one hand holding the phone to my ear while the other tears at my piss-stank clothing. I try to swallow my fury, but my Wolverine almost goes through the wall when I kick it off my foot.

"How's Jack?" comes muffled, and I can hear many voices in the background.

"What are you doing? Git yer ass here!" Anger has me slipping back into a diction that got my ass kicked once I left Rusty Knob.

"How's Jackson?" Bren tries again, voice clearer, background noise disappearing.

"If ya really wanna know, git yer ass up here." With a wrenching motion, I whip my belt out of the loops, tugging my jeans with it. "Now!"

"Don't be a motherfucking pain in the ass, Kaden!" Bren snarls. "Just answer the question, then I will answer yours."

"Wynn is having a heyday," I mutter, feeling like a horse's ass. "You know how much he likes to problem solve. Wynn and Jack are locked in our bathroom, doing whatever they need to do. Jack's tougher than he looks in all ways. He's probably more worried about you and what you saw than anything else that happened."

In boxer briefs and a thermal, I sit on the edge of our bed, too tired to move. "Just talk to me, okay?"

"I don't know where to start, only to say whatever I tell you can't be spread through the grapevine. Dad doesn't even know." The noise returns, louder than ever. "Hey! I've gotta get going," Bren shouts at someone. "If you're not going home, just leave Honor with my dad and Willa." A muffled voice reverberates, but I can't make it out. "Okay, I'm back. Listen. I'm going to chat with you for a minute, then I gotta go talk to Corbin. After that, it's gonna take me an hour to drive to you. So give me two hours before you start wondering where I am. 'Kay?"

"'Kay," I mutter, baffled. "Explain some shit to me." I stalk across our space, kicking my discarded clothing as I go. Bypassing Wynn's clothing in our shared dresser, I grab a pair of pajama pants and a long-sleeved jersey cotton shirt.

"Corbin and I have an odd relationship," Brennan explains– understatement of the year. "That night that Sean hurt everyone… I snuck out of the twins' bedroom window and ran through the woods to Gillette Holler to fetch Corbin. I was– I was with Corbin when he did what he had to do, and that changes people."

"Reading between the lines, you feel responsible for Sean's death?" My inner therapist rises to the fore. "Bren, you shouldn't. You didn't pull the trigger."

"I feel no guilt whatsoever," Bren answers without a moment's hesitation. "None, and neither does Corbin. Sean was a monster. Every nightmare I have ends with Corbin and me saving the day."

"Corbin is not a hero," I mutter wryly, eyes flicking to our bathroom door. Wynn would shit a brick if he heard the hero-worship in Bren's voice.

"Corbin's problems are the Kennedy family's fault." Bren's tone brooks no room for argument. "Dad and Willa know the main story. Granddaddy was fooling around with Birdie Probst and Octavia was made. When Birdie's husband found out, he moved them away to Virginia. Cut to years later, when we got the settlement, Damon and Sean thought they deserved a share by default because of their little sister."

"Then they made our lives a living nightmare." Tugging on my pajamas with too much force, I almost tear through them. "Yeah, I was there, remember? The FBI said Cain was behind it, but he looks a bit too young for that– a bit too much like Corbin."

"Birdie and Octavia were being abused– because she cheated and the proof she cheated. Damon and Sean took after their dad. They were beating the hell out of them, emotionally torturing them. Birdie came to my granddaddy for help, but she found Corbin instead. He took care of it, and Cain was made."

"Took care of it? You mean Corbin took care of the father like he did the son?" Slumping backward on the mattress, I stare up at the ceiling. "I didn't realize Corbin was a contract killer with sex as payment."

"Is it murder if he protects the innocent?" Bren sounds brainwashed. "Damon and Sean thought it was natural causes, so everything they did to us was for the money. They were absolute lowlife scum, thinking they were entitled to anything anyone else had, and they had the right to take it by force."

"Why is the FBI after Cain?"

"I met Cain," Bren admits. "Dad and Willa were in the hospital, Sean was dead, and Damon was on a rampage. You were visiting Dad, and I was milling around the hospital. I found Corbin with a young woman and a boy, and she was begging for help– my Aunt Octavia and Cain. Corbin and I have kept this secret forever, because telling it helps no one, but could hurt my aunt and Corbin's son. Cain had information on the people Damon and Sean were working with, and they wanted it. But having the FBI chase you is safer than ratting out organized crime."

"Why piss on Jackson?" My voice dips low, a flash of memory resurfacing. Flip-flops. Jack's feet sticking out of the bottom of the bathroom stall will always haunt me. "Cain was sucking Jack off, and was liking it too. Then he freaked the fuck out."

"Cain has issues."

"No shit!" I snarl. "No fucking shit. Explain that to our boy."

"Step away for a second and look at this objectively, Kaden." Bren sighs deeply, the gust reverberating the speaker of my cellphone. "The reason you're the best at what you do is because you don't judge, and you can see why people do what they do. Cain is warped. What do you honestly think would make a man do that to another man? Think about it."

"Sociopath is what I conclude." I crawl into bed, suddenly cold to my morrow. I lie on my side with our blankets wrapped around me.

"Yeah," Bren says snidely. "Remember what Sean did to Donny and Dad? Imagine being a little boy and having your own half-brothers do that to you. I gotta go."

"You hung up on me!" I shout to the ceiling. "What the fuck?"

"What's up?" Wynn whispers through the cracked bathroom door.

"Nothing," I grunt, rolling onto my side to face him. "Bren hung up on me, is all."

"Is all?" Eyebrow reaching his hairline, Wynn's not buying the shit I'm selling.

"Your childhood sucked, but you're so kind, and good, and sweet, nothing really ever got you down," I murmur, unable to stop myself. "But what if your life was worse and your personality was darker like mine, do you think you should be given a pass at pissing on someone?"

Wynn looks over his shoulder, and Jack's voice flows inaudibly. After shaking his head, Wynn slips from the bathroom, towel slung over his hips. "Jack didn't take too kindly to me scrubbing the piss outta him in the shower."

"Literally. I didn't suspect he would," I mutter wryly, trying to keep the smile off my face and out of my voice.

Wynn settles on the edge of the bed. "Jackson is my best friend– has been since kindergarten."

"I know that– is this one of those conversations where you think you'll have to choose between us?" I reach over to twine our fingers together, hating how Wynn won't look at me. "I won't make you, you know?"

"I know," Wynn admits without hesitation. "But you need to realize Jack shouldn't have to choose between me and Bren either. We're not talking romantic crap, so don't get your tighty whities in a wad."

"I do *not* wear tighty whities," I mutter, offended. "It's either boxer briefs, or those bikini briefs you picked out because you said they made my ass look good and you loved how my hard-on would peek out the waistband."

"Is Cain my brother?" Wynn rapidly blurts out, not in the mood for my usual banter. "It's what Jack thinks, says he looks like me.

He would know since he's seen me in every stage of life. Now Bren is hanging up on you, and you're asking about how I grew up versus how Cain probably was raised."

Moment of truth, where loyalties crash and burn.

"Bren says Cain is your brother," I admit, and this time it's me who can't look Wynn in the eyes. He squeezes my hand, so I go on. "Bren's known all along, knowing more than even Royce knows. You know how Corbin and Bren are creepy around each other?"

A heavy sigh is the only answer I get, but Wynn does begin stroking my hand with his thumb. I realize I'm an asshole. This is difficult, life-changing information, but he's too worried about comforting me when it should be the other way around.

"I'm not surprised," is all he says. "Not when it comes to Corbin."

"I'm guessing the Probst momma was one of those needy skanks who cried very real tears and only found succor with a dick between her legs– I know I sound disgusting, but as a psychologist, it's a very real personality that taints everything it touches. If your husband is abusing you, you don't go fuck Donald Kennedy and leave the abusive asshole to raise your bastard. You sure as shit don't go screw around with another guy, creating another kid for your husband and sons to abuse– just saying."

"Exactly." Wynn shuffles back until his behind is butted up against my thigh. "If you love your kids, you leave. You don't make more kids with two more men, then allow your abusive husband to turn your sons into abusers to your newest children. Cycle of abuse. Birdie Probst was a worse monster for allowing it to perpetuate, thinking the only way out was by getting another man in her, which is why I refuse to speak to my mother.

"Momma was living with her sister, messing around with my uncle, and got her ass kicked out. Instead of learning something, she's had a string of men in the past five years. Wanting to have sex because it's consensual and mutual is one thing, using it to leech off men is another.

"Warren tried to get Momma cleaned up, moved her in with him, only to have her lash out at Copper like she did us kids. Now she's shacked up with yet another man who can get her what she needs. Selling that worn-out place between her legs and a body to be struck in fits of anger for a roof over her head, food in her mouth, and her vices of choice."

Having heard this too many times to count, I put a stop to it before it evolves into cracked molars from Wynn grinding his teeth. "You've been reading my books?"

"I have," Wynn admits in a soft tone. "I wanted to understand the dynamic in my family."

Instead of replying, I lean forward to lay a kiss in the center of Wynn's back. "I'm guessing here, but I think Birdie Probst came to Corbin for help, crying about how godawful her husband and sons were, and she got in Corbin's bed to twist his head so he'd help. I don't know how old Cain is, so it was either just before Corbin married your momma, or between Willa and you."

"Daddy isn't easily manipulated. So we can't blame Birdie for seducing him into whatever he did. He did it for the Kennedy family, I suspect, with the added perk of willing pussy."

"Since when did you get so foulmouthed?" Snorting, I kiss Wynn's back again. The towel is loose around his waist, and the divots above his ass cheeks are too adorable to resist. I tongue both before a hand is pressing on my forehead.

"Behave," Wynn breathes, but his pupils are blown from lust. "Foulmouthed? I'm a Gillette, no matter what. Jack isn't mad, only humiliated, because he said Cain didn't understand and thought he was protecting Bren from Jack. He repeated everything Cain had said on the video."

"Bren didn't want you to know." I resist the urge to pull Wynn down into our bed and never let him leave. I don't want to use sex to distract him. I just want him in my arms where he's safe and sound– happy.

"We're past secrets and lies." Wynn's voice holds something that won't be denied. "No more lies. If you are to see me as an adult, then I can't keep my head in the sand. I won't blame anyone. I'm going to go to the source tomorrow."

"Corbin?"

"Yes," Wynn breathes. "Then I'm going to force my dads into a civil conversation filled with the truth. Daddy and Royce need to sit down and put it all on the table. I'll leave the family reunion with Cain for whenever we're all ready. Willa's in a fragile condition, so no upsetting her until after the baby is born."

"It's a girl," I blurt out, then add, "No more secrets and lies. I was told to keep it a secret in case something happened. Brynn. It's our names combined. B and R from Brennan. Y and N from your name. N for me. Y for Hayden, Hayley, and our lost baby Royce. Brynn Piper Kennedy– Piper after Royce's mother."

"Damn!" Wynn jerks his head away, voice thick with tears. "Life has been hard for a long damn time, Kaden. Too hard, but it's taught me some shit." He pulls his hand away from mine, where he folds them in his lap.

I don't say a word, needing Wynn to continue, needing him to let me in. He's normally an open book on the surface, but what's buried beneath belongs to him, which is what I do too. We've been trying to move past it for the last few weeks, realizing how stunted our relationship was.

"After moving in with Royce, I did revert back to someone younger than my age. Even I will admit that. So much resentment." Wynn stares at his fingers as they twist in his towel. "I enjoyed the sense of community basketball gave me, I loved studying, but I hated college."

Laughter bubbles up before I can stop it, and Wynn jerks to glare at me over his shoulder. Laughing more, I rub my hands along his back, not making a move on him, but just soothing his nerves.

Wynn has to excel in everything. He performed well on the team, using basketball to connect to his teammates. He breezed through his courses, enjoying what little challenge they offered. What made college a nightmare was how much Wynn did not like the people. Too many people. Too many people who voiced how much they didn't like what Wynn stood for on all fronts. But unlike me, someone who couldn't roll with the stress, Wynn drove right through it by refusing to acknowledge their existence. I won't lie. I'd stop whatever I was doing to engage in battle with the fuckwits.

If there was a stereotype they could use against me, they struck with it, and I was powerless against the assault. Meanwhile, Wynn looked them in the eye, called them ignorant and small-minded, and walked past. I fought my own battles, and his, and everyone else's, and I never won because there was nothing to win. It was all opinion, and you can't dictate emotion and inherent thoughts. It caused me to cut myself to release the pressure, which made me realize Royce and Wynn were right– I had a problem.

"I don't care if everyone back in Rusty Knob whispers behind my back. The queer kid who thought he was a basketball star comes home with a worthless degree he can wipe his shitty ass on." Wynn looks at me, handsome face scrunched with anger. "I've heard 'em. I loved my education, and I'll use it when I'm ready. I'm not taking the job Miriam is offering, at least not yet."

"Miriam said she had to convince old man Harding to retire first, same goes with my position. There's a bunch of retirement-aged faculty, and Miriam wants to replace them with fresh out of college graduates who understand the struggle."

"I just want to go home." Wynn's voice breaks. "I want to go in my barn and create things– create useful things people will put in their houses and pass onto their children, and their children's children. I just want to be useful," Wynn whispers.

"You are." My voice breaks as I reach for him, but Wynn won't allow me to tug him down beside me.

"I know I am. I'm just not ready to work for someone else after the past four years– the stress took a toll on me. To be honest, I'm not ready for kids yet either, Kaden." Wynn turns to look at me, face washed with fear– fear I'll be upset.

"Don't think about what I want, tell me what you *need*," I stress.

"I need time to help get our family healed– heal myself. If it can't be repaired, the taint has to be cut away like I did with Momma." Wynn stares at his fingertips again. "I'm an adult, no matter how naïve you find me. But I'm not ready to be a father yet. I spent my childhood protecting the twins. Now I just want to figure out what I want to do with the rest of my life. The only things I know for certain right now are how I want to be in Rusty Knob, and how I want to be with you."

"Okay." I sigh, relieved. This time I do lean forward, wrapping myself around Wynn's back. "I'll do everything I can to help you get what you need. I'll delay turning in the foster care paperwork."

"No– don't." Wynn grabs my hands, pulling me closer. "It's for emergency placement. It won't be very often, and it's necessary. I'm not that selfish, Kaden. You need it. The kids need it. And I think it will be good for me to see it. We both know how I will only see one side, while judging the other. I'm trying to grow up and be mature about all of this."

"Okay, that's settled then." Peppering kisses to the back of Wynn's neck, I'm relieved beyond measure. "We'll live together, play together, and be together. You'll work in the barn, and I'll work at the center. Both of us will tell Miriam *maybe*. We'll help transition kids from their abusive homes to their forever homes. But not live middle-age people lives, like the one Bren is leading, until we're both ready. I'm only twenty-eight, even if I feel ancient to your twenty-two, and you and I don't need that life yet."

"Thank you," Wynn's voice wavers with the same relief I feel. "Thank you."

"Can I come out now?" Jackson peers out the crack in the bathroom door with a sheepish expression written across his face.

CHAPTER EIGHTEEN
Kaden Marx

"Yeah!" Wynn hops up, his back flushing until the crimson kiss reaches his shoulders and neck. "Sit here."

"Wynn?" Jack tightens the towel around his hips. "I'm not fragile." *Not like Kaden* is riding the air. "It sucks, and I know it wasn't about me, no matter how humiliating it was."

"It wasn't about you. C'mon." Wynn tugs Jackson down onto our bed, until the guy is almost the little spoon to my big spoon.

"I can sleep in my own bed. I ain't gonna freak the fuck out– honest." For all his protesting, Jack gets comfortable by snuggling down in the blankets.

Standing a few feet away, towering over us, Wynn stares down like he can read inside our heads. I'm frozen still, arm just dangling from where it had been touching Wynn moments ago, unsure how to proceed and what is expected from me. Slowly lowering my arm, because I'm starting to feel like a tool, I pat Jackson awkwardly on the shoulder.

"Do you need anything?" Looking down at us, towel barely staying on his hips, Wynn is clearly concerned, and showing guilt for some reason. "Do you hide hooch in our apartment? Do you need it?"

"Wynn?" Jack and I protest in unison. "No."

"Anything– name it." Wynn steps from foot-to-foot, needing to do something to erase what happened tonight.

"Why don't you just sit with us and we'll talk about what we need to pack, what's going to whom, and when you want to officially move?" I offer the suggestion while patting the edge of the bed.

"Okay." Wynn gingerly sits on the edge of the bed, touching neither of us. "We've pretty much been divvying it up as we pack, and the kitchen and bath have to be last. We can start driving our shit down to Rusty Knob."

I finally give up, placing my arm over Jack's bony ribs to rest my hand on his soft belly. He stiffens for a second, but then relaxes into my touch.

"I need a transitional space." Jack tries his damnedest to sound okay, but I can tell by his shivering that he's not. "My room isn't ready at the duplex."

"You could always stay with your folks." I offer while tugging the blankets around me to include Jackson.

Voice hopeful, Wynn gives a horrible suggestion. "You could just stay with Bren."

"Not with Jesse there," Jack growls, always getting pissy when she's brought up in conversation.

"Oh." Wynn sounds deflated because he couldn't help. His tone and eyebrows both hitch with helpfulness. "What about Libby? I haven't met her yet, but you talk about her nonstop. Does she live with her folks, or does she have an apartment of her own?"

"God, that would infuriate Jesse," Jack mutters with glee.

"Okay, if you want–" I look Wynn in the eyes, searching for permission, assuming this is what he wants. "You could stay with us while the duplex is finished. It's not like we haven't shared this space for four years, and it would be a whole house instead."

Wynn's smile speaks volumes.

"Really?" Jack twists to the side to look at me, managing to shift closer against my body. "You'd do that for me?"

"Are you serious?" Insulted, I just stare at Jackass.

"Thank you," Jack murmurs, then turns to look at Wynn. "Thank you both, but I don't want to impose on your honeymoon period at your house. I can crash with my folks and keep my shit boxed up. It's no biggie, but I love that you asked."

Playing nursemaid, Wynn tucks the edge of the blanket around Jack, eyes tracking every inch of flesh left uncovered. "Your skin is red and blotchy."

"Ugh," Jackson grunts, clearly annoyed. "You scrubbed my flesh from bone," he teases. "But I appreciated the effort."

"My brother pissed on you," Wynn grumbles, but I can hear the tears driving the words. "I'ma get some lotion." Hopping up like a jackrabbit, Wynn's in the bathroom before I can blink.

"Wynn doesn't have to–"

"He's going to, though," I mutter into Jackson's ear, relaxing every muscle in my body. "My guess, he's going to Corbin tomorrow because he wants to track down his mental brother."

"He's too..." Jackson's at a loss. Wynn's too much of everything. Everything that makes a person good.

Standing tall, hair sticking every which way, skin glowing, Wynn is too gorgeous for me to describe. Towel barely winning the fight to stay on his hips, Jackson and I are rewarded with a narrow peepshow of a meaty flaccid cock dangling and the juicy balls swinging beneath.

"Jackpot!" Wynn holds a bottle of lotion in his large paw, smiling brightly while presenting it to us.

Wynn is naïve, shameless, and has no concept of modesty after wandering naked in locker rooms for the last half of his life. He doesn't understand how I get hard just thinking about him, yet here he is standing mostly naked in front of me... Jack's ass is pressed up against my hard-on, with only a pair of pajama pants and a towel separating us. I know by the way Jack's shuddering in my arms, Wynn is driving him to the brink.

The towel slips another half inch, displaying the plum-shaped cockhead that drives me to insanity. Jack whimpers.

Wynn doesn't get it, and Jack and I are not immune to his charms.

"Thanks," Jackson murmurs, reaching for the bottle of lotion, only to have it be taken out of his range.

"Nope." Wynn sits on the edge of the bed, looking at me real quick to make sure he's not upsetting me. I already know exactly where this is headed. I may be driving our relationship into the unknown, but Wynn is the passenger with the map, and he's directing us down a dark path. We trust each other, so I'm just going to see how this plays out.

Wynn's smiling serenely while opening the bottle of lotion, and realization strikes that he knows exactly what he's doing. As he said, he is a Gillette, and he knows how to work all of those Gillette charms to his advantage.

"The bastard is seducing you," I breathe into Jack's ear while we watch Wynn pour lotion into his palms. I can only gawk as Wynn laughs like a happy child while he pats the lotion between his hands to warm it up.

A quivering body rubbing up against mine feels too good to ignore, but it's confusing because Jackson isn't my boyfriend. Meanwhile, said boyfriend is grinning down at us as he slowly settles his lotion-slicked hands on Jack's shoulders.

"Mmm... this will make you feel better," Wynn purrs, one tooth sinking into his bottom lip as his hands begin spreading lotion around Jack's chest. Nipple hit, the poor guy jerks with a grunt.

"No tits," Jackson orders, voice rough for a myriad of reasons. "I don't like 'em– avoid touching them."

Wynn's eyes meet mine, and I raise my eyebrow in agreement. *Touch them.*

I was a bony kid until I moved in with Royce and forced him to fatten me up with a dietician and weight training. That feeling has never left me, not even when I look in the mirror, or when Wynn touches me with lust etched across his face. I don't see the man I've grown to be.

Bren was a chubby, short kid, who eventually just became short. In an effort to change what he didn't like, he became a muscle-head.

Jack is a tiny guy, no ifs ands or buts about it. His lean muscles are covered in soft flesh, yet he manages to be skinny at the same time. He does have tiny tits like a girl, and other than surgery, no amount of exercise or starvation is going to change it.

A guy with extra flesh isn't my thing, nor is it Wynn's, but Jackson shouldn't be self-conscious about it. I understand why he is, but I don't think he should be.

Ignoring Jack's tits for his shoulders and neck, Wynn hums to himself while wearing a beatific expression. Oh, he's sporting wood enough to bat nine innings, but he's getting off on caregiving more.

Then Wynn touches them– palms kneading Jackson's tits, and the guy practically goes into convulsions. Jack may hate the sight of them, but he loves them being touched more.

"Jesus!" I hiss between clenched teeth, riding out the sensation as Jack grinds his ass into me. Wynn never breaks my stare while rolling a pair of nipples between the pads of his fingertips. Jackson's groaning, writhing between us, and Wynn's getting his rocks off on how he's playing us both. If Wynn doesn't stop, so Jack will stop, I'm going to make a mess in my pajamas.

Fighting back a smile, the little shit bites his lip.

Oh, we've talked about this more times than I can count. Wynn– good, wholesome Wynn is a dirty talking freak. He'll jerk me off while playing make-believe, spinning fantasies I'm positive he wants as reality. More times than not, they involve my ex-roommate and his husband, because Wynn loves to torture me. My head blows off when he dirty talks, when he has me envisioning how it could be.

I always thought I'd be relegated as watcher, not an active participant. With Jackson, someone we trust and love, Wynn's more than taking advantage of the situation, just like I knew he would. A goodbye to our life as roommates while testing future waters.

Sweating, gritting my teeth, Jack's round ass is curved perfectly to rub against my hard cock, and it's taking everything in me not to pop. Wynn's making sure I won't be sitting idly by, getting off on watching Wynn bloom into the magnificent slut I know he will become.

"That feel good?" Wynn groans– eyes on me, hands on Jackson. "Yeah?" Whose deep, sexy voice is coming out of my boyfriend's mouth, and who is he talking to? "You like that, huh? Don't you?"

I swear to God, Jackson whimpers, "Save me," underneath his breath, having never seen this side of his best friend before.

Blue gaze glazed with lust and power, lips kissed red from teeth digging in, body flushed with heat, towel forgotten with his cock jutting out like a promise, Wynn transforms before our very eyes.

Wynn stalked me, cornered me, and then took what he wanted on our first time together– the first time for each of us. Ever. If an innocent virgin is capable of that, imagine four years of nonstop practice... four years of doing everything in his power to get my dick in him. The only bargaining chip I have left is penetration, and I've done my damnedest to keep that part of me safe for sanity's sake. Once I give it up, Wynn will own every cell in my body.

"Is this what you want me to do with Uriah?" Wynn asks in an innocent voice as his head dips. Eyes bugging out of my skull, I watch in wonder as a pink tongue darts out to taste Jack's nipple. A wet line is dragged over the flesh, and then his mouth opens. Never taking his eyes from mine, Wynn sucks.

"Kill me!" I shout, hips jerking backward to get away from the little spoon grinding his ass into my cock. The towel comes with me, leaving Jackson completely naked as he writhes on the mattress.

Without shame, I break my transfixion on Wynn to look at what was revealed, knowing damned well the little shit's eyes are doing the same. Hard, rosy red flesh is curved to kiss just above Jack's belly button. He's not too big, nor too small, he's just right, and curved in a way that any bottom on the planet would go fucking nuts to have the dick deeply rooted in their ass.

"Too bad he's a bottom," Wynn and I say in unison, then we both snort.

Silently laughing, Wynn not only tortures me, he tortures his best friend while he's at it. "Jack?" Wynn coaxes. "About that blowjob..."

"Holy fuck!" Jack whisper-shouts, eyes bulging from his skull. He doesn't have to deny it, his hips are thrusting into the air like he's already mouth-fucking my boyfriend. At the same time, he keeps scooting back, like it's physically killing him not to feel me against his ass.

I'm going to hell...

I metaphorically yank the map out of Wynn's hands, because he'd navigate us to the point we'd both do something major we'd regret. Like our dicks impaling a begging bottom's ass. Scooting forward to curve my front along Jack's back, I throw our relationship into drive, and then slam my foot on the gas to make sure we go straight instead of veer off on an exit.

"Wynn's a pervert," I warn Jackson, voice husky because I'll never deny that I don't secretly love the fact. "This isn't because he wants to make up for the fact his brother aborted giving you head. No matter how it looks, us being foster brothers and all, we're not into incest." I pause, realizing I better backpedal because now I sound like the freak. "Um... Wynn may not have realized, but he's been trying to suck your dick for a good year now."

Wynn just laughs at Jack's mystified expression, and the poor kid mutters, "Why?"

When it comes to sex, Wynn and I are about as compatible as humanly possible. Every inch of our bodies is a playground to be explored, and all it takes is a look to be in total agreement. Neither of us is going to explain why Jackson appeals to us, or why while he's using us as a last hoorah, we're using him. Let's face it, it's a once in a lifetime opportunity to have a pair of horny boyfriends give you their undivided attention, even if it's playing into their sick and twisted roommate fantasies.

God, I've wanted this scenario since I was eighteen and Dan was fucking girls left and right in our dorm room. Wynn's giving me a gift, while taking the pleasure of his best friend's flesh at the same time.

This isn't a mistake, but it will be if I don't keep my pants on.

"I'm going to taste you now," Wynn breathes, eyes on mine, hand slowly skimming down Jackson's belly... and then his head lowers, back arching.

Leaning forward for a better view, it doesn't even register how my pajama-covered dick is pressing between Jack's ass cheeks. Torn, Jack thrusts backward to feel more of me, but then he thrusts forward, begging for Wynn's mouth. Caught in our spell, he rocks his hips back and forth, silently pleading.

I could lie and say this isn't a big deal as I watch Wynn's mouth open wide as he descends. Neither one of us has ever touched another, yet no jealousy sparks because we're in this together. We love Jackson, not in the romantic sense. Mutual respect and needs collide. Awed yet confused by my visceral reaction, I can't take my eyes away from the sight of Wynn's pink lips being stretched as the ruddy plum of Jack's cock disappears into his mouth.

Never looking from me, Wynn expresses every emotion, leaving himself open and raw– exposed. Lips rolling as they slide up and down, leaving a wet trail on Jack's rosy flesh, Wynn stares right into my soul.

Whimpering, sensations bombard me from all directions. So attuned to Wynn and Jack, I can almost sense what they're feeling. I know more than anyone the exquisite torture of Wynn's mouth on my cock. Not only does the man love his work, he takes great pride in it.

Fingers gripping, twisting in the fabric of my pajama pants, Jack anchors himself to me as he arches his back, mouth open on a silent moan. The more Wynn sucks, the more Jackson grips the pants, the more my pajamas slide down to leave my cock bare– bare against Jack's flesh.

Panic flashes in the depths of my eyes at the sensation of Jack's tight pucker gliding along my length. Moist from sweat or the damp of the shower, I can feel the difference between the chubby cheeks and the needy entrance. Wynn keeps me centered by maintaining eye-contact. Mouth still working Jack's flesh, Wynn's hand leaves the base of the cock to fish underneath the pillow beneath our heads. Then a bottle of lube is thrust into my hand.

Eyes wide, I take the bottle from Wynn's hand, panic turning to pure terror. The little shit smiles around Jack's cock, knowing exactly what I'm thinking, and our little buddy is so lost to the pleasure, he doesn't realize Wynn and I are fighting a battle with no winners and losers.

Lips popping off the cock with an audible sound, Wynn wipes his smug mouth with the back of his hand. "I know you're on the edge of losing control. So test yourself by rubbing your head on his pucker, then shove your fingers in there so your dick won't fit. Ass is on the table *after* we finally tap each other's– just not Jack's ass."

"Oh!" I exclaim in relief. "Thank fuck." I honestly thought Wynn wanted me to… I can't go there, because if my dick controlled my actions, I'd already *be* there.

Knowing I have no control left to test, I tug my pajamas back into place like an armor-plated cock-cage. Wynn's taunting laughter is smothered as his lips stretch tight around Jack's length. With a deep inhale, his nose is buried in light brown pubic hair.

Evidently never experiencing the insane pleasure of a deep-throat queen, Jackson jackknifes off the mattress, sucking in air to prepare for a scream.

Wynn pulls off the swollen dick, a string of precum or saliva hanging from his chin. "No coming," he warns, then his hand is tugging Jack's sack to help fight the battle. "I just showed you what I'm good at, now it's Kaden's turn."

Jackson's response is a whimper while his eyes roll back in his head. Wynn and I share the smuggest look imaginable.

Helpful as ever, Wynn grabs my wrist, forcing me to open my hand, then he squirts lube all over my fingertips, stealing some as he pulls away. "Draw it out, tease him. Then strum him so good his head blows off, and I'll be here to drink him down."

"Am I dead?" Jackson murmurs, clearly wondering if he's dreaming or has died and gone to heaven. A horny Wynn is a sight to behold.

Worried, I shift my hips backward, leaving my chest against Jack's back as a comfort to the both of us. Other than grabbing a blowjob when the opportunity presents itself, I have no idea what Jack has or hasn't done sexually. I know he jerks off in the middle of the night when he wakes to find Wynn and me going at it across the room. But other than that...

"Just relax," I croon. "I promise it won't hurt at all, barely even feel a stretch." I continue to reassure all three of us as my slick fingertips skim along Jack's crack. Dipping one fingertip in, I realize Jack's been playing with the shower toys too. Relieved yet amused, I go for broke with three fingers instead of a pinky.

Arching into me, Jack's mouth is open on a silent scream as my fingers impale the hottest of fires. Tight, slick, soft body sucking at mine, I groan with pleasure. "Wynn, you have no idea how good he feels." Tone deep, it's an invitation to join me since our little friend is more than capable of taking big cock, so our fingers won't cause even the mildest burning sensation.

Laughing at some joke only he can hear, Wynn crawls to kneel on the bed beside where Jackson and I are spooning. "Your pants are losing the fight." Laughing harder, blue eyes laser in on the fact that my dick is not only tenting my pants, it's saturating it.

"You're going to spurt a bit too when you get your fingers in him, Wynn," rolls off my tongue, knowing damned well Wynn is about to lose his shit. Jackson is a new playground we're exploring together, and it's the hottest thing we can share. Being alone with Wynn is transcendence, while taking another person together is an experience to last a lifetime.

One hand gripping Jack's ass, Wynn parts the cheeks to give us the view of my three fingers stretching Jack's pink flesh. Skin pulled tight, it's a beautiful sight as it gives with each thrust of my fingers.

Jackson grunts, wiggles, and accepts the burn as Wynn wedges his middle finger between two of mine, and then pushes in slowly. The combined heat is scorching my palm. A flush washes across Wynn's chest, up his neck, and across his cheeks. As soon as it reaches his hairline, his eyes flick up to meet mine.

"I want this," Wynn says without shame. "I want to be in Jackson's position." Finger sliding along mine, as a unit, we curl to meet the bundle of nerves inside Jack, both of us rubbing his prostate. "But I want it to be two dicks."

Panting, all I can do is stare gape-mouthed as Wynn takes over navigating. His finger guides mine, bringing Jackson so close to the edge, I fear one more stroke will have him blowing apart.

"You," Wynn stresses, eyes holding mine, going beyond dirty talk fantasy. He means to make it reality. For him. For me. For *us*. This is why I haven't allowed him to meet my friends— I said he wasn't ready, but it was me who wasn't. Now we both almost are. "Your dick will be inside me." It's a threat. It's a promise. It's a demand. It's the truth. "Your dick will be inside me, and so will Dan's."

"Wynn!" I shout, the perverted corner of my mind taking over, forcing me to come like it's happening in reality and not some twisted, fucking deviant fantasy. Body jerking uncontrollably, a hot wash spills inside my pajamas.

Wynn crawls over Jack's prone body, our fingers still deeply embedded in his flesh. Getting into my face, Wynn breathes promises across my lips. "You'll finally get to come with Dan." He kisses me to seal the vow. "Then I'm going to tear up his little princess of a husband's ass in front of both of you, and we're all going to like it."

Stunned, my eyes flick to meet Jack's, who is equally floored. We just look at each other as Wynn shifts on the bed. Mind registering, body drained, I'm nothing but a passenger as Wynn moves my fingers along with his, with his mouth drinking down all Jackson has to offer as the guy fractures apart.

CHAPTER NINETEEN
Kaden Marx

Dizzy, barely able to stand upright without lulling to the side, I feel high. Jackson has already cleaned up and redressed. Wynn and I left him sitting on his own bed with his geeky glasses on and some addictive time-wasting video game playing on his tablet.

Trapped in the only space that offers privacy, Wynn and I are hanging out in the bathroom. "You need to look in the mirror." Wynn sounds awed. "You look like you're tweeking."

Catching a brief glimpse of myself, I know exactly how strung-out I look without actually seeing my reflection. My skin is too tight, my cock is still hard, and there is a low hum buzzing through my veins.

"Are we okay?" I blurt out, terrified. "In one night, you've taken two shots, learned you have a half-brother..." I lean forward, whispering like my mind has been blown. Voice warbling, "We just *fucked* Jack."

"And it was fucking awesome!" Wynn– all or nothing Wynn. He utterly terrifies me because he is my addiction. "I know we probably shouldn't have, and we didn't *actually* fuck him." The deluded little shit has it in his head that it's not sex unless a dick enters a vagina or asshole. "We'll never touch him again like that, but it was *sooo* worth it."

"You're high," I point out.

"So are you," Wynn volleys back.

The juxtaposition between us is laughable. Wynn is shamelessly naked as the day he was born while I'm covered from neck to wrists to ankles in a pair of soiled pants and a long-sleeved shirt.

"You're hard." My eyes dart to Wynn's erection– the gorgeous promise is tucked tightly to his belly, all flushed pink and swollen for my pleasure. The furry sack is screaming for the warmth of my mouth.

Wynn reaches to turn on the taps in the shower, adjusting the spray to nice and warm. "So are you– even harder than I am, I suspect."

"Should we feel guilty?" I blurt out. "Do I owe you an apology?"

"I think–" Wynn struggles not to laugh, having to bite into his bottom lip. Blue eyes glazed with a combination of lust and amusement, I fall deeper into love with him by the second. "I'm the judgmental prick, but I'm also a Gillette. So… the only thing I feel right now is like celebrating. Like I want to high-five you or some shit because we're *that* awesome. I feel better than I did when we won the state championship senior year."

"I–"

Grinning at me, Wynn stops fighting his smug laughter. "You liked it?" It sounds like a question, but it's actually a statement.

"I did," I admit without hesitation. "*So much.*"

"No shit," Wynn turns snarky. "You've been pumping out a puddle of precum since we walked into the bathroom." My eyes dart to the ever-growing wet spot on the front of my shirt. "Stop overthinking it, Kaden, and just enjoy it."

"I'm terrified," spills from my lips as Wynn tugs my shirt over my head, and then attacks my pajama pants. Divested of my armor, I'm shoved into the shower. "Aren't you?"

"Of course I am." Naked skin on naked skin, getting damper by the second in the mist of the shower, Wynn pins me to the stall. "We almost killed ourselves, Kaden. We almost *died*. We almost didn't see today, or yesterday, and never would have seen tomorrow. Yes, I'm terrified, but it's feeding me– it's making me feel *alive*."

We move in tandem, grabbing each other, fists clenching hair as our lips meet. "I love you so fucking much," I growl into Wynn's mouth as my tongue sneaks inside the hot depths. "*So much.*"

Pulling away, Wynn pants against my shoulder. "Kaden?" His eyes roll upward to connect with mine. "As long as we do everything together –I don't mean just sexual either –as long as we do everything together and are completely honest with each other and ourselves, there is nothing that can ever sever this." He points to the fact that the only way for us to get any closer was if we could meld our bodies as one.

Kissing, stroking, washing, we reassure one another of our unbreakable connection. Wet, soapy bodies sliding in an erotic dance, I can sense the thread between us weaving tighter– stronger. I feel more connected to Wynn than I ever have.

"Wynn?" I suckle at his neck, tongue gliding down to curl around a hard, pebbled nipple. "Will you work yourself on a dong for me?" I have no idea why it's so important that he does, but it feels different. Usually I get off on watching him work himself, but I don't understand why my body demands he do it now.

"You have no goddamn idea how jealous my asshole was earlier." Voice husky, Wynn's hand leaves my hip to glide behind his back. "Jealous in a good way." Then he moans, all deep and needy, and my eyes roll back in my head. The little shit is fingering himself. "Which one?"

"Purple," I mutter without thought, for some reason calling out the biggest one.

"Yeah," Wynn gasps, heavy weight leaning into me, and I instinctively know he's spearing himself with all four fingers. In this, we are equals. True versatiles. If we could figure out how to be inside each other at the same time, both giving and receiving, we'd die and go to heaven.

Pulling away, Wynn leans out the shower stall to grab our toys from the plastic tote. Handing me his treasure, one purple suction cup dong, he's still rooting around in the box.

"I didn't get to come earlier," Wynn says conversationally, then chuckles when latex splats to the floor. Laughing at him for chucking our toys on the floor, I make a *tsk-tsk* sound in the back of my throat because now we're going to have to wash the whole lot of them. "When I finally do, I'm probably going to blow my brains out the tip of my dick."

Since he's bent over anyway... I drop to my knees, water pouring over my back, and part Wynn's cheeks. He makes a surprised squeak, but the slut wiggles his ass in invitation. I tongue my prize, rimming my favorite place on earth, and Wynn pretends he hasn't already found what he was looking for. We play pretend for a few minutes, until Wynn can barely stay on his feet and he's a heartbeat away from blowing all over the shower door.

Breathing laboriously, I retreat to my half of the large shower, terrified of what my body was urging me to do since I'd prepared Wynn so thoroughly for it. Wynn takes in my spooked expression and quirks a small smile in my direction, then he hands me a dong.

"We do it together," Wynn suggests, and all I can do is nod my head in total agreement. I've lost my voice for some reason I'd rather not explore. "Here." Brandishing a bottle of lube like Eve with the apple, Wynn pours a healthy amount into my palm.

While Wynn dampens the suction cup and slaps the dong onto the shower wall– giggles every dang time while batting at the latex dick like he's a playful kitten with a toy –I go about preparing myself.

Earlier, all I wanted to do was sink into the scorching hot depths of Jackson's ass. This is an urge I deny myself on a continual basis. Now, as two of my fingertips press inside, the burning stretch makes me feel even more light-headed– delirious. Experiencing the most primitive of pleasures, I want this more.

The constant push-pull of both wanting to fuck and be fucked, I lose the fight.

"Ready?" Wynn's on his side of the shower, three feet separating us so we don't unhinge and turn into animals. Watching every move I make, he knows I take a bit more time to get ready than he does, so he presses my dong to the shower wall for me, making sure it's stuck firm but doesn't do the giggle routine.

"Relax," Wynn breathes into my ear, knowing exactly what I need to hear and why I need to hear it. I've already schooled Jack on what he's going to have to do with Bren if he ever wants to switch it up. "Between partners, it all feels amazing, remember?"

Moaning, I move my fingers faster, stretching and relaxing my muscles. Royce's experience was not like this, no matter how terrified he is for us having to do it… I was taught it was a necessary evil of being gay that could be avoided through other means. Intellectually, I know all men have prostates, and it's not a gay, bi, or straight thing. If you're a top, it doesn't mean it won't feel just as amazing as if you were a bottom. Physiologically we are all built the same.

That prostate craves its bell rung.

I won't deny myself one of the greatest pleasures my playground of a body has to offer, no matter how much it terrifies me.

Sensing I'm ready, Wynn moves back to his side of the shower stall, backing up to his dong. With some maneuvering, he presses it inside. Enthralled, all I can do is watch as Wynn bends slightly at the waist, his ass pressing backward toward the shower wall, dong deeply rooted inside him. Thick and ruddy with arousal, Wynn's cock curves tightly to his body– a few beads of precum oozing out the tip. A dick he will refuse to touch for the duration of our fun.

We started this game before we even moved to Morgantown. Wynn and I would sneak over to my house and we'd test the limits of our bodies. Now we stave off our orgasms to build the pressure until it erupts on its own.

Eyes on mine, body rocking back and forth, Wynn moans softly, as quietly as he can possibly contain. When we're truly alone, he can rock the house on its foundation. A louder moan, body swaying, cock slapping at his belly…

"Don't come– promise me," I demand, unsure why I'm requesting it.

Eyelids shuttering the blue of his eyes, arching his neck, Wynn rests the back of his head against the shower stall. Swiveling his hips, he grunts a song of acquiescence.

"Ugh!" flows from between my clenched lips as I slip my fingers from my ass. Without thinking, so I can ignore Royce's indoctrination, I impale myself on the dong suction-cupped to the shower stall behind me. "Oh, God!" I groan in ecstasy, glorifying in the stretch and burn while owning who I truly am.

Seconds, hours, minutes… days– Wynn and I watch each other from across the shower stall, our bond deepening with every intimate interaction. Body sheened with lust, Wynn stares back at me, expression mirroring my thoughts.

"Turn around," I order out of nowhere, in a voice that's no longer my own. "Bend over, pull your cheeks apart, and show me you've stretched your pucker out enough."

Moving swiftly, because I've never asked him to do this before, Wynn is panting so loudly it's echoing around the bathroom. Bent over, ass less than a foot from my groin, he spreads himself in presentation.

Groaning at the sight, I have to pull free of the dong or else I'd risk coming. "Lube," I order, voice going deeper with every word. "I want to watch you finger-fuck your own asshole."

"Kaden," Wynn moans my name, getting off on how much I love watching his ass stretch tight around objects, how he'll clench tightly in a rhythm just before he comes. Fingers deeply impaled, lube leaving a thick coating, I lean forward as the spasms start.

"No coming," I warn again.

Huffing deeply, on the edge of hyperventilating, Wynn quickly yanks four fingers out, but he's not empty for more than a heartbeat.

The primal sound echoing around the room shocks me to my senses. Looking down, Wynn's ass is not only kissing my cock, it's gripping it to the root. "Oh, God!" I gasp in a panic, fingers biting into Wynn's hips to the point of bruising. Eyes flicking around maddeningly, I connect with Wynn looking at me over his shoulder.

A single tear slides from the corner of Wynn's right eye, but the stark relief replaces any panic I feel over its existence. Wynn looks at me like he's never seen me before, and then he speaks. "Thank you," he practically sobs. "*Thank you*, Kaden."

My control snaps.

Together, Wynn and I are horny but playful. We've been in every orifice of each other's body. Mouths and hands on a daily basis. We've fooled around, putting our heads together while we come, trying to see if we could force cum into the other's piss-hole. We've teased each other, tickling cockheads in ears, nostrils, belly buttons, and whispering across eyelids... but nothing could prepare me for the sensory assault of being *inside* Wynn.

The sight of his flesh stretched tight as I impale it will forever be burned into my mind as the hottest image ever. The intense feeling of his body gripping mine, exploding with tiny spasms as it clenches to draw me deeper. The sound— Wynn is sobbing *thank you* over and over again as I pound him so hard he's trying to find traction against the shower wall.

Slipping in the soapy residue and the spray from the shower, Wynn tries to hold onto his dong, hand wrapping tightly around the latex. The grip holds for three thrusts, each one more powerful and consuming than the last. When the suction breaks, we unhinge. Laughing so hard, we can barely stay connected, Wynn forgets we're in our apartment with a restaurant beneath and Jackson on the other side of the door.

Proof our neighbors will hear us back home in Rusty Knob, Wynn rattles the foundation with his grunts, moans, and screams for more.

"Please, don't fucking come," I beg, wrapping myself around Wynn's back as tightly as possible. We're on our hands and knees now, skating around the shower floor. My thrusts are short but deep, and I know he's close because his ass is kissing my dick like he French kisses my tongue, sucking it deeper and deeper. I don't think it's humanly possible to feel anything more pleasurable than this.

"Don't come," I warn over and over in between moans of my own, and then it's me letting loose a wild roar as I pour deeply inside of him.

Eyes slipping shut, I swear to God I pass the fuck out from the intensity. Wynn whimpers beneath me, mumbling how I didn't let him come... or maybe I'm just romanticizing the fact that he just called me a selfish bastard.

Pulling out slowly, I have a sick fascination with watching my dick slip free of Wynn's body– the way my jizz seeps out of his hole. He's red, so no doubt he'll be sore for a few days. I just hope my enthusiasm didn't hurt him too badly.

Slipping from beneath me, Wynn slides to rest his back against the shower wall, face twisted up in a pissed off scowl. His ass must not hurt too much since he's sitting on it.

"I love you," I breathe, meaning it more than I did just moments ago– ten times more than I meant it yesterday. Tonight's declaration will pale in comparison to tomorrow's.

I know he's pissed at me for not letting him come, but I kiss him anyway while slipping to sit in his lap. Anger forgotten, I amp up his urgency by sucking his tongue like I would his dick. When Wynn's so far gone he doesn't notice what I'm doing, I position myself over his weeping cock and slide down until my ass meets his pubes.

"Kaden!" Wynn howls, no doubt trying not to come just so he can enjoy a few thrusts inside of me. "Holy fuck, you're hot! My dick is on fire!"

Chuckling, I rest my forehead against the side of Wynn's neck, arms wrapping around his shoulders for leverage, then I rise and fall in a rhythm that has my eyes rolling back inside my head. I just came and my dick is flaccid, but the feeling of being filled by living flesh is a billion times better than the facsimiles we were using mere moments ago.

"Your dick is my new favorite toy," I pant against the side of Wynn's neck as he gets the hang of counter-thrusting upward. "And your ass. Both belong to me, but I'll share the wealth."

"Sorry!" Wynn tries to shout while laughing. "C O M I N G!" echoes around the bathroom to no doubt spread to the whole building.

Nothing prepared me for the sensation of Wynn spurting inside of me– nothing. The finality of it wrecks me to the point I fall lax in his arms like dead weight.

"You bastard," Wynn snarls, fisting the back of my hair. The band snaps, causing handfuls and handfuls of hair to fall into my face. In the damp of the shower, my hair tightens into dark ringlets. "You made me wait until I graduated! College!"

"I always said I would," I slur, finding a reserve of energy enough to release a taunting laugh. "You skipped the ceremony last week because, and I quote, you refused to stand up with your goddamn asshole classmates, but you graduated just the same."

"Ugh!" a sharp grunt is pulled from me, now that Wynn has a headful of hair at his disposal. "I won't apologize, Wynn."

Squeezing tighter, Wynn wrenches my head until we're eye-to-eye. "Marry me."

"What?" I gasp, shock and awe mixing in my veins. "What did you say?"

Blue eyes laser into mine, more serious than I've ever seen them. "I just asked you to be my husband, Kaden. Marry me."

"I thought I'd ask you," I grumble. "I had *stuff* planned."

Wynn just stares at me, unblinking. "There are no gender roles in our relationship. You should have been quicker on the draw, kinda like you did when your dick took matters into its own hands and got the job done because you were dragging your feet."

"Ha-ha," I mock laugh, blushing so goddamn red my skin feels like it's going up in flames. "I guess you caught that, didn't you?"

One bushy blond eyebrow rises, waiting patiently.

"Yes," I breathe. "I knew this day would come, Wynn. I've known it would since you were eleven years old and I felt like a pervert. Yes."

CHAPTER TWENTY
Brennan Kennedy

Unsure of what reception I'll receive, I stand outside of the guys' apartment for a few minutes, pacing in front of their door. I was waylaid when Cain came to us. The dude walked straight into Dad's party and introduced himself by his rightful name.

Lots of shit hit the fan, and it splattered far and wide. It will be a miracle if Dad will speak to me ten years from now. I could have lied and said I didn't know who Cain was, but he walked up to me and gave me a hug, crying like he hadn't taken his meds– I don't know if Cain takes meds, but you get the idea on how whacked he was acting. I couldn't deny anything when he was sobbing *I'm sorry for sucking off your boyfriend.* He really should have apologized for pissing on him first.

Now I'm scared of what Wynn will do to me, and whether or not Jack will blame me too. I pull up my big boy underwear and open the door. Real sheepish, I tread lightly, closing the door at my back. The apartment is practically empty, not that there was much in it to begin with. Usually when they needed something specific, they'd just borrow mine or do whatever needed to be done at my house– like their weekly laundry. Except Kade, who just bided his time until he went home to Rusty Knob for half the week.

Sucking in a deep breath, I notice nothing but Jack. I was afraid I'd find him torn up emotionally, but I never expected to find him like this. Sitting cross-legged on his bed, he's no doubt playing a puzzle game on his Kindle.

Glowing– the boy is glowing. Completely relaxed and content, wearing glasses when I didn't even know he wore them. His hair is damp and he's lounging around in worn-in sweats and a t-shirt.

Glowing but smug. "You got laid."

Startled, Jack's head rears back, knocking against the wall. Visibly shuddering, Jackson goes from radiant to guilty at the sound of my voice. His little mouth forms an O while hazel eyes widen in fright.

"My brothers fucked you." Not a question, but a statement. I want to be angry, because it's what normal people would feel. I want to be jealous, because that's also the way the world works. But Jack and I aren't together because I'm still married. *Married*. I made out with my wife earlier, with my hand down her pants– sure, it was to prove a point, but still.

In the near future, though... I will allow the anger and betrayal to bubble up, because trust and respect will be broken. Tonight, Jack and I had an agreement, which is how Cain stepped back into my life. It's still tonight, and I have no right to feel anything but relief that Jackson is healthy and whole.

"I'm not angry or jealous. If those two idiots could make you feel so good that you're relaxed and happy after what happened earlier, then I owe them each a big hug and a thank you."

Shoulders relaxing, Jackson flips the cover on his Kindle closed, then looks me straight in the eyes. "Semantics. I could say we didn't have sex, but orgasms were involved."

Stepping forward, "I'm sorry," flies out of my mouth. "What happened to you tonight was my fault."

"Don't." Jack's hand rises to stop me in my tracks. "I was with Cain tonight, Bren. More was said that wasn't on the video. I talked it through with Wynn, we eavesdropped in on your conversation with Kade, and then I eavesdropped on the conversation Wynn and Kaden had. So we don't need a rehash, because your family needs you more than I do."

"That's not true." *Fuck it!* A few strides take me across the apartment with my ass landing on Jack's mattress. I don't touch him, but I take comfort in his nearness. "How are you?"

"Confused." Eyebrows scrunching together, I watch in fascination as Jack pushes his glasses back up with a single fingertip.

Tapping the black plastic frame, "I like these– they're sexy on you." Jackson rolls his eyes, mutters how lame I am, but a blush stains his cheeks. "Why are you confused?"

"Sex versus love versus relationships." Jack flips his hands until his palms are facing up, then he moves them up and down like they're a scale weighing something. "I'm not saying this to be mushy, but everyone knows I'm in love with you, yet tonight I let a stranger blow me in a dirty bathroom stall, and look how well that turned out."

"That was *not* your fault," I bite out. "Any of it. Even if it had been someone other than Cain, and they did that to you as a gay bashing, it still wouldn't have been your fault. At all."

"You want the truth?" Jackson flings his glasses off, revealing tears glistening in his eyes, then he places them on his dresser. "I'm a jealous asshole."

"So am I," I admit. "No shame in that."

"Wynn and Kaden– I just don't understand them. What we did tonight…" Jack pauses, weighing whether or not I can handle it. "Wynn blew me while Kade fingered me," he quickly mumbles almost inaudibly, and I pretend it doesn't gut me. "They got off on it– like really, *really* got off on it."

"I think that's what sex is about, Jack." I tilt my head sideways, confused. "Did you not want them to enjoy it?" As upset as I am, I still wouldn't want any of them to have regrets.

"That's not what I mean," Jack bites out, frustrated. "They love each other, and the twisted shit they were saying… Kade's buddies from college, they're going to fuck 'em. I know damned well that train wreck is on the horizon. I think about how I would feel if you asked to bring another couple in, and I would *murder* them," Jack seethes, spittle flying from the corner of his mouth. "Then I would murder you."

Clearing my throat, I shift on the mattress to alleviate the kink in my dick as it stirs to life over this bloodthirsty side of Jackson Duncan. "I wouldn't ask, Jack. You know damn well that's not how I operate, seeing as how the last person I slept with was *you*– over four years ago."

"I'm a rat-bastard," Jack snarls, this time directed inward. "I was pissed about Jessica– so pissed. I could lie and say the blowjob scheme was because I wanted to assert my independence, or say goodbye to a carefree life, or some other horseshit that Wynn and Kade actually believe in and actually works for them, but that would be a bullshit lie. Because I only wanted the blowjob so I could hurt you."

"I know," I admit without hesitation. "Which is why I'm pretending it doesn't hurt. Intellectually, I get it. Emotionally, it's killing me. Okay?" I try to level my voice so my fury and resentment don't seep through. "Does that make you feel better?"

"It makes me feel *worse*," Jack cries out, so I reach for his hand, wrapping our fingers together. "I don't want to hurt you, but Cain was about hurting you, and that makes me sound psychotic. Kade and Wynn, I gotta be honest, you only flickered in and out of my thoughts during that, because that was about being with my best friend– just the once. Like I was some sacrificial lamb to introduce them into the life of sharing."

"Do you regret it?" I tread carefully, knowing how well the no judgment bullshit works between Kade and Wynn– they're so free with one another, that when one pisses off the other, they will freely say they hate how they're behaving.

I could never be that way, but I'll also never slut-shame Jackson. I have no right to dictate how he uses his own dick.

"Regrets?" Jack looks at me for a moment, then yanks me toward him until we're sitting side-by-side on the bed with our backs to the wall. "Cain? Yes. Wynn and Kade? Sorry, but that was probably the only time I'll ever experience that type of shit, and it was epic."

Growling, my head whips to the side with a feral glare, and Jackson has the balls to laugh at my reaction. "Was it really *that* good?" Jack's eyes glaze over and a blush washes over his cheeks in a rush. "Well, they are my brothers, and I taught them all that I know."

Jackson snickers, and we share a smile. "We both throw out how so-and-so is our best friend, but I gotta be honest with you, Jack. They *were* my best friends, and I'll always feel connected to them, but you *are* my best friend right now. So if you need whatever you need, I'ma step back and let you have it, because that's what a real friend would do."

"Gotta be honest with you, Brennan." Jack head-butts my shoulder. "If I find out anyone but your wife has touched you, I won't be held responsible for shooting them in the head."

"Bloodthirsty, Nurse Jackie, you so sexy," I tease, but I'm not joking. My cock is going nuts. "I don't share– I only said that shit because I felt obligated to say it so you'd think I was a good guy. If anyone but my brothers had touched you, and I met this guy in person, I don't know what I would have done. 'Kay?"

"Oh, we're on the same page." Jack nods his head rapidly, hair falling to cover his forehead. "Jesse has no idea how many times she was gracing Death's door."

"I'm pretty sure she already knows," I tease, snickering. "What the fuck?" Both of our heads turn to face the bathroom door as a deep moan rumbles from behind it. The moaning increases into a bellowed roar.

"Huh?" Jack leans forward. "That's Kade."

"Not cool," I snarl, hating how Jack knows what Kade sounds like in the throes of passion.

"I've lived with them for four years– those horny bastards get each other off like it's their day-job. But Kade is usually silent, and Wynn's the loudmouth."

"Wynn can get loud, all right." Reliving the moment, my head hitches back and peals of laughter spill forth. "First time Wynn fingered himself, he had his headphones on while watching The Try Guys, and Kade, Dad, and I could hear him all the way in the kitchen."

Jack and I share a look.

"Kade!" Wynn's shout rattles the windows. "Holy fuck, you're hot! My dick is on fire!"

"Gonorrhea?" I tease Jack. Expecting a laugh, a startled expression crosses his face instead.

The moaning increases, with Kade just as loud as Wynn for once. Unable to stop myself, I palm my crotch to stop the incessant throbbing. They may be my foster brothers, but my dick is only hearing the siren call of satisfied lovers. I'm not getting off on it; my body is appreciating it.

"Bren?" Jack whispers, eyes blown wide open. "I think they're fucking."

"No shit." I snort.

"No, Bren. I mean, I think they are *fucking* fucking."

We both stare at the door, like we can see through it and into the bathroom beyond. "You sure?"

"Sorry!" Fills the air, not only rattling the windows but hurting our eardrums. "C O M I N G!"

Groaning, hand clutching my package so hard I'll never have another kid, I close my eyes and begin thinking about gross things, like my brothers doing each other in the bathroom… that's not helping. I move along to the locker room at the club, with it filled with old, sweaty men with balls hanging down to their knees and hair in places it should never grow.

Relieved, my eyes crack open to see Jack in misery. There's a wet patch growing on the front of his sweats with his fingers clenching against his thighs.

I've been upset, angry, and it's time to reclaim my man.

"Jack?" I whisper as I lean into him. "What's wrong, buddy?"

Snarling, hazel eyes narrow into a glare. "I just got off with them an hour ago. My dick is somehow hooked up with them, thinking if they're having fun, it should too. Make it stop," he begs, staring down at his junk like it's a traitor. "They screw nonstop, and I can't live like this."

"Was it better with them than it was with me?" Shifting closer, I align the front of my body with the side of Jack's trembling one. "Hmm?"

"That's not– it wasn't even remotely the same," Jack stammers, every freckle on his face erased by a furious blush. "I didn't even touch them at all– it was my body but they were hooked up to each other. Hot in fantasy–"

"Hot in reality?" Chuckling into Jackson's ear, my fingers begin tugging up his t-shirt.

"It's one of those things you only do once to prove you're not a coward." Jack's gaze burns into my forearm as we both watch my fingers dip beneath the waistband of his sweats. "After the last two times, if you don't get me off this time, I'll murder you."

Husky laughter flows from my lips to Jack's ear. "Nurse Jackie, for a healer, you sure are bloodthirsty." Fingers curling around his hips, I tug him down the bed a bit, then I pull down the front of his pants to expose his cock. Swollen to the point he must be in pain, the flesh is more purple than I've ever seen it. "This will be the second worst blowjob of your life."

"Third," Jack says without hesitation, but his voice is thready with need. "Jessica was the worst. The second worst was the only time you gave head. It was the best blowjob because it was you, but one of the worst because you had no idea what you were doing."

"Need I remind you," I mutter with a teasing lilt as I descend. "This is only the second blowjob I've ever given, and you just had a master cocksucker polishing your knob?"

"Deep-throat queen, actually," Jackson tells me without shame. "But he's not you, so get to sucking. My balls are killing me."

"Greedy little bitch, aren't you?" My laughter dies as soon as Jack's cockhead passes my lips. Groaning at the taste I've dreamed about every night as I jerked off, my senses drown in euphoria.

"Not gonna last long," Jack pants loudly, ass wiggling around the mattress while his fingers attack my hair. "Too keyed up." Grunting, he jackknifes his hips forward, shoving his cock down my throat to the hilt. "Your mouth is so goddamn hot."

I thank my lucky stars that Jack's cock isn't as big as mine for two reasons. Right now, I'd be choking on it. Plus, I'm fond of the sensation of his flesh rubbing along the roof of my mouth and how easily I can take him. But also because of our failed attempt at me bottoming. I was terrified after what happened to Dad, and clenched up so tight I was hurting Jack's cock. If he had been bigger, I would have been harmed because neither of us knew what the hell we were doing.

Humming with pleasure, I quickly rock my mouth up and down Jack's flesh, sucking at his head with as much suction as I can muster before the down-stroke. My cock is having a conniption fit in my jeans, but I ignore him because this is about making Jack's cock know it's mine again. Judging by the way the little bastard's veins are throbbing against my tongue and the way precum is pouring down my throat, this isn't the third worst blowjob it's received, but probably not the best one either.

Body arching, fingers twisting in my hair, hips thrusting a spurting cock down my throat, Jack unhinges in near silence– the only sound is the harsh rasp as he grunts and spasms. Then he falls lax with his back to the wall, releasing a loud exhalation.

Suckling at the flesh in my mouth, enjoying the sensation as it turns flaccid, I stare at Jackson's flushed face. Satisfaction roils in my blood, because the guy is glowing ten times brighter than he had been when I walked in here. Pulling off his dick, the tip of my nose nuzzles at his furry balls, his spent cock, and along his thighs.

"You smell so good." My admission is more moan than spoken words. "I missed you so much– missed how connected to you I feel. Missed touching someone and knowing I made them feel good."

Two hands grip my hair, strands breaking, pulling me upright until I'm practically lying on top of Jackson. Then demanding lips are pressing on mine with a tongue breaching my mouth to taste the flavor riding my tongue.

"Best blowjob ever," Jack breathes into my mouth, sounding exhausted– the good kind of exhaustion.

Blushing, I'm flattered he's trying to make me happy. "You don't have to lie."

"I'm not," is gasped into my mouth. "I've wanted you so much, you could have literally blown on my dick and it would have been the best blowjob of my life." Jackson uses my hair against me again, and I decide we're going to have to have a talk about this violent side of the man. "Where exactly did you learn these skills in the past four years? No longer a sloppy mess, hmm?"

Laughing, I nuzzle against the side of Jack's neck. "Jealous?" Blushing harder, I squeeze the man beneath me who has gone frigid with anger. "Practice. Porn. Instructional books. A dong I'd suck off. Our first time was mind-blowing, but also fumbling. After all these years, where I knew you weren't being a saint, I didn't want to touch you and not have a fucking clue about what I was doing."

"I've only ever had sex with you." Jack's words ruffle the top of my hair. "So I have no comparisons beside the intensity of the orgasm. But other than your poor skills at giving head and mine at fucking you, you were fantastic."

"Bitch!" Teeth sinking in, I bite the side of Jack's neck in punishment.

"I wasn't being sarcastic, Bren." Fingers cup my skull and tug slightly, so I give him what he wants by looking him in the eyes. "Just you and me in bed, with you making love to me, nothing will ever compare with that."

Blushing from the compliment, "Well, I did have a lot of practice at putting my dick into holes." I say this to get a reaction out of Jack– face going blank, I know he's on the edge of violence. "But my favorite one was yours."

The bathroom door closing at my back and the way Jack's eyes widen has me sliding to sit next to Jack on the bed. Wynn's walking around buck-ass naked as usual, his sated cock flopping around with his balls as he walks. The dang thing looks huge versus when he's just running around naked like the world is his locker room.

I need to get off, because not once have I thought of Wynn's dick other than as a dick. Sure, I've always been curious to know how big it was hard, because if he's a grower, Kade's either a very lucky or very sore man. But never once did I think twice about if he was good in bed. He's not my actual brother, but the only thing I want for him is to be happy. Right now, he looks pretty dang smug.

"Are you going to get dressed?" Jack's voice is husky, raw. "There's naked, but then there's thoroughly debauched, and there is a difference."

Wynn turns to us, hands planted on his hips, dick swinging like a pendulum between his spread thighs. "What?"

It's hard not to see someone as a sexual being when he's six and a half feet of golden skin covering taut muscles with meat looking more like a promise than a threat. "He has got to fucking realize," I mutter to Jackson, who snorts in agreement.

Then, like the sun breaching the horizon, Wynn's smile spreads far and wide, showing most of his teeth. "Fuck!" Holding his side, he begins laughing hysterically. "Holy fucking fuckity fuck."

"How's your asshole?" Jack uses his best friend powers of deduction.

"Thrilled," is all Wynn says as he walks over to his dresser, dick still making an impressive showing even from behind. Jack and I breathe a sigh of relief that the idiot is finally going to get dressed.

"Powwow at home, so wear actual clothes," I warn when I see navy pajama pants in his hand. "Get Kade his usual armor."

"Kade needs to speak with you in the bathroom, Bren," Wynn says conversationally, like it's no big deal.

"Why?" I stalk over to the Wolverines butted up against the far wall by the door.

"Kade talks Royce down. You talk Kade down." Wynn shrugs as he tosses me Kade's armor. The guy dresses like his dad when he wants to be comforted. Jeans. T-shirt. Flannel. Wool socks. Steel-toed work boots.

It's almost June and eighty degrees tonight.

"Christ!" I hiss, stalking to the bathroom door, terrified of what I'm going to find on the other side.

CHAPTER TWENTY-ONE
Brennan Kennedy

Hands braced on the edge of the sink, knuckles white from the force, Kaden stares into the mirror like he's not looking at himself.

Kaden is Wynn's complete and total opposite when it comes to modesty. Wynn's not flaunting himself– he just doesn't see it as sexual at all. But with Kaden… I have little doubt that Jack didn't even get a glimpse of my brother's skin during their encounter. I don't think anyone but Wynn and a handful of doctors have ever seen Kaden naked. Yet here he stands, lost in the mirror, not even bothering to hide himself with a towel when he knows it's me and not Wynn in the bathroom with him.

Terrified, I place Kade's clothing on the closed toilet lid, taking his boxers with me as I approach him. "Hey," I murmur lightly as I crouch down. "Lift your foot up." First one, then the other is placed in the leg openings of his boxers, then I tug them up to his behind to give him the privacy I know he needs.

Sucking in a deep breath, I'm impressed. At least eight inches taller than me, everything on Kade looks huge from my vantage point. The musculature is in perfect balance with his height. If he wasn't my brother, I'd want to be his trainer.

"I see you have some new ink." I rest my palm on Kaden as I rise to my feet, right over the tattoo scrawled over the landscape of his back. "It's beautiful, as is your father's name. Darien."

Seeing Kaden like this, frozen and insecure, I have no idea how he could even contemplate having sex with anyone but Wynn. For Christ's sake, he made Wynn wait until tonight.

"They called him Dare," Kade murmurs, gazing into the reflection of his own eyes, like he's staring at his father instead. Lips curling, he surprises me. "But he wasn't very adventurous."

Turning to me, Kade rests his behind on the edge of the sink, ignoring the gasp that's torn from my chest. "I'm sure there are subtle differences, but I look exactly how I remember him– minus the hair." He snatches a band off the sink, then bends down to gather a mountain of curls to the crown of his head. "There," he murmurs as he bends back upright. "We look just alike now. My therapist said this should be a comfort, not a curse."

"It's true," I blurt out, eyes not moving from his torso. Blindly reaching out, I grab a washcloth. "Two?"

"One for you– one for Wynn," Kade answers without a lick of remorse in his tone.

"Why me?" I cry out, reaching to wipe the blood away so I can survey the damage. Evenly placed, one-inch tick marks mar each side of Kaden's torso, from his armpits to the bleeding marks trying to soak through the waistband of his boxers. "The left side is deeper than the right?"

"The left one is yours." Kaden sounds proud of that fact. The weirdo knows exactly what each tick mark means, when there are hundreds of them. "You don't need to ask why, because you already fucking know why."

"Goddamn you, Kaden," I snarl, tugging his boxers down so I can see what he's done to himself. I sigh in relief that he left his junk alone, but if he wants to bleed any more guilt, he's going to have to move on to his thighs. "You need help."

"I'm getting help." Batting my hand away, Kade tugs up his boxers, then reaches for a tube of ointment. "They'll be mostly healed by tomorrow– obviously I know what I'm doing."

"I don't doubt you know what you're doing, but I'm terrified over the fact that you're doing it in the first place." I hand him another piece of armor– jeans.

"I broke our trust." Kade won't look at me while he tugs his jeans over his big ass. Buttoning up, he still won't look at me, but I see why rolling down his cheeks. "I didn't know what to do, and I was letting Wynn navigate– we both know Jack is exactly what Wynn likes, which means he's also what I like…"

"Kade?" I try to stop him, but he won't shut up.

"I was terrified over what I wanted– I've held out for so long. My dick was out, and I didn't mean for it to be. I put it back, though, to keep Jack safe." Voice tremoring, tears are dripping off Kaden's chin. "I wanted it *so* bad."

"Hey!" Gripping Kade's neck, I have to physically move him to get him to look at me. This is why Wynn sent me in here, because when Kade gets like this, only I can get him to knock it off. "We're good. Fine. No harm, no foul."

Leaning forward, whispering like it's a scary secret, "My fingers were inside your– Jack. I just spent the last four years playing interference with Wynn to make sure no one but you got in there, then I'm the fucker who took that away from you."

"Jack and I aren't together– never have been. I have no say in what he does or doesn't do with his body. I respect that he never screwed anyone but me. I'm positive you're not the only fingers that have impaled his ass in the past four years since he's a total slut when it comes to that. We're good."

"I lost control," Kade breathes, yet again a secret that isn't a secret. I hand him his t-shirt as a comfort object. "Almost with Jack, but totally with Wynn. I probably hurt him."

Unbidden, a sharp bark of laughter spills from between my lips, and Kade glares at me. "Dude, our brother is out there with Jackson, no doubt celebrating and singing your praises. He's swaggering around, looking goddamn smug. You didn't hurt him– you made his lifetime."

"I ruined it, though." Locating his boots, Kaden tries to ignore my disbelief. "I have *stuff* planned– amazing stuff. I ruined it."

"What do you mean?" I crouch down to his level as he sits on the can to tie his shoes.

"Who loses their virginity in the shower by accident because their boyfriend loses control and shoves his dick in? That's not very romantic."

"Hella memorable, though," I mutter, voice filled with amusement. "Losing your virginity is not meant to be amazing. It is, but not because of that. It's awkward. When Jesse and I did it the first time, ha!" I bark a laugh. "Why don't you go ask Jack about my oral skills, or how after five thrusts he gave up and pulled out of me?"

"But when you were with Jack…" he trails off, making it a question.

"I'ma sound gross, so beware." I look at Kade, amazed how a guy six years older than me needs me to spell this out. "I knew what I was doing when I fucked Jack, not because I was some anal savant, but because my dick had been inside pussies hundreds of times, and the mechanics are *exactly* the same. Don't just shove it in. Make sure it's wet and willing and relaxed, and ease in. I knew I wasn't going to hurt Jack because I knew exactly what I was doing."

"I was blind with lust, so I don't even know if I did a good job or not," Kade cries out, hiding his head in his hands. "I'm pretty sure my body was in charge, because my mind was giving Wynn orders to make sure he was prepped. Wynn– it took him a bit to get the hang of it, but I was on top anyway and I'm a heavy bastard."

"Damn," I murmur in appreciation. "Five-stars for effort on that front, bro." Then I turn serious. "You can't know how to do it until you do it. Practice makes perfect and all that jazz. You're twenty-eight, and I lost my virginity at half your age. You waited too long, putting more and more pressure on it being perfect, and it was perfect because you finally dipped your dick. At least it was Wynn, and not some quick fuck in a bathroom stall. You wouldn't have almost stuck it to Jack if you'd been doing Wynn all along."

"You're probably right about that," Kade cedes, reaching to tug on his flannel.

"I know I am."

"But I had *stuff* planned," he practically whines, and it's off-putting.

"You have something major coming up, dickface," I taunt. "You and Wynn are oddly girly sometimes– don't hit me." I put my arm up to stave off an attack. Kade has beaten the piss out of me since Dad brought him home. "You're moving in together. So carry Wynn over the threshold, up to your bed, light some dumbass scented candles, and then make love to him like he's a virgin on your wedding night. Only it's better this way, because you both know how to do it. First time is for awkward fucking. Second time is for making love. 'Kay?"

"You're the best brother I ever had." Kade smiles at me, tears still lingering in his eyes. "So smart for your lack of education."

"Shut up, fucker!" My fist lashes out in a jab.

After punching Kade's chest, he grabs my hand and presses it to his heart. "I'm sorry."

"Don't be."

"You're hurting– I can feel it, even if you won't voice it."

Kaden's heart beats wildly underneath my palm, and I know this is important to him. I was the annoying little brother, and Dad was the overbearing father, all before Wynn came along. I know Dad and I aren't more important to Kaden than Wynn– we're tied with him.

"I am," I admit. "But it's not your fault. I'll deal."

"How?" Kade releases my hand, then begins buttoning up his flannel, which is a major sign he's upset.

"Jesse and I are finalizing a divorce. Once it's finished, Jack and I will have a talk about what we want. Then and only then, will anything he does with anyone else be any of my business. But since we respect each other, he's been open about it. I know he wanted to hurt me and why, and that's why I hurt. But at the same time, I know I've hurt him too, so it's fair. None of this had anything to do with you or Wynn... or even Cain."

"When you look at me, you'll see what I've done." Shame washes over Kaden's features, and it kills me to see it.

"Explain something to me," I mutter before I can stop myself. "When you thought of sharing Wynn, what exactly did you see?"

Blushing crimson, Kade turns shady and flicks his eyes away from mine. "Wynn and I see our bodies like a playground, and we just want to share our toys."

"Lame," I grumble, rolling my eyes. "Try again. Explain."

"I always had a thing for my roommate, everyone knows that. But I'm incapable of just letting anyone touch me. I've known Dan for a decade, Brennan. *A decade*. We talk at least five times a week, used to goof around online." He glares at me.

"No internet for you, buddy." My voice brooks no room for argument. "No way, no how."

"We've still been meeting twice a month, sometimes with and sometimes without Uriah. Dan's my friend and I trust him– no different than how I was able to touch Jack. Touching me..." he trails off.

"So you want to watch Wynn play with other people, and you just what? Sit there?" My mind is spinning wildly, having no idea how this insanity would ever work.

"No, not anymore." Kade looks at his hands while he makes a confession. "I found out tonight, probably something Wynn already knew, I'm going to want to join in– *some*. The way he bloomed... you have no idea how gorgeous and free Wynn looked tonight."

"And I never wanna know," I mutter quickly. "*Ever*."

"Wynn and I aren't talking about randomly fucking people, okay? Like a long-term arrangement with Dan and Uriah a few times a year. I'm going to have Wynn meet my friends and see where it goes. It's them or no one. I don't trust anybody else. I won't mind if Wynn goes balls to the wall with both Dan and Uriah, and I'd like to touch them both too. But I don't think I'll be able to let anyone else see me naked, or be inside me... maybe Dan if I'm horny enough, but Uriah is not getting near me, not even to suck my dick."

"Is he ugly, or something?"

Face stone-cold sober, Kade just shakes his head no. After taking a deep breath, he reaches over to the vanity to grab his cellphone. After a few moments, he thrust the device in my face.

"Dear God in Heaven–" my eyes bug out of my skull. "Good luck not pitching your modesty at the door when you're around this one."

"Dan and Uriah blocked Wynn on social media so he wouldn't see them until I was ready," Kaden admits, like this is normal behavior for your boyfriend to never speak to your friends in over five years of your relationship. *But* understandable once I've seen Uriah.

"Wynn's gonna wanna fuck this guy," I try to warn him.

"Yeah, I know." Smile flirting along his lips, I've never seen such an expression on Kade's face before. "I can't fucking wait to watch."

"Jesus Christ!" I rise to my feet in a hurry, ignoring the fact that Kade is getting turned on. "You guys are seriously warped."

"Are you honestly saying you wouldn't want a taste of him?" Kade wiggles his phone in my face.

"Don't ever let me meet your friends face-to-face, that's all I can say." Turning to the door, I threaten over my shoulder, "And don't ever let Jack see that Dan guy."

Laughing, looking lighter than he has in ages, Kaden smiles at me. "Why am I dressed like this at this hour? Wynn was supposedly getting me my pajamas."

"Powwow at Dad's," I reveal as I walk back into the main room, leaving the bathroom door wide open. I find Jackson and Wynn dishing it up like two old biddies. "Cain walked straight into Dad's barbeque tonight, and they're waiting for us in his office. Pretty sure Dad wants to disown me at this point."

"Shit!" Kade spits out with feeling.

"Yep, we're neck-deep in shit."

CHAPTER TWENTY-TWO
Brennan Kennedy

"What are you doing?" Jack whispers in my ear, as I press the other one to my parents' bedroom door.

"Shh… I'm listening." Straining, I can hear the voices streaming as Willa watches television in bed. "Okay." I break away, moving down one more door. "You stay out here."

"Where are you going?" Jack looks at me crosswise as I open Hayley's door.

"To check-in with my sister, but you stay out here– she's a grown woman now," I tease, winking as I disappear. Hayley's room is darkened by thick purple draperies, but soft light comes from Dad's ancient lava lamp. The globs cast a glow onto the ceiling. Everything is black and purple in the tween's bedroom, including the real mohawk sticking out above the covers.

Tugging the blanket back, I reveal a button nose and eyelashes casting half-moon shadows on pink cheeks. Satisfied my sister is dreaming happy thoughts, I leave her be.

"Aren't you going to–" Jack hitches his finger toward Hayden's bedroom as we pass Wynn's with mine as our destination.

"Nope."

"Why not?"

Smirking, I stop in my tracks, causing Jack to bump into me. "Hayden is a hybrid of both Kennedy and Gillette stock. Gillettes are horny, charming bastards –as you well know– and Kennedys reproduce just by being in the same room with someone they want."

"Huh?" Jack grunts, confused.

"If you were a girl, you would've started your period when you were sixteen," I tease, snorting as I get the words out. Eyes narrowed, chin jutting out, Jack glares at me in challenge. "I'm not going into any room that boy is in unless it's a communal room— even then, I'd be worried."

Face blank, Jack still isn't getting it.

"I was jerking off at his age."

"No way!" Jack's hands fly up as he shakes his head left and right in denial. "No way."

"Yes way. If I was a girl, I would've become a woman at age nine. Just saying… Not to let out info you don't need, but Hayley's a woman now, and her twin is definitely…"

"Definitely…?" Jack trails off.

"A Gillette-Kennedy hybrid." I turn to walk away, and say over my shoulder, "And that's all you need to know."

Creeping silently into my old bedroom, I find my wife curled protectively around our daughter, both softly snoring. Content. All is right with the world when you gaze upon your sleeping child.

Jesse and I had a real turn around tonight. After our fight, where we got it all out on the table, we came over here to find an impromptu barbeque. Jesse's always held herself apart from my family, and now that we're separating, she sees no matter what she'll always be one of us.

Penny's family and Corbin were all in attendance, and seeing how Dad put his issues aside for the sake of being a big community family, Jesse realized there was nothing she could do on this planet to take their love away.

Royce Kennedy is the epitome of unconditional.

Outside of when it was just her and I, I've never seen Jesse so open and receptive as she was with Penny's mom, Brenda, tonight. They hit it off, and it transferred over into her finally getting along with Willa. Nothing is ever going to have Jesse and Penny liking one another– they know each other's secrets after twelve years in hell known as Kentwood Area School District.

It's a good start.

Ignoring the glowering shadow at my back, I lean down to kiss both my girls on their pouty lips. Honor's curled fist knocks me in the side of the head, but she goes right back to sawing logs. Jesse opens one eye, lips curling into a smile, but she doesn't stir because she senses her adversary at my back.

"Go back to sleep," I barely whisper. "We were summoned by Dad about Cain."

"Is everything going to be okay?" Jesse asks both of us. I don't turn around, but I can feel Jackson wandering away somewhere.

"I don't actually know what's going on, but since everyone I know has been accounted for and in good spirits, I guess everything is going to be okay."

Jesse snorts, holding in her laughter, and I'm surprised the way her chest is rising and falling that it doesn't wake Honor.

Jackson rests his hand on my shoulder, so I step to the side. Ignoring my wife like she carries the plague, he lifts Honor's chubby arm and places a stuffed Nittany Lion beneath it.

Kade had given me that toy, calling me a baby for crying when he went to Penn State. He returned home with the stuffed animal, saying babies needed toys. He was just being a dick, because when he left to go back after the weekend was over, he was misty-eyed too.

Jackson leans down to kiss my daughter, and Jesse has the good sense to move her head as far away as humanly possible. "Sleep well, baby," he murmurs softly, pulling away. Then he surprises the piss out of me. "You too, Jessica."

"Night, Jack." Jesse looks at me, startled beyond belief.

In the hallway with the door shut to our backs, I turn to Jackson with a smirk. "Warming up to her, ain'tcha?"

"Nope." Jack blushes so bright his freckles disappear. "Don't know what you're talking about."

"Someday you'll see Jesse's charms." Wrapping our fingers together, I tug Jack down the hallway toward the staircase.

"I highly doubt that, Bren," he mutters dryly. "Jessica's charms seem to be of the origin to persuade men and women alike, and I don't do women. But, ya never know. Someday we might get along."

"Good." I sigh in relief, releasing his hand to walk down ahead of him.

"Around the time Honor is made a grandmother, I suspect." Jack's laughter has me smirking. "Or maybe I'll hold this grudge until well after I hit the grave."

"Jack?" I caution, not ready to go there just yet. But I know if Jack doesn't get along with Jesse, this will never work. I can't have Honor noticing this resentment, or hearing her mother bad-mouthed.

"Brennan?" Jack tugs me back once my feet hit the living room floor. Standing two steps above me, he leans over my back and nuzzles the side of my face. "I'm just teasing you– I'm trying. I'll behave." Kissing me softly on the side of my mouth, he whispers, "Promise."

Swiftly turning to the side, I steal a kiss, then lope away toward Dad's office.

"Are you sure I'm invited?" Jack suddenly turns insecure of his place in this family. "I'll go hang out in Kade and Wynn's old room."

Reaching for his hand, "C'mon, Jackass," I tug him into the silent standoff between the Kennedys and Gillettes.

Dad glowers at me from behind his desk, lines of betrayal giving him premature wrinkles on his forehead. To cut this shit off at the pass, I drop Jack's hand and stride across the room, avoiding everyone else.

Dad's face turns to watch my movements– at least he doesn't look away in bitter disappointment when I stand to the right of his chair. Leaning down, I rest my forehead against his, and then whisper, "I love you."

Without checking to see if Dad's expression changes, I make my way back to where Jack is leaning against the wall, knowing Dad probably has a dopey expression on his face. Manipulative of me? Sure, but ya gotta do what ya gotta do.

Now that Dad isn't shooting lasers of disappointment my way, I check out what's going on. Jack and I are leaning against the wall near the door. Dad's in his chair because no one else is allowed to sit in it– ever. Corbin's sitting in one of the two other chairs, but he's pulled it off to the side so he doesn't look like a kid being scolded by the principal. Kade's big ass is filling the other seat, with Wynn not giving a shit that he looks like an idiot for sitting on Kade's lap. Just guessing, Wynn's upset and refusing to acknowledge it. Warren's pacing like a caged animal.

The office isn't huge by any stretch of the imagination, but bigger than most. It was meant to be the mother-in-law suite, situated on the first floor for ease, directly off the dining room. The structure was designed after a giant farmhouse with wraparound porch and the needs of the era. The walk-in closet was converted to the file room, and the small bathroom is Dad's– only Dad's. He practically lives in here.

So, with all of us crowded around the desk in a small space, where the fuck is the guest of honor?

Glancing over, I notice Jack's eyes are trained in the same direction as everyone's but mine and Dad's, because Dad is staring at me like he's never seen me before. Following their gaze, I spot a huddled up form hiding in the back corner near the bookcase, with his back to the wall and his mop of hair covering his face. Cain's fraying a hole in the knee of his jeans, rocking a little bit.

"What's going on?" I mutter, and Cain's head snaps up at the sound of my voice, revealing a face that's all Gillette. Judging by the gasp coming out of Wynn's mouth, this is the first time Cain has shown his face tonight.

No DNA test required.

Sun-kissed, flawless skin, bright blue eyes, a button nose giving off false innocence, with a masculine jaw sharp enough to cut, and dimples bracketing plump lips– the face of an angel doing the Devil's bidding.

Every Gillette looks like that, just varying shades of each feature, with my baby brother and sister given the genetic lottery win of great beauty. The only difference is body shape. Wynn is tall with lean muscles, while Warren and Corbin are short and stocky, built to work hard, manual labor and beat the shit out of you.

Cain is almost feminine in stature– where we say Wynn and Kade are fragile emotionally and mentally, this guy is fragile in every way except for the rage burning from his eyes.

"We haven't gotten very far," Dad replies, face scrunched up and all pissed off. "Corbin and I had a long talk while we waited for you, but Cain said he wouldn't talk until you were here. Why is that, son?" is an accusation.

Fuck if I know wants to roll off my tongue, but it seems disrespectful. "I met Cain when you and Willa were in the hospital– I met your sister too. Until tonight, I haven't seen him in person again. I just knew who he was," I admit. "And why it was important to keep that a secret. We've kept in touch some over the years."

"Yer daddy said I thiefed his son away from him, and I told him it was only fair 'cuz he took mine." Corbin's diction shifts, when he's worked so hard to overcome it.

Knowing he's upset because he does care a great deal about what my dad thinks of him, I try to soothe his nerves so he can talk straight. "It's okay, Corbin."

"Don't do that!" Dad barks. "You know I hate how you two always side against me."

"Royce," is an interjection from Kaden, just as I bite out, "Dad!"

I count to ten, then twenty, because Dad's issues with Corbin are far and wide, but are seated with Uncle Donny– Dad wanted all of Uncle Donny's attention, not realizing Corbin wanted to befriend Dad too, not take his only brother away. Since then, there was Willa, then Wynn, but Dad seems to forget Corbin saved his ass– literally.

"Remember what I said to you when I entered your office?" I remind Dad, and he nods his head slightly. "Good– behave."

If Gillettes are gorgeous, Kennedys are jealous. Fact of life.

Feet stilling, Warren directs to Cain, "How old are you? You look like a goddamn baby."

"Twenty-four," Corbin answers, with Cain whispering it in his barely audible, raspy voice.

"What?" Warren snarls, stomping to stand before his daddy. "You've got to be fucking kidding me. I've worked my ass off to get you cleaned up, to get you educated, and this is how you repay me!" Shouting, he points at Cain like he's a dirty mutt.

Wynn slides off Kaden's lap, and then wedges himself between his brother and father. "He can't answer if you don't let him." Walking backward with his hands on Warren's chest, Wynn separates them.

"I'm sorry," is all Corbin mutters in reply, staring at two of his sons while the third stares at me for some reason.

"Cain, why are you staring at me?" My question has the guy shaking his head in a practiced move to shield his face with his hair.

"You look like Octavia, and it's creeping me out," barely projects across the room. "But it's comforting me. Plus, I'm pretty sure you could damage anyone who tried to hurt me. Sorry. I'll stop. It's just– that's what I was taught. Find the person who will protect you and stick with 'em."

"Jesus!" Warren cries out, striding across the floor to land ass-first next to Cain. "No matter how pissed we are, no one in this room will hurt you."

Cain eyes his daddy with an intense look of longing and confusion. "Corbin has always protected me the best he could– Tavia too. But sometimes that's not possible."

"Start from the beginning– now." Dad orders Corbin, losing his patience. "Facts, not bullshit to cover up the facts so you look like a goddamn superhero."

"Fine," Corbin mutters, glaring at Dad head-on. "Yer daddy knocked up Birdie Probst, then they moved away, and we all thought that was the end of that– You were just a kid, but Donny knew," Corbin spits out like a challenge. "Over a decade later, Birdie comes back to town, but yer daddy didn't want nothing ta do with her."

"Calm down and talk like a civilized person." Dad sighs like Corbin's exhausting him.

Wynn's hand lands on Corbin's shoulder out of nowhere. "Don't," he warns. "Royce, don't antagonize him. You know damn well he'll get defensive and start rattling off about how you think your shit don't stink."

From the corner, Warren's snort ricochets around the room.

"Birdie came to me and Donny, saying how her husband was being rough with his boys, and how the boys were almost grown men. Saying how Probst was calling her a whore, and how her daughter was born a whore because of it. Birdie was worried because the boys were getting violent and her husband was taking an interest in Octavia– she was twelve or thirteen at the time. So Donny ran off to Donald with his tail between his legs, and Donald came to me knowing he and his sons were cowards."

Wynn's face whips back and forth like he's watching a tennis match, hand hovering into space, like he doesn't know if he should hold Corbin down, or run as quickly as possible to keep Dad in his chair. It'd be laughable if we weren't all holding our breath.

I don't give two shits about ancient history with my kin– no grudge-holding. Dad and Corbin?

Lord, help us all.

"This is where you become a superhero, isn't it? You want us to pat you on the back for killing a man who had a wife and children?" Dad doesn't rise to the bait, but his words cut deeper. "You're just an uneducated hillbilly who was paid to kill a man with my dad's sloppy seconds."

"Holy. Fuck. Royce." Kade breathes the words, laughing not out of amusement but shock. "Don't say that shit in front of the kid."

"Probst was a goddamn pig," Corbin spits across the desk. "I mean that in all ways."

"He was a cop?" Jack's head jerks back, knocking into the wall. "Fuck."

"Birdie tried no less than fifty times to get him arrested, but his *brothers* wouldn't do it. They'd tell her to be a better wife, and raise better children, while she was hospitalized with broken bones and bruised organs. I want no pats on the back, but I sure as fuck wouldn't allow that man to change his sons into bigger monsters, while sneaking into your sister's bed. I want no thank yous, but I sure as shit don't want you insulting my son's mother to his face."

"And your son was what?" Utterly floored, Dad's tone is beyond incredulous. "A thank you gift?"

"You've never killed a man, you coward," Corbin snarls. "Think back, goddamn you. I wasn't always a drunk. When we were kids, you liked me– you would follow me around and mimic me. When I first married Cora, you didn't want to leave my house when Donny was ready to go. The night I took out a monster, was the night I started drinking."

"So you're blaming us for your alcoholism and how you abused Wynn his whole life? And how you allowed Cora to bitch at and hit your children– *my* children? Explain that away, superhero."

"Awake or asleep, I felt Probst's life draining away, so I drank, and drinking made me ornery. The worse I acted, the worse Cora got. The worse Cora got, the worse I acted. It was a vicious cycle. Cain was made about six months later. Birdie came to tell me about how Damon was starting to act like his daddy, and in grief and shame and guilt, we screwed– that's how Cain was made.

"But Probst was a crooked pig, and his sons were following in his footsteps. Damon and Sean took to a life of crime, to being violent with their mother and nasty with their sister. They were using my son as bait, luring in predators and blackmailing them. Then they found Donny after the settlement came through– their *friends* wanted a bigger pay off instead of two-bit con jobs."

"So we were just a job to them?" Dad mutters, face etched with rage, fingers turning to claws at the edge of his desk.

"No, they believed Octavia deserved all of Donald's settlement, but they didn't plan on giving her a cent she didn't *earn.*"

Dad looks away, the first signs of shame crossing his expression. "Someone should have told me."

"What were you gonna do, Roy?" Corbin snorts, sounding exactly like Warren and Wynn. "You had three kids and my daughter to think about, and you were sniffing around my son, wanting him as your own. So I left you to do just that. Besides– I took care of Sean."

"Wish you were quicker," Dad grunts.

"Yeah, call me a murderer, then insult me for not murdering quick enough, hypocrite. You can't have it both ways, goddamn you."

Resting his head on the back of his chair, Dad rolls his neck until he's facing Corbin. "I'm never going to thank you."

"I know, and I don't want it."

"Bullshit," Dad coughs. "Why is Damon in prison? Why is my brother still in prison? Where did Donny's money go? Where is my sister, and why did Cain show up tonight?"

Knowing none of us have any patience for Corbin's diction when he's upset, I answer instead. "Damon's in prison for a long list of crimes, but mostly the FBI is hoping he'll eventually rat out his *friends.* Uncle Donny's in prison to protect him from said friends who are blaming him instead of Corbin for pulling the trigger on Sean. Corbin and I gave whatever I could find of Donny's money to

Octavia and Cain at the hospital, so they could start a life away from the assholes who had terrorized them."

Dad, yet again, he's looking at me like he doesn't recognize his own son. But he's no longer disappointed. I just have no idea what he is.

"I could have helped my sister." Dad won't look at me. "I could have known her– I would have helped the boy."

"Our families had done enough to theirs, Dad," I answer why Corbin and I did what we did. "Obviously we'd be the first place those assholes would look for them. They were safer away from us than with us– same reason the twins were left in Gillette Holler."

"Why did you show up tonight?" Warren's voice is gentle and coaxing as he speaks to Cain.

Voice barely audible, Cain's whispered words impact like a shotgun blast. "Tavia is missing."

Leaning back in his chair, Dad scrubs his palms across his face. "Details. Please, son."

Cain pauses, thinking Dad's speaking to me, not realizing men in Rusty Knob use the endearment on everyone's sons. I tilt my head slightly to encourage him before Dad loses his patience.

"Octavia's raised me basically my whole life. Mom took off when Damon got bad– we assumed she was killed by him and Sean. Probably an accident." We all lean forward, barely able to hear Cain's raspy voice.

"Tavia was left alone for the most part, because my brothers wanted her to get an education– accounting." Cain snorts, but doesn't elaborate. "I wasn't so lucky– I won't speak their name, fearing it will call them down on us. But they liked to use me because at first I looked older than I was, until I reached that age. Then I started looking younger than I was– not explaining what I mean by that either. After everything blew up on us, the FBI came knocking, wanting me to rat my brothers out. I wanted to, but all of their crimes connected to those I knew to keep my mouth shut about.

"So we just went about our business like death wasn't knocking at our door. Back in Virginia, Tavia's been working for an old-time doctor, with a tiny office in a town not much different than this one. Um... maybe more stable, less poverty. Anyway, Tavia is Dr. Stuart's assistant and bookkeeper. I work part-time at the library shelving books and part-time at the local nursery tending plants. Nothing major. Quiet– peaceful.

"I came home from work this afternoon and Tavia was gone, but her purse, phone, and all of her clothes were still accounted for. The window in the back door had been busted, probably so they could reach the deadbolt. I... I–um... I drove straight here, but I saw you guys going into Adam & Steve's, and I wasn't in my right head at the time– yeah..." he trails off.

Dad leans forward, chair squeaking. "What's Adam & Steve's? And what happened there?"

"Nothing!" comes from every direction in the office, including mine and Jack's.

"Oh, there's a story behind that," Warren murmurs, shit-eating grin plastered across his face. Then he's joining Corbin in a sex-fueled laugh that has me shivering. "Royce? That's a gay bar our boy loves to frequent when his room-date comes to visit all the way from Pittsburgh."

"Room-date? Really?" Kade sputters, blushing. "So very punny."

"Enough!" Dad barks, looking disappointed in us. "Corbin, take your boy into my bathroom and have a talk with him– I doubt he's going to tell us any info we need to know."

Eyes narrowed, Corbin doesn't like being told what to do, especially by Dad, but he does it anyway because it's a good idea. Walking across the office, father stares down at son, and their resemblance has us all doing double-takes.

"You'll tell me," Corbin orders. "You'll tell me and I'll bring yer sister home. If ya don't, we ain't gonna see her again. You git that, right?"

"Yes, sir." Cain accepts the hand up and crawls to his feet. "I'm sick of running, hiding, looking over my shoulder."

"I'll do my best." Corbin sighs, making his way around the desk, giving Dad a wide berth.

"What are we going to do?" Wynn demands the instant the door to the bathroom clicks shut.

Nearly running over top of him, Dad blurts out, "What happened at that bar tonight?"

"What are we gonna do?" Kade parrots Wynn's words to change the subject.

"Well," Dad sighs, easily distracted as usual. Jack smothers a chuckle behind a fake cough. "I wish I knew my sister– had known her all her life. But I don't. She knows Corbin. I have obligations here." Dad points at the ceiling at his bedroom directly overhead. "I've got a pregnant woman and a pair of kids who are almost twelve to think of first. Lord knows, Corbin is capable of anything, and I'm not killing anyone when they could just be put in jail."

"Ya gotta stop judging my daddy," Warren warns. "I can't take the divide no more. I get along with you now, better than I do Kade most days. But I can't be tugged back and forth, neither can Wynn and Willa, or your kids with their papaw."

"We've been working on it," Dad mutters sheepishly. We all know dang well Dad loves Corbin like a brother, but he'll never admit it out loud. His pride gets bent. "Shit like tonight rubs me wrong. I lost Donny to this shit, and I managed to lose a sister I never had. Meanwhile, my son has been lying to me for the last half of his life."

"Dad." Inhaling, I take in a big gulp of air and expel the truth. "You were in the hospital– *broken*. Octavia looks like us, but she looks like Sean too. I didn't want you having to look at your sister and see the man who terrorized you, and I didn't want Octavia to look at us and see the reason why her brothers terrorized her."

"I wouldn't have cared." Dad stares right at me, blaming me, and it kills something vital deep inside me.

"Corbin asked Octavia what she wanted. After everything that happened, it was her right to get to finally choose. You had months of rehabilitation ahead of you. Willa was damn near catatonic. Kade almost dropped out of school to take care of me. The twins were being shuffled back and forth between here and Gillette Holler. You had a business to run, a town to support, and me and the twins to raise. Octavia was a grown woman, and she made the decision."

Refusing to look at me, Dad has me snapping. "Instead of blaming me for being loyal, for keeping my word, blame the criminals that Probst motherfucker got into bed with. I was a kid– yeah, I'm gonna pull out this card. I'm only twenty-two now. A husband and a father, with a circus for a family. What's going on in your sister's life wasn't on my radar. I've got my own sister to worry about– my own daughter."

"Let's just calm down, okay?" Kade turns into the mediator. Standing from his seat with his hands out, he abruptly yanks Wynn to the empty chair because his pacing was driving us nuts. "I get why everyone is upset. But we're forgetting the bigger picture through the trees. A woman is missing. That Cain kid has been through enough, and we can't be bickering and talking down about his daddy, momma, brothers, and sister. Have some compassion."

"After what he did tonight," Wynn snarls. "He ain't no better than the rest of his kin."

"No." Kade palms Wynn's forehead, causing his head to snap back. "Don't you start shit too –we got enough trouble with the dads of the group going postal."

"What did Cain do?" Dad's like a dog with a bone. "What happened at that bar?"

Jackson sinks against the wall, trying to disappear behind me.

"Uh…" Kade and I stare at each other, with Jack slowly sliding behind me until I block him from Dad's view.

"I wanted to have a drink," Wynn lies. *Wynn lies?* "Kade was always going to Adam & Steve's with Dan, and I wanted to go too. We were chatting with the bartender, having a few drinks, getting ready to play pool when a guy walked in– Cain. Jack and Cain shot some pool, while Kade and I played at another table."

"You should see your face right now," Warren mutters, trying his damnedest not to smirk. "You told mostly the truth, but when you lie your face goes as white as a sheet and you hold your eyes wide open. You never blinked. What part of that story is a lie, Wynn?"

"I-I-I–" stammering fills the room as Cain walks back in with Corbin at his back. "I was nasty to Jack, and I feel sick about what I did." Just like his daddy, Cain gives Dad an even wider birth, almost skimming the wall. "I've had it happen to me a lot– sorry!"

"I don't know what you did, or what happened to you…" Warren hooks his arm around Cain's shoulders, squeezing the guy to his side. "But the look on your face says it all."

We all look at Cain. None of us blinking. He's a few inches taller than Warren, but so dang fragile I can't even muster up an ounce of outrage, especially knowing it had happened to him too. I'd been right when I told Kade that.

"Cain's staying here," Corbin announces, moving toward the door. "No one knows what I look like, and the kid would stick out like a sore thumb. Can't have him going home and being a sitting duck. After I say goodbye to my daughter, I'ma go find Octavia, and I won't be back until I do."

"Where's he staying?" Pointing at Cain, Wynn is a wicked grudge-holder. But he'll eventually soften– I hope.

Dad moves to volunteer, because that's the type of guy he is, but Warren beats him to the punch. "With me. Ginger's crib is in our room, and we haven't fixed up Wynn's old room for her yet. Seems poetic to have Cain sleeping on Wynn's cot, doesn't it?"

Blue eyes narrowed, "Eh–" Wynn doesn't seem to think so. He's acting more like a Kennedy right now than a Gillette. Jealous, wanting his big brother all to himself.

Warren's of the opinion that there's more than enough of him to go around. "Say goodbye to me, Daddy." Releasing Cain, Warren crosses the room to give Corbin a back-slapping hug. "Think you'll be back before the baby's born?"

"Hope so," Corbin mutters, eyes lingering on my dad as he gives Warren a final pat on the back. "C'mere, son." Wynn and Cain both freeze, not knowing who he's referring to– both estranged.

Deciding for them, Corbin rubs a heavy palm over Cain's head, mussing up his hair so we all can see the guy's face, then he makes a beeline to Wynn. "Hate me or not, but there ain't no guarantees I'll be coming back– give yer old man a hug."

"Don't drink," Wynn demands, accepting the hug readily. Burying his face against his father's neck, no one but Corbin can hear what Wynn's saying.

Dad looks away, tears of jealousy, agony, or hope– Lord knows when it comes to those two.

"Don't you start drinking," Corbin warns as he pulls away.

"I promise," Wynn whispers shyly, surreptitiously wiping at his eyes.

"Me too," Corbin mutters as he weaves his way around everyone. When he gets to the door, he pats Jack on the shoulder, and then gives me a half-hug.

With a wave, Corbin walks through the door and out into the dining room. "I'll be back," flows back into the room.

"Did he just make a joke?" Mouth hanging open, Kade looks floored. "Asshat didn't say goodbye to me."

I start counting in my head, getting up to ten before Dad's slowly rising from his seat. "Gotta take a piss," he lies, going in the opposite direction of his bathroom.

As soon as Dad's outta ear shot, Cain expresses his fears. "That guy– your dad, he isn't going to get in a fight with mine, is he?"

Laughter rumbles from all of us, with Warren admitting the truth. "I suspect Royce is gonna go steal a hug too."

"Oh," Cain breathes, not getting it. "Are you sure?"

"Yup." I break away from the wall. "Dad's too prideful to do it in front of us. But he secretly loves Corbin, even if he'd also like to kick him in the nuts."

Laughing, Kade and I fight over who's going to sit in Dad's chair, with Wynn dumping us out of it and taking the prize. Hands on the blotter, pretending he's Royce Kennedy, with his face glowing, Wynn says to Cain, "Welcome to the menagerie."

We all pretend not to notice Cain edging his way over to Jack until they're heads are bent close. Kaden, Wynn, and I try to not listen into their intense whispering, but Warren's a gossip whore.

"You what?" Warren shouts. The guys and I share a look, not sure if he heard about Jack getting head or being treated like a urinal. "Alright, I was gonna warn ya off Penny's sisters. Guess that ain't gonna be an issue, is it?"

Head, it is.

"How many sisters does your wife have?" Cain ignores Warren's question.

"Four," we all say in unison, some of us louder than others. Four boy-crazy, clingy Penny clones. So glad Penny grew up when she had kids, because that means there's hope for those girls.

"I don't really like being around a lot of people at one time." Cain visibly shudders, hair sliding to cover his face.

"Ha!" Warren pats him on the back. Hard. "Good luck with that. When you're at home, you can hide out in your room if ya want. I'll take ya to work with me. You said you like quiet?"

"Please," the guy nearly begs. "Do you have a library or a nursery? I have references. I don't want to be near people– at all. Plants and books don't talk."

"Just me and Penny's father and brother at work. Garret and I gab nonstop, so you can spend your time not talking to Jeb." Wrapping an arm around a younger, taller yet smaller version of himself, Warren walks Cain to the door. "C'mon, let's get ya home. You bring any of your shit with ya?"

"Yeah, it's in my car." Cain looks at me and the guys, both asking if he's going to be okay and begging us to get Warren off of him. They slip out the door, and out of sight.

"When an introvert and extrovert collide." Kade's eyes are held impossibly wide. "Imagine that kid hanging around with Warren, Penny, Garett and Brenda, and the Franklin sisters. All in one kitchen with a toddler and a crying infant, with Jeb rocking back and forth in the corner like a PTSD survivor."

"Jesus." Wynn's voice warbles, when a few minutes ago he was furious with Cain. "Maybe we should've offered to help."

"We have too much shit going on right now," Kade stops Wynn's incessant need to help. Yet another trait that's more my family tree than his. "Cain can hang with Jeb and Copper and just chill."

"Copper's chill," we all murmur in unison, then bust out laughing.

"We're idiots." Jack breaks away from the wall. "I suggest we go find Royce– make sure he's not bleeding out somewhere for insulting Rusty Knob's resident drunkard assassin."

We find Dad sitting in Willa's rocking chair, staring at the driveway with tears glistening in his eyes because he's going to miss his buddy– erm, I mean his nemesis. No doubt he wanted to go on the adventure too, and he's finally wishing his roots didn't run so deep in Rusty Knob.

LET IT OUT
Kaden Marx

Walking out to our cars, we don't get two feet off the porch before I cave. Feet slapping as I jog back up the steps, I lean down and engulf Royce into a hug. Strong arms enfold around me in less than a heartbeat, and squeeze with all their might.

"You're the best, Royce," I whisper into his ear, instinctively knowing he's crying, even though I can't hear it or feel it. "You're the best father anyone could ever ask for– and I'd know." The sincerity in my voice is intense, and there's no denying it's my universal truth. "I don't know what's going to happen, but Bren wouldn't have kept this from you if he didn't think it necessary."

Voice rough, there's truth in Royce's tone too. "I know." …And that's all he says.

"Don't worry about Corbin," I add, knowing that's second on a long list of things plaguing Royce. "He's tough, like the Terminator." I earn a chuckle, which makes me smile because I'm helping Royce for once, instead of the billion and one times he's helped me. "He loves you, you know?" I murmur softly as I pull away.

Royce hits me with his concerned gaze, showing me his universal truth. "I know." …And that's all he says again.

Chuckling, I can't stop myself from razzing Royce about his bro-crush on Corbin. "And we *all* know you love him back."

Rich, deep laughter echoes off the porch walls, causing Jack and Wynn to join in from just the sound, but Bren's looking at me curiously, wondering what I'm talking about with his dad.

While Wynn says his goodbyes to Royce, I pull Bren aside with a grip to his massive forearm. Tugging, I draw him down the porch where it wraps around the house near the garden.

"Bren, you gotta listen to me, okay?" I whisper furiously. "Say what you need to say to Royce, but then you've got to get out of here. He needs to lean on Willa– they need each other."

"I know," Bren says solemnly, voice shadowed in the pre-dawn darkness. Then his teeth flash white, grinning for mocking his dad. "Short and sweet, then he's Willa's problem."

"Exactly." We share a chuckle, forever feeling like we did after I first got settled here when I was sixteen.

Brothers– joining forces against the parental authority for all eternity... then beating the shit out of each other because the intimacy was too uncomfortable.

I slide forward, voice barely a whisper. "About Jack–"

"What about Jack?" Bren demands, hands reaching up to grip my shirt.

Shit!

"*I'm sorry*," I stress. "I promise it will never happen again– Wynn too." My shirt only gets gripped tighter in those small but mighty hands of destruction. "I'm sorry I couldn't protect him."

Hands drop from my shirt instantly, but then I'm the one being hugged. It's awkward– the height difference. With Royce, I don't notice that I'm nearly a foot taller because his presence is massive. But with Brennan, no matter how much he bulks up, he's my baby brother, and he can't comfort me like a dad would.

"Messing around with Jack– your fault, but only Jack's call. What happened with Cain– Cain's fault, but still Jack's call. We're good, as long as you don't do a repeat performance."

"Promise," I vow, squeezing Bren tighter for a second, then I let go, stepping backward until I'm leaning against the siding. "You gotta get Jack to talk. Not tomorrow, or next week. No later. It has to be as soon as you leave here. Take him somewhere special to both of you, then force him to let it out."

"Shit!" Bren mocks me, hands digging into his own hair. "Same for you with Wynn, bud."

"Same for me," I agree. Eyes connecting for a moment, we break apart to go do what we have to do, even if it's uncomfortable.

Bren heads straight for Royce, with Jackson leaning against the porch railing, looking as if he's waiting to witness the sun rising. I do my best to extract Wynn from Royce, knowing the man wants us to stick around so he can see us, hear us, and be near us, so there isn't the extra burden of worry with us from his sight.

"Care if I drive your truck?" I direct toward Wynn as I head for the driver's side.

"Nice of you to ask," Wynn drawls, knowing I was merely being polite and not truly asking, which is evident when I get behind the steering wheel without getting an answer first. Chuckling, Wynn slides into the passenger seat. "Can't say I've ever had this view inside *my* truck before."

"Bear with me," I warn, clueing Wynn in that I have my reasons, even if I refuse to divulge them.

In the silent dawn, I drive Wynn's truck around Rusty Knob. With us living in the mountains, the sun hasn't crested above the highest hilltops yet, but it's light enough to see clearly. The fog will descend in about an hour, so it's best to be off the road by then until it dissipates.

The need to feel connected to my roots has me driving the opposite direction from Wynn's land toward mine. I know I shouldn't miss the old bastard, but I do– can't help myself, which is why I understand how everyone is feeling with Corbin leaving.

The ten-minute drive is met with companionable silence, with the view hammering home why we live where we live. It's lush and green, with no flat spaces, creating nooks of tranquility.

For someone like me– like Wynn –urban life would slowly siphon away our center of calm, because we recharge our energy off the land.

"I can't believe I ever wanted to leave this place," I mutter more to myself than Wynn as we pull up the driveway to the rundown house I now own. I spent my entire childhood longing to run away, then ten years denying the urge to truly move back, all because people are brainwashed into believing they're a loser if they never leave their birthplace.

Irony, wherever I ended up would've been someone else's hometown, somewhere teenagers were trying to flee in droves, so that debunks the loser myth. Where you live is what *you* make of it, and not a sign of your worth.

Home.

Granddaddy may have been an asshole, but he was doing what he felt was right, even if it was the wrong thing for me personally, especially with the harsh delivery. With his advanced age, the time and place he was born, he honestly didn't understand what it meant to be homosexual. Before he died, we agreed to disagree, but came to terms with the other's point of view, and we were good. Real good.

Staring at the only place that holds memories of my momma, daddy, and granddaddy, all the way back to when I was a toddler. I don't have many real, clear memories of my mom. Dad filling in the blanks made it difficult to know which were real memories, or if they were gifts from my dad.

But, there is a memory I've forever cherished. I was obsessed with the movie 8 Seconds when I was a little shit. I don't know how I got started watching it, or why we had a VHS copy when we barely had any frivolous items. Looking back as an adult, I kind of wonder if Momma didn't have a crush on Luke Perry, because Daddy always chuckled when I was watching it.

Just another instance where I wish one of them was still around so I could ask them. But those private moments are between my dead parents, forever a lost intimacy. I'll make my own with Wynn, ones no one but us will hold the key to understanding.

Anyway, I was obsessed with 8 Seconds, so Granddaddy made me a bronc out of a sawhorse, and I'd pretend to ride it in the lawn. My only real memory of all of us together is of me riding that sawhorse like an idiot, with my family surrounding me, clapping and laughing with delight– I can still hear it echoing off the land if I listen hard enough.

The sawhorse is still in the shed.

Need, an inescapable urge to jump from the truck and run back into the rundown house nearly overpowers me, but I know once I step foot inside, I can't recapture what's been lost.

My family isn't in there, only lost memories taken away with the dead.

The Marx's house is slanted to the right slightly, slowly sliding down the slope of the land, but everything is in good repair, even with Granddaddy passing just after watching me graduate with my master's degrees. Just like the gnomes appearing in the yard, someone has been maintaining this house for the past year and a half, because they love me.

Granddaddy cared about this land– it meant something to him, so it means something to me, so it matters to Wynn.

It hurts too much to admit the truth, how I was named after Granddaddy, how he wanted me to be more like he was– more like my dad. But I never felt deserving of the name.

All those harsh words made me feel badly about myself, but after working with a lifetime of therapists, I realized the seed was already in place before Granddaddy ever said a word. He might not have understood what being gay meant, but he knew what it meant to own who you were, and he didn't like how cowardly I was being by not being the best version of my Kaden Marx.

Just before he died, Granddaddy said he didn't need a clone– he just wanted a grandson who didn't sulk around, hating himself, and the more I behaved that way, the harder it was not to join suit.

I got it. Then we were good. Then he left me.

Alone.

"I know," I begin, then chuckle because I hear Royce saying it earlier, even if it's meant in a different connotation. "I understand how you're feeling," I mutter to a silent Wynn, who is barely keeping his shit together because he knows exactly what I'm doing.

I wait.

"Don't pull your therapy bullshit on me," Wynn snaps back, eyes never leaving my property in the distance.

I didn't have to wait long for Wynn's usual tagline.

"Hey," I call, turning to the side, but I don't touch him. "This isn't me being a therapist, or your lover, or your boyfriend… this is me being your friend. Okay?"

"Okay," is a soft grumble.

Shifting into reverse, I back up, because the rest of this conversation is going to take place en route to where we're going to let it all go and move forward.

"I miss him almost as much as I miss them." Wynn doesn't have to ask who I'm talking about. "Maybe because I had him in my life the longest. Granddaddy was harsh with me, but it wasn't until the end that I understood why."

Movement out of the corner of my eye catches my attention, but I don't take my eyes off the road. Wynn shifts slightly, wordlessly asking me to continue.

Fingers clenching the steering wheel, I let it out. "Some people rub others the wrong way, and that's the way it was between me and my grandfather. There was no hiding who I was. He was lashing out, not because I was gay, but because of how shiftless I was being. He loathed how I hated myself, so he said all the things out loud that I was saying silently in my head… and he meant them, because nothing is worse than being surrounded by a perpetual victim who is so down on themselves they're tainting everything."

"That doesn't work with chubby people," Wynn says after a length of time. "Fat-shaming them doesn't make them go on a diet and change their lifestyle. Bren knows this firsthand– he says to make them feel good about themselves, and getting healthy will follow. So how is calling you a faggot in your best interests?"

God, Wynn can pull that prick tone out of his ass in a heartbeat, which is where I'm leading with my conversation.

"My dad had the patience to coax me, but maybe I didn't need to be coddled." My eyes flick in Wynn's direction, trying to gauge his reaction. "Maybe I needed someone to put a boot up my ass."

"People are different," is all Wynn gives me.

"Exactly, and Granddaddy couldn't handle a needy, clingy, self-loathing little boy, when I had no reason to be needy, clingy, or self-loathing. No amount of attention was good enough, erasing all the good anyone ever did for me. So he lashed out as a way to put a boot up my ass, because he refused to put up with my bullshit. But I was so stuck in being a victim, to the point I didn't realize he was angry because I hated myself, not because he hated me."

"Are you trying to make yourself feel better?" Wynn turns to me, judgmental asshole tone in his voice. I put the truck into park, but Wynn's so focused on me, he doesn't realize I'm sitting in front of Corbin's house. "He called you a faggot and said you were going to be selling your ass on the street. How is that not hateful?"

"Wynn…" I reach out to cup his cheek in my palm, and he cradles into the touch. "I'm not trying to make myself feel better. Granddaddy told me this shit directly to my face, only I didn't listen until just before I lost him."

"Explain it to me," he demands to understand.

"Because clingy, needy, gay kids who can't get enough attention, especially ones who lost their mother, then their father, they end up on the streets… selling their ass to make rent. That's why. There was no amount of positive attention Granddaddy could give me because he wasn't the one I missed. I needed my dad, not giving a shit that my grandfather needed his son. So instead of negative attention, he voiced my silent thoughts to show he *knew* me. It was the truth– my *real* future. I still hate myself today. For *no* reason."

"It could have backfired," Wynn voices what Granddaddy said was his worse fear, which is why he allowed Royce to take me from him. "He could have worn you down so low, you would have run away and done just that."

Chuckling to myself with irony, I mutter, "Do you ever just want to beat the living shit out of someone who is annoying the piss out of you?"

"Fuck. Yes." Wynn grins at me.

"Exactly– my grandfather was sick of looking at the pitiful creature I was transforming into, simply for no other reason than I was thriving off being pitiful. So I don't blame him."

"Why are you telling me this while we sit outside of my house, when we both know my daddy ain't inside?"

Wynn is smarter than the average bear.

"Because you want to hate Corbin, but you can't, just like you tried to with Royce over the years for the many betrayals he made."

"Corbin. Is. A. Horrible. Human. Being." Wynn enunciates slowly, but the, *"So why do I love him so much?"* is silent.

"Look at it!" I grab Wynn's hand, forcing him to point at the house he grew up in. "Does this look the same? And I don't mean how it has a newer roof, siding, and windows. Look at how your dad is taking care of the place. The trash heap is gone, the yard is mowed, there are flowers in pots and a tiny vegetable garden. Corbin's even decorating," I mutter wryly about the ancient toilet and clawfoot tub filled with begonias.

"Yeah, and he's not drinking anymore, learned to read, and has been picking up odd jobs for Royce..." The prick tone is getting stronger. "You say this shit like it erases everything else that happened."

"When you lived here all together, it was tainted with toxicity. Corbin has done horrific things for reasons he felt were right." I turn to face Wynn. "I've known your family longer than you have, and Corbin wasn't a drunk when you were little– he was a hands-on dad who taught Warren how to fish and hunt and work, and Donny was always around here. Piecing all the shit together, I can see why Corbin took to the bottle to be able to sleep at night, and how it all spiraled from there."

"Shut up!" Wynn snaps, but he releases what I've been waiting for. "Daddy treated Warren like a best buddy, and other than that bullshit with Donny, he defended Willa against Momma constantly. But with me... he beat the shit out of me. He may as well have tortured me."

Furious, Wynn wrenches his seat belt off, whipping to the side to glare at me. "Daddy *sold* me. *Sold me,*" he seethes, spittle flying. "He hit me. Why? Because I'm gay?"

"No," I mutter softly, trying to think of a way to defuse the situation. I need Wynn to let it out in a cathartic way, not funnel his pain and confusion into violence.

Wynn's past with Corbin, his resentment toward Royce, the secrets being revealed, finding out he had a brother, one who pissed on his best friend, then having sex with his best friend, where he lost his virginity to me moments afterwards.

The pressure cooker has to release before it turns to bloodshed. As a survivor, as a cutter, I know what happens when I don't get it out.

"I know he's not a monster, but Daddy treated me differently than the rest of 'em." Fists clenched against his chest, Wynn's voice breaks on a quiver. "*Why?*"

With a deep breath, I keep a sob of pain at bay. "Because there is something about you that annoyed the piss out of him," I answer bluntly, stunning Wynn, and I fear I've gone too far so I keep talking. "You held Corbin to a higher standard. You judged him. You wouldn't allow him to get away with his own shit, when he was trying to hide in the bottle instead of letting his pain go. He was burying secrets and shame, and you weren't letting them remain hidden. You were Corbin's mirror when he didn't want to face his own reflection."

Wynn just stares at me, tumblers falling into place on how I told him about why my grandfather treated me the way he did.

"It wasn't my fault, but it was, just as this isn't your fault, but it is. We're adults now, and we take half of the responsibilities when a relationship fails or succeeds."

"I love him," Wynn admits like the words sting his tongue. "*Why?* If I had a lick of self-respect, I wouldn't. What is wrong with me?"

"Nothing," I say adamantly. "Corbin's your father, that's why. No matter what, you want him to love you back."

"But he doesn't!" Wynn bellows in the confines of the truck cab. "He. Doesn't."

Leaning forward, I whisper into Wynn's face, needing him to get it out. "He does– Corbin loves you– maybe more than anyone. You were the one person whose opinion matters, like it does with Royce. Corbin wanted you out of his face so he could forget, so he didn't have to require more of himself. You challenged Corbin, and he loves you more for it, not less."

"He sold me!" Wynn's voice nearly shatters me before it does him. "He *sold* me! And Royce bought me!" Shuddering violently, his words vibrate. "I don't give a shit what his excuse was for abusing me– he still did *it*. Everyone just writes it off! *Everyone!*" Wynn bellows directly into my face.

Not me, I think but don't voice. "Let it out," I coax instead. "I've got you."

The fists come first, pummeling weakly against my chest, each thump gaining a little more force than the last. Then the silent tears. Finally the sobs. But Wynn's still not letting it out– letting it go.

"I have a goddamn brother he hid from me!" Wynn gasps, fists landing on my chest with increasing intensity, until I'm bracing against the door. "Bren hid my brother from me! BREN!" Enraged, the primal sound of betrayal fills the truck cab. "Then the cocksucker literally sucked Jack's cock… then pissed on him, and I'm just supposed to feel bad for the fucking freak because he had a bad life."

One fist continues to bruise my chest while the other smudges away tears. "I'm not *that* fucking good, Kaden. I'm not that fucking good!"

"Yes, you are," I whisper, breaking the spell.

Exhausted in defeat, Wynn slumps into my arms, with violent sobs wracking his entire body. All I can do is hold on tight as he finally lets it go.

"I want him to come back," Wynn whispers the universal truth all children feel, no matter if they are a toddler or ninety. No matter who they are, or how they've treated us, we want our parents to come back to us, even if we pushed them away.

Sometimes you're lucky like Wynn, where you can say these things to your dad's face. Sometimes you're unlucky like me, where your parents are dead, so your only recourse is to shout and scream and cry at an inanimate object wearing a jaunty hat with blood splatter on its face.

"Why? So you can punch Corbin?" I tease, squeezing Wynn as tight as possible, not giving a shit that he's snotting all over my shoulder.

"No." Wynn sniffles, fists balled up against my chest. "So I can hug him again."

LET IT OUT
Brennan Kennedy

"Dad," I tread carefully, worried my hug won't be accepted. "I–"

"Stop it," Dad orders, practically toppling over the rocking chair with his need to hug me back. "I just…" He releases me, looking lost. "I don't know what to say, or how I feel right now."

Crouching to rest on my heels, I hold onto the armrest of Willa's rocking chair, while staring into my father's vacant gaze. "We all had our own parts to play," I admit, not caring that Jackson is pretending he can't hear us. "It was a miracle the three of you survived–"

"I know," Dad cuts me off again, eyes looking skyward to avoid connecting with me. "I never wanted you to see me like that. If anything haunts me, it's the knowledge that you saw me. But it's not my pride speaking. It's my fear that it changed who you are."

"Yeah, well… watching a ruthless Corbin in action kinda changes a boy," I mutter wryly, causing Dad to growl. "Sorry," I say, trying not to laugh. "You should have seen it from my point of view, Dad. What was happening to you will give me nightmares for the rest of my life, but the cold efficiency that Corbin displayed when he protected you without a second of hesitation–"

"Corbin is not a goddamn superhero," flows out on a growl, and Jackson's stifled chuckle is way too loud for Dad's liking. "He's a murderer."

"Yeah, but he's *our* murderer," I joke, but it falls flat. "In all seriousness, Dad. I needed Corbin in that instant. Without him, I have no idea what would have happened. Maybe we all would've been raped, tortured, and executed. So if I find Corbin's actions that of a hero, so be it. I need to know there are people who are willing to do anything to make sure justice is reached."

"Justice?" Dad and Jack mutter in unison.

"Yeah, justice. Look at Damon rotting away in prison, with Uncle Donny there too. They're playing by the government's rules because those who are supposed to protect us won't. Damon and Uncle Donny are bait, trying to catch the bigtime players in the game. So without Corbin stopping men like Russell and Sean Probst, evil would be held in wait until they were usable and disposable for the "good guys" to make their move. That's not justice– that's an agenda."

"There are laws for a reason," Dad stresses, like he fears I'll turn vigilante. "In the eyes of the law, Corbin is a contract killer. It's a good thing West Virginia doesn't have the death penalty."

"Um... Russell died somewhere in Virginia," I admit sheepishly how Corbin told me that much, but gave no details. Judging by the fury written across my dad's face that was the wrong thing to say. "I'm going to decide to believe that your anger is because you're fearful for Corbin, because you respect him, love him as a brother, and don't want to see him on death row."

Dad's snort is violent enough to make a man bleed.

Crouching down until my ass almost meets the floorboards, I try to think of a way to soothe Dad's bent pride. "Corbin was there when your dad needed him. He was there when Uncle Donny needed him. He was there when *you* needed him. He was there for me when you were in the hospital, giving me a brutally honest viewpoint when everyone else wanted to pat my back and tell me pretty lies. I needed it, so I don't give a fuck if Corbin is the twenty-first century's Charlie Manson. I needed Corbin, and he was there without question– the rest is just history."

Glaring down at me with narrowed eyes, Dad isn't pleased with what I have to say. "I know Corbin inside out and upside down, dumbass." He has the audacity to roll his eyes. "I've known him every fucking day of my life. But what that doesn't explain is you lying to me by omission about my sister and Cain."

"Oh," I whisper, deflated, while Jackson hisses, *"Shit!"*

"They say *oh* and *shit*," Dad mocks, so I know he's furious with me. He'll never hit me, or ignore me, and he'll still comfort me. But the fact that Dad will take whatever shit I throw at him, and never hurt me back, makes it seem ten times worse. "How am I supposed to be the head of this family when I don't know a goddamn thing happening *inside* this family?"

"Yeah, I could see how that would make you upset," I mutter lamely, mind furiously spinning to find a way out of this.

"That was a rhetorical question, Brennan." Dad groans as if he's exhausted by me, then his nostrils flare. "Just explain why," he grumbles in defeat. "Tell the truth, and we won't have anything to forgive."

Trap.

That's a Dad Trap!

"The truth–" Fuck it, I slide to land ass-first on the porch floor, boards groaning in protest under my weight. "I was terrified. My dad, my uncle, and the mother of my siblings were being assaulted in the living room while I was locked in the bedroom with my baby brother and sister. I felt utterly helpless– powerless."

Folding in half, I hide my face against my thighs, trying my damnedest to speak the truth without spiraling down into reliving the nightmare as if it's playing out in reality. Using the meditation techniques my yoga instructor taught me, I breathe while trying to clear my thoughts.

"I acted on instinct, and my legs took me to Corbin." Gazing up to Dad, I try to get him to see it from my point of view. "I just *knew* Corbin would protect me– save us. So cut me some slack. I saw my dad lying on the floor, being raped with a gun to his head. There wasn't a single cell in my body that didn't want to pull that trigger instead. I was simultaneously jealous and hero-worshipping Corbin for blowing Sean's brains out."

"Bren–"

Dad tries to get me to stop, but I don't allow it. "It's time to get this shit out in the open, and then put it to bed– I promised Kade," I add to get Dad to relax. "You were in the hospital, Uncle Donny had been taken into custody by the police, Willa was under a 72-hour psyche hold at the hospital, Sean was in the morgue, and Corbin was being questioned and cleared by the FBI. So when a woman showed up who looked just like me, with a boy who looked just like Wynn, I took charge."

Yeah, that got Dad's and Jackson's attention. Both guys look at me with their jaws hanging, completely captivated with my storytelling abilities.

"I lied– even to Corbin." An edge of pride slips into my tone. "I said I met them when I caught Corbin talking to them at the hospital, but that was bullshit. I met Octavia and Cain in the hospital hours earlier. They were there to identify Sean's body. We talked for hours, every word spoken was important."

"What?" Dad's face turns to the side, looking at me as if he's never seen me before.

"Kennedys are loyal, and Octavia is a Kennedy, no matter what her last name is. I was not breaking your trust by not telling you about her. After talking to Octavia for hours, I did the right thing, even if you saw it as a betrayal. Tavia and Cain needed to feel safe, and it wasn't safe to be around our family– sure as shit wasn't safe around Corbin. The FBI was actually questioning him about what happened to Russell, not what just went down with Sean."

"What did you do?" Dad accuses, and he has every right.

"We set it up for Corbin to stumble onto Octavia and Cain– believe it or not, Corbin didn't know he had another kid until that moment."

"What did *you* do?" Dad tries again with a different inflection.

"Everyone was indisposed, so I did the right thing. I took Octavia's third out of Uncle Donny's money–"

"I've been looking for that fucking money for years!" Dad seethes, spittle flying, and I worry for the first time that he's going to hit me.

"It wasn't your money. Octavia was Granddaddy's daughter, and a third of it was hers. Uncle Donny brought the Probsts back into our lives and he wasn't doing a damn bit of good with his portion, so I decided he should be the one to pay up."

"I've been looking for years!" Dad bellows red-faced, vein in his forehead throbbing.

"And I tried to get you to stop, didn't I?" I raise a brow. "You wanted the truth, so this is it. Hate me, but it won't change anything. I did the right thing. I was loyal to all of us. I was a kid keeping secrets to protect us."

"You sound like I should be grateful," Dad mutters incredulously. "You wouldn't have been a kid keeping secrets if you would've come to your own fucking father." Eyes squeezing shut, the single tear falling down Dad's cheek has my breath catching in my throat.

"It's bad enough that you saw me in that condition, then my recovery afterward. But it's somehow worse, like my measure of a man is damaged, because my son felt I was too weak to help when I was the head of our family."

Scrambling to my knees, I grip Dad's chin between my fingertips so he's forced to look me in the eye. "That's your own bullshit talking, Dad. Don't pull a Kaden," I snarl. "You were medicated to the point you couldn't even move, remember? Had I met them later, I would've brought them to you. But in the moment, when it was just me and Corbin who were mobile, I did what needed to be done, and you should be proud of me, not disappointed in me."

"I'm not–" This time Dad's breath catches in his throat. "I'm not disappointed in *you*– I'm disappointed in *me*."

"As an outside party here," Jackson treads lightly. "I can honestly say this isn't about you, Royce. Octavia's decision belongs to her. This was an out-of-control time, let's not infect right now with those same feelings."

Laughing, I look at Jack with tears glinting in my eyes. "You've been hanging with Kade too much."

Shrugging, Jack smirks, looking a bit terrified, worried Dad will be angry with him.

"You're right," Dad admits defeat, simply because someone who doesn't belong to him brought him to heel. After climbing to his feet, Dad looks down at me. "Brennan?"

"Yeah," I breathe, coming to my full height.

Holding my gaze, Dad doesn't even blink. "Is that everything?"

"Yes," I admit without hesitation. "That's everything."

"I can't help how confused I feel right now," Dad mumbles, as if saying the words physically guts him. "I can't help how betrayed and hurt I feel, but I do understand– I really do. I know it's not about me. My sister made the choice, which was her right. But that doesn't take away how it still hurts that my son kept this from me. How it hurts worse that my sister didn't want to know me– I'll be man enough to admit that."

"I think I can commiserate," Willa's betrayed voice flows from the screen door, then her baby bump comes into view. "Different people, same scenario, with added layers of bullshit."

"Cain," Jack and I whisper in unison, because Dad looks clueless.

"Willa, damn." Royce moves quickly to embrace her. "I'm so sorry. I'm being thoughtless."

I breathe a sigh of relief because Dad's focus shifts from how I'm a shitty son to the pregnant woman who needs him. Nothing makes Dad feel more like a man than taking care of his family, which is why what I did stung so hard.

Thank you, Willa.

"I'm so pissed I could spit nails," Willa snarls, diction shifting. "Since I can't change the past, I'm gonna get to know my brother. We'll worry about your sister and my daddy while we wait for answers."

"C'mon, you should be in bed." Dad ushers Willa off the porch. "This is too much stress for you and the baby."

"So easily we're forgotten." Clutching my chest, I pretend I'm hurt. "Didn't even say goodbye."

Jackson chuckles, which was my desired response. Reaching for his wrist, I tug him off the porch. Jack protests in surprise when

I don't lead him to his car, but instead start across the side lawn toward the back of the barn.

"What's up?" Jack sounds hesitant. "Where are we going? What are we doing?"

"Trust me?" I laugh at how idiotic that sounds after the big reveal tonight, with my dad still stinging from what he sees as the ultimate of betrayals. "I'd never hurt you," I promise.

"I trust you– hell, I trust you more now after what I just learned."

Baffled, my feet still just as we reach our destination. "Why?" I murmur in surprise.

Jackson shifts, pressing my back against the barn, bringing me out of the shadows of the pole light. The sun is rising, but it'll still be a bit before it reaches this side of the barn, with the hills in the way.

"It takes a lot of courage and loyalty to remain quiet to keep people safe, especially when looking at your dad. It had to have hurt you when Royce would bring up the money, and you had to bite your tongue. No doubt you struggled with keeping the truth for years."

Jackson blows my mind.

Moving without thought, I have Jackson pressed up against the barn, bodies so close we're nearly fused together. Lips speaking silent words, tongues more coaxing than dueling.

Kaden made me promise to take Jackson somewhere that meant something. This may be Wynn's barn on the inside, but the back wall belongs to Jackson and me.

"I've got to take a leak," Jack announces for some bizarre reason, and no one pays him any mind. Wynn and Franny are doing an immunity challenge, trying to see who can build a fire from scratch and burn their string in half. Idiots are obsessed with Survivor, and our entire basketball team is doing different challenges around the backyard. Dad's having a field day organizing the fun.

Everyone's been calling me a bum lately because I'm just not feeling it. Life. Not feeling life, and it makes me understand both Kaden and Wynn better. I'm depressed, I know that, but I'd never end it all because someday I might become un-depressed.

I have hope.

Bum that I am, I'm poking the bonfire with my hotdog stick, fretting about Jesse treating me like shit last night and this afternoon. After I found her another victim, she spent all night going down on Dawna while ignoring me. The only way I got my dick touched by Jesse was when I dipping inside Dawna's snatch while Jesse's tongue was doing its business.

I didn't even come.

Haven't in months.

Confession– I have a bum dick at age sixteen.

Then Jesse and I got into a huge fight this afternoon because Dawna said she didn't want to play around with Jesse anymore– only wanted me, Dawna said, which made me the bad guy.

Maybe it's not depression.

Shame.

"Bren, c'mon!" Duane shouts at me, pissed that I won't participate. I only joined the basketball team to be closer to Wynn. Why else would I humiliate myself when I don't have any talent? I love the guy as a brother, and he doesn't even notice me. Wynn just sees me as an annoyance, one he humors on occasion when he notices I'm around.

Whatever.

Squeaking, my finger gets singed, so caught up in my thoughts my stick had burnt to a nub. Jackson's laughter ruffles my feathers. Yet another guy in my life who ignores me. I noticed Jackson during sophomore year, getting a different sort of vibe from him. He's cute and sweet, sweet enough that he's laughing with me right now, instead of at me.

"Do you want me to look at it?" Stepping closer, Jackson gestures at my burnt fingertip.

"I thought you were going to take a piss?" I mutter in confusion, then shove my enflamed finger in my mouth to shut my ass up.

The guy stares at my mouth for some reason. "I... um..." Jackson steps from foot-to-foot. "This is the first time I've been to your house, so I have no idea where it is, and I thought your dad said the inside of the house was off-limits."

Jackson blushes in a way that gets a reaction out of me usually reserved for pretty girls in tight shirts. Now it's my turn to shift around.

"I'll just jog over to my place and take a wiz." Jack walks backward, stammering.

"C'mon–" I grab for his thin wrist, then tug him behind the barn.

"What's up?" Jack sounds hesitant, feet stilling. "Where are we going? What are we doing?"

"Trust me?" I laugh playfully at how idiotic that sounds.

"I trust you," is a breath on the wind, and it shocks me to my core.

I'm the most untrustworthy person on the planet.

"I'll show you my private piss-spot. No one else knows it exists, so you don't have to go in the bushes and stand in everyone else's piss. Ugh! The stench."

"Eww— gross." Jackson mock shudders, and I can't help but find it cute. "Thanks, I have a shy bladder."

"What the hell is a shy bladder?" Pointing at a hidden divot between where the back of the barn ends and the woodshed begins, "The hole in the ground is a drain where a downspout used to be. It flows into the drainage ditch where the other guys wiz." I lean my back against the barn and cross my arms over my chest.

"Um..." The kid sure does stammer a lot. Facing the opposite direction from me, Jack's shoulder brushes against mine as he unzips. "I have a hard time pissing in front of people.

Laughing good-naturedly, I roll to my side, facing his shoulder. "Urinals are out of the question, eh?"

Jackson grunts in response, and more than curiosity enflames me. If the guy can't piss at a urinal, how the hell is he drenching my drain pipe? All I have to do is glance down and I'll get an eyeful of Jack's junk.

Hmm... now that idea sparks some interest in me.

"Shit," I hiss underneath my breath. After finding the courage to look, I catch Jack zipping up instead.

"My turn!" I mutter too brightly, blushing like a virgin on her wedding night. I shoulder past Jack, not giving him time to move before I'm whipping it out. "Not into Survivor challenges, either?" I mutter conversationally.

"I'm– um... I'm not athletic," Jack admits, stammering more and more.

Turning, I act like it's every day I hold my dick while chatting. "You're on our basketball team," I remind Jack, breath fluttering against his cheek. Noticing how large his eyes are held, I follow the path they take. "I suck at basketball, but I do enjoy working out–"

My brain checks in with my eyes, realizing Jack's staring at my dick like he's never seen one before. Unbidden, my eyes flick down, only to witness Jack's bulge looking a bit fuller than a minute ago.

Face paling, reminding me of Willa and Uncle Donny during the nightmare. "Oh, God!" *Jack cries out, fleeing.* "Don't tell!"

"Hey!" *I reach for Jack, not letting him get away, forgetting that my dick is flopping in the wind.*

Batting at my hand, Jackson goes batshit crazy, arms and legs flailing, but manages to keep it down to a whisper so we're not caught. Voice cracking, what Jack says next has my world tilting on its axis. "Don't beat me."

"Don't freak– I'm not going to harm you."

Some decisions are made in an instant, never mind the consequences.

I can't be a cheater, not when my girlfriend came out to me last month. Okay, so I did cheat immediately, and Jesse nearly killed Dori afterwards, but every girl since was for us to share. My pea-sized brain hasn't handled it well. Kind of like how my brain short-circuited the instant I figured Jack was gay and into me.

Huh? So that's why I kept following the guy around, thinking bizarre shit about how cute he looked when he laughed.

Fuck!

"Listen to me, Jackson," *I plead, because the guy is putting up a fight but not going anywhere and not saying anything. Just sort of spazzing out while staring down at my exposed dick.* "Chill, dude. We're cool."

Like a switch being flipped, Jack settles down. "Don't tell," *flows without sound.*

"I can keep a secret," *I mutter wryly since the secrets I keep would put several people in prison, including me. Moving Jackson backward by walking forward, I pin him into the hidden cubbyhole.* "But the real question is can you?"

"Huh?" *Jack's grunt turns to a moan the instant our lips connect.*

So what? I'm cheating on my girlfriend. Fuck her. I just figured out I was bi, and I think I deserve to have something just for me. I'm sick of sharing. Sharing my dad with Kade and Wynn. Sharing my girlfriend with every girl willing to spread her legs.

Jackson.

I'm not sharing Jackson.

Awkward, slobbery, teeth mashing together painfully, this has to be Jack's first kiss. But it's mine too. First kiss with a guy. Even with the bad technique, it's still the most exciting kiss I've ever had.

After thirty seconds of fighting over who's going to lead, Jack gets with the program and learns what I'm teaching him, then what was awkward turns explosive.

"Jesus," Jack hisses, hands gripping my belt loops, drawing me closer, then his fingertips press into my ass. Laughing, he arches his neck, giving me access so I can suck on his skin. "Your whiskers are giving me a brush burn and I love it."

Unhinged, I plaster my body to the front of Jack's, using the back of the barn as leverage. Raw, messy kisses, groping hands, rocking hips, Jack comes first, and I swallow down his cry. With the roll of my hips, my spooge stains Jack's t-shirt and jeans.

Laughing breathlessly against Jack's neck, "I guess I don't have a bum dick after all."

"Huh?" Hella confused, all Jackson can do is laugh with me while I smother him. "I've never done that before," he admits like it's a secret.

"Me, either," slips from my tongue to vibrate Jack's skin, causing him to freeze beneath me. Nothing like soundlessly being called a liar. "I've never dry-humped a girl in my life." I sound surly as all hell. "I may be a man-whore, but not with men."

Mood killed, I pull away to tuck my spent junk into my pants. "I'm sorry I made you messy." Pointing at the front of Jack's soiled clothing, I bite back a groan. The guy looks thoroughly debauched and I've never been so fucking proud in my life. "Fuck," I hiss. "You look good enough to eat."

"Huh?" The stammers and blushes are back in action. "I-I-I–" Jack bursts out in peals of infectious laughter. "My God, that was awe-fucking-some! Ha!" Hitching his head backward, he laughs so loud I fear my dad will check out the sound.

Talk about being bathed in ice-cold reality.

"Listen, Jack." I tug on his t-shirt. "I really like you, okay? I've wanted to get to know you for a while, but you're always shoved up Wynn's ass." Looking heavenward, I ask for answers. "I won't use you the way I treat the girls. I can't. I won't. I like you too much."

"This is a kiss-off, isn't it?" Jack accuses in an expressionless voice.

"I like you. I want to get to know you." I admit the ultimate truth. "Sex feels good, but I'm sick of empty sex. I'd rather be your friend than lose you when Jesse finds out and cuts your dick off."

After I figure out how to cut Jesse out of my life like the cancer she is, I have plans for that dick.

"What did I do?" Jack asks the sky, just as I had. Then he's charging around the side of the barn– the side the guys can't see, no doubt running home, because no one would believe he hadn't just been fucked.

Fucked and fucked over.

Pulling away from our kiss, "Jack?" I pin my best friend to the back of the barn, just as I had so many years ago. "I'm mad at you for touching my brothers– so fucking furious I can taste it. But I know why you did it. I know *why*."

The tears are instantaneous, and I hope they wash the pain of shame away.

"I wanted to hurt you," Jackson admits without hesitation.

"It hurts more to know you did it because you wanted to hurt me. But I understand."

"I'm trying to be all cocky about it." Jack tries to look away from me, but I don't allow it. We need the truth out in the open so we can move forward. "I was still riding the high when you showed up at our apartment. I wouldn't have allowed you to suck me off otherwise. I'm sorry."

"I know," I repeat the phrase of the night.

Tears increasing until I can't see the color of his eyes, Jackson looks on the verge of being distraught, exactly what Kade thought he needed. Release the shame. I long to comfort Jack, to take it away, but I can't.

"I regret everything I did tonight– *everything*," Jackson mutters with conviction. "I shouldn't have tried to pick a guy up at a bar–"

"Jack, no," I murmur softly. Unable to help myself, I tug him into my arms. "No shame. No blame. It wasn't your fault. Guys get sucked off every day, everywhere. What Cain did was wrong, and it's up to him to apologize. But it's up to me to comfort you, because you wouldn't have done it unless I'd hurt you first."

It's my fault. Deep down, that's how I feel. Maybe Kade knew that, and he was trying to get me to say it out loud too.

"Brennan, I'm so sorry," Jack sobs, clutching my t-shirt. The cries change to whimpers as I hold us both up, but Jack's next words weaken me to the point we collapse to the ground.

"I feel so dirty," accompanies the most pitiful sound I've ever heard. Hands tearing at his clothing, Jack tries to shed his shame and guilt. "I want to tear my skin off and grow new." Sobs renewing, "Will I ever be clean again?"

"Yeah," is barely a breath of a sound. "That's why I took you back to a place where you once were innocent. It wasn't your fault, Jack, and I want you to repeat that until you believe it." When Jack doesn't comply, I order him. "Say it with me, *it wasn't my fault*."

"It wasn't my fault," is said in unison, over and over until it finally sinks into our skin to clean the taint of sin away.

What I thought was for Jack alone becomes for both of us. Mistakes are made, but they don't make us who we are.

"It wasn't my fault."

CHAPTER TWENTY-THREE
Kaden Marx

"I see you're using your minions," I tease Warren as I wander by with my arms laden with boxes. Cain and Jeb follow me, carrying the drawers to Wynn's dresser, with Copper bear-hugging our comforter, dragging half of it on the ground.

"I wanna minion," Wynn whines, plucking the baby out of Warren's arms. "He-he," he mock laughs. "Now yer daddy's gotta help and I can sit on the porch chatting with you."

"Gimme my baby back!" Warren reaches for Ginger, but Wynn's large stride takes him across the yard.

"Git my dresser in the house, and I'll give Ginger back." Wynn coos, nuzzling the baby's cheek with his chin. "You love Uncle Wynn more than your old man, dontcha?"

"Weakling," Warren grumbles, stomping over to Wynn's pickup truck. Without breaking a sweat, the stocky bastard manhandles the dresser, then bitches the whole way into my house and up the stairs to my bedroom.

"I'm no weakling," Wynn's telling Ginger as I carry the boxes inside. "But your daddy is more equipped at handling heavy stuff. Remember that in the future when you move a billion times– your daddy will move all of it for ya."

After following the precession, dropping off the boxes in the upstairs hallway, I make my way back down to Wynn, with Warren and his minions trailing me.

When we pulled up the first time, it proved beneficial to live across the street from Warren. He hopped out of his house, carrying the baby, with his little helpers following closely behind. Now on trip four, with only the stuff left at Royce's place to drag over, Wynn and I are almost moved in together.

"Hey." I tug Warren back into the living room, allowing the guys and Copper to wander back outside. "Have you heard from your dad yet?"

After nearly thirty years of friendship, seeing Warren hang his head and refuse to look at me is not a good sign. "Nah, and he ain't called none of us either. I keep asking around. Maybe he's been in contact with Royce."

"It's been three weeks," I muse.

"I know that more than anyone." Slumping to rest his ass on the arm of the couch, Warren just stares off into space while worrying his bottom lip. "I don't ever remember him leaving us, even for a day or two, so I have no idea what happened when he took out Probst, or when he knocked up Birdie. But I'm not feeling right. In here–" Warren rubs his knuckles against his chest.

"I asked Wynn the same thing, 'cuz I remember sensing when Dad was gone, but he said he's not worried."

"Yeah, Wynn said I'm overreacting, that I'm looking for excuses to get stressed out so I can use again. Could be right… could be wrong."

"Worrying about it ain't gonna change anything," I remind Warren, because I think Wynn might be right. Royce isn't upset, and neither is Willa. Wynn won't talk about it, but he's not silently fretting either. Only Warren is stressing. "I'll grab something for us to drink– meet me on the porch."

After always being in and out of this house for the past four years, I don't keep much to eat or drink that isn't prepared or packaged. I'm a tea-drinker, so my fridge is stocked with bottles of unsweetened iced tea, when before it would have had a gallon pickle jar filled with sun-tea. I grab an unopened six-pack of iced tea and a big bag of individually packaged assorted cookies.

Snorting, I take in my movers. Wynn and Warren have their heads together while sitting on the front steps, with Ginger's eyes following the movement of their mouths. Like an angry storm cloud, Jeb's on the sidewalk, unabashedly glaring at the three grown Gillette men who represent everything he hates in the world. Cain's sprawled out in my front yard, sky-gazing while ignoring Jeb's glares.

I make a beeline to the fourth Gillette fella, because he'll want cookies. Copper's sitting in his car a few feet from Jeb, with his shades on and a Creedence Clearwater Revival song playing on an iPod strapped to the dash. Smirking, I notice he's got a travel mug filled with grape Kool-Aid in the cup holder.

I wish I was half as cool at twenty-eight, as this kid is at four and a half.

Head rolling on his neck, copper hair swinging by his jawline, only the package of frosted animal cookies being lowered into his line of sight catches Copper's attention. Lips curling, he doesn't reach out, knowing I have to offer first.

"Here ya go, bub." I pass him the cookies, and he's tearing into them before I can stand upright.

"Thanks, Uncle Kade!" I'd always wondered where Copper got his raspy voice, so quiet you can barely hear it. Now with Cain in our midst, it must be a family trait that never popped out in Corbin, Wynn, or Warren.

Palming the top of the kid's head, I muss up his hair. When I get to Jeb, I break into the package holding the tea bottles together, then pass him one. He's trying to act disinterested in the cookies, but he's a dude, and all dudes love cookies.

Smiling, I open the big bag filled with packs of cookies so Jeb can reach in and grab whatever kind he wants. "Sweet!" he says brightly, taking some Nutter Butters and Nilla Wafers. "Thank you." Jeb likes me– I'm not a Gillette.

The weirdo of the bunch is outlining a cloud with his fingertip, so I shove a drink in his palm and leave without giving him any cookies. Cain and I haven't spoken more than a half dozen words in the past three weeks. But the guy won't eat a dang thing that isn't vegan. Out of all of his problems, that's the one that requires a therapist the most, because it's uncomfortable when he pouts while we eat near him.

Dropping the goodies on the step below Wynn and Warren, I wedge my big ass between them, then take the kid. My boyfriend, my buddy, and the baby, I have to be the center of their attention. Just a fact of life they deal with.

While Wynn and Warren ramble on about what they think Corbin's up to, I stare down at Ginger as she stares back up at me. Copper stopped being cuddly pretty much as soon as he could run and talk. He likes being near us, but he doesn't want to be smothered. Honor's still a cuddle monster at three, and I'm hoping she doesn't grow out of it. This little girl– Ginger's an observer, and she's more than happy to observe as long as she's being held.

After being around every Gillette and Franklin in Rusty Knob, it's wild to look at the baby and see each and every single one of them gazing back at me from the face of a tiny baby. Even gloomy Jeb is present in the shape of Ginger's nose and the arch of her strawberry eyebrows.

The only way I'll ever experience seeing my family again is when I stare at my own reflection. Burying down the loneliness, I check in with the guys chattering at my sides.

"He giving you any trouble?" Wynn's shoving a handful of cookies into his mouth. After a couple of chews, he dumps the crumbs straight out of the little bag into his wide open mouth. Washing it down with some tea, he's reaching for another bag before he's done swallowing this one.

"I'm not made of money, ya know?" Warren plays with the cap to his tea. "The peckerwood will only eat organic. Raw honey. Almond milk? What the hell is that, exactly? How the fuck do you milk an almond? All these foods I've never heard of are appearing in my cupboards. There's this gigantic kitchen gadget on my countertop he's always fiddling with. Sometimes, he won't eat food that's been cooked."

"What?" I snort. "Only sometimes?"

"Yeah, only sometimes. Like only when someone else prepared his food, and he thinks we're sneaking shit into it. He'll say he's eating *raw*. But then later, he'll be at the stove."

"Weirdo– he got any money?" Wynn grabs more snacks. I guess I better feed him soon. We haven't had anything to eat since lunch yesterday. "He's been working for Garrett for three weeks. Ain't you paying him?"

"Yeah, Cain's got some money, but it all goes straight into the cupboards. He's sniffing around the farmer's market, wanting to help. Got in an argument with one of the vendors last week."

"An argument?" I arch a brow, staring at the guy as he sits cross-legged in the grass, now staring back at Jeb instead of the sky. "Other than the pissing incident, he's meeker than a bunny rabbit."

"*Argument*," Warren stresses. "A Corbin-worthy shit fit. Hollering at the vendor, calling him out for being a liar. If he didn't look like us, I would have my doubts. But after his meltdown, I knew he was kin."

"How's the staring contest contestants getting along?" Wynn juts his chin in their direction, then dives into the big bag, coming out with a fistful of cookie packages.

"Cain confuses Jeb. He looks like a Gillette, so he's the enemy. But he's quiet and reserved, and walks like he's hovering on air– sneaky bastard. They ganged up on me and Garrett, now all the nudie calendars have been stowed in a box underneath the desk. The dang shop is now up to Cain's recycling standards. The assholes don't work much– one idiot hides in the office reading, and the other hides in the field out back, staring at the sky and reading books."

"Maybe Royce should re-open the town's library, or make a community garden for the center," I offer as a solution. "Sell the fruit at cost, or let the volunteers divvy it up."

"Neither of those options pay the bills, especially when it costs more to feed Cain in a week than it does to feed my family of four for an entire month, and the kid looks malnourished as it is."

"Legumes? Have you been buying any?" I ask, curious, because Cain does look even thinner than before. He must be terrified for his sister and worried about his dad. Added to that, he's been plucked out of his life, only to be stranded with familial strangers.

"Legumes?" Warren cries out, voice warbling from stress. "What the fuck is a *legume*?"

"Beans." Wynn snorts. "I could go for some right now myself, before I eat my goddamn arm off. Wanna order a few pizzas? Or do you wanna get groceries while I grab the last load from Royce's place?" Wynn rises to his feet, then leans back down to gather up his pile of wrappers. "I'm never moving again. The driving back and forth has eaten up time I could have used to actually *eat*."

Stomping back into the house, a moment later I hear the cupboard doors creaking open.

"Ya better feed him soon– Wynn turns into an ornery bearcat when he's hungry." Warren chuckles, both hands sliding along mine to cup the back of his daughter's head and bottom. Then the warm, comforting weight of the baby is gone. "Grab him a Snickers, eh?"

Snorting, I try to swallow my laughter, then I turn serious. "Your brother is using food as a way to feel in control."

"What?" Warren's eyes flick to Cain, instinctively knowing I wasn't talking about the brother grazing in all of my cupboards.

"Make sure he's getting enough fats in his diet, make sure he eats at least six to eight times a day to get enough calories, and have Bren talk with him. An added level of control is found through exercise, and Bren does the gamut. Even yoga, which is probably more Cain's speed. Bren has done wonders with Jeb, and beneath the surface, they seem to have more in common– Jeb and Cain."

Whatever Warren has to say is cut off by Copper driving up the front walk to stop inches from our feet. Tilting his head, he stares right at his dad. "I gotta take a leak."

I manage to keep a straight face while the kid backs up and does a three-point turn in the middle of the sidewalk, until the hood of his car is facing the street. Laughing with me, Warren rises to his feet, Ginger pressed to his chest.

"You guys can handle all the shit from Royce's, right?" Warren's talking to me, but his eyes are filled with amusement, affection, and pride as he stares at his son.

"Yeah, we're good. Get the feller to the potty."

Resting one hand on Copper's shoulder, Warren makes sure he looks both ways down the street three times, then they cross to their house. Jeb unfreezes, only saying goodbye to Copper and me, then he's stalking down the sidewalk to parts unknown with his head bowed and his shoulders curled.

"Cookie?" I hold the bag out to Cain to be a dick.

Sighing, Cain stretches his arms far over his head, elongating his torso. He's very thin, but those muscles are wiry and strong no doubt. He's just as intoxicating as Wynn, but Cain has this mysterious, intriguing edge of *what the fuck*.

"I'm not deaf, ya know?" Blue eyes peek at me through a thick fall of hair. I have to lean forward on the steps in order to hear him, when he's only ten feet away from me at best. "The reason I know so much about the people who have Tavia... they saw me as an inanimate object. They treated me less than an animal. Disposable. So it didn't matter if I heard or not."

"No one should ever be made to feel like that," I whisper, trying to empathize but falling short because no one knows what Cain has been through.

"I know," Cain rasps. "I just thought I'd let ya know that I can hear well, not just when people are talking about me." Rising to his feet, Cain stretches again, causing his t-shirt to ride up, showing off that he and Wynn have more in common than facial features.

"I know you're terrified for your sister, worried about your dad, missing the life you used to have, and trying to find your place amongst strangers who look like you. I just want you to know I understand why you're feeling as you're feeling– to a certain extent. If you ever want to talk, you know where to find me."

"You're a therapist, right?" Cain squints, trying to get a read on me.

"I'm working on my licensing right now– my options are open. I'll be hosting group sessions at the center, and I'm on the fence on whether or not I want to be a guidance counselor with one set of degrees I have, or use the other set and go into private practice."

Grabbing a fistful of hair, uncovering his entire face, Cain stares at me, and I have to smother the surprised gasp that tries to erupt.

"Whatever I say will be confidential? The Feds won't be able to force you to repeat what I say? In court? Anywhere?"

"Precisely."

"We'll talk after you're licensed." Cain heads toward Warren's house.

"Eat some goddamn food!" I shout at him, and he actually chuckles the exact same sound Wynn makes for me countless times a day.

"A Gillette that don't eat?" Wynn appears behind the screen door, hand buried deep in a bag of chips. "Must be he got his appetite from his momma."

Leaning backward until I'm resting on the porch floor, I gaze up at Wynn. "Remember when you couldn't hold your food down, and Royce kept having to make you smoothies?" Bag fisted in his hand, he looks like he's going to be sick. "I'd wager that kitchen gadget Warren mentioned was a little gift from Royce, eh?"

"Guess Cain got his appetite from the Gillettes after all," Wynn murmurs, looking lost and sad. "What do we do?"

"We do what we're doing." Righting myself, I hop to my feet. "I like your idea about me getting groceries while you get the rest of your stuff from Royce's house. I should be back with everything put away before you are."

"It's three blocks from here." Wynn looks at me like he thinks I'm losing my mind. "It's not like I'm driving to and from Morgantown like the last five trips."

"Yeah, but Morgantown didn't have Royce… or Willa… or the Twins. You ain't getting outta that house without a meal in ya, a few hugs, and a lot of help."

Blushing to his hairline, Wynn huffs a laugh. Screen door slamming after him, he shoves the chip bag in my hand. Salty lips press against mine, curving up into a smile. "I wrote a list– it's pinned to the fridge door. Sorry it's so long, but I'm starving."

"Huh? Imagine that, another Gillette who's gonna eat someone out of house and home," I tease.

"Gotta keep my strength up for tonight." No pressure. No pressure at all. With a saucy wink, Wynn jumps into his truck. The passenger side window buzzes down. "R E A L maple syrup," Wynn demands, then he pulls away.

CHAPTER TWENTY-FOUR
Brennan Kennedy

"I feel kinda bad we're playing while the guys are moving." Jack doesn't look guilty, though. He's sitting cross-legged in his leather recliner, controller clutched in his hands with his eyes glued to his seventy-inch television.

It's early afternoon, so we're just tooling around, not actually playing with our online buds.

"They did help us move," I murmur, not sounding the least bit guilty either. I have to lean back quite far to get a good look at Jack because of the way we set up the basement. Most games don't allow dual-screens anymore, and it felt a bit like cheating. So we have two game systems set up on two different televisions, with our own comfy chairs. I can't see Jack's TV, and he can't see mine.

All's fair in love and war, and our games are most definitely war.

"Should we?" Jack freezes, guilt finally breaking through. "Should we go help, ya think?"

"There wasn't much to begin with." Unable to help myself, I laugh at Jack. "You boxed up the apartment for them. I helped load it into Wynn's truck. Warren and whomever he rustled up was the welcome wagon. It wasn't the same as moving my entire house into two, because Kade already lived in his house and it was just odds and ends and Wynn's shit."

"You're right– Wynn had even less than I did." Jack tosses a soda cap at me. "Hey, thanks for making your guys work overtime to get the duplex ready so I wouldn't have to crash with my folks."

"No thanks necessary." I pick up my controller, signaling the end of that conversation.

Jackson and I are in buddy-mode, neither of us willing to delve too deep into emotional territory. We both know why I had them rush, because I couldn't wait to have Jack all to myself, so it can go unsaid. Other than giving him head all those weeks back, we haven't touched more than simple affection. We're working through the hows and whys of this arrangement.

Our half of the duplex is empty besides the essentials, since I gave all of our furniture to Jesse, and Jack only has personal belongings. Jesse picked everything out and loved it, so it belongs with her. The country chic theme wasn't my thing anyway. I figured after Jack and I moved to the next step in our relationship, we could start picking up things here and there to make the place feel like *our* home, not just some solution to a major problem that derailed us before we even had a chance to begin.

Being back in Rusty Knob has made this feel *real*. For all of us. With my folks next door, Jack's only two streets over, and Jesse's across town, we're anchored now instead of just floating in the wind.

"We should throw a welcome back to Rusty Knob party," Jack mutters conversationally, completely at odds with him dropping me with a headshot.

"Dick!" I taunt, waiting to respawn. "I have some gossip, ya know?"

"Do ya, now?" the smile in Jack's voice is thick, and it has my lips curving up.

"Yup. Let's test how strong your BFF bond is with Wynn versus my brother bond with Kaden."

"I like them odds." Jack actually swivels in his chair so he can see my face. "Winner gets to pick out the kitchen stools?"

"Ugh!" Grunting with disgust, I don't know if I want to take this bet. We've been going back and forth for three days. I want wrought iron swivel stools with thick padding for my ass. "If the upholstery gets stained, we'll just get them reupholstered."

"It's gross– allergens breed in butt cushions, especially when dropped food is involved. Wood can be wiped down and disinfected against all those farts."

"Farts? No fun," I grumble. "I don't want my ass to ache while I eat my breakfast."

"Carry a butt donut around, dummy," Jack taunts me in a husky voice. "We in, or not?"

"We're in." I turn to the side in my chair, with Jack doing the same, so we can look at each other. The basement is dark, the only light being cast from the huge televisions, the staircase, and the emergency lights above the door leading to Jesse's half of the duplex. My gym equipment looks like prehistoric dinosaurs roaming in the distance.

"You tell me what your secret is, and I'll tell you if I know already or not." Jack leans forward, an eager light flashing in his eyes. "I promise not to lie and say I know– I can't lie for shit."

"Hmm... I smell bullshit." I grin wide, knowing my teeth glow in the dark. "So Wynn thwarted a bunch of Kade's plans, but Kade's going to go through with those plans anyway."

"What are you talking about?" Confusion is thick in Jack's voice, so I know his bestest buddy did not tell him the epic news.

"Wynn asked Kade to marry him," I mutter smugly.

"WHAT?!" Jack squawks, arms rising in the air in utter disbelief. "He did? He didn't tell me he was even planning to. What the hell?" Deflated, Jack doesn't like how his buddy froze him out.

"Pretty sure it was the after-effects of losing his virginity, just saying... anyway, Wynn ruined a bunch of romantic horseshit."

"I hate that shit," Jack grumbles, and he's telling the truth. Neither of us is into it. "Just say what ya want and take it. They waited five years to get laid for shit's sake."

"I know, right? Kade's going through with his romantic plans since Wynn didn't give him a ring, but at least he knows Wynn will say yes since he asked first."

"Wow..." Jack just stares at me in stunned silence with a bunch of emotions scrolling across his face. "Just... wow."

"I have no idea when they plan on doing it, with how everything has been so chaotic lately. Kade's the type to want a huge production, but he might decide against that because of how Wynn is."

"It would cause fights between them," Jack agrees. "Wynn would hate every penny spent on needless shit, but Kade will want the attention. We should throw an epic bachelor party for them here at the house."

"What about Jesse?"

"Have Royce and Willa watch Honor. Jesse might as well join in because we'll invite our classmates."

"Really? Thank you." Jackson has been working very hard to include Jesse, or at the very least not badmouth her or be condescending.

Eyes going wide, smile going even wider, I can sense Jack's excitement. "We need to sync this shit up with Franny's arrival. Then he could be here for it!"

"Yes!" I shout, clapping. "YES!"

"Ten bucks says we're the best men," Jack murmurs smugly.

"Nah, not ten bucks. Winner gets to pick the lawn furniture."

"Oh, that's major. But since I just lost, and I know you'll be Kade's best man... there's a chance Wynn won't pick me."

"Wynn will, and I know I'm betting against myself here. But with so many brothers and a sister, only his best friend should have the honor."

"Thank you." I can't see his blush, but I know he is. No doubt the smattering of freckles are now washed away by a pink tint.

"About those kitchen stools, ya wanna know the real reason I want padded ones?" Even I'm shocked at the sexy quality my voice takes on. "I'm not one to make a huge production out of shit, with declarations and *stuff* planned. But it's been two weeks, and you've yet to do anything but put sheets on your bed. All of your stuff is still in boxes, why's that? Even your toiletries in the bathroom."

"You know why." Jackson whispers like it's a secret. "Explain the cushions."

"Well, since your shit needs to be unpacked… in *our* bedroom and bathroom, I'm being proactive. Sitting on wooden stools the morning after would be torture, ya know?"

"The padded stools are for me?" Jackson sounds flustered, and it makes my pants feel too tight. "I want that… In fact, I think we shouldn't be like Kaden at all. Why wait?"

"Why wait?" I whisper, reaching down to hit the lever on my recliner, hard dick getting pinched in the process.

"Hey, guys!" Libby shouts from the cracked open door. "You down here?"

In stilled silence, Jack and I stare at each other, questions swirling.

Do we answer?

Will Libby go away if we don't?

Should we run to our bedroom and start unpacking Jack's shit?

How quick can we jerk each other off?

Would this recliner hold our combined weight as Jack rode my dick?

Sighing, Jack gives first. "We're in here, Lib! We're practicing for our next tournament."

"Sweet!" Libby bounds across the basement, and I now regret how I put a door on each floor combining our sides of the house.

Why wait? Because my wife's girlfriend wants to chat. That's why.

"Oh… wow…" Libby is in awe. "I just–" trailing her hand down the side of Jack's television, she looks about ready to jerk it off. "It's perfect."

"You play?" my voice pitches high with surprise.

"Just a little," Libby mutters bashfully.

"Here!" Jack gets up to sit on the arm of his chair, giving Libby space to sit. "Let me log out, and you can log-in with your Live profile."

"This is a sweet setup, guys," Libby murmurs dreamily, and I know damn well if she and Jesse end up going for the long haul, there will be a third gamer station set up down here, with Libby's chair of choice.

Libby steps to the side, and I can finally see what she's wearing. Always a flowered dress and a pair of leggings covering her slightly pudgy body. She has a mass of curly hair with blunt-cut bangs above thick black glasses like Jack's.

Libby's a nerd. No way in hell does she play *just a little*.

She's about to hand me my ass, and Jack knows it.

I flash Jack a look that screams *you're sucking me off for this*, and he grins in agreement.

Two hours later, I got more than I bargained for. Jack and I wanted to practice, but you're only as good as your competition. Jack and I are about the same level as a gamer... Libby just kicked my ass nonstop for two hours, and I feel like a better gamer than I was before the beating.

My cellphone vibrates in my pocket, so I quickly toss Jack my controller and give him my seat. I step away to the other side of the basement for privacy, because Jack and Libby are bad-mouthing each other as they play.

"Hey," I answer. "You okay?"

"Why does everything have to be so complicated," Corbin complains. "All the leads have taken me to D.C. but the road system is bullshit."

"Road signs giving you problems?" Not only is Corbin dyslexic, he never learned to read until a few years ago. It's harder for him than it was for Warren, because Warren hadn't been conditioned to do things the wrong way for over forty-five years. It's a struggle.

"Problems? Pfft..." The background noise gets louder, with Corbin talking to someone. "Trying to get directions, but it's slow going."

"Just take your time," I encourage. "Did you call my dad?"

"Yeah, I called him first." Corbin's been texting Dad, and has called me twice, but he didn't want us to tell anyone until he had something concrete. "I saw Octavia yesterday– the assholes have her working off a debt her family owes."

"Corbin," I cry out softly, suddenly terrified.

"Not like that," he protests. "Her accounting skills, or whatever the hell that is. Anyway, I know where she is, but I can't take her home with me. I'ma have to stick around until they let her go."

"They're going to let you do that?" Pacing, I find myself near the staircase.

"The creep guarding Tavia yesterday found me today, and he gave me an offer to cut her time in half."

"Corbin," I warn. "Don't go down that road."

"I'll be home soon. Just tell my kids that, okay? I'll bring Royce his sister– don't I always follow through for your daddy?"

"Corbin," my voice shakes with fear.

"Be a good boy, Brennan. I'll be seeing ya real soon."

"Dammit!" Hand wrapped around it, I glare down at my cellphone.

"Everything okay?" Jack projects across the basement. As soon as they figured out who I was talking to, they shut down the game systems.

"As okay as it can be." I walk toward them just as Jesse comes in the door from her basement. "Corbin found Octavia, but they can't come home yet."

"Where's Honor?" Jack tries very, *very* hard to keep the condescension from his tone.

Jesse wiggles the baby monitor in her hand– it's hooked up to a nanny cam. "Napping– thanks for always taking good care of my daughter, Jackson." Jesse has found ways to thwart Jack's rivalry by making him feel welcome to parenting our daughter too, but sometimes it comes out sounding sarcastic to even my ears.

Fun times.

"I stole your girlfriend." Jack's tone couldn't get any smugger... then he kisses Libby on the cheek just to twist the knife in Jesse's back. "She's an expert gamer. I doubt she's ever going to want to enter your side of the house again."

Sitting her perfect ass on the arm of the chair Libby's sitting in, Jesse beats Jack at his own game. "Yeah, but my side of the house has tasty pussy, and it's about to be served."

"Oh, my God," Libby breathes in a rush, voice quivering. "Excuse me, fellas, but I'm starving."

"I'm thinking after I make a few phone calls," I say to Jack, who looks ready to commit homicide or puke, "Maybe we should unpack."

"Unpacking? Yes. Yes, I think we should do that." Jackson is so focused on me, he doesn't even care that Jesse is swatting Libby's ass as they jog across our side of the basement. "Why wait?"

CHAPTER TWENTY-FIVE
Kaden Marx

We had unpacked each load, putting it in its rightful place, before going to get the next load, so I don't have much to wrangle before heading out to get groceries. While Wynn is waylaid by Royce, I quickly run to the store, put the food away, and then unpack everything from the last load. I didn't want our first night in this house together to be a stressful one, especially with how OCD Wynn can be about order.

I'm not a romantic– really, I'm not. But I think things should feel special. I'm still upset about how our first time had gone down when I had so much planned. We can fuck every day of our lives, but these rites of passage should be memorable. Wynn assures me it was more than memorable, going as far as to laugh at me. He's been pissy lately because I refuse to go there again– our second time *will* go as planned.

"Did you really organize the pantry?" Wynn's voice has me jumping out of my skin. "When I left here, it was a disaster." Folding around me from behind, he rests his chin on my shoulder, both of us staring into the cupboard. "I expected to have to do this."

"I expected that too." Hands resting over his as they hold me, I run my fingertips along the fine hairs on his forearms. "I'm selfish– I want your undivided attention tonight."

"Selfish is good," Wynn purrs, more relaxed than I've seen him in weeks. "My dad called Royce while I was there, and he talked to Willa, me, and the kids."

"Wow!" I turn around in his arms, noticing the stress has melted from his facial expression. Everything had felt forced from Wynn the past few weeks, and I knew I couldn't fix it, no matter how much I tried. "I'm relieved. Is Corbin coming home?"

Voice breaking with worry, "He said he had something to do with Octavia, then both of them would be coming home. Maybe a few weeks to a month or more– he didn't give a definitive date."

"That explains why you look relieved yet terrified." Dammit! The selfish side of me wants to throttle Corbin for putting a stain on Wynn's and my first night living together. But the other side of me, the more prevalent side, wants to help him do whatever he has to do to get back here with his family, bring Octavia back to Cain and Royce, and make sure the cost isn't too high to pay and ruins his sobriety.

"Did you eat too much at Royce's?" I ask instead, deciding to take a page out of Corbin's playbook and accept the things I cannot change. I can't change what's happening right now, so I move along with my plans.

"It was a total hubbub over there, so no vittles to be had." Leaning forward, Wynn's lips press against mine, but he doesn't make it more. "Starving– for whatever you're willing to give me," is a double entendre.

"Well," a wide smile breaks across my face, "I unpacked everything, but your dresser still needs to be organized and your shit needs to be put away in the bathroom. So how about you do that while I get supper on the table?"

"Mmm…" Wynn steals a kiss before stepping away. "I like the sounds of that. You're turning over a new leaf for me, cooking and cleaning."

"Ha!" I bark a sharp laugh. "Expect the filthy fucking hog to make a reappearance tomorrow, but I'm trying to be better at it."

"Trying's better than not," is Wynn's parting shot as he swaggers to the staircase.

Standing in the center of my tiny kitchen, I give myself a minute to become centered. When I first moved into this house, I felt like such an adult, but now I feel younger than I did then. I never felt alone before, just Perty and me in this house. Over the past four years, I've missed the home-life feeling, where you tool around the house, buy something big or small to make it feel like home, and just exist in your own space. When I'd come back to Rusty Knob, I was reluctant to leave the center or Royce's house and come back here all alone. I was used to the loud chaos of Royce's and my roommates in Morgantown.

Without Perty's nails clicking on the linoleum, his snores coming from his doggy bed, and the need to take him on walks, there was a level of loneliness I couldn't shake. But hearing Wynn overhead as he pulls his drawers open and closed, a blanket of serenity falls over me.

I'm gay, but not all those stereotypes bigots toss out at us. I'm not girly just because I love a man like a woman would. I don't need flowers and bullshit. I don't want to be the housewife or the mommy. So it's a struggle as I fight the need to nest, like it somehow makes me less masculine, because there is nothing in this world I want more than to cook Wynn a good meal and watch him enjoy it. Then I want to clean up the dishes together, take a walk together– go to sleep together and wake up to face another day with Wynn at my side.

As I light the gas grill, then get out the serving wear, I come to terms with how those things aren't masculine and feminine– gay or straight. They are human traits. There are straight men out there who want those things, living an unfulfilled life because they would be called weak for wanting it. There are women who want to be the provider but are belittled for not wanting to raise children.

Humming to myself, I place plates and utensils on the small table on the back porch. I've never eaten out here with a guest– but Wynn isn't a guest. This is his home, and I finally feel like it's mine because he's living in it.

I go about mundane tasks of home living, like getting the mail. As I'm sorting through the bills and advertisements, I spot a note tacked to the screen door.

No Visitors Allowed!
(NO exceptions)
That means you!
Gillette. Kennedy. Duncan. Franklin. Even you, Miriam.
Come back tomorrow after 9 a.m.
Don't call or text unless it's an emergency. You can live without us for 16 hours.

Heart exploding with warmth, I laugh softly as I chuck the mail into a basket resting on a side table. It feels good to know Wynn wants this as much as I do.

Wynn wanders downstairs, head peeking out the screen door to the back porch, just as I'm resting the steaks on a foil-lined tray. "I'm salivating."

"Nothing too special," I murmur, trying not to blush. "I didn't have time, and you know I'm not the best cook, so I just ordered up some sides at the deli. Pasta salad. That green fluffy salad with the marshmallows in it you love so much. Anybody can grill a steak."

"Not anybody–" Wynn steps onto the porch, fresh from the shower, wearing a pair of well-loved cotton shorts and nothing else.

"Jesus," I whisper underneath my breath, for the billionth time wondering what the fuck this kid sees in me. It's physically difficult to look away, but if I don't, supper won't be served– ass will be.

"I put a note on the front door to stop Warren from invading us. No doubt he can smell the steak from across the street. Penny can't cook if her life depended on it, and he can't grill for shit."

"Cain can make them smoothies," I tease with a wink as I take a seat at the table. My blush blooms even brighter as Wynn takes in how I'm using brand-new plates with matching bowls filled with deli sides, and I even lit a citronella candle.

Wynn has the good sense not to comment on where they came from, who paid for them, or why I'm being a sissy for trying to romance him. Alright, I know Wynn doesn't think that and my insecurities are talking, but I'm just happy he doesn't mention it.

"Everything looks so delicious, I don't know where to start." Wynn whips his cloth napkin to unfold it, then places it on his lap. He doesn't comment how everything matches– white and blood-splattered with little zombie gnomes.

You can find just about anything on the internet. If you can't find it, you can custom-order it. My shopping addiction has waned since I've been cut-off– from the internet, not Bren's trust.

Bren gives me whatever I want, saying I'm a good trustee so I deserve a wage. My trust is long gone thanks to a decade of higher education and this house. Wynn won't touch his trust, not a penny of it. His scholarship paid for tuition, and Bren paying me paid for our housing costs– Jack lived rent-free too. My stipend from the center pays all of the bills on this house, so we're good, not needing to mooch off anyone. But I miss buying awesome shit like my gnome dinnerware.

Smiling to himself, Wynn takes in every detail on his plate, then his eyes flick up and widen. "Suicidal Tendencies has friends," he murmurs, expression fighting between amusement and fear. My fingers wrap tightly around my fork, waiting for a lecture, followed by an epic fight, ruining our night. "You don't need forty gnomes to talk to, do you?"

Sighing in relief, I thought Wynn would judge me, but he was only worried about my mental health. "No, I'm good– well, my version of good. The gnomes, the mushroom houses… they have been arriving on their own, placing themselves in the lawn."

"What?" Wynn laughs, leaning forward to take a big scoop of pasta salad. "They just showed up? You didn't buy them?"

Pouring carefully, I fill our glasses with sun-tea. First thing I did early this afternoon was wash out my pickle jar, fill it with water and teabags, and plunk it in the middle of the front walk in direct sunlight. I've missed this comforting tradition.

"Every time I'd come home from Morgantown, there would be another gnome, or house, or something gnome-related in the back yard. I thought about setting up a game camera to catch the culprit. But truth be told, I didn't want them to stop doing it. I don't know…" Murmuring, I blush bright red, "Made me feel special, I guess. Like someone was thinking of me."

"Many people think of you– nonstop," Wynn assures me, and I believe him. "I'm still curious as to who the sneaky snake is, and whether or not they will still do it now that we live here."

As we hold a conversation, we manage to avoid all the pitfalls we usually fall into, which always result in passionate fights. This carries through while we clean up the supper dishes. Wynn's ignoring things that usually trigger him, like spying new gadgets in the kitchen, maintaining a playful edge to everything he does.

Rubbing the sting away from being snapped in the ass with the kitchen towel, "What do you want to do this evening?" My eyes flick quickly to note dusk is slowly falling.

"I have something on the porch I want to show you." Wynn tugs my hand, pulling me through the house, his smile infectious. "I've been waiting to do this all day."

"Waiting for what?" I'm not sure where all of his confidence is coming from. Usually Wynn is only forceful when he's angry or horny. But since he came home with the last of his stuff, it's like he's bloomed into my equal. Our relationship has shifted, and our personalities seem to be trying to match.

Feet hitting the front porch, "Whoa…" I bat Wynn's arms away when he tries to lift me. "What the hell are you doing?"

"Carrying you over the threshold." Wynn smirks, blue eyes holding more mischief and pleasure than I've ever seen before.

"No, this *was* my house," I stress. "Now it's *our* house. If anyone should be carried over the threshold, it's you." I poke Wynn in the chest.

Grabbing my finger, laughter filling the air, Wynn surprises me yet again. "Three rounds of rock-paper-scissors. Winner carries the other over the threshold first, then loser takes his turn."

"Are you being serious?" Blushing, my eyes flick across the street to note Warren sitting on the porch and Cain is yet again sky-gazing. Copper's playing mechanic with his car and a toy gas pump.

"Serious." Wynn chuckles, looking at me while I look at his brothers and nephew.

Leaning into him, I whisper, "It's cheesy."

"One. Two." His fisted hand pumps in the air, and drawn to the challenge, I mirror him. "Three. Rock."

"Paper." I smirk. "Best outta three, you say... One. Two. Scissors."

"Rock!" Wynn smiles brightly. "Tied."

"One. Two. Three. Paper… goddamn it," I snarl. "I thought for sure you'd do rock again, you twisted fucker."

Wynn scissors his fingers, pretending to cut the side of my palm. "I win!" is the only warning I get before I'm levitating off the ground.

"Ha!" I taunt, expecting Wynn to struggle to pick up my huge ass, but he does it with little effort. "Life's not fair." Sighing, I ignore Warren's cackle from across the street. With my feet set firmly on the living room floor, Wynn's not even breathing funny or breaking a sweat.

I am, though.

Grasping the waistband of his shorts, I tug Wynn out the screen door to the front porch. Before I get the chance to bend at the waist to pick him up, he's grabbing me instead. In front of his family, the entire neighborhood, the old biddy walking her teacup poodle, and God Himself, Wynn practically sucks my face off. Truly getting into it, Wynn's fingers clench my ass, pulling me tight against a hard dick, and then his hips grind rhythmically against mine.

Licking a path across my neck, "You asked what I wanted to do tonight…" Wynn shows me to the background soundtrack of Warren pretending to wretch, Copper asking if he's okay, and Cain's uncomfortable laughter.

Inhaling deeply, I scoop Wynn up, and I don't exhale until long after the screen door clatters behind us, not even as my feet pound on the stair treads. When I inhale again, Wynn's bouncing on our bed, face alight with pleasure.

Moving, my shirt is torn from my back, and I fling it wherever the hell it lands. Crawling over Wynn's prone, chuckling body, I kick off my shorts.

What plans?

I had plans, but they slip my mind as I yank Wynn's shorts off, finding out he's been commando all evening. Hard. He's been hard all evening too, even if I tried to ignore the gorgeous sight of his cock tenting the gray fabric, with a small wet spot dotting the front.

My perverted need for all things Wynn Erastus Gillette has my nose trailing along his flesh, from his left instep, along his furry calf, past his fleshy thigh, burying itself in his groin for a long detour. Wynn's musky, masculine scent of sweat, his natural woodsy odor, and the salty tang of precum. Inhaling deeply the entire journey, the tip of my nose trails his side, taking another long detour in his armpit, before I end the trip at the apex where his shoulder meets his neck.

"You smell so fucking good." Groaning, my own breath flutters back to fill my nostrils as I speak against his flesh. "Just one whiff and I'm hard yet comforted. I can't get enough."

My world tilts on its axis, Wynn reverses our positions until my back is pressed to the mattress with his body covering mine. "Kaden," he moans a split-second before his lips connect with mine, tongue delving deep.

Gripping, clinging, we devour one another for Lord knows how long. All I know is just kissing this man is delivering me to the brink. Pulling away, Wynn's face is flushed, his lips swollen, and he's panting laboriously.

"Open your mouth," Wynn purrs huskily as he slides to kneel on the bed next to my head.

Eyes held wide, I do as I'm told. This is the Wynn from the backseat of my old Durango. The Wynn who stood up for me on stage when I was fired. The Wynn I've seen off and on for the past five years. The Wynn who took control of his own best friend and gave him pleasure.

Adult Wynn is terrifying– intoxicating and getting stronger and stronger every day I know him. In this moment, I realize it's been me hung up on our six-year age difference, because Wynn's already more man than I'll ever be.

For once, my insecurities don't get ruffled. I *need* this version of Wynn.

"Wet your lips," Wynn demands, and I do. Tongue quickly dabbing out, it swaths across my lips. "No teeth," he warns, so I wrap my lips inward. Only ever touching Wynn, we've explored to the point of knowing exactly what the other needs. But it also meant we knew nothing in the beginning, and teeth happened. When I get overly excited, teeth happen still.

Leaning into me, Wynn grasps his cock at the root, and then paints my lips with his precum. Unable to help myself, my tongue quickly darts out to steal a taste. "Suck…" he purrs, slowly pressing in. "You're the one who taught me to suck dick, so don't pretend it's about licking. Suck."

Cheeks hollowing, I add as much suction as I can with a cock thrusting between my lips and down my throat. Groaning, just touching him, making Wynn feel good, is drawing me toward the brink. Wynn shifts, going deeper. My eyes slip shut, so I don't realize the reason he moved until I hear the bottle being opened.

"Please," I try to murmur around the intrusion, causing a shudder to work its way down Wynn's spine.

Gripping me in his fist, a saturated hand spreads sticky lube down my shaft, all over my balls, and then dips even lower. Wanton, scissoring my legs around, I widen my thighs in invitation.

Fear slams into me, causing me to stiffen up and close my legs before Wynn can touch me. Reading me like an open book, "Relax…" he coaxes, sticky palm pressing on the inside of my thigh. "Wanting this doesn't make you a girl. You're just a guy who wants me to touch him."

Whimpering, I pant through the fear as Wynn navigates me past my insecurities. "It's not a *boy pussy*," he sneers, hating that saying as much as I do. "Just because we're gay doesn't make us women and the straight guys real men. Your ass is *not* a vagina. You're a *man.*"

With a dick shoved between my lips and three fingers thrust inside my ass, I believe Wynn. My dead grandfather's words can't reach me, nor can the rest of the assholes in Rusty Knob, or my ex-fuckface professor who tried to make me hate who I am and where I came from.

"Wynn?" I gasp when he pulls away, dick and fingers leaving me feeling empty.

"Feet flat on the mattress and lift your hips," Wynn commands, voice a sexual rasp that has my cock throbbing. I do as he bid, and a pillow is shoved under the small of my back. "Draw your legs to your chest and wrap your arms around the back of your thighs."

"What-I–" stammering, all I can do is watch as Wynn moves to kneel between my legs. "I had plans. Really good plans." Plans that involved Wynn in this position with sultry music and cheesy candles, with drinks and snacks to quench us before round two.

I fucked up our first time and wanted to make our second time perfect. Wynn has his own plans, it seems.

Arching an eyebrow is Wynn's only reply. Forgetting all about plans, I'm awestruck as he fists the base of his cock, and then leans into me. Mouth lax, eyes glazed with intense lust with his blown pupils, Wynn takes what he wants from me, giving me what I need in return.

"Kade," is a benediction from Wynn's parted lips as he pushes inside me. The stretch and burn have my eyes holding wide, my mouth forming a pant, and my body going bowstring tight. "Not gonna wait no more– the pressure to perform wasn't doing us any good."

A heavy weight covers me as Wynn pitches forward. I release my legs, allowing his body to keep mine open to him. Curling around him, arms and legs gripping at his back and hips, emotions slam at me from every direction.

"We're not allowed to get chubby." My joking words cause Wynn to falter. Grinding upward, I try to show him why I said what I did. Cock being rubbed by our primal dance, Wynn's striated abs and my hard stomach is better than any handjob could ever be.

"Later tonight, tomorrow, the next day…" Wynn pants in my ear, breath moist and hot against my flesh. "You won't freeze me out. If we want this, we're going to do it. Understood?"

"Yeah!" A grunt is torn from my chest as Wynn rolls his hips in an expert move, and I have no idea where he learned it. Stretched tight, slightly burning but enjoying the fullness, I can feel every vein in Wynn's dick. "You're kinda big, so maybe give me a few days break."

Chuckling evilly, "You can do me next."

"UGH!" Lifted, my legs are hooked over Wynn's shoulders and his cock is pegging the hell out of my gland. "Don't stop! Good God, don't you fucking stop!"

"Now look who's being bossy," Wynn teases me, but it's cut off on a moan. "Not gonna last long– you feel too good."

Wynn's inside me– in my body, my mind, my heart and my soul. Wrapped up tight together, our sweat-slickened bodies gliding against each other, I let go first, with Wynn joining me seconds later.

This time, I'm louder than Wynn, and I don't doubt the neighbors heard me screaming Wynn's name.

Breathing slowing, synchronizing with Wynn's, my plans for the night filter in. With a shaking hand, I reach for the drawer pull on our nightstand, but fingertips bracelet my wrist, stopping me.

"Just lie here and let me take care of you." Wynn pulls free from my body, and I miss the pressure immediately. My legs flop to the mattress, completely useless after such a thorough fucking. "I'll be back in a minute." Then he is disappearing out of our bedroom, just as I lose the fight with my heavy eyelids.

Regaining cognizance, a warm, wet, soothing stroke is between my buttocks. "No," I protest, mortified. "I'll get up and change the sheets after I shower."

"Stay–" Wynn presses my shoulder back down, then he bats my hand away as I try to stop him. "Kade, you taught me how to douche– did it for me. Me cleaning up the mess I made of your body is no big deal." He smiles down at me, amusement his passenger. "All done!" The dirty rag splats on the hardwood.

"Did you… did you just do that? Mr. OCD, did you just toss a rag covered in your jizz and my butt juice on a pristine hardwood floor?"

"Why, yes, sir." Still buck-naked, Wynn crawls on the bed next to me. "I do believe I did." A champagne flute is thrust into my hand.

"What the…" trailing off, I stare at the golden bubbles. "You had plans?"

"Yup." Wynn grins at me.

"But what about *my* plans?" I contemplate the champagne, then say the hell with it and take a sip. "Mmm…" the bubbles pop on my tongue, waking me up.

"Kade?" Wynn turns to face me, lounging in the center of the bed with a flute in his hand. "You're the one who needed the bells and whistles– I didn't."

"But I wanted you to have 'em." Dumbfounded, I just stare at my partner while he smirks at me. "I wanted it to be special."

"Wasn't it? Since the Durango, what hasn't been special? Every minute has been because it was you and me. We're wandering this life together, making mistakes and learning from 'em. *You* needed the special treatment and extra attention, so I'm giving you what you need."

All I can do is stare at Wynn in total shock. He twists to the side to retrieve a tray that was hidden behind his back on the mattress. "Strawberry?"

"Chocolate-covered strawberries?" I snort, "Cheesy," but I secretly love it. Judging by the knowing gleam in Wynn's eye, he knows I do too.

"Just because you're older, doesn't mean you have to make the plans, Kaden." Wynn chomps on a berry, eyes closing as he chews. "It doesn't relegate you as the man and me the woman, or vice versa. We're not going to be slipping gender roles by who takes it for the evening– we're both men. You can surprise me next time."

"I have something for you…" I turn back to the nightstand, but Wynn stops me.

"Have a strawberry, Kade," is a demand I can't ignore. I reach for one with a lot of white chocolate drizzle. "No, this one." Wynn moves the tray under my hand until I pick the one he wants me to have.

"What's up with you?" Taking the berry, it feels odd between my fingertips. Cold. Metallic. "You asshole!" I shout, flushed with a crimson kiss. "I wanted to give you yours."

"Touch that drawer again, I'ma smack your ass," Wynn warns. "I asked you– you said yes. I get to give you a ring first."

"Holy shit!" I know when to pick my battles with him. Examining the berry, a platinum band is sitting around the stem. All I can do is stare with my mouth catching flies.

"Being that we live in a town called Rusty, I wanted to give you something stainless. I don't mean steel, either. You deserved something pristine, without taint– a ring only you've ever worn. One to last forever."

"Wynn?" I hate how breathy I sound, but Wynn seems to be enjoying my shocked reaction. "Do I wear it now? I wasn't sure. I mean… we're not girls, so it's not an engagement ring. I wasn't sure what to do when I gave you yours. Wear it now, or is it the rings we exchange on our wedding day?"

"Kade?" Wynn relaxes, getting more and more comfortable the more awkward I get. "We don't follow the rules– we make 'em."

From now until nine a.m. the next morning, we make up rules for our life. We compromise with a ceremony involving all of our friends and family, instead of the elopement Wynn wanted and the large affair I wanted. We decide no one gets to dictate how we live our lives, because once you've not only knocked on death's door but let him in, every second thereafter is a gift you don't squander.

CHAPTER TWENTY-SIX
Brennan Kennedy

Pacing. Life is all about pacing. Normally I would have pushed myself to run miles more, then regretted how depleted I felt. Normally I would have gone balls to the wall on my new gym equipment, but regretted how my muscles seized up. With Jack in my life, life is all about pacing.

Jack's good for a two-mile jog in the evenings, while I'm used to running full-out for miles on end. Our compromise has us jogging two miles, and walking two miles home. It's a great way to end the day, able to talk to each other without interruption. Plus, there's the added benefit of Jack in tiny jogging shorts and a tank top.

Balance. Jesse needs time early in the morning, because she wakes up inspired. So I have Honor in the mornings, coming into work later than I should. Jesse has Honor in the evenings, giving Jack and me some much needed alone time.

"What's your schedule for the rest of the week?" I'm barely breaking a sweat, let alone out of breath, but Jack is struggling. In a few more weeks, with our jogging and walking, his endurance will increase. "Same shit, different day for me. My foreman– Jim's getting a bit peeved with me because construction starts early in the morning and I'm supposed to be apprenticing so he can retire."

"I can handle Honor in the morning, getting her dressed and fed and off to preschool," Jack offers, but that wasn't why I was venting.

"That's not why–"

"I know," Jack stresses, wiping his face off with the bottom of his shirt, giving me a nice view in the process. "You know I see Honor as my daughter too. I'm not saying that because of whatever you and I have going on– it's just how I've always felt."

After taking a large guzzle of water, I reply. "I don't want to burden you. You're still studying while holding a fulltime position at the hospital."

"I won't be the only nurse with a kid," Jack reminds me, smirking. "Especially since I'm a labor and delivery nurse studying midwifery, dumbass. I'm in the business of babies."

Flipping around, I walk backwards down the sidewalk so I can look at Jack as we talk. "I'm not saying you won't be great with Honor. I was only asking your schedule so I knew when we could hang out."

"I know." Jack tries to suppress his smug grin, but fails. "I want to spend time with you too, and I know the sooner you go to work, the quicker your entire crew gets to go home in the evenings."

"It's also cooler in the morning– Jesus Christ, it's hotter than Hades. Swamp muggy. By the end of the day, I feel like my nutsack has turned into melted flesh and dripped down my leg to pool on the roof. If you think it's hot on the ground, try being two stories up when it's ninety degrees in the shade… only you're above the shade and have to wear protective clothing that doesn't breathe. Torture. Pure fucking torture."

"Get your ass to work at five a.m., dipshit." Jack just shakes his head left and right at me. "I'm working days for the next three weeks. With two nights a week for summer session classes. We'll revisit this conversation when my schedule changes. But from now on, I'll take care of Honor's needs in the morning."

"Thank you," I breathe, heart stuttering a beat at how amazing Jack truly is. He's such a good human being.

"HA!" Jack laughs at whatever dumb expression is on my face. "I'm not entirely being altruistic. If you're exhausted from the heat, I don't have it in me to force you to spend time with me."

"Force?" Judging by the way Jack's face goes blank, there must be a naughty gleam in my eye. Stopping in the middle of the sidewalk, I won't let Jack pass. "We make a great team, you and I. Don't you think?"

"Yeah, we do," comes breathy, but not from exertion. A loud bellow fills the air, causing both Jack and me to jerk our heads around. It takes a few seconds to put two and two together.

"Was that… was that Kaden?" Jack snorts, and snorts again when Wynn's shout hits our ears.

All I can do is swallow my laughter as I stare at the exterior of a tiny blue house with two idiots inside alerting the neighborhood to their sexual exploits.

"I've never been more thankful for earbuds in my life," rasps from directly behind me, causing me to jump and squawk. "They are exhibitionists."

"Holy shit, Cain. You scared the piss out of me." Jack's holding his chest. "You walk like a ninja… or a ghost."

Earbuds dangling from his fingertips, Cain flashes us a sneaky grin, causing Jack to look flushed and me to feel flustered.

"They've been going at it for two hours," Warren projects from across the street. He's sitting on the porch reading a magazine. "Fools carried each other over the threshold, then went at it like rabbits. But first they wouldn't share their steak." Warren glares at his brother for being vegan. "I'm a red-blooded male who needs some barely dead meat. I want it to still be mooing when I put my knife and fork into it. Fuck raw vegetables."

"They made a sign for us." Cain points at a note on the door. "Like anyone in their right mind would interrupt." Visibly shuddering, he walks back across the street, and then picks up a worn paperback off the porch's bottom step.

"Either they soundproof their house, or I'ma force 'em to move." Warren's in a rare mood, flicking the pages on his auto magazine with brutal force. "No man should have to listen to his buddy banging the hell outta his baby brother... just saying. Have some respect for my sensibilities."

"And on that note—" Jack takes off jogging again, his laughter trailing after him.

"Have a good night!" I shout as I jog after Jack.

"Remember what I said," Warren warns. "Yer daddy is your neighbor. Don't fuck with his head like that."

"Never happen," I shout back as I jog away. "Never gonna happen."

I catch up with Jack at the end of the block. He's bent at the waist, holding his side, while laughing his head off. "Those two are shameless, I tell ya!" Chuckling and shaking his head, Jack's eyes are bright and shiny. "I don't get them at all. Not one bit."

"They need to apologize to Warren at least," I grumble, feeling bad for the guy. It's not homophobia, but just good old-fashioned big brother syndrome. "Maybe fix him something to eat."

"Yeah!" Jack leans from side to side with one hand on his hip, stretching out his back. "Kade better fix Warren a giant prime rib, put it on the front porch, ring the doorbell, and run like hell."

"Yeah– that!" I join Jack in stretching by grabbing the front of my foot and drawing my calf back toward my ass. "I really have tried to understand Kade and Wynn, but I just can't."

Dropping my leg, I start walking again to avoid the teenage girls who are peeking at us from their front window. Jack joins me in contemplative silence for a few streets.

"I know you probably don't want to hear it... but as the only person they've let into their *world*, they're not doing it against the other– they're experiencing it together. I was someone they both trusted and cared about enough to let in. But it wasn't about me at all, and I understood that."

"I know we're–" fumbling, I'm not sure how to say what I need to say. "I know we're not together *together*. But I can't wrap my mind around being madly in love with someone and being okay with them going off to fuck someone else."

I don't say it, but I think it, and I know Jackson hears what I'm thinking. I know how it feels to know the person you're in love with is somewhere else, seeking something they want from someone else when you're more than willing to give it to them. I've tried to hide it, how upset I was knowing Jack wanted to go off and get a random blowjob from a stranger. But just as I felt with Jesse and the pregnancy, how it was her choice to do what she wanted with her body, I felt the same way with Jack.

I wanted my child, I wanted Jack, but I had to have faith in the relationships I had with both of them to know they would make the right choices, for all of us.

If Jack didn't want it, he wouldn't have been doing it. I understood he was punishing me for dicking with him from the end of junior year until everyone else had graduated from college. I understood it and I learned from it, but I will never go through it again. I'm not a doormat, and I won't allow anyone to turn me into one. I know Jack respects me and himself enough never to do this to *us*.

If I'd known Jack was going to mess around with Kade and Wynn, it wouldn't have hurt as much in the moment, because I was terrified something like what happened with Cain would happen. It actually helped that Jack learned a valuable lesson while I did. No, I don't blame Cain, or Kade, or Wynn for what they did with Jack, because it's Jack's body and it's his choice.

Possessive jealousy is just another form of abuse, and I agree with both Kade and Wynn on that. While it's hot to think someone wants you *that* much, it's just controlling bullshit. I understand why Jack was being petty, playing games to teach me a lesson, but I can't respect Jack disrespecting himself in the process.

Fucking a stranger isn't a bad thing as long as it's what Jack wanted, but he did it to hurt himself and me.

I'm no saint, so I can't judge Jack for fucking it all up. Lord knows, I've been doing a bang-up job of it myself.

"I know what you're thinking." Jack refuses to look at me, remorse etched across his features. Even his shoulders curl as his head bows in shame. "It's not like that for them, Bren," Jack defends Kade and Wynn, voice going a little icy. "I couldn't live that way, but I *do* understand it. It's not going off to fuck someone else. It's like you can never truly understand what it's like to be a nurse, and I will never understand what it's like to work manual labor, with thirty guys lives in my hands, and a client to impress."

Totally thrown at the odd subject change, my voice pitches high. "Yeah, but we talk about it, ya know? We make sure the other one understands what's happening in our lives. Every day."

Jack puts a hand on my chest to stop me, and my heart accelerates to reach out to him. "But the difference is how they don't have to talk about it. It's a shared experience. They're in it together. I've never seen them more connected, and that tie has strengthened since."

"It's so baffling," I whisper, staring at my sneakers. "I-I-I–"

"It will never be with people they don't love and trust. That's not who they are. But shouting so loud that everyone, including their own brothers, heard them, that's because they truly want to share what they have with the world."

"I guess I'm too private," I mutter, trying to understand but failing. "Modest, maybe? After having threesomes and seeing the devastation, never again. I want you all to myself." Jack blushes, so I take that as invitation to continue. "I don't want to share your affection– your love."

Five years, maybe even longer if I think back, I've been shut off. Jesse and I were never the type to kiss and tell. Sex was about sex. There was no hand-holding, no stolen kisses in public, or in private. Obviously I get why now, but after a lifetime of not just reaching out and touching someone, I don't even when I want to.

Going against what's been ingrained, I reach out to pass my fingertips through Jack's, wanting to hold his hand for the first time in public as a couple. Baby steps. I had a lot of sex in high school, all of it behind closed doors, and absolutely no affection or sex in more than four years. These little tastes of Jack lately, they made me want more.

I'm starved, but I've gone so long I don't know if I can handle being hit all at once with sensation.

Standing in the middle of the sidewalk, Jack stares down at our linked hands with a look I can't decipher written across his face.

Then he tugs me, and I worry I've done something wrong. But all he does is align his body to the side of mine, cheek pressed close to my lips.

Warmth floods my system, drowning me. Every nerve in my body sparks to life, quivering to get closer to Jack. My eyes flutter shut from the sense of belonging.

"I'm not sorry I was with them, Bren," Jack whispers in my ear. Then he squeezes my hand in comfort. "It wasn't about you. It was all about me, something I needed for myself, and that's why I get them, even if I'm not wired the way they are."

"Explain it to me," I breathe back, nose softly caressing Jack's jawline. The subtle scrape of whiskers against my skin makes my knees go weak.

"Brennan, for people like us, every moment we're closer to death. But for survivors, it's another moment to celebrate how they lived. We can never understand, because we take our time in this life for granted, while they see all the good *and* bad as a gift they never thought they'd experience."

"Jesus!" I cry out, turning my head to capture Jack's lips, not giving a shit that I'm kissing him in public, right in the middle of the sidewalk. It's not the brutal actions of a starving man– we fall into our embrace as easy as breathing.

Not understanding my brothers, I decide I'm willing to try. I will never share Jack, never share myself, but I don't want to go through life as an apathetic asshole who is just biding his time until death. No more taking anything for granted.

Arms clinging, fingertips biting in, the rough rasp of whiskers abrading my neck, my cheek, my lips, all I can do is hold on as our need erupts. Stroking and rubbing, breathing hard, neither of us knows where to begin.

Palming the back of Jack's head, I draw him down to my lips for a real kiss, but as soon as we connect, a throat clearing has us jumping apart.

"Oh, shit! I'm so sorry," I mutter as Jackson releases a string of curses. Blushing, he turns his back to face the street. "After I promised Warren, goddammit!" I chastise myself.

Chuckling softly, Dad stares at me as he crouches in the garden. "I figured you didn't realize whose house you were in front of, but thought I better stop ya before clothing was shed."

"Going home now." Mortified, Jackson takes off up the sidewalk, and I watch as he nearly collapses to sit on the bottom steps to the duplex.

"I'm guessing you heard what we said." Turning, I face my dad but I won't look at him. I do a quick scan to make sure Willa and the twins are inside though. "Just pretend you can't read between the lines."

"Where do you think you got your bat-like hearing, son?" Dad's voice gets closer, and the amusement in his tone gets thicker. "I'm not an idiot, ya know? I do know more than you think."

"Don't tell me that." I turn away from him, hiding my mortification. I glance at Jack, and he quickly looks away from me, but I can see how bright his blush is all the way from here.

"Kade does talk to me. About everything." Dad's hand lands on my shoulder, fingers clenching in a soothing massage. "Warren also just called to beg me to drive a wrecking ball through their house, and to bring him a steak while I was at it."

"Oh, Lord," I groan. "They are shameless."

"I think it's great–" I move to cut him off, but no one cuts off Royce Kennedy. "I know what you're thinking, how you assume I'm in the dark. I'm not, son. I'm not. Let them do whatever they want to do, because you need to take care of your own business."

"This said by Rusty Knob's micromanaging patriarch?"

Dad only laughs at my sarcasm, having found a thick vein of humor since Willa and the twins came to live with him. The loss of baby Royce actually made Dad more lighthearted. An epiphany strikes, and I realize Dad thinks like Kade and Wynn do now, probably Willa too.

Thankful for every breath taken– every agonizing moment is still a celebration how they still live.

Shit!

"That kid sitting over there–" Dad points at Jackson, who's sipping on his water bottle. "He's waiting for you to make the first move, son. No one is going to argue about why Jack did what he did with your brothers. So maybe you ought to make sure it doesn't happen again."

"How?" I breathe out, the remembered pain resurfacing.

"He's your best friend, right?" Dad tugs me to look him in the eye. "Ever since Franny left Rusty Knob, you and Jack have gotten closer and closer, but it changed what had started to build when you were in high school."

"This is so *creepy*," I mutter, rolling my eyes. "Having this conversation with my father."

"Who better else, son?" Dad chuckles some more, tugging me into the grass so we're not hanging out on the sidewalk becoming fodder for the gossiping old biddies. "You're going to want Honor to come to you for everything. Remember that."

"Fine." I sigh heavily, sounding put out, but I really do want this type of closeness with Dad. "Lay the advice on me."

Dad glows, happier than a pig in shit when it comes to spreading his advice town-wide. "Being friends is a fundamental building block of any relationship. If you're in it for the long haul, you better make sure you can stand 'em, right?"

Laughing, I blurt out, "Right."

"What drew you to Jack wasn't friendship, though. I remember how fucking batshit you both acted around each other. It was like watching one of Hayley's favorite shows."

Eyes flicking, I take a good, long look at the subject of our conversation. Slumping on the steps, head hanging, bottle sloshing back and forth like a metronome from his fingertips, I've never wanted anything as much as I've wanted Jack.

"I still feel that way, Dad," I finally admit. "I just hide it."

"Why hide it anymore?" Dad says as if the answer is that easy. "You and Jessica respected each other during your marriage, and I respect you both for that. But what's done is done, and what is now can change your life."

"What?" I squeak out, hating how high my voice pitches in surprise. "Look at you, all romance guru or some shit."

"I just said I have to listen to Kade, remember?" Blushing, Dad laughs at himself while simultaneously making fun of Kaden's romantic streak. "If you want to go the long haul, ya gotta be friends. But you also have to be lovers, and I don't just mean sex. Have fun in and outside of the bedroom."

"Dad," I drawl out, more than mortified now.

"Brennan Honor Kennedy," Dad chastises me. "Do you want me to kiss your ass, or do you want to be happy?"

"Happy," I mutter begrudgingly.

"So listen to your old man, then." He mock-punches my shoulder. "If you don't want Jack playing with your deviant brothers, then maybe you should clue the kid in on how you see him as your partner. I don't mean that in gay terms, either. Plenty of straight marriages are not partnerships, and there are too many divorces."

"You're not married," I remind him.

"But Willa's my partner. She's my best friend, but she's also my lover. You need both for a partnership to work."

Mystified, I just stare at my dad with my jaw hanging low, catching flies. "You're telling me to go screw Jack? *You*?"

"Don't be gross, Bren," Dad chastises me. "Your walks have been good for the two of you. That's intimacy. All I'm saying, maybe you better go tell Jack you want to be with him, and touch him while you're at it. Quit friend-zoning your boyfriend."

"Get off Facebook!" I shout aghast. "No forty-two-year-old should speak like that."

"I've got tweens in my house, son." This time Dad's punch feels a little too real to be playful. "I'm on Facebook more than you, and I watch waaaayyy too many shitty TV shows. I'm down with the lingo." Leaning in to whisper in my ear, "I'm not old, asshat. Right now, you and I are in the same boat, floating in the same shitty lake of raising kids."

"Uncle!" I shout, stalking away. "You win! Royce Kennedy is always right."

"'Bout time you admitted that, son." Dad's laughter is taunting as he goes back to gardening. "Have fun tonight. But, unlike Warren, I do own a crane with a wrecking ball attachment. Keep it down."

"Why won't the ground open up and swallow me?" I ask Jack as I stalk up the sidewalk toward him. "That was worse than having the sex talk when I was ten."

"Ten?" Jack's eyebrows hitch high in surprise. "I was fourteen."

"Already established that you started your period at sixteen," I mutter in a teasing tone.

Sitting on the bottom step, Jack reaches up to fist the center of my shirt, tugging me down to his level. "You suck," he whispers against my lips.

"Let's get inside and I'll prove it," I whisper back, not turning it into a kiss. "Wanna go steady? Be my boyfriend? Ya know, live with me, share a life and a home and a little girl who wouldn't be here without you? Be my partner, so I have a reason to feel this level of insane jealousy and you won't go looking for what I am more than willing to give ya?"

"Umm… yeah–" Never have I managed to stun Jackson, until now. "I'm totally down for that."

"'Bout time." Modesty getting the best of me, I've used up my allotment of public displays of affection. "Let's go shower, 'kay?"

"That, I'm totally down for." Jack springs up like his ass is on fire. "You know, we're blessed with having a giant shower."

"I like this *we* in which you speak," I tease. "If Wynn and Kade can have a honeymoon because they moved in with each other, than you and I can celebrate you finally moving into our room and unpacking your shit."

"Deal!" Jack trails as he runs up the steps, only to bump into Jesse coming out.

"Shit!" Jesse backs up, hands out in a stop motion. "Never mind."

Jackson notices exactly what I do, the concerned look in Jesse's eyes. "What's up?"

Eyes cast down, Jesse stares at her sandals. "I don't know how to say this without pissing you off, Jack. But I know that lust-crazed look in Bren's eye, so I don't want to ruin what you guys were gonna finally do."

"Out with it," Jackson demands, managing my wife better than I ever could. "What's going on?"

"Honor hasn't felt good today, and I was going to have you check on her– see if we need to take her to the doctor or not." Sheepish, Jesse still won't look at us. "I don't want you to think I'm making shit up to stop this–" she points between us. "I want that for you, truly I do. But Honor–"

"Symptoms?" Jack demands, cutting Jesse off. He's already on his way up to Honor's bedroom with Jesse explaining a tummy ache and fever, with me trailing behind. "I'm sure she'll be fine, but let's make sure she can keep fluids in her."

"Thank you, Jackson." Jesse's voice warbles, a mix of fear over our daughter being ill and continually walking on eggshells around Jack. But I feel this will be a turning point. One good thing out of having my heart beating out of my chest for my daughter, at least.

CHAPTER TWENTY-SEVEN
Kaden Marx

I planned on getting up before Wynn, which is a feat because the guy rises easier and brighter than the sun. Assuming he's doing his morning jog routine, I get my day started. Wynn's the only one of us who fled Morgantown for Rusty Knob who doesn't have a job tying them down.

Jack's still studying while holding a fulltime position at the hospital. Bren started up with Kennedy Construction a few weeks back. Jessica is working on her paintings while raising Honor, and no one is going to argue that she is living a life of leisure– Honor is a handful, and even I will agree preschool was the best idea. I work four days at the Center, and I could stretch it to last the full week if I cut my hours down, or shorter if I worked harder. The center runs itself for the most part, with me doing all the administrative duties. I'm not yet licensed to run the group sessions, but I do sit in while local therapists volunteer their time to lead the group. Believe it or not, Penny keeps the operation running smoothly.

Wynn, when he was a kid, he worked day-in and day-out. But as an adult, he hasn't held a job. His basketball and school careers are finished, and he's refusing to take any more classes to get his teaching degree, at least not yet. He just wants to be left to his own devices in the barn. Truth be told, he wants to be within shouting distance of Willa after everything that happened with baby Royce, but no one will admit this aloud. I don't blame Wynn. Royce manages everything from his home office, never leaving the property unless Willa is with him.

While I plate up two omelets, my gaze drifts to the kitchen chairs– no way in hell is my ass going to take sitting on wood after last night's pounding. Wynn was in rare form, taking me three times and not letting me return the favor. He said tonight was my turn.

Fighting a blush just at the memory, I gaze out the window over the sink to the back porch. The wrought iron dinette set has cushions– just what my poor ass needs.

"What the…" murmurs softly from between my surprised lips. I catch sight of Wynn in the backyard, glancing over his shoulder while carrying something, acting all shady. Hands pressed to the edge of the sink, I lean forward to get a better look out the window.

Wynn steps over the small fence my secret admirer installed about a month ago, then he crouches, eyes flicking in all directions because he can feel me gazing at him. After some rearranging, a tree trunk gnome house is placed, with one of the straggler gnomes tucked in the doorway. Standing, he brushes off his hands on his shorts, and then steps back over the fence. He gives Suicidal Tendencies a pat to the top of the hat, and starts for the porch.

Mind spinning in a billion different directions, I lunge for the stove, where I pretend to be plating an omelet. Instead of jumping when the screen door creaks shut with a slam, I try to force my muscles to be relaxed and fluid.

"Mmm… smells good," Wynn purrs, coming up behind me. I hear him saying how gender roles are bullshit, and try to remember that as he wraps his arms around my waist and kisses me on the side of the neck.

I'm not a girl. I'm not a girl. I'm not a girl.

Just because I cooked Wynn breakfast after letting him fuck me all night, that doesn't make me a girl. In a few minutes, I'm going to go out in the big, bad world and become the provider. Hunting and gathering to bring home more food to cook. In other words, I'm going to go sit at my desk and do my job so I can get paid money that will pay the bills on this house.

For the past five years, longer still if you count the fact that I've known Wynn since he was born, I've wanted to be the one in control– the mentor. Somehow the little shit I've grown to love is now more than my equal. He's asserting himself to prove he's my equal, but he's managing to be more than I can ever be, and it's utterly terrifying.

What's utterly terrifying is how easily I could slip into becoming dependent on Wynn, needing his strength and goodness, when all along I thought it would be me in charge.

Last night while we were lying in bed, Wynn kept reassuring me how bottoming to him, wanting romantic bullshit, and cooking for him, how that didn't make me less of a man. My grandfather kept superimposing over top of what Wynn was saying. Somehow, in the middle of the night, my father joined in, only he told me to let this shit go and enjoy how my relationship with Wynn is everything I want and more. But, then again, I don't know if it was my dad or me, since we look and sound just alike.

Talk about a royal mind fuck.

"Stop," Wynn breathes into my ear. "I'll make breakfast tomorrow. Quit thinking about that horseshit. Believe me," he purrs, hand sliding from my waist to cup the bulge hardening in my trousers. "This is all man." After a teasing squeeze, he reaches for his plate, and then swaggers out to the porch.

How is it humanly possible for me to want to get off again? Growling with annoyance, I adjust myself, and then grab my plate and two bottles of water.

"What time will you be home tonight?" Wynn asks conversationally, but he's glowing bright with happiness. Day two of our honeymoon period seems to be setting a good trend. "I'll make sure dinner is ready for when you get home."

"Probably later than usual– I have quite a bit to take care of after not going to the center for almost a week. Plus, for some reason, the instant I set foot in there, people flood my office, wanting attention."

"It's good to be wanted." Wynn winks at me, the little shit. No one denies my constant need to be the center of attention, even if it gets annoying at times. "I'm just going to go hang out with my sister, then tool around in the barn. I'm not going to start a project until after I've taken inventory of my supplies."

"What kind of project are you thinking?" I stab my omelet, trying to eat slowly even though I'm starving after last night.

"One project to pay some bills and give me some cash to start another project." Wynn shrugs. "On the side, I'll start working on upgrades in the house. That is–" he looks away, turning sheepish. "If you still want to do what we planned."

"Yeah." I nod, knowing we're playing this by ear right now. I haven't turned in the paperwork to children services yet. I'm going to wait a few weeks until after we get settled in. "I'll talk to Bren. He did a damn fine job with the duplex. He can help us design the upstairs, and you and I can do the work on it ourselves."

"I like that." Wynn's smile stretches far and wide. "This does feel like home, ya know? Not a layover like I felt across the street, or at Royce's, or in Morgantown. Even though this was your house first, it feels like it's *ours*. I've never felt that way before, always loathing Gillette Holler."

"I thought it felt like home before." Gazing down at my plate, I admit the truth. "At first I liked being alone. Then Perty came, and it was a comfort to have a dog happy to see me when I came home at night. But these past few years, this house has felt more like one of your layovers. It's like, yesterday when we were moving your stuff in here, I was moving home too. Because–"

"Because?" Wynn reaches over to rest his hand on mine. "Because we're each other's home."

"Yeah." A huff of laughter bubbles up when I realize it's the truth. "Yeah, my home is with the guy who sneaks around my yard, delivering gnomes."

"Nope, don't know what you're talking about." Wynn looks everywhere but at me or at the zombie gnome horde in the yard. "Me?" he points at his chest. "Me? The stingy bastard? Would I waste money on grotesque yet cute statues?"

"Yeah, you would." Leaning across the table, I flutter a kiss to his surprised lips. "Because you love me."

"Shit!" Wynn blushes bright red. "You caught me!"

"You had the others sent to Warren, didn't you? He delivered them when you were at school." Smiling, I quickly gobble up what's left of my omelet.

"Wrong," Wynn sings. "Like I'd trust one of my brothers to do a dang thing."

Laughing, I know exactly who Wynn would trust. Rising to my feet, I steal another kiss. "I'll be home around five, but I have to be back at six. We have a few classes happening this evening, so Penny and I have to tag-team.

"How about I bring supper to you? We can camp out somewhere in the building, and I'll help with the classes tonight? I've been thinking of adding a woodworking class twice a month to the schedule, once I get my projects sorted out."

"Like, like, and like," I murmur against his lips. "All of your ideas are always perfect, Golden Boy."

"I prefer it when you call me little shit."

"So do I," I rasp huskily. "So do I." With a backward wave, I lope down the back steps to the yard, then make my way around the house. "I'll say hello to your gnome delivery partner in crime, little shit!"

Even after a five-minute drive through town, I'm still grinning ear-to-ear when I enter the front door to the center. Surrounded by Rusty Knob's rich history, Penny's always the first face I see, with it being a crapshoot on whether or not any tiny Gillettes are clinging to her.

"How many more gnomes are hiding at your place for special delivery?" Smirking at Penny's stunned expression, I walk past the reception desk and sneak a peek at Ginger snoozing in her portable crib.

"Whose ass needs ice this morning?" is Penny's snarky comeback.

"Not Wynn's," I mutter with a smirk, and my reward is Penny's gobsmacked expression.

"What?" Tiny jaw unhinged, Penny's brown eyes bulge from their sockets. "I was just joking. I figured you were doing the usual."

"The screaming bloody murder didn't clue you in?" Biting back laughter, I have to turn until Penny's no longer in my peripheral. If I witness her shock, I'll bust out laughing.

"I couldn't hear it in the house– I honestly thought Warren was making a joke." Penny busies herself by grabbing the file with my daily schedule. "Really? Huh? I thought for sure it would be the other way around."

"Don't sit on your porch tonight." I take the file from her. "Or else you'll find out for sure, being that it's Wynn's turn."

"Oh, my God!" Penny shouts. "Bleach. I need to bleach my brain!" follows me all through the center on my way to my office in the outermost building.

Still silently laughing when I take my seat, my wince has it changing to vocal guffaws. While my laptop boots up, I quickly scan today's schedule, groaning when I see Miriam actually made an appointment this time.

Relentless.

Even Jessica penciled me in for some reason.

Before I can examine the why, my first appointment is already knocking on my open door. "Come in, Miriam." I sound exhausted, even to my own ears. All the warm and fuzzies from Wynn, the high from last night's epic sex, and the amusement at torturing my future sister-in-law, it all evaporates when a classy forty-something woman crosses the threshold into my office.

"I see you made an appointment this time." With a fingertip, I flick the file closed. Miriam's nosy enough as it is. "It's good to see you," I admit as I rise to my feet, quickly bussing her cheek.

"Such a liar." Miriam rumbles a laugh as she takes her seat. "It is good to see you, Kaden. I know our professional business has interfered with our personal business, but I do want you to be happy to see me."

"I am," and the sincerity in my tone is hard to deny. "If you want to have a personal relationship, I'm more than happy to have one. How's Tyler? Any plans to visit the area this summer?"

Intelligent eyes narrowing, Miriam humors me as usual. "Tyler's thinking of visiting near the end of August. He's hard-pressed to find a job out east. So right now, he's just trying to figure out if he should come back home where the cost of living is ten times cheaper."

"It's an epidemic, really." I lean back in my chair, refusing to bring up Wynn. He's just one of thousands who graduated this year who won't be able to get a job with their degrees. Their only recourse is to continue their education, racking up more debt, or fight others for a job just to make rent.

"Tyler's first student loan payments will begin shortly." Miriam gazes at her hands, looking lost. "So much for the American dream, right? My son was one of the brightest in his class, not that it means a damn thing. They're all worthy of a profession. There just aren't any to be had."

"I'm surprised you're not passing out employment opportunities like it's candy. Tyler's your son, so why go after Wynn and me instead?"

"I can only work with what I have to work with, Kaden." Miriam does that momma shake of her head– the one that means they're disappointed in you. "I can offer teaching jobs to young men and women as my current staff ages out to retirement. But I can't give my son a job when teaching is not his thing."

"What is Tyler's thing?"

"Fuck if I know– it would be easier and cheaper for both Tyler and me if he'd move back home. No job while living in my house, with me footing his student loan payments, versus Tyler racking up more debt while working a dead-end job to pay for a postage-stamp of an apartment for two grand a month, when the equivalent is four hundred in Kentwood County. He needs to get his shit together, so that's why I'm here."

"What does Tyler have to do with me?" I mutter in amusement.

"I need to be around someone I've mentored who does have their shit together– finally, anyway," Miriam murmurs quietly. "I feel like a failure at this rate. I'm now in a position to make a positive change, evolving Kentwood from being backward and narrow-minded. I've been offering our local graduates teaching positions. I want educated, open-minded people moving back to the area to teach the kids who are being raised by their backward parents. The fact that you're dragging your feet and waylaying me isn't helping matters, Kaden. I have to have this coming school year's roster of teachers in by the end of July. An entire school district of teachers, both elementary and high school for Rusty Knob, Hillock Corners, and Furrow Creek. Don't dick me around anymore."

"Wynn–"

"I'm not talking to Wynn– I'm talking to you." Eyes bleeding fire, Miriam is not going to take no for an answer. "Wynn and I already have an arrangement. The fact that he's back in his barn is telling, isn't it? You guys love kids. You want to make a positive change in our area, and you've been through a lot. You have a lot to offer. Wynn will make a great addition at Rusty Knob High School as the industrial arts teacher. But we have two years to wait. I need a guidance counselor *right now*."

"Miriam–"

"Your daddy and I were friends in school. We hit it off because Dare was calm and kind and I was bossy. One day my second cousin was visiting, and Darien came over to visit. I didn't believe in love at first sight, Kade. But your daddy and momma… I know you lost her early, too damned early. Lydia was my kin, and I've always taken a special interest in you. I tried to get you, but Royce beat me to the punch, saying you should stay in Rusty Knob with your friends at your school."

"And you've been a thorn in my side ever since." Miriam's not telling me anything I didn't already know, but she's persuading me like a master manipulator. I know she's only trying to get me to do what everyone but me is willing to admit.

I do want the job, if only I could swallow my pride long enough to take it.

"Kade?" Miriam leans forward, snatching my hand up in hers. Squeezing gently, I know I'm not going to like what she has to say. "Kentwood Area School District needs you. The kids at Rusty Knob High School need you. Your town and our county needs you. But I think you need this job more than we need you. Got it?"

With a quick intake of breath, I close my eyes and count to fifty. Still unsure if I can open my eyes and not have tears slip out, I speak with them squeezed shut. "Okay."

Not hearing me, Miriam's on a roll. "I worked very hard to expunge the real reason you were let go from your last position. After blackmailing nearly half of the current school board, we rewrote history with you leaving to continue on with your academic career. I did all of that, going against my own code of ethics, so I could hand you this job when it became available. Don't make everything I've gone through for nothing."

"Okay," I say louder, trying to break into Miriam's lecture. "I get it, okay? I said yes."

…An hour later, I find myself staring at the back of my eyelids–heart beating out of my chest, with every emotion inundating me. I didn't think it was possible to feel guilty, ecstatic, like shit, and proud of yourself at the same time. But I manage it.

"Kade?" Jessica's voice comes soft from the open door. "I can go if you need to be alone." My eyes flick open to take in the nearly six feet of lithe, blonde woman standing before me. "Penny said it was okay to come on back here. She told me to give you this."

Snorting, my smile is genuine. "Well, how can I deny the power of iced tea?" I take the bottle from Jessica's outstretched hand. "Have a seat. I'm curious to know why you made an appointment versus just texting me. You know anything that happens between you and Bren is between you and Bren. You and I, we're always going to understand each other."

"Are you okay?" Jessica is being sincere, taking time away from whatever agenda she has to check up on me first. I've always seen what Bren sees in Jessica, even when their relationship was at its most toxic point. Jessica is an awesome person, as is Bren. Together, not so much.

"Truthfully?" Sighing, I lean back in my chair, and then break the seal on my iced tea bottle. "Never better. Everything is wonderful, and it's scaring the piss out of me. Wynn and I… I've never felt more in tuned with another human being. Moving in together, evolving in our relationship. Now I just took the job I've wanted for over a decade."

"Waiting for the other shoe to drop, ain'tcha?" Jesse has my number. "If you're thinking Willa, don't. That woman is strong. Her pregnancy is not high-risk, and this baby doesn't have congenital birth defects. And if anything does happen, it's not your fault because all the pieces in your life are finally falling into place."

"It does sound rather narcissistic when you say it." Chuckling, my face blooms with a wicked blush. "I'm sitting here, terrified that somehow my good fortune will cause someone I love bad fortune, when that's like saying I'm so awesome that I control the ways of the world and Fate itself. Narcissistic in the extreme. Thank you."

"You're very welcome." Jesse smirks at me, showcasing how gorgeous little Miss Honor is going to be when she grows up.

"Now… about me." We both start laughing at the irony. "First, I brought the designs to give to your tattoo artist."

"Awesome!" I nearly shout, face splitting into a grin wider than I thought possible. "My day just keeps getting better and better."

"Second, while I was working on the mural in Honor's bedroom, it got me to thinking about Rusty Knob's kids. Maybe we could have an hour on Saturday mornings for art here at the center. It would give me a good idea who has natural talent, and I could tutor them more. At the very least, it's a positive outlet for the kids. If it hadn't been for art, you know I wouldn't have made it through my teen years."

"I know." Sighing, Jessica was one of the lucky ones. Bren didn't realize the stress he put on her, and no one is ever going to clue him in. Jessica truly loved him, and telling him she was a lesbian was more difficult than any kid coming out to their parents. Not only was Jesse coming out, she was destroying whatever future Bren had visualized.

Jessica was the first person I mentored for our old Facebook group, and I was terrified she would think taking her own life was easier than facing Bren and telling him the truth.

"He loves you, you know? He loves you no matter what." There's no need for me to say who he is. "He's happy because you're happy, and now he's comfortable enough to find what will make him happy too."

"I think Jack has finally figured out that I'm not the one standing in the way. I'm still the cheerleader he used to know, standing on the sidelines of their relationship." Jessica sighs, then fidgets in her chair. "Besides, last night while we were tending to Honor, Jack and I got over ourselves."

"Is Honor okay?" Clutching at my chest, I'm terrified over every sniffle and sneeze since Willa lost her last baby.

"Jack figures Honor picked up a stomach bug at preschool— par for the course." She shrugs her shoulders. "Jack called off work today, wouldn't let me sit vigil."

"So instead of being a nurse, he's playing nursemaid. He pulled out the nurse card to get you to leave the house, didn't he?" Chuckling in a mix of amusement and relief, I finally relax.

"You bet." After opening her large shoulder bag, Jesse extracts a sketch pad. "So here is my design for your sleeves. I spent a lot of time with Penny in the welcome center, and you know how difficult that was for me."

My sharp bark of laughter echoes around my office. "I can only imagine. Oil and water."

"Exactly." Jesse covers her mouth with the back of her hand, trying to catch an escaping giggle. "So I thought you would appreciate a few of the scenes from Rusty Knob's history, intermingled with branches of familial lines."

"Whoa…" is the only word I'm good for when I take in the design. Jesse had gone as far as to measure my forearms before beginning the design. Each arm will be covered with mountains, branches of family trees, and a road map. The sleeves are meant to cover the horrific scars bisecting each of my arms. "This is incredible, Jessica. I'm speechless. I would feel proud to show my arms… the world is a more beautiful place with you in it."

"Thank you." Jesse dabs at her eyes. "I thought it time for something else, Kaden. So don't be angry with me for doing more than you asked. But after designing a semicolon for all of us to wear, I felt it time for you to say goodbye to your cutting. Here–"

As Jessica flips through the pages of her sketch pad, I shore up my emotions with great difficulty. Wynn and I took the leap to end our sentence, yet we were saved unexpectedly. But there were others in our community who were suffering with the decision as well.

Jessica battled with the decision, suffocated by the knowledge of how Bren would take the news of her being a lesbian. If I hadn't started up the LGBTQ group when I did, Jessica admitted to me she would have rather 'left' than stuck around and hurt Bren day in and day out.

There are three schools in our district, in one of the most intolerant counties in the country. The major reason I wanted to become a guidance counselor was because I wanted to save the lives of those who were battling with themselves and close to losing the war.

Bren believes Jack saved Honor's life. If it wasn't for me, Jesse would have been long gone before Honor was ever conceived, and I'll take that knowledge to my grave. Bren looks at the world through a wide lens, but it's impossible for him to see what Jessica has sheltered him against.

Bren's love hurt Jessica, because Jessica's natural persuasion couldn't accept Bren's love. Together, they were toxic.

Jesse takes a deep breath when she finds what she's looking for. After a moment's hesitation, she passes me the notebook.

"These tattoos will cover the sides of your torso– say goodbye to cutting, Kaden," she demands, when not many are willing to do so.

On the pages is the Serenity Prayer, mirrored for both my left and right side. It's stunning, possibly too beautiful for someone like me to wear. But maybe it will make me feel more comfortable in my own skin.

"I know the prayer is for those in recovery, but I think the sentiment should be used by everyone." Suddenly nervous, Jesse's voice breaks. "When you look in the mirror, I want you to see it, to read it, and to put it into practice, Kaden. No more hurting yourself until your outside looks like your inside. I know this better than anyone."

"I-I-I– I just…"

"I understand," Jessica says softly in a soothing tone. "Unless you want anything tweaked, I have the final versions for the tattoo artist to use. Ignore me for stepping my bounds, but I've included the forearms, the wrist tattoo, and the torso tattoos. Do them whenever you want, but know they're there for whenever you're ready."

Jessica passes me a shaking folder, either she's the one trembling or I am, but there's no way to tell.

"Thank you–" the rest of my words are cut off by the telltale tapping of Perty's nails as he scampers toward me. Yelping a bark, his tiny feet rest on my knees, begging for me to pick him up. "There's my boy! Daddy wuvs you so much, Perty Werty."

"He's not your dog," Willa reminds me, having obviously misplaced *my* dog. Jesse is to her feet in an instant, grabbing a hold of Willa's hand to pull her into the vacated seat. "I'm not an invalid, but I appreciate it. Thank you." Groaning as if in horrible pain, Willa stretches out her legs. "Damn baby is riding my lungs today. I'm only good if I'm standing, which hurts my feet, or lying down, which hurts my back. Getting close."

Mind going on vacation, I block out the ladies as they invade my manly space to talk about things I refuse to acknowledge. Instead, I accept excited kisses and hiney wiggles from my favorite four-legged beast.

"I missed you so much, little man. Daddy wuvs you lots and lots." Perty wiggles more the more I baby talk. "Daddy's little potato. You look like a chubby potato. I'm gonna bake you up for supper."

"Put my dog down," Willa demands, pointing at the floor. "Can't stand it when you talk like that."

"Somebody's being a bitch today," I mutter to Perty, and he wags his hiney even more. But then he wiggles free of my arms, jumps off my lap, and runs over to his new master. "Traitor," I pout.

"There's no dog on this planet more spoiled than this one," Willa deadpans. "Get over it. I'm growing a life over here."

"You really are a bitch," I grumble. We don't actually hate each other, but this brother-sister animosity runs deep. We don't get along, but we love the hell out of each other. Probably kill for the other, but we call each other bitch and bastard and ride the other's asses just because we can.

"I'd call you an asshole, but from what I hear... yours is pretty sore," Willa volleys back.

"And with that, I gotta go check on Jack. Gotta make sure Honor hasn't run him ragged." Jessica disappears as quickly as she came.

"Did you tell Royce?" I stare at my blotter and the corner of the file folder Jesse left behind. "Ya know, about my ass."

"I take it there was no need to call an ambulance," flows in from the other room ahead of Royce. Then the stocky man comes into focus. Smiling smugly, he leans on the door casing. "I heard a rumor congratulations are in order.

All right, you know you've got a lot going on when you're not sure which event your foster dad is talking about, so you keep your mouth shut, lest you ruin a surprise.

Face straight, I look Royce right in the eyes. "Congratulating me because Wynn didn't fuck up fucking to the point we needed an emergency room visit?" Okay, I couldn't let that opportunity go.

Face blooming with an epic blush, Royce surprises me with a laugh instead of a glare. "I deserved that." Willa's snort is ladylike, which is an oxymoron. "Congratulations on your new job, son. You deserve it– proud of you."

It's amazing how hearing *I'm proud of you* will make you burst out bawling, when mere seconds ago you were laughing right along with them. But I'll deny it ever happened, especially in front of Willa.

CHAPTER TWENTY-EIGHT
Brennan Kennedy

Feeling grubby, I sneak into our side of the house after visiting with Jesse for a few minutes. Honor was down for the night, but not because she's sick. The little minx tore through the house all afternoon. Her daddy could take a nap too, but after he showers off the stench of sweat and construction dust.

I find Jackson sitting on our newly acquired stools at the kitchen island– wrought iron with big cushy seats. "Tired?" I whisper in his ear, taking a peek at what he's doing. The kitchen is messy from whatever Jack's cooking, but he's doing his homework while something simmers on the stovetop.

"Shit!" Jackson hisses, clutching at his chest. The pen he was holding clatters to the countertop. "You scared the piss outta me– is it really *that* late?"

My eyes flick to the clock on the stove, noticing it's after eight, almost nine. "Yup. Sorry about that. We only needed two more hours to complete a job. So it was either stay late, or end up getting a late start on tomorrow's project."

"Makes sense." Relaxing into me, Jackson rests his back against my chest. Taking that as invitation, I wrap my arms around him, luxuriating in the fact that I can do this whenever I want now. After five years of ignoring how I felt, it's a relief to just be myself without restriction.

"I hope I didn't ruin dinner because I was late." Sighing, I squeeze Jack tighter, getting a whiff of his natural scent. Running the tip of my nose along his jawline, my mind turns to other appetites. "Have you ever been so hungry, you lose the craving for it?"

"I think I know what you mean." Lips caress my forearm, then whisker stubble follows its path as Jackson rubs his cheek along my skin. "Like you wait too long to eat, so you're past the point of hunger and no longer crave food. But the instant you get a taste, you're voracious."

"Exactly." Using the tip of my nose, I nuzzle along Jack's shoulder, pushing the collar of his t-shirt to the side.

"We're having chicken enchilada soup– it's a new recipe I saw on my Facebook feed. I'll get you a bowl."

Voice husky, to the point it no longer sounds like mine, "I wasn't talking about food." Lifting Jackson up off the stool, I place him on his feet with his stomach to the island. Reaching down with one hand, I plunge into his shorts, while I grope his nipple with the other.

"Christ, Brennan," Jackson cries out, head hitching backward. "Leave my tit alone, though. You know I hate it."

"Liar," I breathe into his ear while rolling his nipple between my fingertips. "For someone who hates it so much, why is your dick getting harder the more I do it? Jesus, you're leaking against my palm– *so hot*. Why are you panting and grinding your ass against my cock? Hmm… your body is contradicting your words, Nurse Jackie."

"Goddamn!" Jack shouts. "Tug on it. Harder."

Laughing evilly, I cup his balls while brutalizing his nipple.

"You rat-bastard, you know I meant my dick!" Jack protests, so I touch him even lighter. "Tit! Fine, I meant my tit!" Jerking his head to the side, he tries to reach for my mouth, needing to taste me as much as I need to taste him.

We're both short, but Jack's an inch or two taller than me. I'm thankful, because there's no struggling to reach for each other when we're practically the same height. Lips merging, tongues surging, the small taste has my hunger exploding.

With a sharp tug from me, Jack's shorts meet his ankles. At the same time, Jack's reaching back to work at the fly of my jeans. Struggling with it, I decide to lend a helping hand before my dick is wrenched in two.

"Hurry," Jack breathlessly pants, reaching across the kitchen island for some reason. Not that I'm paying too much attention, because his perfectly round ass is grinding into my crotch. While he's doing whatever he's doing, my eyes focus on my hands massaging his ass cheeks. So fleshy, my fingertips leave white marks when I press too hard– so I press harder, slightly parting the cheeks.

Moaning, my dick has its eye on a destination, when I'm not sure we're ready for the trip. Jack slides back to his feet, managing to rub my cock between his ass cheeks with the motion. Shuddering, I count to ten in my head, because with just that small touch, I'm close to exploding.

Heads turned to the side, our mouths connect again. Concentrating on all the points our bodies connect, it's almost too much. Our mouths, the way our hands grope any body parts they can reach, the rasp of hair rubbing along my dick as I slide it in the crack of Jack's ass.

Jack fights me as I wrench his t-shirt over his head, getting his chin stuck in the process. Laughing together, our clothing flies to wherever it lands. After fumbling with something, Jack grabs my hand. The slick wetness has me trying to jerk back, but his fingers bracelet my wrist, keeping me immobile.

The light scent of olive oil hits my nostrils, causing my eyes to widen in wonder. "Is this for what I think it's for?" stammering, my words barely make sense.

"It sure as fuck isn't for us to jerk off with, Bren." Impatience makes Jackson surly. "Goddamnit, don't make me wait any longer."

"Are you sure this won't hurt you?" I might be asking, but my hands have a mind of their own. The oil-slicked hand is rubbing along Jack's crack, fingers targeting their prize.

"When I was experimenting, I didn't have lube. Kinda hard to explain to Mom and Dad how I needed lube to finger-fuck my own asshole. Kinda opens up too many questions, ya know?" Jackson has me laughing when this is supposed to be hot. But the more I laugh, the hotter I get. "Fuck me, Brennan. Now!"

"Bossy little thing, ain'tcha?" Pucker pressing into my fingertip, Jack lets me in. In one smooth movement, I sink two fingers knuckle-deep. Eyelids slipping shut, a moan flows from between my parted lips. "Ignore the stream of precum gushing down the back of your thigh. I promise I didn't just come." Embarrassed, I hope to God I'm telling the truth, and pray my dick stays hard.

"You're such a bullshitter, Bren," Jack taunts me. "Enough trying to stretch me out– I'm a total anal slut, and I jerked off and fingered myself before you got home tonight. Best hurry before we find out you actually just got off on my thigh."

"Shh… that didn't happen," I whisper in Jackson's ear, causing him to quiver. Swallowing my embarrassed laughter, it's amazing how affected by me he is.

"It's the most flattering thing I've ever had happen to me, Bren– honest."

"It's been a long while for me," murmuring against his neck, I slowly slip my fingers out of his hole. Before I can miss the snugness wrapped around my fingers, I'm pressing my cockhead to his entrance. Without hesitation, he presses back against me, making it easier to enter him.

This.

This I'm good at. Virgin idiots when it came to anal sex, last time we just fit together perfectly. My practice with girls did come in handy, because it meant I wasn't thrusting blindly with painful results. When you're a virgin, everyone expects the guy to be some horny savant who immediately knows what he's doing. Case in point, Jack was horrible at it. With some practice, I'll let him try again. My first time with Jessica is hilarious now, but it was mortifying then.

Guys are not born with the knowledge. That's why first times suck.

Second times, though…

Slipping inside without any struggle, I inhale through my mouth and exhale through my nostrils, because the feeling of Jack's snug ass kissing my dick is enough to drain my sack dry. "Jesus," shudders out when I'm seated fully. "I've missed you so much. Missed sex, but missed sex with you more."

Laughing, which makes his ass constrict on my dick, Jackson has me on the edge. "Fuck me, Bren. I've been waiting just as long as you have been. Can't wait any longer– don't torture me."

Our lack of height difference is in our favor as I fuck Jackson up against the kitchen island. Every ram of my dick has him grunting with his oily fingers scrambling to hold onto the countertop. To add to the torture, I grope his tits, rolling his nipples between my slick fingertips.

My little accident earlier has me lasting longer than I would have, but not by much. It's too much stimuli, too much Jackson, causing all of my senses to light up with the need to climax.

Rutting roughly, we manage to tip one of the wrought iron stools over with a heavy bang, but neither of us gives two shits enough to make sure the floor tile didn't get chipped.

Hand wrapped tightly around his dick, jerking himself off, while I grope his tits and fuck him from behind, it's Jackson's animalistic keen that has me falling over the edge. No doubt it's the feeling of me letting loose inside him that has Jackson following me, jizz spurting on the countertop in front of us.

Breathing heavily, we slowly come back down, neither of us moving away from the other. I think of the theatrics between Kaden and Wynn, and chuckle how the loudest noise we made was the stool tipping over.

We may not have screamed and shouted to be heard by the masses, but every grunt and gasp was driven by primal need.

"That was the best sex I've had in over four years," I compliment Jackson... waiting... waiting for him to get the punchline.

"And they call me the jackass," he taunts back. "That was the only sex you've had in over four years."

"True." Peppering kisses to his neck, shoulders, and back, I get lost for a few moments. "Still better than most of the sex I've ever had."

"Insulted," Jackson snarls, but he doesn't try to move away from me.

"You shouldn't be, as I was including the night of nonstop fucking between us. You know, the last time I ever had sex."

"I guess you're forgiven, then." Turning his head to the side, Jack steals a kiss. "If I was Kaden, I'd be crying about how this wasn't romantic enough."

"Memorable though, right?"

"Fuck, yes." Jackson pulls away from me, my cock slips free as he moves. We both ignore the messiness. "I'm not Kaden." Facing me, Jackson and I can finally kiss without cranking our necks to the side. "This was perfect, but I've got to shower."

"I'll join you!" I shout as Jack waddles from the kitchen, shorts clutched in his hand to hide his ass from view.

"Turn off the burner on the stove!" Jackson shouts back at me.

Doing as I was bid, I take a long sniff of the yumminess I'll be enjoying after our shower. My cellphone rings, and Jack's does at the same time.

"Dad's calling!" I shout in Jack's direction. "I'll be a minute."

"Fuck!" Jack runs back to the kitchen to answer his phone. "That's the hospital's ringtone on mine."

"The baby!" we cry out in unison, voices breaking.

CHAPTER TWENTY-NINE
Kaden Marx

"Why, Kaden?" Wynn's tone isn't accusatory, when it should be. He doesn't sound disappointed in me either. More resigned than anything. "Why?"

Dr. Carlin called me earlier, and I spilled the news on how I took the job Miriam offered. He preceded to tear into my psyche, torturing me with how I was a bitter disappointment. This wasn't the first time Dr. Carlin treated me this way since I left school, but it will be the last. I finally saw how his harshness was actually abuse. What I once thought was motivational was actually manipulative.

My ex-professor told me I was dead weight, how it would be better if I just killed myself since I wanted to stay in Rusty Knob. How I was destined for greatness as a college professor, but now I'm wasting my education by trying to make a difference with kids— kids who didn't deserve it because they are born in an ignorant wasteland.

In that moment, I finally saw Dr. Carlin for the small man he truly is. He was frustrated, lashing out, all because I refused to stay in his abusive grip, allowing him to feel powerful. In Rusty Knob, I'm surrounded by a solid support system who allow me to be my own man. Dr. Carlin wanted me to be his cerebrally fucked minion.

Rusty Knob isn't an ignorant wasteland, not with so many people wanting to open the eyes of its residents. I'll do it for them because they are worth it. They deserve it, even if I don't believe I'm deserving to be their mentor.

Head bowed, I clutch the sink with my fingertips while ignoring the wash of crimson flowing down my thigh from the cut near my left hip. "I took the job," I confess, voice barely a rasp.

"I know." Wynn doesn't move to stop the bleeding, or clean me up, or help me redress. He doesn't play nursemaid when I do my cutting bullshit. He forces me to clean up my own messes and doesn't coddle me afterward. "Everyone is happy for you, so explain to me why you just cut yourself because of it. It looks pretty fucking deep too, shithead."

"I don't want to fight," I whisper, hoping to head Wynn off at the pass. We fight. We're not abusive to one another– not really. We each give as much as we get. Most of the time we can talk it out, but sometimes we can't. Usually we temper our physical brawls by turning the anger into lust, ending our fight with intense frotting.

"I'm not going to fight with you over this, Kaden." Refusing to be ignored, Wynn leans against the sink, making sure I have to look at him. "We've talked about this over and over again, and I've done my best to ignore it while understanding. But this is black and white, Kade. People don't cut unless they're having problems. I'm not going to ignore it anymore– I'ma call your therapist, is what I'm gonna do."

"Don't threaten me," I sigh, exhausted. "Dr. Amherst already knows. Okay?"

"Why'd you cut this time?" Voice level and calm, Wynn's trying to coax me into honesty.

"I don't deserve the job, that's why," I admit without hesitation, ignoring the tears sliding down my cheeks. I've been a wreck since Royce said he was proud of me, but it was made exponentially worse when Willa agreed.

"You've got eight fucking years of college under your belt, you dumbass. I'm positive you were going for a doctorate or two in something or other when we stopped you. You are more than qualified for the job– over-qualified is more like it."

"I don't want the job." Eyes flicking to my reflection, I stare in the mirror at a stranger. The stranger looks like Darien Marx, but my father would've never pulled the destructive acts I've done. Ever since this visage said he was proud of me in my dreams last night, I've been an emotional wreck. I don't know if I'm proud, or if Dad was sending me a message. I don't know where Dad ends and I begin.

"The first real conversation you and I had was on the back steps of this house. You stared at Suicidal Tendencies the entire time as you spilled your guts about how badly you wanted to be the guidance counselor, because you wanted to make a difference in the lives of these kids. You were running the LGBTQ Facebook group, because you thought that even helping one kid would make a world of difference. So don't feed me a line of shit about not wanting this job."

"There are kids here who need help– hell, I can see how Jeb and Cain are in serious need of help, but maybe I'm not the man for the job. Maybe I'm too fucked up myself."

"Maybe being who you are makes you the best man for the job, because you understand better than someone who hasn't had a single tragic event befall them." Wynn tugs me away from the mirror, his touch firm and resolute. "You're talking to me right now, Kade. Not yourself. Not your dead dad. *Me*."

Terrified, I gaze at the one person who means more to me than my problems do. "I'm ashamed of myself because I used you– I used you to get fired. God, how I wanted you. Wanted you so fucking bad, and I knew you wanted me too. I knew if we had each other, I'd get fired. I didn't do it on purpose. I may be an attention whore, but not enough to warrant school board meetings and public hazings with dog shit flung out car windows and hate letters stashed in my mailbox."

"It was subconscious on your part." Wynn sighs, resigned. "We all know it, even if you won't admit it. Self-fulfilling prophecy. You didn't think you deserved the job, so you made sure they would fire you. Now, no matter who tells you differently, you don't believe you deserve the new position because you feel guilty. Do you honestly think Miriam doesn't know you did it on purpose?"

"She knows?" my voice pitches high in surprise. "If she knows, why the fuck would she try to give me another job? I'll just fuck this one up too, only I could do more damage this time around."

"Your bullshit was the precipice for change in our school district– in our towns. A lot of kids came out right then. It's not so taboo anymore, even if the hillbillies are cringing when we pass by. You deserve the job, Kaden. Your past mistakes need to stay in the past, and you need to learn from them. Stop bleeding for sins a different version of you made– you're not that Kaden anymore."

"I'm not?" Head tilting to the side, I hate the childish hope filling my voice as I gaze at Wynn.

"You're not. I'm not the same guy who enabled my own family. Right now, I'm terrified for my daddy, and I'm angry at him for not telling me about Cain, but I'm not sticking my nose in shit that doesn't have anything to do with me. I'm getting to know Cain as a person first, a brother second. I'm worrying about my daddy in private, and talking to him when he calls. I'm worried about Willa, but hovering ain't gonna do nothing about it. The baby will come, and the baby may live or die. But my actions don't sway the way the world turns. So I'ma go about my business, doing what I need to do for myself, and see how it all plays out."

Snorting, I remember my conversation with Jesse from earlier today, where we joked about how thinking if our lives were going good it would cause other people to suffer bad. It's narcissistic in the extreme, and total horseshit. Wynn and I loving each other, planning a wedding, and my new job, that's not going to cause Willa to lose her baby. It just won't.

"I'm getting some new tattoos." Wynn's thrown by the subject change, head jerking back in a startled motion. "Jesse designed them for me. They go here." I run my fingers along my forearm. "And a semicolon goes here." I touch my wrist. "But the most important ones go here." Running my hands along my torso, my fingertips hit the feathering of cut marks telling the history of my sins. "Once these are covered, I'm never going to cut again."

Wynn sags against the sink, relief washing the terror away, and the need to cut one last time overpowers me. The craving to slice into my flesh because I've upset Wynn beyond measure with my cutting. Irony: punishing myself with the very thing that caused Wynn to worry.

I won't. I won't go there again. I may not be more important than my issues, but Wynn is. For Wynn, I won't cut again. The fact that Wynn has never asked me to stop is the reason I will.

"You better get yourself cleaned up and tended to." As always, Wynn doesn't coddle me by playing nursemaid, for which I'm thankful. "Why don't we... I don't know. Let's just take a walk or something. Clear our heads while talking about whatever comes up."

"Yeah." I reach for a washcloth, then dampen it in the sink. "Yeah, I'd like that." In some places, the blood has dried already, so it takes some fierce scrubbing. By doing so, I accidently break open the cut that had started to scab over. A fresh wash of blood seeps from the wound.

"Good." Wynn busies himself by grabbing the ointment and a bandage because this cut is deeper than the rest. "It's a nice, quiet night out–" our cellphones ringing stops that line of conversation. "So much for that." Wynn snorts, tugging his cell from his back pocket.

Scrambling forward to grab my phone from my discarded trousers, a premonition strikes. "It's the baby," I mutter, voice breaking, as we both answer our phones. "It's the baby."

—*—

"Shh… calm yourself," Wynn tries and fails to soothe me as we jog through the hospital. "My sister is fine. The baby is gonna be fine." We almost take out a mother and her two children who are loitering in the corridor. I don't feel the least bit bad when she blurts out a homophobic slur. Even Wynn's apology dries up.

"Willa's due date wasn't for another three weeks." Palms sweaty, I almost lose my grip on Wynn's hand as I yank him through the corridors. "How can you be so calm?"

Wynn's blue eyes cut in my direction. "Have I ever overreacted? About anything?" His chuckle has me wanting to punch him in the nuts. "Kaden, this is my sister and niece. If I truly felt there was a problem, I would be worried but I wouldn't show it. This is no different than when we sat around waiting for Jesse to deliver Honor. No different. This isn't Willa's first rodeo. This is the fourth baby she's birthed."

"Okay. Mr. Voice of Reason," I grumble underneath my breath. "I want to be calm like you, but I can't stop the anxiety."

"Just breathe." Wynn squeezes my hand tightly. "We'll have answers in a few seconds." Then he pulls me into the waiting room. The twins are the first sight I see, and I relax by a billion degrees.

To be young again and not give two shits about anything that isn't on my cellphone. Sitting up with earbuds in and her cellphone in her hands, Rocky's wearing My Little Pony pajamas that totally clash yet manage to match her purple mohawk. Laying with his head in his twin's lap, Hayden's tapping away on a video game on his cellphone while rocking his legs back and forth over the arm of the small sofa.

The only other person in the room is Bren, and he's fast asleep in a chair, with his neck at an uncomfortable position. OCD, mother hen Wynn tears off his hoodie, and shoves it under Bren's head.

"What?" Bren mumbles, wiping drool off his chin with the back of his hand. "Oh, hey! Did I fall asleep? Must've. Been a long day."

Impatient, I stand before my brother with my hands fisted against my hips. "Willa? The baby?"

"Where's Jack?" Wynn talks over me, looking amused. "Did you call Warren?"

"Yeah, Warren's on his way– had to wait until Penny got out of the shower before he could go so the kids weren't unattended." Stretching his arms above his head, Bren looks to be in pain. "Muscles cramp up so easily. Got any water on ya? Nurse Jackie says I don't hydrate enough."

"Baby!" I shout, fed the fuck up. "News– gimme."

"Jesus, you're in rare form tonight." Bren continues to stretch while Wynn takes off in search of water. "I've been up for twenty hours, worked manual labor in the boiling hot summer sun all day. Give me a second to get my head on straight, will ya? Then I'll answer you."

Wynn's return saves me from a murder conviction. "Didja eat anything?" he asks, passing Bren a bottle of water and a granola bar from the vending machine. Then he's gliding across the room to pass out bottles of juice and packs of fruit snacks to the disinterested twins.

"Nah, Jack had some soup on the stove, but we got sidetracked." Bren blushes, and it piques my curiosity. "Got the call as soon as we were going to… anyway. Willa's going through labor." Bren glares up at me, brown eyes narrowed. "Would you please sit down? You're like an angry storm cloud ready to open up and pour out on me."

"Fine," I allow, sitting. "But don't stop talking." Wynn sits next to me, then passes me a Snickers.

"You looked hangry," Wynn teases, not even bothering to stifle his insane giggle. "Eat a Snickers so we can get back the Kaden Marx we know and love."

"Asshole," I whisper, tearing into the wrapper, then I bite the candy bar in half. Eyes slipping shut, I can already feel my heart rate slowing as I chew. "Next time, bring me more than one cheese steak for supper. I weigh two-fifty– don't starve me."

"I'm pretty sure it's the blood-loss and stress making you act like a cunt." Wynn never puts up with my shit, always calling me out on it. "Not the fact that you didn't have two cheese steaks. Not to mention you took down an entire family-size bag of chips, a two-liter of Coke, and an entire package of Oreos– minus the one I ate before you wrenched it out of my hand."

Ignoring Wynn, I draw attention back to the matter at hand. "How's Willa? Since Wynn doesn't care about his own sister, and by the looks of her other two ingrate children over there–" Hayden and Hayley are popping fruit snacks into their mouths, eyes still glued to their phones. "They don't either."

"They're a few days away from being twelve, leave my baby brother and sister alone," Bren chastises me. "Willa's great, other than being in labor. This isn't her first time, ya know? She wanted Jack in there with her, and he pops out every so often to give us updates. I guess due dates aren't all that accurate, and it's perfectly normal with it supposedly three weeks early. No fear. Dad even came out here once to check on us."

Heart beating out of control, I slump back in my chair, confused as to why no one else is as panicked as I am. My thoughts drift as Bren and Wynn chat softly and the kids communicate without actually speaking. I worry so much, I swear I can feel every lash mark on my torso throbbing with phantom pain.

Anxiety. Panic attack. Whatever you call it, I now recognize it's not rational. With that thought, I'm able to slow my breathing instead of lashing out at everyone in my vicinity or pacing around like a caged beast. As my fingers eventually unclench, I realize it was Wynn's thigh I was brutalizing. My senses come back online, and I notice Wynn's been rubbing the nape of my neck the whole time, fingertips digging slightly into my skull.

Feeling drugged from the attention, my eyelids droop and my jaw unclenches. Ever so slowly, I start to drift until my head is leaning against Wynn's shoulder. "Mmm… that feels nice," I murmur absentmindedly.

"Yeah, I can come around in the next few days or so," Bren's saying. "We have another project starting tomorrow, but it's a small one. I can fit you in after that, if that works for you?"

"Thanks, Bren. I appreciate it. Not having a bathroom upstairs is a literal pain in the ass, if you know what I mean." Wynn and Bren share a masculine laugh, but I don't bother opening my eyes to look at them. My own lips curl in response, though. "Nothing like having to go down a flight of stairs and through the house to get cleaned up in the middle of the night. Bathroom down there is dinky, too. No way we'd both fit in the shower together."

"Don't diss our house," I murmur, smiling for some reason. "I miss our shower from the apartment too."

"There's three small bedrooms upstairs. I'd like to turn it into a master suite if it's possible. I don't know which walls are load-bearing. I assume your foreman could figure it out, right?"

"Yep, I can show you how to figure that shit out. You're good at building stuff as it is, so it will come in handy in the future."

"Hey, guys!" Warren's voice jars my eyes open. He swaggers in carrying a bag of pork rinds in one hand and Cheetos in another. Cain eyes the snacks with complete disdain, edging away from his brother like he carries the plague. "I'm becoming great at this waiting for babies hullabaloo. Wasn't I just here a few months ago? How about some snacks?"

Cain makes a beeline to the twins, where he sits on the floor, using their sofa as cover. Legs pulled to his chest, arms wrapped around his knees, hair covering his face, Cain doesn't like being in a hospital. Yet again, I worry about him, and decide to send a therapist his way.

"I call Cheetos!" Leaning forward, I snatch the bag out of Warren's hand. Without shame, I open the bag and shove my face in the top, inhaling the cheesy goodness. "Mmm… thank you. That Snickers wasn't enough. Wynn's neglecting me."

"Fat ass," Bren teases me. "Do you even work out anymore?"

"Yeah." I pop a handful into my mouth. Crunching, I talk with my mouth full. "In the bedroom."

"Eww…" Warren shudders, snatching the bag away as punishment. "None for my baby brother's fucker."

"Kids!" I point at the twins, who aren't listening with earbuds shoved in their ears. "Don't say stuff like that around 'em."

"When I was their age–"

"No!" Wynn heads that off at the pass, knowing any Gillette stories would have Royce in an early grave. "No. That didn't happen until you got married and had kids."

"Don't lie to them," Cain interrupts with his barely audible raspy voice. "That makes it worse. Just educate them, give them gross facts, and they'll behave."

"And you know this how?" Wynn goes where he shouldn't.

"My body parts have never belonged to me, that's how." Cain buries his face against the tops of his knees, blocking us out.

"Damn!" Wynn hisses with feeling. "Sorry, brother."

"S'kay," Cain murmurs, one vivid blue eye gazing out at us from across the waiting room. "You don't know any better– you didn't do anything to me."

"Let's not go there." Warren's surprisingly the voice of reason. "So… who wants to take bets? Hmm? Willa took forever to birth the twins, but there was two babies. Baby Royce took forever for other reasons." The silence in the room is thick with shared pain. "Penny popped little dude out within an hour of getting to the hospital, but Ginger took twelve hours. Let's place bets to occupy our time."

"Gross," Wynn grumbles, hating the Gillette side of himself right now, no doubt.

Proving the earbuds were a prop, scrambling up from his sister's lap, Hayden lunges across the waiting room, hand shoved down his front pocket. "I'm placing a twenty on Brynn within the hour." With a sharp slap noise, the money connects with Warren's hand.

"I'm proud to call you nephew," Warren praises, causing Wynn and Cain to grunt the same sound of exasperation.

Digging his wallet out, "I'm in," Bren announces, then a twenty is flicked in Warren's direction. "Four hours– Hayley, make a record of the bets and times."

Hayley's earbuds drop in a heartbeat, but it's the naughty smirk she flashes us that has Bren chuckling.

"What the fuck?" Wynn glares at the twins. "We were saying shit you shouldn't hear."

"Never forget, bro." Bren reaches over to rub Wynn's shoulder. "Those mongrels are Kennedys, and we're sneaky, crafty assholes. This new baby is going to be a monster."

Laughing while typing quickly on her cellphone, Hayley mutters absentmindedly, "Hayden for within the hour. Bren for four hours. Who's next?"

Warren tugs a wad of cash out of his front pocket, hand really jabbing deep to locate spare change. After counting out, he smiles wickedly. "Double or nothing– within twenty minutes. Hayden's bet doesn't count within that time frame."

"Jesus," I murmur with pride. Arching off my ass, I reach for my wallet, but a hand stills me.

"No," Wynn glares.

Rolling my eyes, I ignore him. "Hour one to hour two," I pick, slapping a twenty in Warren's hand.

We all look at Wynn, who closes his eyes in defeat. "You guys suck. No."

As silent as a ghost, Cain flows to his feet, then crosses the floor, bare toes sticking out from beneath frayed jeans. "Triple or nothing, next five minutes."

"If you're wrong, that's sixty bucks, bro," Warren reminds Cain, causing the man to nod his head until his hair reveals his Gillette features.

"But if I'm right, that's sixty bucks from each of ya," Cain's raspy voice is filled with calculated risk.

"Little hippie badass is definitely my daddy's son." Warren turns to Wynn in bitter disappointment. "Clearly you aren't– pussy."

"I'm in," comes from varying sources around the room, including me, with Wynn pouting in the background.

"Hey, guys." Jackson pops into the room, huge smile on his face.

"Well, aren't you as cute as a button," Warren drawls, smirking at Jack's pink scrubs covered with cartoonish chubby babies.

Laughing, Jackson's middle finger flicks up without hesitation.

"How's Willa doing?" Wynn asks before any of us can get a word out. "These asshats are taking bets instead of fretting." I get eyed– judged.

"You told me to quit stressing, now you're bitching at me for not stressing. Make up your goddamn mind, man," I growl, feeling the early stirrings of either an epic fight or brutal fuck on the horizon.

Wynn winks at me– the bastard.

Brutal fuck it is…

Chuckling, Jackson steps to the side, "See for yourself."

"Brynn!" Hayley shouts, dropping her phone to the sofa, then she's propelling herself across the room to her dad.

Royce makes it about a foot into the waiting room before we're all on our feet swarming him. Shining with pride, tears in his eyes, he's holding a swaddled baby in his arms.

"Reenact the Lion King– c'mon, ya know ya wanna," I taunt, using my height to my advantage to get the first look at the little girl. "Hold Brynn up and present her."

"Dick," Royce chuckles, sounding relieved. "Willa's doing good, by the way," he mutters snarkily. "Thanks for asking."

"She looks like a pink potato," Hayden sounds disappointed the baby didn't come out of Willa full grown. "How long until we can tell who she looks like?"

Cranky with all these funny faces staring at her, Brynn starts to wail. "Like mother, like daughter," Wynn laughs, more relief than happiness riding his voice.

"Hey!" Hayley proves her nickname by punching her uncle in the hip. "Dad's not exactly sunshine and rainbows."

"Thanks," Royce mutters dryly, finding a more comfortable position for the baby, and she instantly stops fussing.

"Simba," Bren murmurs, rubbing the tip of his nose against his baby sister's. "I'ma call you Simba from now on."

"Oh, Lord," Hayden growls. "You're such an idiot."

Royce notices how Cain holds himself apart, while everyone else is oblivious. "C'mere, son, and greet your niece."

After wiping his hands on the front of his jeans a dozen times, Cain tucks his hair behind his ears, giving us an unimpeded view of his face. Terrified, he wears a funny grin just like the one gracing Wynn's face. Then Cain walks slowly toward Royce as we part like the sea.

"I've never seen a newborn before," Cain rasps in awe. "Hi." Evidently freaked out, he quickly backs up when eyelids snap open to reveal blue eyes peering out at him.

"Aww– Brynn has Gillette eyes," flows from a few people at once.

"Okay, new dad." Jackson pats Royce on the shoulder. "Time to get the little one back to her momma. It's time to see if she'll latch-on."

Royce gives us a wave, with Jackson following behind.

"What does that mean?" Cain murmurs softly. "Latch-on?"

Warren pats Cain so hard on the back, the guy stumbles forward. "Not to make you squeamish, little bro... since you probably don't like titty like some of us do. But our sister is going to feed our niece."

Head whipping around, his hair moves like a living veil. "Feed?" Cain is clueless.

"Giving the kid some boob." Hayden laughs, retrieving his twin's cellphone, only to have it snatched out of his hand.

"Oh." It takes a few seconds, then Cain's face is twisting up. "Eww... I don't do dairy."

"Three minutes, forty-two seconds," Hayley announces, wiggling her cellphone. On the screen is a timer stopped. "Winner. Winner. Chicken dinner."

"You don't even know what that means," tumbles from my throat. "You're my favorite person, Rocky."

"Ante up, boys. My brother has an insane grocery bill to pay." Warren digs into his pocket, getting out another forty bucks to break even. "Buy some legumes, or whatever the fuck you call 'em."

"Make it rain– make it rain," Bren purrs, flicking bills at Cain, and everyone follows suit.

"I'm not a stripper," Cain grumbles, sounding and looking like Wynn when he's grumpy and thinks I'm being an immature ass. Dropping to his knees, the guy starts counting to make sure no one short-changed him. "You could have handed me the money."

"Where's the fun in that?" Bren stalks off, shouting over his shoulder. "Anyone from Willa's vag, come with me. The rest of you bitches will have to wait your turn." Waving like a dick, "Bye-bye until visiting hours tomorrow."

"No fair," I mutter begrudgingly. "The baby will bond with him." Grumpy, I want the baby to love me best. "Wait a goddamn minute!" I start to charge forward, then realize I left someone behind. Grabbing for Wynn, I drag him behind me. "We're Royce's kids. Technically that baby is our sibling– we're allowed in there right now too."

"Do you have a Whole Foods?" Cain's raspy voice hits my ears.

"Ain't no brother of mine," Warren grumbles, causing Wynn to snort as I tug him into Willa's room.

Finding Willa in bed with the baby bundled in her arms, "Gimme that baby," I order, shutting us in together. "You've held her for nine months– stop being so selfish. It's Kade time right now."

Laughing, Willa flips me off, looking exhausted but highly amused. "Make your own dang kid and stop stealing mine."

Sad, pouting, I walk toward Willa's bed. "Can I at least watch you feed her?" Wigging out, I look around the room to find Bren giving Royce a neck rub and the twins more interested in their phones than the new life. Wynn pulls away from me to go chat with Jackson, who's writing something in a chart.

"Yeah, git over here, dummy." Willa pats the bed next to her. "Yet another kid to add to your godfather duties. You best hope nothing eradicates us, or you'll end up with my kids, War's kids, and Honor."

Heart stuttering in terror at the loss of them, it simultaneously fills with love. "Don't talk such horseshit." Gingerly, I rest on the edge of Willa's bed. "Hi, goddaughter. Uncle Kade will take care of ya– promise."

CHAPTER THIRTY
Kaden Marx

Sitting in her rocking chair while holding Brynn, "Well, don't you fellas look dapper," Willa's voice flows from the front porch as Wynn and I carry a new jointer to the barn.

"Thanks!" Wynn jerks his head to the side, moving the hair off his forehead. It's hotter than Satan's asshole out today, and we're both sweating. "We'll be out in a second."

"We couldn't have done this tomorrow morning?" I mutter sardonically, sweat dampening my collar. "You waited until I was wearing a suit, fucker."

"I couldn't relax until it was where I wanted it." Ass hitting the door, Wynn kicks it open, and then continues to back in. With a deep breath, we lean down in unison to plop the jointer to the floor.

"Well, now you'll stop bitching about how the other one wasn't working right." Yanking a hanky from the inner pocket of my suit jacket, I dab the sweat from my forehead.

"Dude." Wynn stares at me, not taking the shit I'm dishing out. Gesturing with his hand, "Look around, asshole. Would you want to make an entire kitchen full of cabinetry with a piece of shit jointer? This is a job about precision."

"It's gorgeous," I mutter in awe, eyes taking in all the work Wynn's been doing. After hesitating no longer than thirty seconds, I grab his hand. "C'mon– we'll moon over your carpentry skills tomorrow."

"Dick," Wynn whispers, but there's no venom in his tone.

"Thanks for offering, but I'm busy right now." I earn a chuckle for my efforts. "Don't you dare start a conversation with Willa– if we're late, I'ma blame you."

"Me?" Wynn points at his chest, and I'm momentarily distracted by how smoking hot the man looks in a white dress shirt and a navy vest. "I'm Mr. Punctual. You took fucking forever working on your hair."

Tossing my curls, I bite back a grin when I stun Wynn, pupils blowing with lust. "I'm the one wearing a jacket– you pussied out by wearing a vest."

"I look good, though." Wynn's voice warbles with insecurity as his hands pass over his chest. "Right?"

"You're killing me, little shit," I murmur in appreciation, ignoring the red hot lust firing straight to my cock. "That cut of the vest ought to be a felony– it's positively lethal."

"Fuck me," Wynn mutters, and I'm about to respond with '*yes, please,*' but the direction of his gaze stops my tongue.

Breathing in Wynn's direction, "There's not a snowball's chance in Hell we're going to be on time."

"Hey, Royce!" With a wave, Wynn keeps walking. "No time to chat. Gonna be late."

"Where the fuck you going dressed like that?" Willa shouts to still our feet.

"The wedding isn't for forty-eight hours," Royce reminds us, like we don't know that after spending the better part of the summer planning the dang thing.

I always thought I'd want a huge affair, because I'm an attention-whore, with Wynn wanting something conservative with only family and friends. We settled on using Bren's backyard and taking a tropical honeymoon during winter break.

Between the center, wedding planning, getting licensed, and gearing up for the new school year, I don't have time for anything. Wynn's been playing carpenter around our house and working with Kennedy Construction with custom cabinetry and woodwork.

We said fuck it all and allowed the best men to plan everything– Lord knows what Bren and Jack are going to put us through.

"We know," Wynn and I mutter in unison, after having every single detail shoved down our throats. "We're going out to dinner."

"Ah, that's so sweet." Royce picks up Brynn. The girl is almost two months, getting chubbier by the day because her mouth is always attached to Willa's boob. Bren calls her Simba, but I'm an asshat by calling her the Michelin Man. Someone ought to make Cain take dairy, because clearly it works on fattening up humans.

"Royce?" Willa turns, but I can see her rolling her eyes. "Those bastards are up to something. Who you meeting?"

"I-um… I'm–"

"See?" Willa points at her brother having a coronary, unable to mutter the truth.

"Dan and Uriah are here for the wedding," I say without a thread of shame.

It's not like we're going to fuck 'em tonight or anything.

"Goddamn Bren for his loose tongue!" Wynn snarls in reaction to Royce's eyebrow raise, like the all-knowing dad can read our minds. "Is nothing private?"

"In this family?" Willa laughs. "I'm guessing it's bad luck to fuck someone else, like a groom seeing the bride before the wedding– keep your dicks in your pants," Willa warns, and she's deadly serious.

"Jesus, sis!" Wynn rocks backward like he was struck. "What do you take me for? We're meeting up because the first time I meet them shouldn't be at our wedding. I'm not a fuck on the first date kinda guy."

"What kind of guy are you, then?" Royce teases, mirth shining in his eyes, while more than half of his attention is on the pink, babbling bundle in his arms.

"Third date." Wynn drops the mic, walking to the Land Rover, leaving us all stunned, me included. "C'mon, we're gonna be late."

The hour drive takes just under forty-five minutes, and thankfully speeding-ticket-free, with us arriving right on time. In other words, we're late after parking.

"C'mon." Fingers wrapping with Wynn's, I tug him up the sidewalk to the swanky, fancy-swancy steak and seafood restaurant. "What's up? Why are you dragging your huge feet when we're already late?"

"I'm nervous." Wynn gestures with his hand toward the restaurant's façade, tan face paler than usual. "Intimidated."

Taking a deep breath, I pull us to a stop by the front door. Taking a moment to calm my nervous fiancé, Dan and Uriah can wait. If it hadn't been for the fact that I've eaten here a good dozen times, I'd be nervous too. I can understand how a guy like Wynn must feel after the hellhole he grew up in, because I grew up in a shack too.

"This is one of our haunts– Morgantown really, because it's the halfway point between Rusty Knob and Pittsburgh. An hour and fifteen minute drive for Dan on a good day, and an hour for us on a bad day. This isn't a foreign land, Wynn. You lived here for four years, and it's just a town."

Eyes staring up at the exterior of the building, the green awning no doubt intimidating the guy who still sees himself as a hillbilly boy, when he's an amazing grown man. I know the feeling– constantly.

"This place is only expensive for the sake of being expensive, when it ain't worth it. Expensive sign made by an artist no different than our Jesse. Expensive food that tastes no different than any other food. Expensive chairs and tables made of the same wood you craft every day. This three-story stone building's frame is no different than the entire block of the Life Skills Center. Rich and educated, Dan's no more educated than I am, and not as wealthy as Brennan. Hayley could take Uriah, and Dan's the same height as Jackson, and he's not much bigger either. The restaurant is a restaurant, and Dan is just a good-looking dude with a soothing personality, while Uriah is… Uriah."

"I pictured Dan in my head looking like you." Wynn blushes, eyes drinking in my massive frame. We're nearly the same height, but I've got a good thirty or more pounds of solid muscle on Wynn. "I can tell Dan always makes you feel safe. How does a regular-sized dude do that?"

"Dan's intelligent, confident, caring, giving, and kind. But he was born with a spotless silver spoon in his mouth, so his affect is kind of suffocatingly intoxicating. Dan emits an '*I'm in charge*' vibe, and I needed a protector at the time. Now I just find it a low background buzz that's soothing."

Breathing heavily, I try to remain in the present, not going back to the first day of freshman year at Penn State. Royce left me alone, and I wanted to bawl like a baby I was so terrified. Skinny like a scarecrow, zitty face, scarred, and gay, I knew I was in for a shitty time.

Dysmorphia– my outside doesn't match my inside. There are days when I feel tiny and weak. Worthless.

"Dan didn't befriend me, okay? He was my roommate– my *babysitter*, more so than my friend. Dan would make confidence-boosting comments, and later on I'd find out how he took care of anyone who tried to hurt my feelings."

"Took care of?" Wynn trails off, eyes wide with terror.

"Not like Corbin takes care of people." I laugh at the insanity, but then realize it's our reality. "Ya know, Dan has a way with words. Instead of coming off smarmy, it's genuine."

"Way with words?" Wynn starts walking forward, grabbing for the door handle, but a greeter meets us instead, ushering us inside.

"Lawyer," I mutter in explanation to Wynn, then turn to the host. "We have a reservation– we're meeting Daniel Bishop and Uriah Crane."

"Right this way, sirs," the host walks slowly, weaving around tables in a nearly empty restaurant.

Wynn relaxes as we walk through the restaurant, realizing the décor, menu, and pricing is only an excuse to dress up and feel important and special for a few hours. In this economy, in this town, this is a special occasion location.

Wynn walks ahead of me, with my hand resting on the small of his back. Steps faltering, I know damn well he's spotted Uriah. I can't see around Wynn, but I know exactly what he's seeing– Uriah is androgynous in a way that makes every head turn, purely out of curiosity and intrigue. Memorable and arousing. Gorgeous.

I kept my friends apart from my boyfriend for a few reasons. Mostly I didn't think Wynn was mature enough to handle Uriah's intensity or the odd intimacy Dan and I share. I also liked having people just to myself, because we share everyone else and Wynn has friends he calls his own. But I'm ready now that Wynn's ready.

Tucked in a dark and secluded U-shaped booth at the back of the restaurant, Uriah comes into view first. Androgynous: Raw masculinity from a jawline sharp enough to cut, with a bladelike nose, and wiry muscles hidden beneath genderless clothing. Soft femininity from large, brown doe eyes fringed with thick lashes and a pouty mouth meant to kiss and suck cock.

Uriah glows so brightly he would still manage to stick out in a light bulb factory, especially with him wearing a silk blouse, skin-tight red leather pants, and kitten heels.

Dan is mostly straight, with the exception of his fascination with Uriah, who calls himself gender fluid. When they hooked up is when Dan and I truly got close, because my buddy couldn't handle the way his world tilted on its axis. Dan wasn't in denial. He wasn't closeted or bi, or ignoring his baser impulses because of societal, familial, or religious reasons. Dan was a pussy fiend, and Uriah put him through an existential crisis of epic proportions. Boy. Girl. Boy. Girl. Uriah hit all notes with the poor guy– with time, Dan fell in love with the extra dangly bits between his boyfriend's legs because he loved Uriah.

Wincing, I hope to God Wynn doesn't notice how I light up when I see Dan, reading more into it than there is. Dan's fit, average height, with dark curly hair. Hiding behind a pair of thick frames is a captivating, commanding pair of blue eyes.

"Hey." Now it's my turn to be bashful. I ignore Uriah and Wynn, because my fiancé is being eye-fucked and rendered speechless and motionless under the gaze. Uriah is like injecting pure sex into your veins.

Dan had slid out of the booth when he saw us approach, waving off the host. Now he strides toward me, pulling me into a manly, back-slapping hug. "Long time no see, soon-to-be married man."

"Hey," I repeat, hugging Dan tight, enjoying the way he feels solid beneath my arms and how safe I feel around him. He makes me feel good about myself– makes me see the person he sees when he looks at me. "Was the drive in okay?"

"Yeah," Dan breathes into my ear. "Uriah was a chatterbox the whole way, couldn't wait to meet your guy." Pulling away, he holds me at arm's length, never failing to make me feel younger than him when we're the same age.

I've never said this to anyone except for the man in question, but Dan elicits similar emotions in me that my dad did. The comfort. The security. The safety. Things, that up until recently, I didn't get from Wynn, but am getting more than I bargained for now.

I want to feel shame or guilt, but I can't. Wynn gives me everything I need and more, and I love him inside and out on a cellular level. After dealing with this discombobulating feeling for the past five years, I still can't explain it, but I'm not ashamed of it.

Dan and I love each other. There's an intimacy between us that transforms into sexual chemistry that wouldn't normally bloom because I'm not Dan's type. At all. As I said, he's straight, and Uriah is half feminine, and I'm not.

I get hard when I snuggle down in a warm bed, blankets up to my ears, and a song in my heart– that's how Dan makes me feel, and I him. We're looking at each other now, silently communicating while our partners have a standoff, both of us hard.

Wynn makes me feel like I'm dangling off the precipice of an erupting volcano after shooting up meth. No doubt Uriah makes Dan feel the same level of insanity.

Our relationship is safe and comforting, whereas our partners give us a thrilling dose of life. Both of us selfish, needing a hit once and a while, we both managed to choose exhibitionists who will help us meet our mutual needs.

It was Dan and Uriah, or never. Jackson was a test to see if we could go through with it– a test we couldn't fail because it was Jack.

I don't want to fuck Dan, and I sure as hell won't touch Uriah. Sex is emotional for me. As hot as Dan's husband is, I don't even want a taste. I just want to be held while watching them play together. That's all I want. Dan and I are too much alike, neither of us able to meet every need of our partners, either because we can't or we don't want to.

"Stop it," Dan chastises, hands dropping from my shoulders. Then he turns to Wynn. "Does Kade still mentally checkout nonstop."

"Not as often as he used to, thank fuck," Wynn mutters with a sly smile. Hand jutting out for a shake, "Wynn Gillette. A.k.a. Kade's little shit."

"You're an awfully big man for someone called little." Laughing, Dan shakes Wynn's hand, and I breathe a sigh of relief. They're both men's men, and I know they'll get along as buddies. "Kade called you that from the moment I learned you existed. One drunken night, Kade spilled why he thought he was a pervert."

"Hey, now." I step around them, blushing to beat the band. "There'll be none of that bullshit talk." Leaning down, I peck a kiss to Uriah's pouty mouth. "So… thoughts?" I ask, half listening in as Dan and Wynn make acquaintance.

Jaw dropping low to catch flies, Uriah just stares at me, then he whispers like it's a secret, "Thank you." Shaking his head, silky hair flying, "You always give the best gifts."

Sharing a laugh, I stare into Uriah's vivid eyes, happy to help. Dan's straight, emotionally driven like I am, and his adventurous side isn't as strong as Uriah's, nor is his sex drive. The first and last time they messed around was the limo ride, with Dan focusing on me to get through it. On another drunken night, Dan confessed how much he hated every second of it. Not Uriah enjoying himself, or me whacking off, but having to participate when he didn't know the stripper or want him at all... It's been a barren five years for them sexually, and I know I can't meet Wynn's voracious appetite day in and day out for the next sixty or seventy years.

We negotiated for four times a year, with Dan and me watching. But Uriah and Wynn are both naughty and intoxicating, and will do anything to make us engage with them. We'll see where that goes— if it happens at all.

"Thinking again," Dan sings, sliding into the booth. "Sit your big ass down, bub. I'm starving."

"That vest, Wynn…" Uriah trails off as he slides in next to Dan. "Are you wearing something similar in the ceremony?"

"Yeah." Tan skin flushed pink, Wynn's soaking this up like a sponge. I slide into the U-shaped booth so I end up sitting next to

Dan, with our partner's facing each other for ease of chatting. "Why?"

"Because…" Uriah shakes his head, humming to himself, he has the sexual subtlety of a wrecking ball. "Damn. That vest was made just for you to wear it."

Chuckling underneath my breath, I notice Wynn's ears are the last thing to turn pink. Resting my hand on Wynn's inner thigh, I drag it up out of curiosity, not shocked to find a hard dick riding along the inside of his right thigh.

Coughing into his hand, instead of moving away like I expected, the little shit presses up into my palm.

"Shameless," I mutter for only Wynn to hear, squeezing his length through the trousers before pulling away. "I like it."

Grabbing for a menu, I pretend to check it out when I already know what I'm getting. "Were you guys nervous before the ceremony?" I ask absentmindedly as I make sure what I want is still on the menu. "I'm not nervous."

"Nope," Dan answers without hesitation. "Not a single doubt."

"I was a fucking basket case," Uriah admits, leaning forward like he's sharing a secret. "It's like… every muscle in my body was shaking, and I felt like I had to take a piss even though I just did. Teeth where chattering."

"Cold feet?" Wynn leans into Uriah, like a flower reaching for the sun, which is ironic as I see Wynn as the sun in my life.

"No." Uriah folds his hands on the tabletop. "Performance anxiety. With Dan's family, we had to have a huge wedding– over five hundred guests. I think if we'd gotten married first intimately, and we were already husbands when we did the big production, I would have felt more comfortable."

"Like losing your virginity," Wynn's saying as the waiter arrives, when ordinarily he'd be bashful about that sort of thing. "The first time is awkward, and the next is as natural as breathing."

"Exactly," Uriah is now leaning across the table to get closer to Wynn, and it's as cute as all get out. "But who gets married twice?"

"Divorced people," Dan and I say in unison, sharing a private laugh.

"Shall I give you a moment to decide, or would you like to hear tonight's specials?" The waiter is patient, the same one we usually have, and he likes a nice tip. "I can take your beverage order while you peruse the menus."

"Shall I order for the table?" Dan asks, gaze connecting with each of ours in turn. He's Wynn's and my complete and total opposite with how we grew up and were raised.

"You know what I like, and Wynn pretty much eats the same as I do– no beer, though."

Dan picks a few entrees, saying we'll share them family-style, and then picks up the conversation where it left off. "I see enough divorces every day. The reason I had no reservations was because I was in it for the long haul, and I knew Uriah was too."

"Ah– thank you, babe." Dan earns a kiss to the cheek for his romantic words. "Performance anxiety was my only issue. I mean, sure…" Uriah runs his hands down his flat chest, rolling his hips a bit. "I'm confident in my own skin, but I don't want to be stared at while experiencing the most profound event in my life. That ought to be private, ya know?"

"I had the fantasies of a little girl for the longest time," I admit, blushing until my skin catches fire. "The terror of what you just described nipped that blushing bride bullshit in the bud."

"Plus, it's a waste of money," Wynn adds in, voicing what always has us arguing, but this time I agree with him. "We're having a ton of people, everything informal, so no pressure. But I get what you're saying about how it should be private."

"That's one of my regrets," Uriah confesses. "I was so nervous, with all those eyes on me, I can't remember what happened when we took our vows except for being relieved it was all over, and that's not fair to Dan and me."

"You said you see a lot of divorces?" Wynn accepts his glass of red wine from the waiter with a thank you, then takes an experimental sip. After a heartbeat, he makes a humming noise and goes for more. Everything the man does is utterly fascinating, and I love watching him experience new things. "What did you mean by that?"

Dan looks at me crosswise, a funny smirk flirting with his lips. "Kaden didn't give you my details, I see. I'm a divorce attorney."

"Really?" Wynn's eyebrows reach his hairline. "Who thinks to themselves, *when I grow up, I want to be a divorce lawyer*?"

"I did." Dan snorts, reaching across the table to pat Wynn's hand when he flinches. "No harm, no foul. I thought it was witty what you said. Speak your mind around me and don't edit yourself… I'm a third-generation divorce attorney at my family's firm. So I never worried about what I'd do since I already knew."

"Did your family pressure you?" Wynn's compassion seeps into his tone. "Did you want to do something else?"

"No on both accounts." Dan takes a sip of wine to wet his throat. "I'm good at it, and I love my job, and nothing else ever crossed my mind."

"Are your parents still married– damn!" Wynn covers his mouth, the small amount of alcohol already lowering his inhibitions. "Forget I asked that. I feel like I'm interrogating you. But I've heard the really personal shit, but none of the usual stuff people share."

"As I said, don't edit yourself," Dan warns, chuckling darkly. "My grandparents have been married for nearly sixty years, and my parents are going on thirty-five years. We learn from our clients' mistakes. Half the time, I could fix their marriages if only they'd let their pride go, so I carry that over into my own marriage on a daily basis. It's not perfect, but what is?"

"God, Dan's parents are insanely in love. To a creepy level." Uriah blushes, so he must have some juicy stories. "I want to grow up to be like them."

"Ha!" Dan's belting out laughter as the waiter delivers our salads. There's a lull in conversation as everyone makes yum-yum sounds while taking a few bites. "Have you gotten your office in order at the high school yet?"

"Off-limits conversation." Wynn's eyes cut in my direction. "Kade turns into a stress monster, and I can't have that until after the ceremony."

"I'll behave," I whisper softly in Wynn's direction. He hasn't stalked me in the bathroom, but I know he secretly fears I'm cutting again from the stress of it all. When we make love, he runs his hands down my sides and hips, and it's not in a loving gesture. I don't blame him, because I broke our trust.

"Yep, school starts next Wednesday for our district, and I'm all up and running. Even have my internet privileges back– with limitations."

"How do you survive?" Uriah gasps in horror, but he's not teasing me. "What limitations?"

Wynn takes this one. "Amazon, but only for purchases and no reading the comments on reviews. Facebook, but only as our LGBTQ group moderator. He's not ready for threads and comments from keyboard warriors. Wikipedia and Google search. No interacting with anyone yet. He has to earn that back."

Dan and Uriah look at me in horror, like I'm being controlled by my future husband, and it would be humorous if it wasn't necessary.

"Strangers, who have never met me and know nothing of me, were making me feel bad about myself– bad for being who I am, just because they could. Without a threat of consequence, they were telling me and others to kill ourselves, or fuck off and die. Telling someone who has attempted suicide to kill themselves is the ultimate of triggers. Calling us assholes, sluts, whores, ugly, no one would ever love us– demoralizing and dehumanizing us. I didn't go looking for it. Recipes. Funny meme. TV show recaps. Product reviews. Discussion threads on obedience training for pets. *Every thread* has a pack of dogs in the comments section, waiting to go after anyone with an opposing viewpoint. Most people laugh it off–"

"You couldn't," Dan confirms how he knows me, then he looks at Wynn. "Good. Don't let him back on unless it's absolutely necessary. That gnome's name belongs to Kaden– never forget that."

"Yeah, that's exactly why," I mutter, feeling ashamed of myself. Staring down at my salad plate that's still full, I've suddenly lost my appetite. "I didn't recognize it, but my usual coping tendencies weren't working, and I had a professor who was mind fucking me to get his own shits 'n' giggles. If I'd harmed myself, he probably would've felt like his dick grew a couple inches."

"We discussed that shit before, Kaden." Dan sighs, already having done a tour with me at Penn State for that very reason. "You don't plan on going back for more degrees, do you?"

Ashamed, all I can do is shake my head.

"Hey." Wynn wraps his arm around me. "I've told you time and time again how it's not your fault. You're not a wimp who needs to be tougher. It's an infection spreading, and I've even felt the need to lash out like those assholes do. It's a form of arrogance. The more we say, the more we think we have the right to say, the more we think people give a fuck about what we have to say. Then when someone doesn't care, shit hits the fan and disgusting words are said about the person, attacking their looks or their job, or a life we know nothing about. All of it to validate ourselves, to give us meaning, when it's just the fucking internet."

"Freedom of speech does not mean what people think it means," Uriah interjects. "I run a web magazine for the LGBTQ community, and every word I publish has to be within the law. Freedom of speech is the right to voice your political views without fear of prosecution, in all its forms, to protest without rioting, and exercise your artistic expression or advertise, with limitations. When someone tells you to fuck off and die, that is a terroristic threat. When someone says they have the right to say whatever they want about you, it is defamation, and it's punishable in a court of law. Ignorant people hide behind freedom of speech."

"I'm rubbing off on you," Dan mutters with pride, chuckling softly. "You talking law is making me hot. Uriah's right, Kade. If someone attacks another online, causing harm such as suicide or a mob mentality to bodily seek out the person, there is legislation passing to prosecute them to the fullest extent of the law. That's not under freedom of speech. Cowards. If it's against the law to say it to someone's face without getting a citation, you can't say it on the internet."

"I can't get up, get into our waiter's face, and scream about how he should go off and die." Uriah leans across the table, trying to get close to Wynn and me, trying to explain color to the blind. "I'd be taken away in handcuffs."

"Just because it's behind a screen doesn't make it legal," Dan hammers home. "I'm not saying we need people to police the internet and arrest these assfucks. Just leave them to their negativity. I had a thirteen-year-old girl argue law and dick with me last week. I'm an attorney, and I have a dick, neither of which she had, but she felt the right to argue about what I know and she'll never experience. I didn't find out how she was a child, until she was calling me an ugly bastard, since she had a man's name in a private group of adults. You have no idea who is instigating. It's gross, and the parents need to have their asses kicked, because these kids turn into the adults who are doing it even worse. Your professor is probably raising sociopaths for children."

"I catch myself doing it too," Uriah admits, voice filled with shame. He looks at Wynn, because Wynn admitted the same earlier. "But I stop myself. Debate is one thing, but once slurs are thrown, moral and religious statements are made, or physical attributes are defamed, I leave. I welcome a different viewpoint, but I don't welcome anyone saying I don't have the right to my private convictions and thoughts. I won't allow someone to make me be that type of person. I can debate facts, why I feel or think what I do, but I won't go down that dark path to nowhere."

"I'm getting there, but I'm not there *yet*," I stress. "I was actually relieved when they pressured me to get off the internet. But the anxiety has been creeping in now that I have to be available to my students and their parents."

"Shit," Dan hisses.

"Yeah," Wynn replies, chuckling sardonically. "Some of the parents don't like us. I have access to the email account, and I delete anything that isn't about school before I let Kade see it. Makes me sick."

"I can take it," I growl, pushing my salad plate away.

"No, you can't." Wynn reaches over to squeeze my thigh. "There is no shame in that. Those parents need to have their heads examined, and their vile words would infect how you do your job. After reading some of the bigoted mail, I wanted to hate their kids on principle."

"You're too good for that." The server removes our salad plates and leaves behind an appetizer platter. Dan likes to make dinner a strung out affair with lots of conversation.

"You're a better man than me. Why do you think I'm avoiding Miriam?" Wynn's fork spears a stuffed mushroom. "It's still too fresh. The kids I'd be teaching were in school when I was, or their siblings were, or their parents flung dog shit and bible verses at me. I'd fail them just to get a sense of vindication… and I'd be around power tools. Saws that could amputate fingertips of little bigots."

"That's hot," Uriah whispers from behind his napkin while he wipes his mouth, then he changes the subject. "Did the master suite get finished in time for your honeymoon period? Dan said you've been camped out in the living room on an air mattress."

"Oh, it's gorgeous." Wynn glows with pride. "Bren hooked me up with help when I couldn't figure it out myself– plumbing and electrical. But I did the rest myself. It was finished last week, and it killed my jointer."

"We got you a new one," I mutter wryly, causing Wynn to chuckle. "We've been too busy to christen the new bedroom. I was finally allowed to shop online to outfit the spare bedroom we made out of my old home office. It's got swanky new bunkbeds."

"We were going to do two bedrooms, but we wouldn't have had a living room of any kind." Wynn's enthusiasm for how I've always seen our life warms my heart. We're holding off on the foster care paperwork until we're married, and both of us are applying.

"If we take in siblings for emergency placement, it will be fine. But not if we end up with opposite sex nonrelatives since it's the one room– no sharing. I doubt we'd ever get more than one family of kids at a time anyway… and not for long."

Wynn reaches over to tug me to his chest, then he whispers in my ear. "You're the good one between us." Pecking my lips with a kiss, he pulls away laughing. "Don't even say how I make you good. I am who I am, but you're not who you think you are."

Rolling my eyes, I take the chastisement in stride. Catching me drooling over the Caprese salad, Dan pushes it toward me.

"Hun, why don't you tell Wynn about our place, or whatever else you think he ought to know, since our boy has been so tight-lipped," Dan commands in a wry tone. "Kade and I have to have a powwow over here."

"Okay–" Uriah gears up, turning into the chatterbox he's known to be. The guys at Adam & Steve's are baffled yet blown away when Uriah walks in. Even here in the restaurant, people are staring. "So we just have an apartment in the building where the legal firm is located. No commute times and I work from home. Now, Wynn, do you like to dance? You've got to come to Pittsburgh. There's this one club…"

"Be happy Uriah released some of it on the ride down here." Dan chuckles as he slides closer in the U-end of the booth. Wynn and Uriah are basically interrogating each other across the table, affording us some privacy. If Warren was thrown in the mix, they'd be fighting to get in a word edge-wise.

"Listen– I'm sorry for not telling Wynn all about you guys–" Dan stops me with a potent look.

"I get it." Sighing, Dan slumps deeper onto the backrest, then reaches for his wine glass. "Are you sure about us staying at your house for the next few nights? We can get a hotel room somewhere nearby."

"We're not going to– ya know…" I trail off.

"Kaden," Dan admonishes softly, eyebrows scrunching together in the center of his forehead. "If you can't even say it out loud, then we sure as hell won't be doing it. But it's your wedding, and we shouldn't be imposing."

"You won't be staying on the night after the ceremony, so it's a moot point." I know he won't drop the subject, so I stab my fork into a hunk of mozzarella. "Bren and Jack are planning something tomorrow night. It's like a bachelor party and reception rolled into one, since our ceremony is the next morning with whomever sticks around."

"What's happening?" Dan laughs, completely baffled by how my family operates. Being affluent, he's used to a different sort of lifestyle. *Waaaayyy* different.

"Tonight, you guys can take the living room. We just bought a microfiber sectional with a really sweet pullout bed. Tomorrow night, because my brother has a twisted sense of humor, Bren thought we'd get cold feet. To avoid that, he's planned a campout in Royce's and the duplex's backyards, with the kids in Royce's yard with responsible adults, and the rest of us in his backyard being heathens. Then when we wake, we get married."

"Wow…" Eyes bugging out behind his glasses, Dan tries to hide his laughter at bay. "I've never– just wow. That's so–"

"Hillbilly? Redneck?" Laughing at myself, a wicked blush reaches my hairline. "It's fucking fabulous, and absolutely nothing like how I envisioned it my entire life, but exactly how Wynn probably did. Dish-to-pass, a pig on a spit, bonfires, and tents, with booze only in Bren's backyard, with our rehab folks in Royce's yard. Bren even made a tunnel through the tree line so it was easier to go from one yard to the next. The tents are already being pitched as we speak."

"I'm actually excited, believe it or not." Now it's Dan's turn to laugh at himself and blush. "You know I've never been camping." Leaning in like it's a big secret, "Uriah is going to flip his shit when he learns this. HA!"

Noticing our partners are no longer volleying information back and forth across the table, Dan and I turn quickly to catch Wynn blushing and Uriah catching flies.

"We should take a picture while they're quiet. Quick! Get your phone out." I shoulder bump Dan, and he moves into action.

They actually pose for us. Wynn pretends to fork the camera, with Uriah flipping us the bird while wearing a cat that ate the canary smirk.

"Gimme!" Uriah wrenches the phone out of Dan's hand. After a second, he flips the phone around. "That will do, I guess. I look deranged, but Wynn looks hotter than Hades. Your turn– scrunch together."

Laughing, eyes connecting, Dan and I look at each other. Before we can pose, the picture is being taken, and Uriah and Wynn are both muttering, "Whoa…" With Uriah continuing on with, "Would you look at that connection? I ought to be jealous, but I'm happy instead."

The rest of the several hours long dinner goes off without a hitch. With too many glasses of wine drank and two drivers, we decide to walk around town to sober up before heading back to Rusty Knob.

Summer is drawing to a close with Labor Day a blink away, so the nights are getting chilly. Ahead of us, Dan and Uriah walk hand-in-hand, giving Wynn and me some much needed privacy after our dinner date with them.

"Penny for your thoughts?" I murmur out the side of my mouth to gain Wynn's attention, with a squeeze of his hand for good measure.

"That saying takes on a whole new meaning when you have a sister-in-law named Penny," Wynn mutters wryly. "I'm good. Damn fucking fine, actually. I was terrified to meet them, but they're both awesome. I feel like I understand you better now."

Eyeing our companions, I whisper absentmindedly, "Good," but end up chuckling as Uriah squeezes Dan's ass, then kicks him in the back of the calf with the toe of a kitten heel. "Never a dull moment with those two. Dan's really reserved. Calm. The day Uriah popped into Dan's life–" an explosion sound vibrates my lips.

"I'm not blind." Wynn squeezes my hand when I wince. "I'm not jealous that you're half-assed in love with him. If Dan's that awesome, then I want to befriend him too. I know that's the real reason you didn't have us meet until tonight. I know you love me, will never leave me, and we'll be happy together forever. But a few years ago, even a few months ago, seeing the way you and Dan are together would have made me doubt."

"Not now?" Stopping in the center of the sidewalk, music pouring out from a nearby bar, I'm honest with myself. "Yeah, I waited, figuring our marriage would be all the reassurance you'd need. Dan and I love each other, but it's not the same as it is with me and you and him and Uriah. We're not compatible."

"I'll pretend that I don't beg to differ on your compatibility..." Wynn trails off, tugging me until I start walking again. "But I won't argue on him being nuts over Uriah." Turning to look at me, a smile lingering on his lips, "And I know–" Wynn fists his chest. "I *know* how you feel about me, can feel it in my bones."

"Just don't be jealous, okay?" Pulling Wynn to me with our clasped hands, I wrap my arm around his shoulders, spinning him like we're dancing. "I don't want to share my life with him– parts? Sure. I don't want to share his bed, either."

Chuckling darkly, Wynn's blue eyes shine with irony. "Keep lying to yourself, Mr. Marx. Keep lying, and keep believing the lie, but no one else believes it, including Dan."

"I don't know what the fuck you're talking about," I mutter defensively, good mood evaporating.

"Dan wants to fuck you," Wynn blurts out bluntly. "Dick allergy or not, he'd be good with yours. Not mine, or anybody else's but Uriah's. But he wants yours. Probably always has. Probably wanted you before Uriah swaggered into your lives."

"I– what?" Squinting sideways, I try to get a read on Wynn.

"While you were in the john and Dan was settling the bill, Uriah and I had a little chat, and neither of us are anything but blunt."

"Fuck!" Neck arched, I look to the night sky for an answer. "Nothing good could possibly come from the unholy union of Rusty Knob's golden boy and Pittsburgh's deviant wet dream."

"A lot of good can come from it." Wynn winks at me– the little shit. "I've been thinking."

"God, help us all."

"Ha!"

"About what?" I slow up, because Dan and Uriah have turned around and are headed our way. The kitten heels make Uriah's nonexistent hips sway, but it's the eyes locked on Wynn like a predator spotting prey that has me taking notice.

"Wow, they are something else," Wynn mutters with appreciation, lust and bashfulness warring in his tone. "I was thinking about how you put so much pressure on us over losing our virginity, and I want to enjoy the festivities Bren and Jack have planned. No stress. No anxiety."

"What the hell are you talking about?" I tear my eyes away from Dan quirking an eyebrow above his glasses in my direction. No doubt my confusion is evident, and he's wondering what's going on.

"I say we elope," Wynn proves just how blunt he can be. "Tonight."

CHAPTER THIRTY-ONE
Brennan Kennedy

"Bit much, ya think?" Jackson wiggles the tulle bundle in front of my face as I go over my check list. "Sample-sized flavored lube, three condoms, and a breath mint?"

Snorting, I hold my tongue on whether or not it's too much. "These favors can't come out until well after dark and the parents and kids are on the other side of the boundary line."

"I'm not an idiot, Bren." Jack finishes tagging the naughty adult favors, and begins on the regular ones. "Is it too childish to have noise-makers and tiny bottles of bubbles? I was gonna do chocolate, but it would melt."

"All or nothing," I mutter absentmindedly as I mark gathering enough chairs off my list. "I feel bad that Corbin won't be here."

"Still radio silence?" Jack leans over me as I sit at the kitchen island, finger tapping my list. "I already dragged a couple tents over to Royce's, and Hayden and Hayley promised to erect them, then do the ones in our yard. Oh! That too– Libby is in charge of the yard games."

"Okay, good." I take a deep breath, amazed at how much work this best man gig is, unable to contemplate an elaborate wedding and reception. "Jesse's doing the decorations, and Willa's been making food for days."

"Hope Penny didn't try to help. HA!" Checking off more things, Jack demands my undivided attention.

Impatient, Jack proves how we should've bought the stationary wooden stools he wanted. Swiveling me until I'm facing him, he grabs the pen out of my hand, and it lands somewhere near the kitchen sink.

"We have a lot to do," I caution, raising an eyebrow at the lusty expression crossing Jackson's face. He's so fucking hot when he wears his glasses. "Too much to get distracted."

Palms sliding up the column of my neck, Jack cups my jaw– romantic, sweet, hot. He's controlling me– he knows it, I know it, and I like it.

Hesitating, Jackson makes me wait, staring deep in my eyes, then he moves in for the kill, lips pressing into mine with violent force. "Want you," escapes between my parted lips to flow into Jack's mouth. "Been too long, too busy."

Unhinged, hands fist hair as lips mash together. Moans fill the air as greedy hands explore, yanking t-shirts and tugging at shorts. Tearing himself away from me, Jackson leaves me breathless.

Lips swollen from our kiss, Jack pants out the words, "Here's a lesson in delegation, especially when you have a billion relatives. Half of the items on this list, I gave to the Franklins. Do you know where Penny got her bossiness?" Rhetorical, obviously. "As the mother hen of our bunch, Brenda copied your list, then enlisted the women in our families to delegate it down the ranks. We're good."

Reaching behind me to the countertop, Jack retrieves something, only to press it into my hand. "Read the tag, Brennan. *Read it*," is a breathless command.

Unbidden, I hold the adult favor in my palm. Fingers twisting, I turn the wedding bell-shaped tag over to reveal **FUCK ME! NOW!**

"God, yes!" I shout, suddenly impatient. Tearing the tulle, I get the bottle of lube out and have it saturating my fingers in an instant. The rest of the contents hit the tile floor with a smack. After yanking Jack's shorts to his ankles, with one hand I grab his hair, drawing his lips to mine, while my sticky fingers seek his ass.

Hands struggle to get my dick out of my shorts– so hard it won't bend. "Ugh!" we grunt in unison for varying yet exactly the same reasons. My fingertips impale Jack's heat the same instance his hand wraps around my cock.

"Ride my cock or be ridden from behind," I barely gasp out between kisses.

"Ridden." Jack pulls his lips from mine, freckles gone behind the crimson kiss of lust. "Wrought iron or not, that stool won't withstand how hard I want to be fucked." Moving far enough away that my fingers slip from his body, "Bend me over the stool, spank my ass, then fuck it. Now, Brennan. Now."

Shuddering with need, I grab the nape of his neck, and wrench him forward until his forehead lands on the cushioned seat. Jack reaches out to stabilize himself, fingers wrapping around the backrest of the stool.

"I'ma fuck your brains out," I gasp out breathlessly, cock already on the edge of erupting and it hasn't gotten anywhere near Jack's ass. "You bossy bottom bitch."

"NO!" we shout in unison as the doorbell rings. "Go away!" In quick succession, the doorbell is pressed dozens of times. "Not now– it's been weeks."

"Whoever the fuck is on the other side of the door," bloodthirsty Nurse Jackie rears his violent head, "Owes me an epic orgasm."

It takes less than fifteen seconds beneath the constant onslaught of the doorbell to get our clothing righted. Jack takes off before me, rage giving him an extra burst of speed. The door is wrenched open, then a high-pitched squeal fills the air, when I didn't think Jack was capable of such a noise.

Not pain. Shock.

"What's going–" is all I get out before my eyes finally register what they're seeing. "Better than an orgasm." Not bothering to yank him away from Jackson first, I use my strength to pull them both into my arms. "Welcome back to Rusty Knob."

"Can't…" Franny tries to tap out, hand patting me on the back, and I pretend it's his version of a bro-hug. "Breathe."

"You're suffocating Francis underneath all that muscle," Sage's sarcastic voice hits my ears, making the shock of seeing Francis that much more real. "Nice place, and I'm not being sarcastic. Saw your dad's place on the way in. What are you guys, the top dogs in Rusty Knob?"

"Thanks– I think." I pull back, holding Francis at arm's length, with Jackson still attached to him like a monkey. "Wow… you're really here."

Ignoring the emotional moment, or perhaps unable to deal with it, Sage keeps up a constant barrage of snooty commentary in the background of our reunion. "You should see our place– it's on the Pacific. Can't stand being landlocked, no matter how majestic your mountains and woods are. Even back in Mass, we're near the water. Prefer the Atlantic, though."

"You look–"

"Mind-blowing," Jackson finishes for me, stepping away so we both can get a good look at Franny. "I expected you to be in queen-mode," is a comment on the tasteful trousers rolled up past his ankles, flip flops, and a concert t-shirt Francis is wearing.

Smiling at us, Franny tucks his chin-length hair behind an ear, showing off a diamond stud in his earlobe. "It's hot out– didn't want my makeup to melt."

"Did you expect a drag show?" As a unit, we turn to Sage, who is wearing khaki without a perfect hair on his head mussed up. He looks like he stepped directly from an Abercrombie and Fitch ad. "We just did a tour from Massachusetts through Upstate New York, with a sojourn in Amish country. Now we're in backwoods West Virginia. Francis is not stupid."

"Some of my designs are in my luggage." The Franny we know and love makes an appearance with a single arch of his eyebrow.

Sage and Franny are friends only, sometimes lovers, because they'd murder each other as partners– too much alike. Both tops, breaking the ridiculous stereotypes about small framed men automatically being bottoms. Their personalities are commanding, demanding, and cat-fights ensue.

Stepping to the side, Sage reveals a mini-me out of nowhere. "Got a place I can stash my sister until we leave?"

Stunned, Jackson and I stare gape-mouthed at a little girl around five or so, with a brown ponytail and huge eyes like a Precious Moments figurine. "What's your name, sugar?" Jack's quicker on the uptake than I am. "How old are you?"

"Gemma Fischer," she announces in a melodious voice more befitting of a woman. "I'm five."

"Question for you," pops out of my mouth before I introduce myself. "If you could pick a playmate, do you want a little boy or little girl?" While Gemma mulls that over, I do the introductions. "I'm Bren, by the way." Pointing over at Jack, "And this fella is Nurse Jackie. We grew up with Francis."

"Gemma likes to network, so just toss her in with any kids you have on hand," Sage says as if we breed children like one does livestock, but the fucker is taunting us into engaging him in verbal battle. If our weekly video game sessions have taught me anything, it's that Sage gets off on a lively debate. If you won't engage him, he'll instigate one out of thin air.

"How about if I call up Warren to bring Copper over, and you guys can have a sleepover with Honor?"

"Jesse will be so peeved." I shake my head, mulling over the fallout.

Grinning like a villain, "I know," Jackson drawls while reaching for his phone.

"Some things never change." Franny giggles evilly, patting Jackson on the back for being a rotten douchebag.

"First question," Sage directs at me. "Who is Copper? Second question, where is this sleepover taking place."

"Copper is on the upswing toward five, and the coolest little dude you'll ever meet." I point to the door next to us to put Sage at ease. "Right there, with my daughter and soon-to-be ex-wife."

"Good, just so Gemma's out of earshot." Clearly Sage wasn't worried about undue influence. "I'll go grab her bag."

"Sage!" Gemma bellows, chasing after her brother, tiny shoes tapping on the sidewalk. I fear she doesn't want to be out of his sight, but she surprises me. "Don't forget my squishy pillow in your luggage."

"Um... what's up with that?" I point at the Lexus with the GAYSAGE license plate, directing the question to Franny.

Laughing, Franny tugs me back into my living room. "That is an upset Sage. Lots of shit went down in his hometown. Back when Sage was still in high school, his dad got some twenty-year-old chick knocked up, and the man was in his late sixties. Cut to now, the girl ran off, leaving the kid behind. Sage was lured home with the promise of seeing Weston, but Weston didn't show up. So when we got to Boston, Byron –Sage's dad –abandoned the little girl, signing over custody to Sage."

"What?" Jackson whisper-shouts, furious. "Why?"

"Oh, this is Sage after destroying his family, trying to get his mother to take the girl in, and having a mental breakdown. Sage always said he knew from the instant he learned that Aubrey chick got pregnant, he'd end up raising the kid."

"What's he going to do?" I draw Franny down to the sofa, eyes watching as Jack stalks out of the house, no doubt collaring Jesse for sleepover duty.

"Well, this won't be the last you see of me." Leaning back on the sofa, Francis looks exhausted. With a sigh, brown eyes open to level on me. "We're moving to Boston as soon as we find our way back to California. We have to pack and quit our jobs. There's no way Sage can do this without his mother's side of the family, even if they aren't actually related to the girl. I'm not staying in California without Sage."

"Are you guys together now?" Confusion rings in my voice. "Last time we spoke, you said you weren't."

"Fuck no," Franny grumbles, laughter in his voice. "I sure as shit refuse to be alone. We'll still be living in a major US city, just a couple hours' drive to NYC. That's all I need in order to do my job. I can ship anywhere in the world. Sage is going to have a hard time finding a job, though. He was set to substitute in our school district, hoping for an in. But with the school year already starting, no way can they accommodate him."

"Sage's mom is going to help out, then?"

"*No*," Franny says firmly. "Opal's great, but she has her own life, and I don't blame her. It's the kid her ex made and then tried to pawn off on her to raise. Plus, she's a few hours away in some Podunk town called Fairport."

"Podunk?" Laughing wryly, I stare at Franny, trying to see the vestiges of the guy I grew up with. "Sage is wearing off on you."

"Good or a bad thing?" Francis asks, looking as if the answer truly matters to him.

"Good," I answer with all honesty. "You're sophisticated. Classy. Hot," I tack on, blushing.

Leaning forward, hand resting on my forearm, "You ain't seen nothing yet, sugar," Franny turns on his accent with a bat of his eyelashes. Eyeing me for a heartbeat, he makes sure the flirty routine isn't rubbing me wrong. "Get me lubricated, and I'll pull my tricks out of my luggage."

Of course, I'm fanning myself with my hand when Sage walks in. "Does lubricated mean something else around here? Jealous, because you won't bottom for me."

"Oh, yeah, darlin'," Jack says from behind Sage as he walks in the front door. "Lubricated means intoxicated."

"Perfect." Sage grins like the Cheshire cat. "I have three cases of wine from the Finger Lakes we picked up on our way out of New York into Pennsylvania."

"As a joke, we picked up a bottle of maple syrup every time we stopped at a place that sold it." Franny has us all laughing, knowing exactly who's going to be the recipient of all that liquid gold.

"Yo!" the tiny smooth dude pipes in from the front door. "Somebody lose a chick?"

"Chick?" Franny's eyes go wide with awe as he takes in Copper– the kid is even rocking his pajamas.

"There's some strange chick drawing on the sidewalk." Copper hitches his thumb behind him, as if it's the most bizarre thing he's ever seen. "What do we do with her?"

"You go play with her, little dude." Warren palms the top of his son's head, steering him outside so he can get inside. "Don't be stingy, go get Honor." Face lighting up like Christmas, eyes glued on Francis, Warren shouts, "Pen! Pen. My God, git your ass in here. You're never going to fucking believe this shit."

"What?!" Penny shouts back from parts unknown.

"It's bizarre seeing the little dude without his car," I murmur while wearing a smile.

"Copper looks like the type to cruise for some strange," Franny teases after I've told him countless tales from Rusty Knob over the years, many involving the budding badass.

"Yeah, strange chicks." Warren's snicker is sadistic, then his attention is drawn to Sage squeezing into the house around his solid frame. "Who the fuck are you?"

"Strange chick's brother," is Sage's answer as he drags his luggage in the front door. "Get off your bubble butt and get your own bags," he issues to Francis. "Not your bitch."

"You need a drink," Francis volleys back. "I'll grab a case of wine from the trunk."

"Bring it all– too hot in there. Don't forget the liquor, either." Sage huffs and puffs. "Remind me to downsize when I pack next." Dropping his bags wherever they lie, the effeminate tyrant falls to the sofa next to me. "Exhausted. So goddamn exhausted. Hope you have a spare bedroom in this place."

"I'll go make up the bed," Jack's a lifesaver, causing Warren to turn into an ass.

"Ah– Jack's the wife. We had bets going."

Flipping Warren off, Jack takes it in jest. "I'll never deny it. My house. My man."

Gaze roving from Jack's toes to the top of his head, and then back down again, Warren looks at Jackson like he's never seen him before. After an audible gulp, "Ain't no shame in that, I guess."

"Good," is Jack's reply as he snags Sage's bags without breaking a sweat, proving how tiny our houseguest truly is.

"I'll go round the kids up and herd them to Jesse," Warren offers, still blushing from Jack's response.

Head turning slightly on the back of the sofa, Sage's intense stare pins me. "Who was the beefcake?"

"You thought Warren was hot?" Franny laughs from the other side of me. "Oh. My. God. No way, no how. *Gross.*"

"Go get your shit," the grump mutters, clearly a control freak.

Ignoring the bitch on the sofa, "Wait until you set your eyes on Wynn, then." Francis chuckles evilly, making the hair on the nape of my neck stand on end.

"Leave my brother alone," I mutter, sounding as annoyed as Sage. "Oh, I forgot to tell ya, there's another Gillette in the family. So if Sage thought War was hot–"

"Is this mystery man rough and tumble?" Animated, Sage comes to life.

Talking over Sage, "Bottom?" there is hope in Franny's voice.

"Bottom?" I mull that over, hating how I'm being stereotypical with my guess. "Probably. Rough and tumble? No way, no how. Copper could take his uncle down for the count."

"Oh," they both sigh in disappointment, with Sage adding, "I like dominating a huge guy."

"They're like finding a unicorn in the wild." Franny snickers. "When I'm in queen-mode, I like ramming a dude until he screams."

"My brothers are huge, and both are versatile. But if you so much as bat an eyelash their way, I'ma bury you both." Fragile, they seem easily manipulated, which is why I'm terrified about their dinner date tonight. After putting in all this time, energy, effort, and money, there better still be a ceremony taking place.

"Mentor KM and Wynn are so out of our league anyway." Sighing, Francis braces his palms on his thighs in preparation to rise from the sofa, but he's taken down by a ninety pound, squealing redhead.

"Franny!" Penny finally figured out why Warren wanted her to come in here. Sitting in his lap, peppering kisses on his cheeks, poor Francis is assaulted by Penny. "Welcome home– we've missed you."

"Your kid," Francis gasps out, "Is the best kid I've ever seen."

"Hey!" Sage is insulted. "Since he won't get off his fat ass, I guess I'll go empty the rest of the shit out of the car. Enjoy being mauled by this hillbilly spawn."

"Your man seems nice." Penny rumbles with laughter, causing Sage to take notice.

"Okay, I love sarcastic bitches." Sage pats Penny on the shoulder. "You're my new best friend, and your kid does seem like a badass."

"Bedroom's ready," Jack calls out as he descends the staircase. "Get the wine chilled for our prissy houseguests. I want a couple of shots while we finish off these favors." Stilling at the bottom step, Jack takes in the scene on the sofa. "No vagina allowed. Out!" he points at Penny. "Love ya, girl. But we're playing with condoms and lube and talking about dick tonight."

"I know dick," Penny purrs seductively, then laughs like a hyena. After climbing off our buddy, she gives a little wave. "See ya in the morning, girls"

"Um… so are we having an orgy?" Sage looks around for hidden gay guys, clearly not as worldly as I thought him to be. As hot as he is, Sage's ass is safe from the likes of me.

Calling out over his shoulder as he steps into the kitchen, "You'll see." Jackson's laughter is infectious, and I find myself across the room before my mind checks in with my feet.

"Love you," I whisper, stealing a kiss, then I sit on the stool I almost got to fuck Jackson on, noticing the spilled lube on the floor.

Blushing, Jackson quickly cleans up the evidence. "Should we help unpack the car?"

"No." Eyes intent, I stare at Jack while fingering the tag that says **Fuck Me! Now!** "You're on music duty, and I'll get the shot glasses. Delegation, remember? We've got a party to host."

CHAPTER THIRTY-TWO
Kaden Marx

Panting wildly, standing in the middle of our living room, laughing with insanity, Wynn and I don't register how we have guests.

"I just… I can't fucking believe it," Wynn stammers, eyes glossy, face glowing brighter than ever before.

"You look so fucking high right now," I murmur, half-ass wondering if I'm in shock. No doubt Wynn's expression is mirrored on my face.

"I've never been high, but I doubt it feels this fucking fantastic. Wow…" Shaking his head in mystification, Wynn just gazes into my eyes. "No wonder my brother and sister were drug addicts. Holy fuck! I feel goddamn alive like I've never felt before."

"I just… I just– fuck!" Neck arching, I toss my head back and laugh at the ceiling.

"I'm not exactly what you'd call impulsive," Wynn's still babbling, like he has been for the past hour and a half since we committed this insanity.

Grabbing for Wynn's hand, I twine our fingers together, then raise our hands before our eyes. "I'd say that was pretty damn impulsive." Eyes zeroing in on the rings on our left hands. "Holy fuck, you're my husband."

"I know, right?" Wynn's still shaking his head, to the point he's going to get a crick in it. "I was what, eleven? Twelve when you first noticed me? It's been a decade, Kaden." Insanity bubbles up from Wynn's throat, the laugh so intoxicating my entire body lights on fire and begins to shake.

"Bren's gonna cut our balls off," real fear is injected in my voice, fear of disappointing my brother.

"Nah– ain't gonna tell Bren," Wynn slurs, and the wine wore off a while ago. "This was for us, so we could enjoy ourselves tomorrow at the campout, then not freak the fuck out during the ceremony planned. No one has to know. It was to release the stress and make our union about *us*, no one else."

"No expectations," I muse, then get hit with reality. "The minister will want to sign the license," I point out, trying to be logical when I'm thinking with a foggy mind.

"Tell him we're doing a ceremony for in-state guests because we got married somewhere else." Wynn leans into me, smirking. "Fucking lie– I don't give a shit."

"Lie?" This time I laugh so hard my ribs hurt. "Do you hear yourself, Wynn? You never lie. You're never impulsive. What's up with you?"

"The more you go off the rails with stress, the more I don't give a flying fuck about anything anymore. I just want what I want– what you *need*. I just want to play with my saws and fuck you."

"That's... creepy yet fucking hot," I mumble, bizarrely turned on right now.

"I'm twenty-two years old. I almost killed myself– strike that. I *did* kill myself, but there were no shells in the shotgun. I feel like a man who's had five years of experiences I wouldn't have. I almost didn't know a world with Copper and Ginger. I never would have held baby Royce as he struggled to survive. Brynn wouldn't be stealing my heart. Honor– I've watched childbirth, for fuck's sake. That changes a man."

"That was *so* gross." Skeeving out, I shudder in revulsion. "I can't believe Jesse let us... ya know, see her vag... as it turned into something from Aliens and ejected a human being. That's got to be the moment Jackson went from calling her a breeder to wanting to be a midwife. He was fascinated."

"Stay with me, here." Wynn shakes me, because unlike him, I have been drinking since our walk. Liquid courage. "We've been fucking– and it's so goddamn good too –and the world didn't implode. We're living together– the first married gay couple in Rusty Knob, and it didn't poison the water supply."

"We ought to–"

"My dad is missing. *Poof.* So is Octavia, and I wish Dad would find her just so creepy Cain would maybe follow her somewhere and never come back."

"Cain's awesome."

"Go home– you're drunk," Wynn manages to say with a straight face. "I want to hold him down and shove a steak down his gullet as vengeance for pissing on Jack."

"Or because you're jealous he's your brother– just saying."

"Follow along, Kade. You're making me lose my train of thought. So... shit happens. I can't change it. I could stress, and wallow, and let it rule me. Fuck that shit. I've only got this one, very *short* life to lead, and nothing is going to get in my way."

"So you now drink, asked about smoking weed, debating on fucking Uriah, and had us elope? I fear you're acting out."

"No therapy bullshit," Wynn growls at me. "I have never felt better in my entire life, because I'm the only person who is making my choices, and they aren't made out of fear or necessity. I'm chasing happiness, Kaden, and I'ma pull you along for the ride, whether you're stressed, freaking the fuck out, or eager to be with me."

"I must confess, I'm kinda getting off on this new side of you." Hand moving on its own accord, I find my fingers fiddling with the buttons on Wynn's vest. "Don't get me wrong– you terrify the piss out of me, but in a good way."

Hand gripping the back of my neck, Wynn jerks me forward, mouth brutalizing mine. "Whoa…" I release in a panic as I freefall backward, only to ass-plant on the sofa. Scrambling, I try to get back up, but Wynn's palming my forehead.

"You stay right there and rest while I get your present ready." Wynn literally talks down to me, then grabs his junk– like really squeezes the bulge in his pants.

"What the hell?" I mutter, confused.

"This is a dick," Wynn cups himself, adjusting until there's an outline of the shape of his cock down his left leg. "Not a vag. I'm all man, and I have needs I'm gonna fulfill."

"Alrighty then." Terrified. I'm utterly terrified where this is going.

"Sit tight." Wynn leaves with a bright and airy vibe, disappearing somewhere with Uriah in tow. With my new husband not in the room, I finally notice I'm sitting next to Dan. "Either Wynn is suddenly bipolar, or I'm drunker than I realized."

"You are *lit*." Dan's rumble of laughter vibrates the sofa. "Don't you remember how I had to drive the Land Rover, with you guys in the backseat sharing a celebratory bottle of Jack, with Uriah following us in my car? Well, Wynn took a few sips to your guzzles."

"Um… no, I do *not* remember that." Head lulling to the side, my vision is whacked and all I see is the side of Dan's glasses and the hair curling around his ear.

"Yeah, so whatever you're thinking, saying, or doing, might not be reality." Laughter again. "It's hilarious to witness, though. I've never seen you like this."

"Like what?"

"Free."

That single word rocks my world.

Blinking, I find Dan standing over me, with a bottle of water extended between his fingertips. "Drink up– hydrate some sense back into ya, and maybe ward off tomorrow's hangover."

"Wynn can get out of control sometimes, and he won't regret it–"

"But you might," Dan finishes as he sits on the cushion next to me. Reaching over, he twists the cap off my water bottle. "I'm completely sober, which I did on purpose. I won't let anything happen that we haven't discussed previously. Probably none of that, either. After all, it's your wedding night."

"Wynn wants to tear up Uriah's ass– his words, not mine," flows without a filter.

"I know. Uriah knows. Half of Morgantown knows. Your entire street, including the Gillette family across the road knows."

"Oh, Christ. What did I do?"

"Nothing." Dan chuckles sinisterly, and I know I'll never live down whatever mischief Warren witnessed. "Kaden?" he shifts on the sofa to face me, voice coaxing. "Wynn might not realize it, but seeing us together freaked him out. He knows you love him, and he wants you to be happy. But it's hard to swallow enjoying the company of a man who wants to make love to his husband."

"I'm sorry Wynn said whatever he said about wanting to screw Uriah," I mumble with shame, alcohol removing the filter from my thoughts.

"Backward, Kade. Got that backward. No doubt Wynn wants to conquer Uriah's ass– who wouldn't? But he senses the real reason you didn't allow him to meet me, and it wasn't how hot my husband is– fucking scorching."

"I prefer to use the word intoxicating to describe Uriah."

"You would, you lush," Dan teases me, when most of his college career was with a bottle in his hand. "Black and white– I don't want to fuck you."

"I know," I mutter resolutely.

"No, you don't. You purposefully hedge around it. Fuck, as in bag and run. I've avoided the subject on purpose, but our husbands aren't fucking stupid, and they love us enough to try to make sure they give us what we want and need, which includes us probably at some point screwing each other's brains out, and starting something that is terrifying."

"Oh… I thought you were straight, and Uriah just pinged 'girl' for you since he's gender fluid." I couldn't sound more confused if I tried, or maybe it's the whiskey sloshing around in my belly. "Maybe it's the high heels and occasional dress and pearls he wears."

"That man could wear a burlap sack and turn heads," Dan murmurs with a mix of pride, lust, and adoration. "I'm pushing the elephant out of the room by stating the obvious to a drunk man. We have four people with four different views on what is expected out of this, and I don't mean tonight. Uriah and Wynn are probably a close match, with you and me terrified because shit we want to ignore will be revealed if we do more than watch and cuddle."

"I can't." Suddenly sober, I beg, plead with my eyes. "I can't."

"We won't," Dan promises. "Tonight, my little drunkard, our husbands want to put on a show. Wynn will touch you, Uriah me, and nothing else. We'll enjoy the view. But at some point in the future, it will spin out of control. You have to accept that as fact."

"Are you straight?" I sound like a lost little boy, simply because my world is changing around me and I'm not.

"You're hung up on labels, aren't you?" Sighing, Dan tries to get comfortable. "I don't have a label. Am I straight? I lived to the age of eighteen being obsessed with pussy. Still love it. Sometimes miss it, but it's no big deal. Never looked at a guy, wasn't in the closet, never felt a lick of attraction. Then over the course of four years, I fell for a guy and it freaked me out. It wasn't sexual, but emotional. Then I met a girly guy who confused me, so I brought him home to the gay guy who was in love with me too, only that blew up in my face, because my dick was obsessed."

"Did you have a hard time dealing with Uriah's dick? Be honest," I beg for the truth.

"Yeah, at first. It was pure lust, attraction at its core. But I could only touch Uriah's dick if I was insane with need, when I couldn't overthink it." Head turning to the side, Dan stares at me, eyes searching. "Not gonna lie, I struggled between what I wanted and who I thought I was. Then I went through a period where I said the hell with it, and just enjoyed it. But as I fell in love with Uriah, had to love *all* of him, I had some soul searching to do."

"What'd you find out?" I ask because Dan goes silent, and that's not fair to leave me hanging like that.

"Straight? Sexually. Yeah, pretty sure I am– the not confused half of me is, anyway. Probably never would've noticed a guy if I hadn't fallen in love with you, to be honest. Wasn't sexual. Emotional. Uriah and his trippy gender bending confused the piss out of me. I mean, I can look at Wynn and know he's probably a gay guy's ultimate fantasy, straight women's too."

"Nothing?"

"Absolutely nothing down here." Dan cups his crotch, erection belying his words. "Don't laugh," he warns. "My only conclusion was that I was sexually attracted to the female half of Uriah. So I'm straight, yet also demisexual when it comes to being with another guy– the male half of Uriah and all of you. I mean, emotionally, I *get* you. I love you. I want you. I can't fuck you, but I'd have no issue loving every inch of your body with mine. But that's no way to live. So this is going to be a fine line to walk for us, giving in to our husbands' insane need to test our limits and give us what we both want but are too goddamn terrified to enjoy."

"Earlier, when I was in my head, I was thinking of how amazing it would be to watch Uriah and Wynn while you held me– naked, maybe inside me but not moving." Looking away quickly, tears flick down my cheeks from admitting something so painful.

"I knew what you were thinking, Kaden, as did Wynn. Your elopement was for many reasons, but that was a major one of them."

"It wasn't a mistake," I quickly say, because it wasn't. It didn't take Dan saying the reason out loud, because I felt it the second Wynn brought up eloping. If I said no and waited another thirty-six hours to get married, I would've broken Wynn's trust. By agreeing, Wynn knew I believed in *us*. Which led to celebrating too hard with the bottle. I hate being tested, even if Wynn didn't realize he was doing it.

No regrets.

"I wasn't saying that, Kade. You'll be married until the day one of you dies, hopefully in your old age and at the same time. With all your degrees in psychology, you know human emotion is not cut and dried. It's complex, and it drives us to do rash things. All parts of me love Uriah, just as all parts of you love Wynn, but that doesn't mean my capacity to love and lust is gone for other people."

"That's what we're taught– a soul mate for everyone. To even think about how good it would feel to touch or be held by someone, or screw them, or just hang out, that's cheating. If you truly love someone, it's physically impossible to want anyone else."

"That's fairytale bullshit that ends up ruining more marriages, and I would know by my profession. The truth might hurt, but it heals and it keeps shit real. Marriage is a fulltime job."

"Scary thing to hear on my wedding night," I tease, laughing. "Sorry, I know it is. We haven't been married, but every day for almost five years, Wynn and I work at our relationship."

"Exactly. I love my family, my friends, my coworkers, and care about my clients. Does that mean I don't give all I've got to Uriah? Does that mean Uriah getting hard while watching a movie with a hot actor somehow negates how he feels about me?"

"Human nature," I mutter from my teachings. "It's human nature."

"To stifle oneself is to be miserable, within the limitations of being respectful and self-respect– obviously," Dan mutters, probably worried in my drunken state, I'd do something I can't erase or come back from. "Just don't worry about anyone but you and Wynn, and the impact your actions have on your family. That's it."

"Am I getting this spiel from the attorney, or the friend?" My eyelids automatically slip shut to stop the ceiling from swirling. I'm at the point where I'm either feeling the best I've ever felt, or the absolute worst.

Being drunk is great– or it sucks.

Laughing, no doubt because of something idiotic I did or said, Dan leans over and presses his lips to my temple, lingering. "I just want you to be happy, Kaden," is whispered as he pulls away, just as Wynn walks in.

"We weren't– I wasn't– Dan wasn't–" cheating is what I'm trying to say, but bomb spectacularly. "It's not sexual–" on Dan's part.

Lips tilted, Wynn knows exactly what I'm thinking and feeling in the moment. Eyes focused on his mouth, I fail to see what's right in front of my face until I register Dan's sharp intake of breath.

"Oh... wow," I slur like an idiot. Wynn's standing right in front of the sofa, only wearing a pinstripe vest and a pair of tiny underwear that look like a tuxedo– nothing is being left up to imagination.

"We need to get you a vest in every color of the rainbow." Eyes traveling southbound, "Jesus Christ, Wynn." I jerk on the sofa as if electrocuted with pure lust. "Your cock is..." the underwear are too small to contain Wynn's hard-on. There's a flash of shaft where it's pointing toward his belly button, the vest barely covering his cockhead.

Leaning forward, "Can I kiss it? Lick it?" My reaction has Wynn blushing and Dan bellowing laughter at the ceiling.

"Uriah didn't account for my size when he bought me these underwear," Wynn blushes, but there is a newfound confidence in his voice that has an addictive quality. "He said you liked your one and only lap dance, so he's going to teach me."

Mouth suddenly dry, no words form. Dan taps my water bottle to get my mind functioning again. After a sip, I lean back on the sofa, sliding my ass forward, making room for Wynn on my lap.

"Lord, save us all," rumbles out of Dan's mouth to draw my attention to Uriah prancing into the living room. Prancing, he does.

Uriah is naked as the day he was born, without a single hair on his body, except for his chin-length multi-colored hair, wicked eyebrows and eyelashes, and a manicured line of facial hair along his jawline.

Petite, with long, lean muscles and no body fat, Uriah is androgynous in the extreme. Tiny pink nipples are flush with his flesh– everything is flat except for the divot of his belly button.

My eyes are drawn back to Wynn, getting more and more aroused by the second, because I love the way the muscles in his legs are striated, and the smattering of hair all over his body.

Whimpering, I wiggle a little on the sofa, only to have my eyes drawn back to the pink bow riding Uriah's flaccid cock. Hanging soft, a small cock is nestled atop completely hairless pale balls, with a pretty bow sitting where pubic hair should be.

"I thought it best if I was naked, so Wynn could see the fluid movement of my body and duplicate it," Uriah explains as he comes to stand in front of Dan, next to Wynn. The man is gorgeous, he has to know it, but the lack of confidence in his voice is startling. I'm so used to being around Wynn, who never second-guesses, doubts, or has a lick of insecurity.

Wynn would use the world as his own private locker room if he could, feeling no shame in wearing his birthday suit.

"I love the bow– you have a very pretty cock." I sound absurd, but Uriah blooms underneath my compliments. Maybe Uriah is intimidated being around Wynn– size-wise. Sometimes I'm even jealous of Wynn's body, looks, personality, and cock.

"We okay doing this?" Uriah asks Dan, whispering quietly, as if he doesn't want us to overhear, but the flicking eyes in my direction is a dead giveaway. I've known him since senior year at Penn State when I was only twenty-one. I'm getting closer to twenty-nine with every passing heartbeat, and in all that time, I don't remember Uriah being insecure.

"Yeah, love. Your idea is amazing." Dan reaches for Uriah's hand, tugging him closer. Then he leans forward to nuzzle the tip of his nose along Uriah's inner thigh, across pale balls, and all over that tiny cock until it fills with blood.

Turning to rest his cheek on Uriah's hip, Dan flashes me a pointed look, and I get the hint. Wynn and Uriah were taking a page from Bren's playbook, probably listening to us talk from the safety of the kitchen. The depleted confidence was no doubt over revealing how Dan had to learn to love Uriah's cock.

Pulling away, Dan kisses Uriah's cockhead, then settles back to the sofa. "Your body is amazing when you dance. Teach Wynn, and make Kade jealous over how I stole you away from him."

Experiencing a full-body blush, "I was never Kade's, silly," Uriah stammers. "My recollection is different from yours, even if you dragged me back to your dorm room to draw Kade out of his shell."

"Never doubt your appeal, Uriah," I mutter self-deprecatingly, laughing at myself. "I popped three seconds into the lap dance."

"Oh, that I do remember." Uriah laughs at the memory. "Most flattering thing in my life that's ever happened."

Good to the core Wynn comes to the rescue. Turning to the side, he rests his hand on Uriah's shoulder, eyes drinking in every inch of the smaller man. "Everything on you is perfect. Now show me what to do, because I'm only good at being blunt. I have no idea how to seduce."

"HA!" is torn from my mouth, turning to chuckling. "You're going to kill me if you start behaving like Uriah, while still taking what you want without threat of consequence."

Cocking his head to the side, mouth curled into a smile that doesn't reach his eyes, Wynn shows me there's a fissure in his confidence too.

Some private conversations should remain private. Sometimes curiosity kills the cat. Eavesdropping while a pair of close friends have a private conversation is stupid. I offer Wynn unlimited privacy, both inside his thoughts and conversations he has with other people. I don't own him, and I know sometimes what he's thinking or saying isn't exactly complimentary. Wynn has a lot to bitch about when it comes to me, because I'm not perfect.

"You're killing me now, Wynn," I say in all honesty. "I can't imagine how lethal you'll be in about twenty minutes, since you excel in all that you do." Leaning forward, I grab for Wynn's wrist, wanting to pull him down to my lap. "Gimme a lap dance, you little shit."

"Watch me," Uriah commands, confident in the instruction he has to offer. "This isn't a strip club. No such thing as the bullshit rule about touching. Anything goes." Turning to face the television, with the sofa at his back, Uriah wiggles his ass in Dan's direction.

"Your ass–" the garbled moan flowing from Dan's throat cuts off whatever else he has to say. Eyes flicking in his direction real quick, I note a blissed out expression marring his manly face with his hand extended, fingers curled with need to touch and squeeze.

I choose to watch Wynn instead of Uriah's instruction, simply because Wynn's reactions to yet another first is priceless. Eyes glazed, epically aroused by Uriah, Wynn's rocking on his feet to a song only he can hear.

"Give a couple booty pops once their eyes are drawn to your ass." Laughing lightly, Uriah's joy has a grin spreading across my face. "Doing this naked gives an entirely different view of the real estate, if you catch my drift."

"Don't you mean, catching a draft," Dan murmurs with wry amusement.

Eyes leaving Wynn momentarily, lusty laughter spills from between my parted lips. Uriah's pucker, smooth balls, and flopping cock are wiggling in Dan's face.

"You try," Uriah demands, causing me to shift on the sofa.

Wynn's firm ass takes up my entire view. With jerky movements, it's awkward at first, but this is Wynn. By the third try, I'm tugging on my pant leg to stop my trousers from cutting the circulation off to my dick.

Arousal and hilarity war as I watch Wynn learn to twerk inches from my smirking face. The tuxedo underwear shift, until half an ass cheek is exposed, and I'm tempted to reach out and pick Wynn's wedgie.

Everything else becomes background noise as Wynn mirrors everything Uriah is doing to Dan. Unable to stop myself, my fingertips skim along the back of Wynn's thighs, playing with the hairs. Curling my fingers, I just barely stop myself from squeezing Wynn's ass cheeks and pulling them apart.

Now I wish Wynn was naked, but I understand his need for modesty while he learns.

"Roll your hips in Kade's lap like this," Uriah is murmuring breathlessly. But I could give a shit less what he's up to, because Wynn flips around, body whispering above mine. "Just a little pressure. As you've no doubt heard, my first lap dance, I fucked that part up. If the guy blows, game over."

"Hey!" I shout in mock-outrage when the implications of what Uriah is saying hit my ears. "Never mind, I'm a one-pump chump no matter what."

Eyelids ghosting shut, all I can do is feel as Wynn grinds his ass into my crotch, underwear shifting until it resembles a G-string. A hand wedges itself beneath mine, fingers weaving with mine. It takes me a moment to realize Dan's holding my hand for support, muscles straining in his arm.

"Not gonna last long, Ri," Dan groans, fingers clenching mine. "Rub your ass on my belly while you show Wynn, because my dick can't take much more."

Grunting from the pleasure of Wynn's firm ass rolling across my cockhead, my free arm weaves across his chest, pulling him down into my lap. Laughing at Wynn's shriek of surprise, I bury my face against the side of his neck.

"You smell so goddamn good," purrs from my lips as my hand ventures south, dipping beneath the waistband of his underwear. Squeezing roughly, then rubbing up and down, I press Wynn's length against my forearm.

Lost in the moment, my mouth takes on a mind of its own, sucking marks along Wynn's shoulder. Nose moving the fabric of his vest to the side, I bite his shoulder. Hard. Teeth sinking into delectable flesh, I brand my husband.

Screaming, Wynn bucks in my lap, nearly shoving me over the edge of orgasm. Cock jerking in my hand, I reach down to cup his balls to stop the jizz from escaping.

"Christ, they're hot," Uriah gasps roughly. "Okay, Wynn. Next piece of advice. Since you aren't a stripper, and Kade is your husband, you don't need to disconnect yourself by doing this reverse. Turn to face him, like you would if you were riding his cock."

"Oh, no," I mutter in a panic, knowing I just lost the upper-hand so to speak. When on top, whether he's riding me or I'm being ridden, Wynn's always in charge. "I'm going to stain my trousers."

"Like this?" Wynn asks coyly, ever the student, as he shifts around to face me. Definitely on purpose, with the roll of his hips, his erection grinds into mine.

"You know exactly how this plays out, you little shit," I snarl, grabbing the back of his neck to yank him down to my lips. Mouths fusing, my hand cups Wynn's ass, finger splaying beneath the fabric of his underwear. Only then do I realize Dan's hand is still twined with mine, and his ridged fingers are trying hard not to touch my husband.

As soon as I release Dan's hand, Wynn's ass is getting a hard thwack, jiggling his flesh. Then the sound is repeated on a different ass.

"Is Wynn shy?" Uriah must be asking Dan, because I sure as shit am too far gone to answer. "Is Kade?"

Thrusting upward, I shift Wynn until his dick is fucking my abs and mine is trying to impale him through several layers of clothing. Chin tilted up, I try to reach Wynn's mouth, begging for a kiss.

"That's Ri's way of asking why you aren't naked," Dan murmurs in a sluggish voice, the metal-on-metal sound of a zipper lowering drawing my attention. "You've seen my dick a billion times, so it's coming out to play now before Ri makes me spooge in my pants."

Wynn stills above me, scaring me that this is too much, too soon. Popping one eye open, I gaze up at Wynn, noticing his attention is drawn away. Following the line of his sight, a wry chuckle is pulled from my throat.

Eyes flicking back to mine, "Well, I haven't seen it yet." Then he looks away, waiting to see what Dan's cock looks like.

"And here I always called myself the pervert–"

"There's a man getting naked in my living room. First, I'm gonna look. Second, I ain't gonna throw him out. Third, if he wants to show me his dick, I'm not gonna insult him by not looking… good God, that's…"

Reaching down between us, I quickly unzip my pants, then shove my hand into my boxers. Nearly breaking it off, I yank my cock out. "Suck me off while you stare at Dan. It's our wedding night, and you ain't sucking his cock tonight."

"I wasn't–"

"You're drooling."

Wiping the back of his hand across his mouth, Wynn flashes me a shameless look. "Okay, so I was."

"Was what?" Uriah asks absentmindedly while tugging Dan's pants down his furry thighs.

"Was imagining your lips wrapped around my buddy's cock, you little cocksucker," I answer, voice highly amused, remembering how Wynn bloomed with Jackson.

"Drooling," Wynn mutters, trying to sound pissed off. A second later, his comforting weight is gone from my body, but it's replaced with hot lips slurping down my cock.

"Feel free to drool some more." Lifting my hips with a groan, I feed Wynn my cock, pressing to the back of his throat.

"I've never–" Dan turns tongue-tied, voice sluggish. "I've never seen Kade's cock. He always jerked by the cover of darkness."

"Or thrust his hands down his pajama pants," Uriah mutters with great annoyance. "I once tried to tackle him, tugging at his pants, but he was too strong and thwarted my efforts."

Popping off my cock, not giving a shit how I'm beyond modest when it comes to my body, Wynn manages to do something he tried to do with Jackson but I wouldn't allow it. Hand wrapping around my cock, Wynn jerks me while showing Uriah and Dan my goods.

Closing my eyes, taking a deep inhalation of breath, I force the anxiety to float away. This is Dan. This is Uriah. I've known them forever. This is Wynn– my husband –and I've known him since he was born.

I'm safe.

"It's not as big as mine," Wynn isn't gloating while he presents my cock. "But it's thicker. Thicker is better, but Kade's is nice and long. Only has to be long enough to hit my gland, but it's gotta be fat enough to make me go insane."

"Jesus Christ!" Uriah shouts, sounding shocked. "Can we keep him?"

"Wynn's on loan," is a grunt from between my parted lips. "Stop! Gonna shoot if you don't stop."

"Don't stop, Wynn," Uriah begs. "That is something we've never seen. He'd even hide his orgasm face. We used to joke how Kade must have a misshapen cock and an ugly orgasm face."

"Both are perfect," Wynn assures them while backing off to stand before me. "I think I would like to be naked."

"You're always naked," I tease, reaching out with a foot to tap his thigh. "Get naked. I'm keeping my clothes on."

"Pull your pants off at least," Wynn negotiates.

"That I will do— for you." Hesitating a moment, I feel stupid having to ask, but I better. "Are you okay with this? Are *we* okay?"

Fingers stilling on the vest buttons, Wynn looks at me for a moment, truly thinking over what I asked. Then he pops the buttons one right after the other. Tossing the vest to a nearby chair, Wynn shows off the newest ink covering his left shoulder.

"Until me, watching them was the total of your sexual exploration. For four years, you watched Dan fuck, a year of that with Uriah. The fact that you let me suck you off and show them your dick says a lot about how safe you feel. So I want to do this with you, with *them*. I want to know how you felt— still feel."

"C'mere." Rising slightly, I reach for Wynn, pulling his ear down to my lips. "I get it, but if at any time you feel uncomfortable, say *abort*, and we'll stop. No blame. No judgment."

Smirking, one blond eyebrow reaching his hairline, Wynn issues me a challenge to see how far I'll take it, because there is nothing that will make that man cry uncle.

The Gillette in Wynn is erupting, God love him.

Still holding my gaze, Wynn drops trou, underwear hooking around his left ankle. With a flick, the shorts fly to parts unknown, completely forgotten.

With a palm on my forehead, Wynn shoves me back to the sofa roughly. "I think we need to start at the beginning. Sit back, relax, and enjoy the show. Wait—" I stiffen fearing the worst. "Pants off, old man."

"Shit," I hiss with feeling, hoping he'd forget. Struggling, I'm punished for trying to get away with leaving my pants on. "No," I beg as Wynn shows off his wiry strength, knees pressing into my thighs. "Wynn," I order harshly, but my wrists are gripped in one hand, while the other wrenches my dress shirt apart, buttons flying everywhere.

"You are so goddamn gorgeous— I'm not going to put up with you hiding anymore. Year after year I watch you get dizzy and light-headed in the summer heat because you're always wearing too many shirts. You have nothing to be ashamed about. Be free, Kaden."

Gasping, my shirt is yanked from my back, arm getting caught in the sleeve. With a sharp yank, I'm almost propelled from the sofa, but the fabric rents from my flesh.

"Be free," Wynn orders, leaving me completely naked— raw.

Exposed.

Shivering with nerves, I fight the urge to fold my arms over my chest to cover my nakedness.

"Jesus, Kade," Dan murmurs in appreciation, fingertip reaching out but never lighting on my skin. "Magnificent."

"Jesse didn't design this, and Torque didn't ink you, for you to hide it underneath a shirt. You're wearing one of my muscle shirts to the campout," Wynn orders, and I stifle a shiver from the need to give into him– to be free.

"We need the number to this Torque fellow," Uriah murmurs in awe. Less worried about my discomfort, he actually touches me versus outlining my tattoos a hairsbreadth from my skin like Dan is.

Each of my arms are covered in a full sleeve, with my torso completely inked from my pelvis to the bottom of my pecs. The scars aren't gone, merely hidden beneath a story Jesse weaved for me. Altering the original designs, the reasons why I cut myself are tattooed across my flesh. I no longer have the desire to split my body open and watch it weep red.

My skin isn't covered in sins I've atoned, or insecurities felt. Outside forces caused me to cut, to bleed for things I couldn't change. Now I realize there was something wrong with them, not me, and I no longer want to change who I am.

I thought I was embracing every flaw I possess, but two people tonight have told me to be free, so I still have work to do.

Leaning back on the sofa, pretending I'm perfectly comfortable with three sets of eyes on me– Wynn reading my expression while Dan and Uriah openly gape at my body. "I believe we were starting this lap dance from the beginning," I remind Wynn, earning a smirk of challenge.

Uriah showcases a hidden talent by humming a song, when I didn't even know he could sing. Staring me down, Wynn sways on his feet, creating his own beat. Swiveling until his back is facing me, Wynn shows moves Uriah didn't make earlier.

Muscles rippling with strength and flexibility, Wynn weaves, lulling me yet exciting me with the slow movement. Silent tempo changing, flicking forward like a whip, Wynn twerks his ass.

Naked twerking gives a different view. "Oh, my God." I have to grab my balls to stop the expulsion. "You didn't."

Neck cranking to the side, Wynn looks at me from over his shoulder while dancing for me. "I did. You like?"

"I like," rumbles in a tone no longer sounding like my own. Unable to stop myself, I lean forward, thumb pressing the center of the butt plug. Grabbing the base, I rotate it, causing a tremor to work down Wynn's spine.

Hands gripping Wynn's ass, squeezing until I leave fingertip dimples behind, I lean forward to sink my teeth into his right cheek. Sharp pain causes Wynn to jerk, so I lave him with my tongue in a long, wet line that extends to where the plug disappears in his body.

"Oh!" Uriah sounds like he's breathing through a straw. "Wow. That looks– that looks like it would feel good."

"I need you– can I have you?" voice filled with need, my fingers shake on Wynn's skin.

Moving quicker than I can register, the plug is dropped on the floor at the same instant Wynn's heavy weight presses me down. Shock is replaced by pleasure as my cock is enveloped in intense heat.

"Now you have me," Wynn whispers a heartbeat before kissing me. The intensity ought to transfer over to violence, instead we slow down, kissing softly while holding each other. Breath rasping against my lips, Wynn is content to just have me resting inside him.

Uriah's whimper draws my eye, eclipsed by Dan hissing, "Fuck."

"Look at the longing written on Uriah's face," Wynn breathes into my ear. "Play along, please."

"What?" I mutter in confusion.

"Do you find me manly, Dan?" Wynn asks out of nowhere, while sitting on my cock like it's nothing but ordinary to hold a conversation like this.

Shifting on the sofa, an uncomfortable, "Umm– yeah," flows our direction from Dan.

"Gay. Straight. Bi. Every color of the rainbow, if you were born with male sex parts, you have a prostate. It's not about being manly– it's about being an idiot."

"What are you talking about?" I ask Wynn, eyes seeking first Dan, who looks guilty, then Uriah, who looks ashamed.

"We heard you say how difficult it was to accept Uriah's pretty cock." Wynn's voice holds a silent, '*shame on you.*' White Knight Syndrome. "You'll fuck him, but you won't finger him or rim him. You'll let him suck you off, but not go past your balls."

"That's not fair," Dan defends himself.

I go to intervene, but Wynn beats me to the punch. "No, it's *not* fair. It's not fair to either one of you. You can't say you don't like it unless you try it. You *can't* know, so that means you've got some gender bullshit at play, where the one being fucked is the girl. I'm no girl. It took me a long time to break Kade from feeling like a girl for enjoying the things we do for each other, and that includes regular life bullshit. Straight men fingering themselves and getting pegged by women aren't girly. There's nothing wrong with being a woman, but Uriah's asshole is not a vagina. We are men– we have a prostate. To ignore it out of homophobic fear is idiotic. It's your right not to like it, to not engage in it, but you can't say you don't like it until you try it."

"Um…" mouth gaping, all I can do is stare up at my husband in awe. When Wynn is furious, he glows hotter than the sun. "This isn't our business."

"Uriah and I had a talk too, ya know?" Wynn reminds me. "As payment for teaching me to dance for you, I said I'd make Dan stop being uptight about assholes."

"Out of context, that sentence means something dramatically different," I mutter wryly.

"As a lawyer, we'll negotiate," Wynn offers. "You'll let me teach Uriah how to touch you in a way you'll enjoy, and I'll let you kiss my husband."

"What?" I squawk, but get ignored.

"Every word Kaden speaks, your eyes are glued to his lips. Yet when I showed off his cock, you looked out of curiosity, but that's it. So you meant what you said when you guys talked earlier. It's not sexual, but it is. You'd rather kiss Kade than fuck him."

"I'm conflicted," Dan murmurs, refusing to meet anyone's eyes. "If I say yes, it will send the message to Uriah that I'd do anything to kiss Kade, but that's not true."

"We've never– *I've* never told Dan that I felt…" Now Uriah won't look at us.

"I'll do it, but not for the kiss. Because had I known, I would have tried earlier. Okay?" Dan tugs Uriah into his lap, arms wrapping around the smaller man. "You should have told me."

"I don't know how to touch you, you know that," Uriah whines. "You know my past."

"My friend, Jack," Wynn jumps in to save the day, noticing the agony on their faces. "The one and only time he tried to top, or do anything else like that, it was a failure. So now he won't try. I've been talking him through it. Practice makes perfect, and the first time sucks."

"Hey," I growl, insulted. "It didn't suck for us, did it?"

"We had nearly five years of practice," Wynn points out. "We have a dude who keeps saying he's straight, and a gender fluid person who has never touched a man beside suck cock and take it up the ass."

"Way to be blunt, Wynn," I murmur, scared shitless he overstepped bounds by insulting my friends.

"Uriah's fluidity meant he would never attract or completely be attracted to a gay guy. One look at him, and I knew he was relegated the girl by a long string of homophobic asses who wanted his ass. So I'm not going to let his husband be that *guy*."

"I only know what I know," Dan whines, voice tight with shame. "I have no idea what I'm doing, and it doesn't come natural to me. I just know how to get us off, using what works. So I'm game to learn, just don't think I did it on purpose."

"If you ever take Miriam up on her offer, I fear for your students," I ramble in awe over Wynn's growth these past few months. He keeps getting stronger and stronger in all ways. "I fear for our future children. You are…"

"My hero," Uriah adds, and we all pretend tears aren't shining in his eyes. "I'd like to do what Wynn was doing." He points at the butt plug on the floor, which means they had this conversation while Wynn was working it into himself. *Fuck!* Wynn's freedom scares me. "I've never been rimmed, either. I wouldn't mind trying things on Dan, but I doubt I'd want to top him."

"Ever?" I blurt out, knowing how Jackson at least wants the option, even if he prefers to bottom. Between Royce's anti-anal rhetoric and the bad experience, Bren and Jackson are terrified of even attempting again, but they know it's a possibility.

Uriah's blush is answer enough– he wants the option. Everyone wants to have options.

Closing his eyes in defeat, Dan rests his head on the back of the sofa. "You're going to have to suck me off, because I'm too uptight to just let you shove your finger in my ass– no butt plug."

"Get to sucking– I'll be right back." Wynn levers himself off my cock, and I shudder with a mix of pleasure and loss.

"Come back," I beg, flaccid cock cold.

All Wynn does is laugh, hand snatching the blue plug off the floor in one fluid movement, then strides into the kitchen to clean it.

Out of curiosity, with only a thread of arousal simmering in my veins, I watch as Dan throws his head back in ecstasy, glasses askew, and mouth open on a moan. Uriah kneels between Dan's spread thighs, slurping a thick cock between his pouty lips.

It's not something I haven't seen before, so the beauty of it isn't thrilling or perverted. This should feel uncomfortable for me, but after all of senior year, and then again during their wedding, this was what my sex life consisted of until Wynn– Uriah and Dan sharing the view of their lovemaking while I watched from afar. But only this time I have Wynn, and I hope he's not uncomfortable.

Bopping me in the forehead with the plug, I feel like an idiot for wondering if Wynn is uncomfortable. My little shit wasn't fantasizing all these years– he was telling me what he wanted. Tonight is marking a few of those fantasies off the sexual bucket list.

"We okay?" Wynn asks, plug in hand, one eye trained on Uriah and the other on my lips. I know what he's actually asking.

"Pretty sure you taught Uriah how to insert a butt plug earlier," I mutter wryly, without a thread of jealousy or anger. "Might as well return the favor."

Not a trace of shame, Wynn shrugs one shoulder, but the blush creeping up his chest belies his confidence. Nothing is sexier than a man who knows what he wants, but still possesses his innocence.

Intoxicating.

"Make sure Uriah shifts to the side a bit," I tease. "I want to watch you work."

Lips curling into a private smile, Wynn winks at me. "Sit sideways on the cushion."

Dan's so far gone to getting head, we could open the front door and usher in our neighbors and he wouldn't notice. Moaning, hips rocking up and down, cock passing between Uriah's lips, Dan's trying his damnedest not to blow his wad.

Lowering to his knees on the carpet, Wynn chuckles at some private joke playing out in his head. "Couch lube?" he calls out to me, and I act on instinct, hand automatically fishing underneath the cushion for the in-case-of-spontaneous-sex-acts bottle of lubricant– one of a dozen hiding around this house.

"Hand," I order, popping the top.

"Not my hand," Wynn murmurs wryly, letting me onto what's amusing him so. "After hearing you talk, I'd strived to be as adventurous as those two. Come to find out, they've been one-trick ponies. They're in sore need of some sex lessons, and Dan is pliable enough to learn now."

After taking a deep breath, I join the fray by grabbing for the hand palming Uriah's ass cheek. Dan doesn't swat me away, but he also doesn't comply. One at a time, I pry his fingers off Uriah, then flip his hand over until his palm is facing upward.

Gaining Dan's undivided attention, I can't help but stare back as I hold his hand. It's a discombobulating feeling. Some men might see the geek. Some women might see the successful lawyer. All see the commanding yet caring personality.

Glasses askew, hair curling from sweat along his forehead, face ruddy with lust, eyes burning with passion, Dan opens his mouth on a pant, almost a silent invitation.

Right now, all I want to do is to kiss Dan, and that's why it's a discombobulating feeling. I shouldn't want to, not with Wynn here. Not when I love Wynn, want Wynn, lust after Wynn like a goddamn madman.

The sound of lube squeezing out of the bottle startles me into realizing Wynn is gripping my hand that's holding the lube, while positioning Dan's and my entwined hands to receive the flow.

"Make sure most of it is at the fingertips," Wynn cautions. "You don't just do Uriah dry, do you? How have you not played with that sweet hole of his?"

"First few times, yeah." Dan clears his throat a couple times, blushing with shame and embarrassment. "Um– I was kinda used to self-lubricating sex partners."

"I'm sure you used a tongue to get them there." Wynn is not amused on Uriah's behalf. As one of the people present during that fucked up marathon of sex during their first time, I can tell you there was no pain to be had– no rational thinking either. Uriah got plowed and Dan entered an existential crisis of epic proportions.

"I didn't– okay, call me stupid, but I've heard tossing the salad jokes, and I just couldn't figure out how that would feel good."

This time I interject, "You're deluded," vowing this man's ass is gonna get licked and probed tonight.

"I came home from class one day to find a bottle of anal lube on my bed." Eyes dart in my direction. "And a book."

Wynn has a hardy laugh at my expense. "So Bren wasn't the first guy you pawned books on."

"Shush," I whisper, burning bright. "Dan was using regular lube, and that ain't gonna fly."

"I just use my cockhead to stretch Ri out." Dan looks down at his husband, an apology held in his gaze. "I do know when he's ready, and I don't think there are any complaints on getting off."

"I do like being stretched that way." Giant eyelashes flutter up at us. "Keep doing what you're doing."

Wynn has that intense look in his eye– Teenage Asshole Wynn, now called Confident Adult Wynn –and I know we're in for it now.

"Sometimes a man just wants to frot with a pair of fingers scissoring in his ass– we lived off that for years. Kade?" Wynn orders, and I obey.

Using both hands, I massage lube onto three of Dan's fingers, then pull until he's curled around Uriah's back, with Uriah's head going back to town giving head. "Push back against the pad of his fingertips."

Dan's grunt of shock suggests Uriah knows how to take an order. "Just finger him– I know you know how to do that," I grumble, hinting at the nonstop pussy-fest in our dorm room up until senior year. I'm probably the only gay guy who has never had straight sex but knows what girl cum smells like. Nonstop. Pussy. Fest. Every night. Revolving door on weekends. Tiny dorm room with no escape.

Leaning away, I watch my husband kneel on the floor while wearing nothing but a mischievous glint in his eye. Humming to himself, one eye trained on me, one trained on Uriah's stretched pucker, he rubs lube onto his favorite butt plug.

"You are *so* bad." Amazed laughter bubbles up my throat. "I never in a million years would have expected you to be the bad influence. I was the selfish pervert, manipulator, and you were Rusty Knob's golden boy– pure as virgin snow."

"You're neither selfish nor a pervert," Wynn murmurs conversationally, truly getting off on stroking his plug. "Manipulator? Fuck yeah. But I don't have to manipulate. I ask, and people just do it." Asshat actually shrugs. "I'm not being a pervert, or selfish right now. This is one of the most selfless things you and I could be doing. We're helping a marriage, giving them tools–"

"No premarital counseling speak." I shudder in horror over the '*tools*' comment. The minister officiating our ceremony required we go through six hour-long premarital counseling sessions before he'd agree to marry us.

Funny how it was easier to find an ordained hipster in Morgantown to do the deed for fifty bucks instead.

"Ha!" Wynn and I share a grin. "Look at them, then ask yourself if we're being selfish."

Back arched, finger-filled ass in the air, head buried in Dan's crotch, Uriah is wiggling and groaning and going fucking nuts, and Dan isn't faring any better.

Wynn shifts, plug in hand, and we have a moment. Acting in tandem, I extract Dan's fingers and Wynn fists Uriah's hair, pulling until Dan's cock pops out Uriah's mouth.

"This is my gift to our houseguests," Wynn murmurs wryly. "You can keep it." With sure movements, Wynn is pressing the plug into Uriah's ass, and I've never found anything more titillating or fascinating in my entire life. Enjoying his work, Wynn presses on the base, tilting the plug at an angle, forcing a grunt of immense pleasure to flow from Uriah's throat.

"Feel good?" Wynn purrs, blooming into that same man who made his first appearance with Jackson in the beginning of summer. "Does, doesn't it? I love this plug. Could wear it for hours on end." Flashing me a pointed look, I move into action.

"Here," I grab Dan's hand, pulling until he's curled over Uriah's back again. "Move it around and watch Uriah's reactions to see what does and doesn't work."

Not giving a shit if Dan obeys, Wynn finds himself dragged to the floor with my body draped over his. "Love you," is whispered against his lips a heartbeat before I annihilate him with my tongue and teeth.

Hips jerking, cocks rubbing together, mouths fused, I give Wynn exactly what he asked for earlier. We frot like old times, rolled on our sides, with one hand pressing against the small of his back, while the other thrusts three fingers in his prepared hole.

"One more lesson," Wynn gasps against my lips, with a groan following. "Then I want you in our bed."

"Deal." Shoving off the floor with my palms, I retake my seat next to a crazed Dan on the sofa.

"Keep sucking Dan's cock like that, and you won't get to the sex." Turned on by long hair –sometimes I go to work in the morning with a sore scalp –Wynn yanks Uriah off Dan's dick, shoving his head down farther. "Suck the sack, roll the balls on your tongue. Then nibble the taint. Once you get to the hole, lick, suck, and impale like you're starving for tasty ass. Then use your fingers."

A furry-knuckled hand reaches for mine, fingers clenching tightly for support. Dan's terrified, cock softening. Breathing heavily, he winces, too anxiety-riddled to enjoy it.

"Kiss him," Wynn orders.

"I can't," I issue as a denial, shaking my head. "I shouldn't kiss a guy on our wedding night, and Uriah shouldn't have to always wonder if it was me or him turning Dan on."

"It's about comfort, not sex," Wynn gets it. "Comfort him, and don't make me go back on my word. We negotiated this, remember?"

"Fuck!" I hiss with feeling.

"Do it!" Wynn commands, Dan's whimper of fear accentuating it.

"Don't get upset if Pandora's Box flies open," I warn, sliding to rest on my knees on the cushion.

"I'm not blind or stupid, Kade– kiss him." A hand rests lightly on the small of my back, then a kiss lands on my hip. "This is for *them*– for Uriah."

Jesus Christ, who did I marry? The patron saint of sexual exploration?

With a deep breath, I burn our lives to the ground. If they're not your partner, never passionately kiss someone you're emotionally connected. Ever. There's a reason prostitutes find the kiss the most intimate act.

Leaning over Dan, I raise his face up to mine with a fingertip beneath his chin. Gazing down, I'm asking for permission as much as looking for an answer.

Lost in the land of indecision, Dan kisses me in answer. Palms fly up to cup my face, pressing my lips to his. Half moan, half sob, we each suck in a deep breath, taking the oxygen away from the other. It's awkward, desperate, filled with longing.

Time stills, transporting me back to my first day at Penn State. Emotionally distraught because Royce had just left without me, I couldn't handle it when a kid popped into my dorm room, looking for my roommate. He called me the scarecrow faggot when he didn't find Dan. I met Dan a few minutes later, while I was curled up in the fetal position, bawling like a goddamn baby. He rubbed my back, made me feel safe, and told me that guy would never speak to me again– and the promise was kept.

I imprinted on Dan like a baby bird.

Fast-forward ten years later, I come to sprawled across Dan's naked body, hard cock pressed against his side, with a tiny hand patting my ass in a '*there-there*' soothing manner, with Wynn rubbing my calf.

I'm sobbing like a goddamn baby again.

"I think my fingers are too short," Uriah's voice filters in, startling me.

Looking pained, like he's trying to hold in a moan, Dan runs the pad of his thumb underneath my eyes, then kisses me again. Soft, exploratory, the tip of a hot tongue swipes across my lips, followed by a sharp grunt.

"I can't reach," Uriah sounds like he's struggling.

"Kade's gonna have to help you out, because I can't this time around– probably never on this end." Wynn's sharp bark of laughter has me pulling back from Dan's lips to investigate. But first I notice the blissed out, confused look etched across Dan's face.

"What?" I mouth, then understanding dawns. "Oh." Embarrassed over my behavior, I'm relieved to see Uriah and Wynn preoccupied with something that must have been dividing Dan's attention.

"Need some help?" I direct to Dan, not the two idiots looking for a prostate gland like it's the lost city of Atlantis. No way would Dan allow Wynn to help out on this. "You okay with me showing him? Trust me, it will take the burn, sting, embarrassment, and awkwardness away if I do."

"It feels funny." A queer little grin curls Dan's lips. "I'm not so sure I like this."

"Trust me," I repeat. "If you don't like what I show him, then Uriah will give you credit for at least trying."

Dan nods his head yes rapidly, but I'm pretty sure he mouths no while doing it.

"We okay?" I ask Wynn, who flashes me a cat that ate the canary smirk. "Take that as a yes… and you say you don't want to be a teacher," I mutter wryly.

Sliding from the cushion to the floor, I land on my knees, resting my chest on the outside of Dan's thigh. "Relax, both of you." Uriah is sweating, looking demoralized because he can't find what he's looking for.

"I'm too… I'm not enough… maybe I shouldn't bother." Poor Uriah has lost every ounce of confidence he gained while dancing, and his courage too. No wonder the White Knight warrior has made its presence known. Wynn will do anything for anyone, including allow his husband to finger-fuck another guy's asshole.

Again.

"Let's see." Closing my eyes, I inhale through my mouth and exhale through my nostrils. Easily sliding a finger alongside Uriah's, I'm stuck between marveling that this is my reality and humor because the guy might as well be playing with Dan's bellybutton he's so far off the mark.

"I'm the deep-throat queen," Wynn says without pride or bragging. "Kade's the master of ass," is most certainly filled with pride. Patting Dan's thigh, he actually fucking says, "You're in good hands," like this is a doctor's examination.

Three of us huddled between his legs, Dan flashes me a potent look loaded with disbelief, causing me to snicker evilly.

"Ready to witness a magic trick, boys and sometimes-boy-sometimes-girl?" Curving my finger, I take Uriah's along for a ride. Within a split-second, Dan's squeaking in surprise, back arching off the cushion.

"Oh…" Uriah drawls. "OH!"

Scary Wynn returns with a vengeance. Curled around my back, hard-on a promise against the cleft of my ass, he whispers into my ear for all to hear. "Dan's tight, isn't he? Bet you jerked off to fantasies of this for the past decade, huh? Is his ass scalding your finger? Is he pulsing around you?"

"Fuck," I hiss, body shuddering in waves. "Dirty talking Wynn needs to be quiet, so I can tell when I'm strumming the right chord."

Wynn's voice is filled with innocent curiosity. "Are you tapping or swirling Dan's gland?" Which has Dan almost bursting out of his skin.

"Concluded tapping isn't the password," I mutter with amusement, ignoring how breathy and aroused my voice sounds. Curling slightly, I rub the pad of my finger lightly in a circle, since tapping with force didn't do anything.

"Right there!" Dan shouts, cock dribbling a stream of precum onto his taut belly.

Laughing with joy, I kidnap Uriah's finger, using mine to show him what to do. Once he has Dan writhing, I slowly slip out.

Sharing a look with my husband, we say in unison, "Bedroom?" Wynn pulls me to my feet in answer, then twines his fingers with mine.

Walking from the living room, Wynn calls out over his shoulder, "You know what feels a billion times better than a finger?"

"What?" sounds slurred and drugged from both their mouths.

"Using your dick," is Wynn's parting comment, effectively having a hand in popping Dan's anal cherry. Thrilled to have exercised his deviant nature, Wynn allows me to take over for the rest of our wedding night.

Wynn even lights a scented candle, but I ignore how he calls me the romantic. I can't complain, though. In the missionary position like virgins on their wedding night, Wynn turns passive and affectionate, giving me the illusion that I'm actually his equal.

My outside and inside don't match, but it's no longer body dysmorphia. I accept that I look like my father, but I'm not strong like he was. My body is tall and built to work and protect my family, but my heart and mind are soft, needing to be protected.

I've finally come to terms with the fact that I need someone to make me feel safe, to be my anchor, someone who doesn't need from me what I'm incapable of giving because I need it from them instead.

My little shit has grown into the man I knew he'd always become. The age difference is no longer the issue, because now Wynn's the one who's stronger, smarter, and bigger than me, and I find the comfort and security everything I've ever needed and more.

CHAPTER THIRTY-THREE
Brennan Kennedy

Gazing out into my yard and beyond to Dad's backyard, I'm proud of how wonderful everything looks. Tables are lined up in tidy rows, thanks to Sage's organizational skills. Franny decorated in all the colors of the rainbow with crepe paper, and instead of trashy-cheesy, it's gorgeous– that design degree hard at work. The smell of roasting meat fills the air, and a concession table is set up with side dishes, with coolers stocked with every kind of beverage imaginable. At the end of the lawn, near the field, a row of tents is erected, with the grooms' tent way in the corner of my property, far, far away from the rest of us. Dad's been running around, manning three separate bonfires, with a shit-eating grin splitting his face. The twins have wrangled up anyone under the age of eighteen, with Penny's oldest sister as chaperone, to organize games and music and light citronella torches.

Days away from Labor Day, it's harvest time in our neck of the woods for fall fruits and vegetables. Cain found Dad's garden, and has been wallowing in it like a pig in shit for the past few weeks. Brother-sister bonding time, Cain and Willa added vegetarian fare to our carnivore diets, but at least Cain isn't see-through anymore. Not so sure those sides will be eaten during the party, not with a pig on a spit and chicken halves and brisket in the smoker.

"Without everyone's help, I'd be lost." Exhausted even before the party starts, I slump into a folding chair, unable to kick back because I'm far from done. Jackson stands behind me, squeezing my shoulders since I did all the heavy lifting. "Thanks for teaching me the errors of my ways."

"Delegation is man's best friend," Jack mutters with amusement.

"They better appreciate it," Sage grunts begrudgingly, staring at his fingernails. "Ugh– dirt."

"You are such a diva," Jack grumbles, not Sage's biggest fan. Francis assured us Sage isn't usually this big of a douchebag. After being lured home and not seeing his guy, then Gemma being dropped in his lap, I can understand Sage's frustration. Having to quit your job and move cross-country, I forgive the constant whining and bitching.

Sage is good help, in the way a conquering dictator is helpful. Delegation is Sage's best friend, and we are nothing but his minions.

"Where's your aunt-stepmom-brother's sister-sibling's baby momma-hillbilly incest… whatever you call the woman– I forgot her name." Sage moves into my line of sight, nary a hair on his perfect head out of place. The young guy is prematurely white-haired in his early twenties, but he pulls it off.

If Sage got any whiter, the silver spoon shoved up his ass would be visible.

"Willa?" Jackson snarls, insulted for the both of us. "Why?"

"I like her," Sage mutters with a shrug, still using a thumbnail to clean dirt from underneath his other nails. "I was going to see if she needed any help, and had any suggestions on how to raise Gemma. My mom raised a boy."

"And she did such a wonderful job at it, too," Jack's tone is filled with sarcasm.

"I know, right?" the asshat ignores the sarcasm and takes it as a compliment. "I like the sense of community here– it's less stressful than how my family treats everyone. Grandfather already has plans for Gemma, and she doesn't have a drop of Sage blood in her. I need advice on how to stop him."

"Kade's friend is visiting– Dan's a lawyer from Pittsburgh." I'm glad Jackson's taking over for me, saying what I'm thinking, because I'm too fucking tired to do it myself. "Divorce lawyer, sure. But they must know every law about guardianship with parents fighting over kids."

"Thank you," Sage sounds relieved, and I can actually see the stress melt out of his wiry muscles. "I've always had what you'd call visitation with Gemma. She's stayed every summer with me, and I'd fly home for holidays. But I don't want my dad or Aubrey, or even my grandfather, snatching Gemma away after we've gotten settled. I didn't want this, but I will fight for it."

Sage is not an asshole.

Jackson pouts, no doubt wishing he could hate the douchebag but can't. "C'mon," he grabs for Sage's hand. "If you want maternal advice, you go to the kitchen. If you want paternal advice, locate a fire source. No matter how stereotypical, it holds true. The yard is bursting with advice."

"I don't know where to begin," Sage mutters, both sounding and looking lost. His eyes are vacant, albeit a bit spooked.

Putting the guy out of his misery, "You don't have to start at all. Just walk up to anyone who has a kid. If it's a dad, they will put a drink in your hand– a mom will feed you. Doesn't matter which, unsolicited advice will follow before you can take a sip or bite."

"But you didn't do that," Sage points out, "And you're a dad."

"I fed you while your wine chilled, then we got busy doing all this shit. If you stay past tomorrow, I won't be able to stop myself with the verbal vomit."

"We're staying for three more days." Laughing at the look of horror written on my face, Jackson escorts Sage away, laughter trailing behind them.

My peace is short-lived.

A beer bottle is wiggled in front of my face, then a hairless arm follows it– the arm is attached to a freshly showered and painted Franny. "Sage is actually a great person once his defenses are down," he assures me.

Tilting my head back, I take in Franny's ensemble. He may design clothing and dress drag queens for performances, but Francis Parker doesn't dress like that on a day-to-day basis. He's always a classy mix of softened masculinity.

At an inch or two taller than me, Franny's yet again dressed in tailored linen trousers and a flowy silk blouse, but this time his eyes are lined and his lashes are accentuated.

"You look pretty," I murmur with a smile. "I'm glad you're here."

"Me too." The top is popped off the beer, then it's shoved into my hand. "Why are the guests of honor late? Geez, don't they realize I traveled halfway around the world to say congratulations."

Laughter makes me feel lighter, more awake, and ready to get the party started after so much planning and preparation. "Wynn's like the ultimate alpha male now– if he didn't look like himself, I wouldn't recognize him. They're so in love with each other and themselves, they hardly take notice of their surroundings, but I think it's amazing."

"Selfish?" Francis pulls a chair out beside me and takes a seat. "That's not the Wynn and Kade I remember. Both were like the crusaders of rightness."

"No, not selfish. Wynn's always with Willa and the kids, working in the barn. Kade is always helping Royce. Divide and conquer. But when they get into one another, they are blind to anything else. I think it's sweet, and I want it so fucking bad– to feel intoxicated."

"Jackson?" Unable to help himself, Francis reaches out to finger-comb my hair. "Last night, you two were... lost in each other," he says politely about how we tried to be quiet in bed but must have failed.

"We're getting there. Once the divorce is finalized, and we work the kinks out of going from friends to lovers, I think we'll be as stupid as Kade and Wynn seem to be."

"I can't wait for some man to make me crazy." Brown eyes going wide, Franny's jaw drops. Flipping around quickly, I catch sight of what has Francis in a tizzy.

"Our guests have finally arrived!" Yanking a stunned Francis, I tug him across my backyard. "Holy shit! What the fuck, are they turning into nudists?"

"Who is that precious man?" Franny's all eyes for Uriah. If I hadn't met Uriah this morning, I'd probably trip over my own two feet. "You have to introduce us," is said with occupational lust.

"Bro!" I mock-punch Kade in the chest as soon as he's in arm's reach. "You're naked." Tugging at his muscle t-shirt, I can see down from the front and the sides. The neck and armpits are cut out of the gray shirt, all the way to an inch from the bottom. "If this was mesh, I'd say you're wearing a dang pinny. I take it Wynn's on the skins side in gym class."

Looking at me sideways, none too pleased, Kade grumbles, "Bodily force placed this godawful thing on me."

"It's ninety degrees in the shade, and you were putting on a fucking thermal and flannel shirt when I found you." Wynn's only wearing a pair of cut-off sweats, flip flops, and a smile. "I want to *see* my husband. Next time the armor comes out when it's hot out, you'll be walking around in a pair of underwear."

"I'd say I was pussy-whipped, but we're minus one pussy." Kade is not impressed, using pissy humor to hide his discomfort. "My wolverines are locked in Royce's safe until snow flies. I'm not sure how we missed Wynn's sadistic tendencies when it comes to punishing away my unhealthy coping skills."

"You look good, though," I admit without hesitation, taking liberties anyone else would lose a hand over. Lifting up Kade's shirt, I check out his new ink. "Just make sure you use sunscreen– don't want to fade this masterpiece. Maybe we ought to run before school and work every morning." Pinching less than a quarter inch on his hip, "If you gain any more weight, the tattoos will warp as your skin stretches."

"I'm *not* fat," Kade growls, eyes narrowed to slits. Head jerking to look away from me, he mutters out the side of his mouth, "Six a.m. three times a week– I'll meet you on the sidewalk."

Chuckling evilly, Wynn palms the nape of Kade's neck to draw him in for an ego-soothing kiss. "You have no idea how badly I want to tear this shirt off you." Eyeing him up and down, "The pants too."

"Please stop," I beg, hands out to ward off what I'm witnessing. "No. I worked so hard on this party, and I want to be able to eat the meat, when I woke up at four this morning to get the coals ready. No. Just no."

A soft huff of laughter draws my gaze, and I locate Uriah. Kade being naked, and Wynn always being naked, had occupied my attention. "Wow… you're so pretty." Hair slicked back to his skull, Uriah's face is on display, but nothing is as eye-catching as the slip of fabric he's wearing that resembles a sundress. "And cool. You look like you attract the breeze."

"Thanks," Uriah blushes, eyes darting to gaze at his husband, who looks like he stepped off the cover of Golf Digest. We already had the conversation this morning on what pronoun I was to use, because when I met Uriah, he was wearing guy clothes. "I was worried about how everyone would react, but I didn't want to fucking melt. I'm not built like Wynn– someone would tell me to put a shirt on."

Unable to stop myself, my eyes rove over Uriah's body, finding it nothing but a straight line– neither male nor female. I could see the gender confusion if he walked around half naked like Wynn.

Stepping out from behind me, "Are you going to introduce me?" Franny gets impatient. Walking right up to Uriah with his hand out, "I'm Francis Parker of Frantastic Designs, and you would make the best fucking hanger I've ever seen."

"Hanger?" Jackson rumbles from behind me, coming from parts unknown. "That's not nice, Francis."

"That's the highest compliment I can pay a person." Eyeing Uriah with lust in his eyes, Francis gets down to business. "Hanger, as in clothing hanger. The point is to show off the design, not the body."

We all share a look, finding that to be a grievous insult, but Frances looks high and Uriah looks proud, so we keep our traps shut.

"I'm in need of legal advice." Sage will not be denied. Hand out to Dan, "Sage Fischer of the Sages of Boston– the only liberal gay Sage in the family."

"Daniel Bishop of Pittsburgh." Dan doesn't even smirk as they shake hands, causing Wynn and me to share a loaded look of utter disbelief at the practices of rich bitches. "I met your family at a political fundraiser last spring. Come– we'll chat over here." Realizing he's leaving his husband to the wolves, "Are you okay, Ri?"

"I'm fine." Uriah chuckles. "Francis says he wants me to try on some of his designs in Bren's house. I'll be out in a bit."

Four of our party guests divide, leaving the hosts and the guests of honor to stare at one another. "This is creepy odd," Jackson whispers in my ear, resting his chin on my shoulder. "Want something to eat. Play a game? They ought to mingle."

Eyes darting around, I decide the party is a success, even if we have business being conducted. The kids are running around, screaming like their heads were cut off. Gemma took to Jesse in a heartbeat– they're creating an elaborate wedding scene on the back patio with sidewalk chalk. Honor's playing tuggy with Perty, while Copper is driving his car around the yard, rounding up Penny's sisters. The twins tied empty beer cans to the back of the car with twine and crepe paper, and soaped *just married* on the tiny windshield.

Pandemonium.

Cain is shucking corn by the bushel to put up for the winter, with Jeb glaring at him from across the yard. It would be comical if it wasn't for the tension riding in the air between those two. They've perfected the air of silent staring contests– to this day, I doubt they've shared a single word. It's more than the Gillette hatred on Jeb's part. He saw the video, and I have a sneaking suspicion Jeb's been hazed in the past.

Dad and the rest of the men are huddled around the smoker, the spit, and the bonfires, with a scattering of women chatting wherever conversation was struck up. Then there's Miriam making her way toward Kade, and I'm a rat-bastard for pretending I don't notice until it's too late.

"No," Kade grumbles, running his hand through his long, curly hair. I notice something glint, but I'm too distracted by the fact that Wynn must have hidden all of Kade's hair-ties. "Miriam will want to talk about my dad and mom, how proud they would be, and I can't take it."

"What the fuck is on your hand?" Jack's heavy weight leaves my back, arm whipping out to grab Kade's wrist. "Why are you wearing a wedding band?"

Kade is pale, and Wynn is tanned, but their blushes rival one another's. In a guilty gesture, left hands are shoved in pockets and hidden behind backs.

"What's up?" I ask with more than mild curiosity, finding their behavior strange across the board. "Couldn't wait, so you're practicing?"

"Couldn't wait," they mutter in unison, sharing a private smirk, then Kade juts away from an advancing Miriam. But he only makes it three feet, because Willa and Dad appear out of nowhere to step in his path, with Perty walking Honor with his tuggy rope.

Reaching down, my daughter is hefted into my arms, snuggling down happily because she knows what's coming next.

"We have to give you your present before we eat," Dad is saying, with Willa speaking over top of him, "Before it gets dark."

"You're giving me my dog back!" Kade kneels on the ground, taking possession of the chubby pug. "Perty Werty, Daddy wuvs how you wiggles your hiney-winey for me."

Rolling her eyes, Willa shakes her head in disgust. "Don't talk to my dog like he's a moron."

Miriam comes to a standstill next to us, but remains silent, because Kade is always a trip when he's uncomfortable.

"Here!" Dad holds up a big cardboard box, glowing with pride and happiness. "Open it!"

"Now?" Wynn scrunches his blond eyebrows in the center of his forehead. "We just got here. We were fortifying ourselves to go mingle with the shitload of guests y'all invited. I don't know half of 'em."

"Open it," Willa demands, pulling Wynn's puppet strings. Perturbed that Wynn listens to Willa but not to him, Kaden reaches for the box first.

Everyone jumps backward when the box moves, flap opening on its own. "The fuck?" Wynn and Kade slowly lean in, looking in the box but prepared to retreat fast.

Willa, Dad, Jackson, and I share a private smile... waiting for it.

"Babies!" Kade shrieks, causing the two tan heads to sink back into the box. "Perty Werty is a proud papa." The dog in question is resting his front paws on Kade's leg, trying to get closer to his puppies. "Two babies."

"Ah," Wynn purrs, tears of happiness glistening in his eyes for Kaden. "They look like two potatoes."

"I'ma call them Tater and Tot." Kaden reaches into the box, and comes out with a wiggling puppy in each hand. Pausing, he realizes a mistake, handing Wynn one of the puppies. "Unless you want to name one."

Kaden is making progress.

Smirking, Wynn shakes his head, then Eskimo kisses the puppy. "No, Tater and Tot is adorable. But who is who?"

"They're both boys, but one has a bit more white on his tummy," Willa explains, running a finger along the little fella's belly. "Tot, because he's not as potato looking as Tater."

"Okay," Kade acquiesces quicker than usual, all because a puppy is resting in his palm, belly in the air. "Do you like your sons, Perty?" Kade kneels to show the pug his pup. After a sniff and a lick, Perty isn't impressed.

"I have to take them back in the house now. Too many kids underfoot, the toy car, the fires..." After easily taking Tater, Willa tries to pry Tot out of Kade's hand, but he won't let go. "Their sister is probably crying for them."

"Sister?" Kade perks up. "They have a sister?" Then he looks down at Perty in awe, like the dog is a stud.

"Six pups, actually. Loraine Baxter only needed three puppies for her family, so she asked if we wanted to take three, or if we should split the proceeds if we sold them."

"What's their sister's name?" Tot is already spoiled, disappearing inside that mockery of a shirt.

Dad's sharp bark of laughter just barely edges out mine and Jack's. Willa smirks at us, using the distraction to slip Tot out of Kade's shirt. Quickly, she walks away with a pup in each hand toward her house.

Flashing us a glorious Gillette smile, Willa announces over her shoulder, "Tater and Tot's little sister is named Werty."

"Hey!" Kade's bellow fades, as does Willa's laughter, because the newest arrival to the party has time stopping.

Hell, I think the earth stops spinning on its axis.

If I wasn't holding Honor, I could stop what happens next. But Kade and Wynn react faster than I ever could, with Jackson releasing a startled cry of panic.

Face whiter than a freshly laundered sheet, Dad's knees give out, landing on the packed soil with a thunk, the cardboard box barely breaking his fall. But he's saved from ass-planting by strong hands gripping him underneath the armpits.

"Donny?" Dad breathes through blue-tinged lips.

A furious apparition comes to a stop before us, with a man in a blue suit behind him. "Where the fuck is Corbin?"

Coming Soon– Rusty Knob visits Pittsburgh

POLISHED

· RUSTY KNOB · BOOK FOUR ·

Daniel Bishop

"Hey," Kade whispers, like he can sense why I'm calling. "You doing okay?"

"No," I answer without hesitation, never once holding anything back from Kade. "Are you free to talk?"

"Yep." A loud bang echoes through the speaker on my phone, reverberating my ear. "Even if I wasn't, I'd make sure I was for you. Wynn's taking an online course at the kitchen table, and I'm cleaning out the basement."

"*You*? Cleaning the basement?" I chuckle with wry amusement. "We roomed together for four years, you filthy fucking hog."

"Wanting to get laid ever again will have a man do the damnedest things." Laughing sinisterly, another loud bang sounds in the background. "All kidding aside, we need a home-office, and my need to foster kids took ours from the first floor. Compromise– I clean out the basement, and Wynn will renovate it for a shared office, especially with him trying to pick up credits for a teaching degree."

"Win-win," I mutter with appreciation. "Can't really concentrate at the kitchen table. I have to admit, that makes me jealous."

"What does?" Silence rings, Kade must have stopped moving.

"How you and Wynn work through your shit," I answer after a few moments.

"You mean by fighting and fucking?" Kade jests. I know they fight and fuck constantly, but when it matters, they get right to the heart of the matter and fix it immediately. "We just accept that we're going to hurt the other's feelings by telling the truth. But it goes both ways, until his pain is mine. It's almost punishing, until we're thinking of each other more than our own needs."

"Yeah, but–"

"I'm a selfish bastard, Daniel," Kade calls me by my actual name, so I know I'm in for it. "The more selfless I become, the more selfish Wynn gets, until we're balancing each other… Wynn told me the other day how he either had to go to Bren's, or he was going to punch me in the nuts."

"What were *you* doing?"

"Annoying the piss outta him." Kade chuckles darkly. "So I learned a lesson on how to control myself, or else it will either emotionally hurt when Wynn runs away from me, or physically hurt when he punches me."

"I… Uriah and I can't be like that," I mutter in mystification, never once resorting to violence or manipulation in our relationship. "What works for you guys, most definitely won't work for us."

"How about you tell me what's going on, and I'll try to fix it?" Kade's voice is coaxing, a tone he mastered way after we roomed together. I'll admit it to Uriah, but never Kade, but the sound goes straight to my dick, even if it confuses the piss out of me.

Sighing, I lean against the railing, eyes cast downward to the river below and all the chaos in Pittsburgh. All those people with lives just as fucked up as mine.

"Listen, Dan," Kade orders, when it's usually me in charge, with Wynn doing his damnedest to out alpha dog me, which I allow with great relief. "It's always been you taking care of me. Let me return the favor. It's what I was trained to do. Lay it on me."

"I need your help," I admit at great length.

"'Bout time."

NATIONAL SUICIDE PREVENTION LIFELINE

1 (800) 273-8255

http://www.suicidepreventionlifeline.org/

-ACKNOWLEDGEMENTS-

A lot of work goes into writing a novel, and it isn't just by the writer herself. **My parents:** for their unconditional support. **My readers**: thank you for reading my twisted words and spreading my books to the masses. For without you, no one would have ever heard of my stories. My readers are my lifeblood. A shout out to the members of the **M&M of Restraint Group on Facebook**: thanks for the endless entertainment and inspiration. Thank you to my street team: **Erica Chilson's Deviants!** You guys ROCK! **Wicked Reads**: (in all its incarnations) **Angela G.**, thank you for taking over and making Wicked Reads better than I could have done by myself. & thank you for helping promote my work and the work of other authors. Angela? Have I told you lately how much I appreciate you? A huge thank you to the **Wicked Writer's Betas** for keeping me grounded and encouraging me to keep trudging along when I get frustrated. Your thoughts and observations are invaluable. ((Hugs)) Beta readers: **Kris | Suz | Darcy | Sandy | Di | Angela | Diane | Jacki | Linsey | Alexis | Alicia | Billie Jo | Shelby | Tassie | Caroline | Judith | Jodi Lynn | Jodi | Lakecia | April |** Someday, I'd love to meet you all in real life– it would be the experience of a lifetime.

ABOUT THE AUTHOR

Erica Chilson does not write in the 3rd person, wanting her readers to *be* her characters. Therefore, writing a bio about herself, is uncomfortable in the extreme.

Born, raised, and here to stay, the Wicked Writer is a stump-jumper, a ridge-runner. Hailing from North Central Pennsylvania, directly on the New York State border; she loves the changes in seasons, the humid air, all the mountainous forest, and the gloomy atmosphere.

Introverted, but not socially awkward, Erica prides herself on thinking first and filtering her speech. There are days she doesn't speak at all. If it wasn't for the fact that she lives with her parents, giving her a sense of reality, she would be a hermit, where the delivery man finds her months after expiration.

Reading was an escape, a way to leave a not-so pleasant reality behind. Reading lent Erica the courage she gathered from the characters between the pages to long for a different life. Writing was an instrument of change, evolving Erica into the woman she is today- a better, more mature, more at peace thinker.

Erica has a wicked mind, one she pours out into her creations. Her filter doesn't allow all of it to erupt, much to her relief. Sarcastic, with a very dark, perverse sense of humor, Erica puts a bit of herself into every character she writes.

I love hearing from readers. If you would like more information on release dates, works in progress, teaser chapters, and random bits of madness, please visit my Facebook Fan Page:
https://www.facebook.com/thewickedwriter
my website: ericachilson.com or please contact me via email:
wickedwriter.ericachilson@gmail.com

DEVIANTS ONLY, if you'd like to join Erica Chilson's closed Facebook group, M&M of Restraint:
https://www.facebook.com/groups/MistressandMaster/